William Blake

William Blake was born in Broad Street in 1757, the son of a London hosier. Having attended Henry Parr's drawing school in the Strand, he was in 1772 apprenticed to Henry Basire, engraver to the Society of Antiquaries, and later was admitted as a student to the Royal Academy, where he exhibited in 1780. He married Catherine Boucher in 1782 and in 1783 published *Poetical Sketches*. The first expression of his mysticism appears in *Songs of Innocence* (1789), which, like *The Book of Thel* (published in the same year), has as its main theme the constant presence and power of divine love even in the midst of evil.

Blake's visionary ideas are developed further in his chief prose work, *The Marriage of Heaven and Hell* (1790), where he denies the theory of eternal punishment and the reality of matter. His revolt against authority is expressed in much of his subsequent writing, and in *Songs of Experience* (1794) he protests against restrictive codes and celebrates the spirit of love. The chief works which Blake produced during this decade are mythological and are intended to expose the failings of the moral code. His final symbolic works are 'Milton' and 'Jerusalem'. The minor poems that followed include some exquisite lyrics, notably 'The Morning' and 'The Land of Dreams'.

Little of Blake's work was published on conventional form. He combined his vocations as poet and graphic artist to produce books that are visually stunning. He also designed illustrations of works by other poets and devised his own technique for producing large watercolour illustrations and colour-printed drawings. Blake died in 1827, 'an Old Man feeble & tottering but not in Spirit & Life not in the Real Man The Imagination which Liveth for Ever'.

Alfred Kazin is Distinguished Professor of English at the Graduate Center of the City University of New York and Hunter College. He is the author of *On Native Grounds*, *New York Jew*, and *An American Procession*, among other books.

Each volume in The Viking Portable Library either presents a representative selection from the works of a single outstanding writer or offers a comprehensive anthology on a special subject. Averaging 700 pages in length and designed for compactness and readability, these books fill a need not met by other compilations. All are edited by distinguished authorities, who have written introductory essays and included much other helpful material.

The Portable

Blake

*Selected and arranged
with an introduction by*
ALFRED KAZIN

PENGUIN BOOKS

PENGUIN BOOKS
Published by the Penguin Group
Penguin Group (USA) Inc., 375 Hudson Street, New York, New York 10014, U.S.A.
Penguin Group (Canada), 90 Eglinton Avenue East, Suite 700, Toronto,
Ontario, Canada M4P 2Y3 (a division of Pearson Penguin Canada Inc.)
Penguin Books Ltd, 80 Strand, London WC2R 0RL, England
Penguin Ireland, 25 St Stephen's Green, Dublin 2, Ireland
(a division of Penguin Books Ltd)
Penguin Group (Australia), 250 Camberwell Road, Camberwell,
Victoria 3124, Australia (a division of Pearson Australia Group Pty Ltd)
Penguin Books India Pvt Ltd, 11 Community Centre, Panchsheel Park,
New Delhi – 110 017, India
Penguin Group (NZ), 67 Apollo Drive, Mairangi Bay, Auckland 1311,
New Zealand (a division of Pearson New Zealand Ltd)
Penguin Books (South Africa) (Pty) Ltd, 24 Sturdee Avenue, Rosebank,
Johannesburg 2196, South Africa

Penguin Books Ltd, Registered Offices: 80 Strand, London WC2R 0RL, England

First published in the United States of America
by Viking Penguin Inc. 1946
Paperbound edition published 1956
Reprinted 1959, 1960, 1961, 1962, 1963, 1965 (twice),
1966, 1967 (twice), 1968, 1969 (twice), 1970 (twice)
1971, 1972, 1974 (twice), 1975
Published in Penguin Books 1976

31   33   35   37   39   40   38   36   34   32   30

LIBRARY OF CONGRESS CATALOGING IN PUBLICATION DATA
Blake, William, 1757–1827.
The Portable Blake.
Reprint of the 1946 ed. published by The Viking Press, New York.
Bibliography: p. 700.   Includes index.
I. Kazin, Alfred, 1915–   II. Title.
[PR4142.K3   1976]   821'.7   76-47594
ISBN 978-0-14-015026-1

Printed in the United States of America
Set in Linotype Caledonia

Acknowledgment is made to the edition of Makers complete writings edited by
Geoffrey Keynes, issued by the Nonesuch Press, London, and Random House,
New York.
Thanks are due to the National Gallery of Art, Washington, D.C, Rosenwald Col-
lection, for permission to reproduce from its set of the engravings for *The Book of
Job* and to the Library of Congress, Rosenwald Collection, for those from *The
Gates of Paradise*

A LINE is a line in its minutest subdivisions, straight or crooked. It is itself, not intermeasurable by anything else. Such is Job. But since the French Revolution Englishmen are all intermeasurable by one another: certainly a happy state of agreement, in which I for one do not agree. God keep you and me from the divinity of yes and no too—the yea, nay, creeping Jesus—from supposing up and down to be the same thing, as all experimentalists must suppose.

BLAKE: April 12, 1827

CONTENTS

VI. THE PROPHETIC BOOKS

VII. ON ART, MONEY, AND THE AGE

VIII. THE OLD BLAKE

CONTENTS

EDITOR'S
ACKNOWLEDGMENTS

The selections for this volume have been taken almost entirely from the "Nonesuch Press" edition of Blake's complete writings in poetry and prose, edited by Geoffrey Keynes, (Nonesuch Press, London; Random House, New York). I cannot easily express my indebtedness to Dr. Keynes, who did the real work for this volume, and to his American publishers, Random House, Inc., who have facilitated its publication. The selections from Crabb Robinson's *Reminiscences* have been taken from Arthur Symons's supplement to his *William Blake*, London, 1907, where the notes on Blake were printed as a separate unit for the first time.

I should like to express my indebtedness to John Sampson's edition of Blake's "Poetical Works" (Oxford University Press), for guidance in making my own selections from *The Four Zoas, Milton*, and *Jerusalem*. I am equally indebted to D. J. Sloss and J. P. R. Wallis, editors of the Clarendon Press (Oxford, 1926) edition of Blake's Prophetic Writings in two volumes. Without their editorial analysis, list of variants and unique glossary of Blake's symbols, my own work would have been far more difficult.

I owe a great debt to many pioneer scholars in the field of Blake scholarship. In particular I should like to acknowledge, with gratitude and pleasure, the work of Swinburne; Joseph Wicksteed; S. Foster Damon; Max

Plowman; Alexander Gilchrist; Mona Wilson; Arthur Symons; William Butler Yeats; John Sampson; Ruthven Todd; Geoffrey Grigson; J. Bronowski.

I should like to thank Pascal Covici for suggesting this work, and for his friendly encouragement. I am deeply grateful to Dr. Ruth Bunzel for many valuable suggestions. I owe much to John Marshall and David Stevens of the Rockefeller Foundation, and to Louis Wright and the staff of the Huntington Library, San Marino, California, for making possible a study of Blake manuscripts. And emphatically not least, I should like to thank here my students and friends at Black Mountain College, North Carolina, with whom I read Blake in the Fall quarter, 1944.

A. K.

INTRODUCTION

The real man, the imagination.

In 1827 there died, undoubtedly unknown to each other, two plebeian Europeans of supreme originality: Ludwig van Beethoven and William Blake. Had they known of each other, they could still not have known how much of the future they contained and how alike they were in the quality of their personal force, their defiance of the age, and the fierce demands each other had made on the human imagination.

It is part of the story of Blake's isolation from the European culture of his time that he could have known of Beethoven, who enjoyed a reputation in the London of the early 1800's. The Ninth Symphony was in fact commissioned by the London Philharmonic, who made Beethoven's last days a little easier. The artistic society of the day was appreciative of Beethoven. It ignored the laborious little engraver, shut off by his work and reputed madness, who was known mainly to a few painters, and held by most of them to be a charming crank.

It is hard to imagine Blake going to concerts or reading accounts of Beethoven's music. He never traveled. Except for one three-year stay at a cottage in Sussex, he hardly went out of London. Like his father and brothers, he lived the life of a small tradesman—at one time he kept a printshop. He was always very poor, and generally worked in such seclusion that at one period, near the end of his life, he did not leave his house for two years, except to go out for porter. Blake had instinctive musical gifts; in his youth and old age he spontaneously, when in company, sang melodies to his own lyrics. Musicians who heard them set them down; I wish I knew where. Even on his deathbed, where he worked to the last, he composed songs. But he had no formal musical knowledge and apparently no interest in musical thought. Self-educated in every field except engraving, to which he had been apprenticed at fourteen, his only interest in most ideas outside his own was to refute them. He always lived and worked very much alone, with a wife whom he trained to be the mirror of his mind. The world let him alone. He was entirely preoccupied with his designs, his poems, and the burden—which he felt more than any writer whom I know—of the finiteness of man before the whole creation.

Beethoven's isolation was different. He was separated from society by his deafness, his pride, his awkward relations with women, relatives, patrons, inadequate musicians. He was isolated, as all original minds are, by the need to develop absolutely in his own way. The isolation was made tragic, against his will, by his deafness and social pride. At the same time he was one of the famous virtuosos of Europe, the heir of Mozart and the pupil of Haydn, and the occasional grumpy favorite of the musical princes of Vienna. His isolation was an involuntary personal tragedy, as it was by necessity a social fact. He did not resign himself to it, and only with the greatest courage learned to submit to it. If he was solitary, it was in a great tradition. As he was influenced by his predecessors, so he became the fountainhead of the principal musical thought that came after him.

Blake's isolation was—I sometimes think it still is—absolute. It was the isolation of a mind that sought to make the best of heaven and earth, in the image of neither. It was isolation of a totally different kind of human vision; of an unappeasable longing for the absolute integration of man, in his total nature, with the universe. It was the isolation of a temperament run on fixed ideas; and incidentally, of a craftsman who could not earn a living. There are analogies to Blake's position in a world which has so many displaced persons as our own; but they are inadequate. Blake's isolation may be likened to that of the revolutionary who sits in his grubby room writing manifestoes against a society that pays him 'no attention, with footnotes against other revolutionaries who think him mad. It was that of the author who prints his own books. It was that of the sweetly smiling crank who sits forever in publishers' offices, with a vast portfolio under his arm, explaining with undiminishable confidence that only through his vision will the world be saved. It was that of the engraver who stopped getting assignments because he turned each one into an act of independent creation. Blake was a lyric poet interested chiefly in ideas, and a painter who did not believe in nature. He was a commercial artist who was a genius in poetry, painting, and religion. He was a libertarian obsessed with God; a mystic who reversed the mystical pattern, for he sought man as the end of his search. He was a Christian who hated the churches; a revolutionary who abhorred the materialism of the radicals. He was a drudge, sometimes living on a dollar a week, who called himself "a mental prince"; and was one.

There are other points of difference between Blake and Beethoven, important to recognize before we can appreciate their likeness. With Beethoven we are in the stream of modern secular culture. Beethoven, the enduring republican and anti-Bonapartist, the social dramatist of *Fidelio*, the jealous admirer of Goethe, the celebrant of Schiller's call to the joyous brotherhood of man, is a central figure in *our* history, as Blake never has been. We remember Beethoven the moralist, the Beethoven who felt so gratefully at home in the world of Kant that he copied out a sentence, probably at second-hand, and kept it on his work-table—"The starry heavens above us and the moral law within us. Kant!!!" To Blake the "moral law" was a murderous fiction and the stars were in the heavens because man's imagination saw them there. Beethoven speaks to our modern humanity in tones we have learned to prize as our own and our greatest, as Blake has not yet; he is uneasily religious and spiritually frustrated, in a familiar agnostic way, where Blake is the "immoralist" and "mystic" by turns. Beethoven could not hear the world, but he always believed in it. His struggles to sustain himself in it, on the highest level of his creative self-respect, were vehement because he could never escape the tyranny of the actual. He was against material despotisms, and knew them to be real. Blake was also against them; but he came to see every hindrance to man's imaginative self-liberation as a fiction bred by the division in man himself. He was against society *in toto*: its prisons, churches, money, morals, fashionable opinions; he did not think that the faults of society stemmed from the faulty organization of society. To him the only restriction over man are always in his own mind—the "mind-forg'd manacles."

With Blake, it would seem, we are off the main track of modern secular thought and aspiration. The textbooks label him "mystic," and that shuts him off from us. Actually he is not off the main track, but simply ahead of it; a peculiarly disturbed and disturbing prophet of the condition of modern man rather than a master-builder. From any conventional point of view he is too different in kind to be related easily to familiar conceptions of the nature of the individual and society. Blake combines, for example, the formal devotional qualities of the English dissenters with the intellectual daring of Nietzsche, the Marquis de Sade, and Freud. No Christian saint ever came to be more adoring of Jesus, and no naturalistic investigator was a more candid opponer. f traditional Christian ethics. He was one of the subtlest and most far-reaching figures in the intellectual liberation of Europe that took place at the end of the eighteenth century. But he had no interest in history, and easily relapsed into primitive nationalism. To the end of his life his chief symbol for man, "the eternal man," was Albion; the origin of "natural religion" he located among the Druids; he hated Newton and despised Voltaire, but painted the apotheosis of Nelson and Pitt. Like so many self-educated men, he was fanatically learned; but he read like a Fundamentalist—to be inspired or to refute. He painted by "intellectual vision" —that is, he painted ideas; his imagination was so original that it carried him to the borders of modern surrealism. Yet he would have been maddened by the intellectual traits of surrealism: the calculated insincerities, the defiant disorder, the autonomous decorative fancy, the intellectual mockery and irreverence. That part of surrealism which is not art is usually insincerity, and to Blake any portion of insincerity was a living death. As he hated church dogma, so he hated scepticism, doubt, experimentalism. He did not believe in sin, only in "intellectual error"; he loathed every dualistic conception of good and evil; the belief that any human being could be punished, here or elsewhere, for "following his energies." But he thought that unbelief—that is, the admission of uncertainty on the part of any person— was wicked. He understood that man's vital energies cannot be suppressed or displaced without causing distortion; he saw into the personal motivations of human conflict and the many concealments of it which are called culture. He celebrated in *Songs of Innocence,* with extraordinary inward understanding, the imaginative separateness of the child. He hated scientific investigation. He could say in his old age, when provoked, that he believed the world was flat. He was undoubtedly sincere, but he did not really care what shape it was; he would not have believed any evidence whatsoever that there were many planets and universes. He did not believe in God; under all his artistic labors and intellectual heresies he seems to have thought of nothing else. He is one of the most prophetic and gifted rebels in the history of Western man—a man peculiarly of our time, with the divisions of our time. Some of his ideas were automatically superstitious, and a large part of his writing is rant. There are features of his thought that carry us beyond the subtlest understanding we have of the relations between man and woman, the recesses of the psyche, the meaning of human error, tyranny, and happiness. There are chapters in his private mythology that carry us into a nightmare world of loneliness and fanaticism, like a scream repeated interminably on a record in which a needle is stuck.

Yet Blake is very much like Beethoven in his artistic independence and universality. Like Beethoven, he is a pioneer Romantic of that heroic first generation which thought that the flames of the French Revolution would burn down all fetters. Like Beethoven, he asserts the creative freedom of the imagination within his work and makes a new world of thought out of it. There sounds all through Blake's poetry, from the boyish and smiling defiance of neo-classic formalism in *Poetical Sketches,*

The languid strings do scarcely move!
The sound is forc'd, the notes are few!

to the vision of man the divine in *Jerusalem* that lyric despair mingled with quickness to exaltation, that sense of a primal intelligence fighting the mind's limitations, that brings Beethoven's last quartets so close to absolute meditation and the Ninth Symphony to a succession of triumphal marches. What is nearest and first in both men is so strong a sense of their own identity that they are always reaching beyond man's conception of his powers. In both there is a positive assertion against suffering, an impatience with forms and means. As Beethoven said of the violinist who complained of the difficulty of one of the Rasumofsky quartets—"Does he really suppose I think of his puling little fiddle when the spirit speaks to me and I compose something?"—so to Blake the forms he uses in his last Prophetic Books, even to their very narrative coherence, are nothing before the absoluteness of his vision. In both life becomes synonymous with the will.

There, however, the resemblance ends. For Beethoven does not block our way by asking us to read him in symbols of his own invention. He is subtle, moving, reflective, in a language which we share because he has made it possible for us to share in it. Out of a limited number of musical tones and devices, he has organized his thought and impressed his conception in such a way that his difference is all *in* his art. When we have grasped his meaning something has enriched our lives without dislodging them. Beethoven is as luminously human as he is creatively independent; he can be gay; he parodies; he introduces a little Russian tune to compliment a patron; he is fond of bearish jokes. He is often difficult, but never impossible. He does not challenge man's submission to the natural order; he finds his place in it, and often in such deep wells of serenity, of happiness in his own struggle, that the song that rises from him almost at the very end, in his last quartet, is for a dance. "Must it be?" he wrote on the manuscript. "It must be. It must be." He may have been thinking of something less than man's ultimate relation to life. But the idea that something *must be* is what is most hateful to Blake's mind.

For Blake accepts nothing—not the God who is supposed to have proposed it this way, or the man who is constrained to dispose it in any way he can. Blake begins with a longing so deep, for all that is invisible and infinite to man under the dominion of God, matter, and reason, that he tears away the shell of earth, the prison of man in his own senses, to assert that there is nothing but man and that man is nothing but the highest flights of his own imagination. With his little tradesman's look, his fanatical industriousness, his somber qualities of the English dissenter and petty-bourgeois, he begins with so absolute a challenge to the religion that was dying in his age, and to the scientific materialism that arose in it, that he transcends them both—into a world that is exalted and often beautiful, but of which he alone saw the full detail.

To understand this is to pass up the usual tags. Blake is seeking something which is analogous to mysticism, but he is not in any ordinary sense a mystic. He is very much in the stream of thought which led to naturalism, but he is not a naturalist. It is more important, however, to show what he shares with us rather than with the mystics. Only those who want to make a Blake easy to explain and apologize for, convenient for the textbooks, can see him as a queer and harmless "mystic." As D. H. Lawrence said of his work, "They'll say as they said of Blake: It's mysticism, but they shan't get away with it, not this time: Blake's wasn't mysticism, neither is this." Even at the end, when Blake celebrated Jesus as his great friend and deliverer, we have in "The Everlasting Gospel:"

> The Vision of Christ that thou dost see
> Is my Vision's Greatest Enemy:
>
> . . . .
>
> Thine is the friend of all Mankind,
> Mine speaks in parables to the Blind:
> Thine loves the same world that mine hates,
> Thy Heaven doors are my Hell gates.

Christian mysticism is founded on dualism. It is rooted in the belief that man is a battleground between the spirit and the flesh, between the temptations of earth and God as the highest Good. The mystic way is the logical and extreme manifestation of the spiritual will, obedient to a faith in supernatural authority, to throw off the body and find an ultimate release in the God-head. Christian mysticism is based upon a mortification of the body so absolute that it attains a condition of ecstasy. To the mystic, God is the nucleus of the Creation, and man in his earthly life is a dislodged atom that must find its way back. The mystic begins with submission to a divine order, which he accepts with such conviction that earthly life becomes nothing to him. He lives only for the journey of the soul that will take him away, upward to God. What would be physical pain to others, to him is purgation; what would be doubt to others, to him is hell; what would be death for others, to him is the final consummation—and one he tries to reach in the living body.

Blake has the mystic's tormented sense of the double-ness of life between reality and the ideal. But he tries to resolve it on earth, in the living person of man. Up to 1800 he also thought that it could be resolved in society, under the inspiration of the American and French Rev-olutions. Blake is against everything that submits, morti-fies, constricts and denies. Mystics are absent-minded reactionaries; they accept indifferently everything in the world except the barriers that physical existence pre-sents to the soul's inner quest. Blake is a revolutionary. He ceased to be a revolutionary in the political sense after England went to war with France and tried to destroy the revolution in Europe. That was less out of prudent cowardice—though like every other radical and free-thinker of the time he lived under a Tory reign of terror—than because he had lost faith in political action as a means to human happiness. Even in politics, however, his libertarian thought became a challenge to all the foundations of society in his time. Blake is not only unmystical in the prime sense of being against the mystic's immediate concerns and loyalties; he is against all accepted Christianity. He is against the churches,

> Remove away that black'ning church:
> Remove away that marriage hearse:
> Remove away that place of blood:
> You'll quite remove the ancient curse.

Against priesthood:

> And priests in black gowns were walking their rounds,
> And binding with briars my joys & desires.

Against the "moral law." He denies that man is born with any innate sense of morality—all moral codes are born of education—and thinks education a training in conformity. He is against all belief in sin; to him the tree in Eden is the gallows on which freedom-seeking man is hanged by dead-souled priests. He savagely parodied a Dr. Thornton's new version of the Lord's Prayer:

> Our Father Augustus Caesar, who art in these thy Substantial Astronomical Telescopic Heavens, Holiness to Thy Name or Title, & reverence to thy Shadow. . . . Give us day by day our Real Taxed Substantial Money bought bread, deliver from the Holy Ghost whatever cannot be taxed. . .

He is against every conception of God as an omnipotent person, as a body, as a Lord who sets in train any lordship over man:

> Thou art a Man, God is no more,
> Thine own humanity learn to adore.

He believes that all restraint in obedience to a moral code is against the spirit of life:

> Abstinence sows sand all over
> The ruddy limbs & flaming hair,
> But Desire Gratified
> Plants fruits & beauty there.

Blake is against all theological casuistry that excuses pain and admits evil; against sanctimonious apologies for injustice and the attempt to buy bliss in another world with self-deprivation in this one. The altar is a place on which the serpent has vomited out its poison; the priest is a blind old man with shears in his hand, to cut the fleece off human sheep. Sex is life, and no one can be superior to it or honestly content with less than true gratification:

> What is it men in women do require?
> The lineaments of Gratified Desire.
> What is it women in men do require?
> The lineaments of Gratified Desire.

Restraint, in fact, follows from the organized injustice and domination in society:

The harvest shall flourish in wintry weather
When two virginities meet together:

The King & the Priest must be tied in a tether
Before two virgins can meet together.

He is against all forms of human exploitation, and all
rationalizations of it in human prejudice:

And all must love the human form,
In heathen, turk, or jew;
Where Mercy, Love, & Pity dwell
There God is dwelling too.

Against war, especially holy ones; against armies, and
in pity for soldiers; against the factory system, the labor
of children, the evaluation of anything by money.

In "London," one of his simplest and greatest poems,
Blake paints the modern city under the sign of man's
slavery, the agony of children, the suffering Soldier and
the Whore:

I wander thro' each charter'd street,
Near where the charter'd Thames does flow,
And mark in every face I meet
Marks of weakness, marks of woe.

In every cry of every Man,
In every Infant's cry of fear,
In every voice, in every ban,
The mind-forg'd manacles I hear.

How the Chimney-sweeper's cry
Every black'ning Church appalls;
And the hapless Soldier's sigh
Runs in blood down Palace walls.

But most thro' midnight streets I hear
How the youthful Harlot's curse
Blasts the new born Infant's tear,
And blights with plagues the Marriage hearse.

"Charter'd" means "bound." In his first draft of this poem, Blake wrote "dirty Thames," but characteristically saw that he could realize more of the city's human slavery in describing the river as bound between its London shores. His own place in the poem is that of the walker in the modern inhuman city, one isolated man in the net which men have created. "I wander thro' each charter'd street." For him man is always the wanderer in the oppressive and sterile world of materialism which only his imagination and love can render human. In a more difficult poem, characteristic of his deeper symbolism, he speaks of the world of matter as

> A Fathomless & boundless deep,
> There we wander, there we weep;

In "London," however, the wandering is not a symbolic expression. In the modern city man has lost his real being, as he has already lost his gift of vision in the "fathomless and boundless" deep of his material nature. Blake here describes one man, himself, in a city that is only too real, the only city he ever knew—yet the largest in the world, the center of empire. The city stands revealed in the cry of *every* Man, in *every* Infant's cry of fear. The wanderer in the chartered streets is concerned with a social picture and, in the face of so much suffering, with the social evil that some create and all permit. The extraordinary terseness of the poem stems from Blake's integral vision of the suffering of man and his alienation from institutions as one. His indignation gives him the power of movement; it also leads him into the repetitions which dominate the tonal order of the poem —the *every* cry of *every* Man, the Infant's *cry of fear,* till his tender vehemence swells into the generality of *in every voice, in every ban.*

Every is magic to Blake. Poetically he cannot go

wrong on it, for it carries such a kernel of glory to his mind, it points so immediately to his burning human solidarity, that in using it he knows himself carried along by what is deepest to him. The *mind-forg'd manacles*, as central to his thought as any phrase he ever used, follows with a triumphant sweep right after it, and for an obvious reason. For he is one with every voice, every ban, and can now make his judgment. On this fresh creative impulse he leaps ahead to what is so complex, but for him so natural, a yoking of images:

> How the Chimney-sweeper's cry
> Every black'ning Church appalls;

The young Chimney-sweeper is always dear to Blake, especially when he is condemned to get the soot out of the churches—an impossible task. He is the symbol of the child who is lost. He works among the waste-dirt of the Church, itself black with dogma and punitive zeal, and his own suffering makes it even blacker. *Black'ning* is a verb of endless duration in present time for Blake. In his drawing to this poem, the Chimney-sweeper is shown in one corner struggling before a black flame. At the top of the page he stands in defiance before the blind and tottering old man, the fossilized Church, who seems to be pouring out fresh soot. The walls are the stone blocks of a prison. The whole page is marked, like the turn of the hand on a vehement signature, by a fierce black border. Pictorially and verbally we thus rise to a climax at the word *appalls*. The Church is not appalled by the Chimney-sweeper's cry; the cry of the child, out of the midst of the Church, makes the Church appalling. Blake's thrust is so swift and deep that he characteristically puts the whole burden of his protest, with its inner music, into four words. Every black and blackening Church is appalling, and in every way. The tone of *palls* to his ear, carrying the image of death, the grief and shame that will not rest, clangs with reverberations.

The unhappiness of the Soldier is not that of a man bleeding before a palace of which he is the sentry. Blake means that the Soldier's desperation runs, like his own blood, in accusation down the walls of the ruling Palace. Blake's own mind ran in so many channels at once, his vision of human existence was so total, that it probably never occurred to him that *blood* would mean anything less to others than it did to him. "Runs in blood down palace walls" is what Blake sees instantaneously in his mind when he thinks of the passivity and suffering of the Soldier. Blake is too much abreast of the reality he sees to use similes; he cannot deliberate to compare something to another. And he is equally incapable of using a metaphor with self-conscious daring. He saw the blood running down the ruler's walls before thinking of blood as a "powerful" image. There is no careful audacity in him, the preparation for the humor of T. S. Eliot's

> I am aware of the damp souls of housemaids
> Sprouting despondently at area gates.

Blake's poetic urge, it is clear, was not to startle, to tease the mind into fresh combinations, but to make tangible, out of the wealth of relationships he carried in his mind, some portion of it equal to his vision of the life of man. How swiftly and emphatically he turns, at the first line of the fourth stanza, to

> But most thro' midnight streets I hear

But most stands for: what I have described thus far is not the full horror of London, my city; not anything like what I have to tell you! And he then gives back, in eighteen words, the city in which young girls are forced into prostitution; in which their exile from respectable society, like the unhappiness of the Soldier, expresses itself in a physical threat to another. The Soldier accuses the Palace with his blood; the prostitute curses with infection the young husband who has been with her; the "plague" finally kills the new-born child. The carriage that went to the church for a marriage ends at the grave as a hearse. Nothing can equal the bite of "blights with plagues," the almost visible thrust of the infection. And thanks to Blake's happy feeling for capitals, which he used with a painter's eye to distinguish the height of his concepts, Marriage stands above the rest in the last sentence of the poem, and swiftly falls into a hearse.

These are some of the poem's details, but they are not the poem. For the poem is to be grasped only by the moral imagination, as a shuddering vision of the mind. The title is a city, as the city is the present human world on the threshold of the industrial revolution. We are to read from the title to the last word, from London to its inner death, in one movement of human sympathy and arousal. This, in its simplest sense, is the key to Blake's meaning of vision. Vision is his master-word, not mysticism or soul. For vision represents the total imagination of man made tangible and direct in works of art. And as the metric structure of the poem encloses, in each line-frame of sharply enclosed syllables, the sight of man entering fully into the city with all his being—*hearing* "the mind-forg'd manacles," the harlot's disease *blasting* "the new born infant's tear," so the whole poem carries us along, in a single page, while the border designs meanwhile extend the vision by another art.

Blake was artist and poet; he designed his poems to

form a single picture. Trained to engraving as a boy, he invented for himself a method of etching a hand-printed poem and an accompanying design on the same page. Only two of his works were ever printed—his first book, *Poetical Sketches,* most of which he wrote between the ages of twelve and twenty-one, and a long and declamatory celebration of the new world after '89 called *The French Revolution.* Neither of these works was ever published. *Poetical Sketches* was run off for him, with a patronizing and apologetic preface by a Reverend Mathew, who with his wife formed a provincial intellectual society that Blake burlesqued in *An Island In The Moon.* The *French Revolution* was printed by a bookseller, Joseph Johnson, who was the center of a radical circle in London that included Blake, William Godwin, Mary Wollstonecraft, and Thomas Paine. After England became embroiled with France and a reactionary witchhunt set after radical intellectuals and sympathizers with the French Republic, Johnson became panicky and left the book in proof. Some of Blake's greatest poems—"The Everlasting Gospel," "Auguries of Innocence," the lyrics that follow *Songs of Innocence and of Experience*—were found in "The Rossetti Manuscript," which was bought by Dante Gabriel Rossetti for ten shillings from an attendant at the British Museum. Blake's most famous works, *Songs of Innocence and of Experience* and *The Marriage of Heaven and Hell,* along with his Prophetic Books—*The Book of Thel, Visions of the Daughters of Albion, America, Europe, The Book of Urizen, Milton, Jerusalem,* etc.—were done entirely by his method of "illuminated printing." Blake said he got the inspiration for this technique from the spirit of his dead brother Robert, the only member of his family with whom he had common sympathies. This may be true, but it is a pity that Blake had to say so, for it has given people the idea ever since that Blake's visions were of the kind limited to a séance.

Blake's general technique is now clear. He etched his poems and designs in relief, with acid on copper. He corroded with acid the unused portions of the plate—characteristically, this became a symbol in *The Marriage of Heaven and Hell* of the corrosion of dead matter by the visionary human imagination. Each print-page as it was taken off the press was colored by hand. Each copy of a work was planned in a different color scheme. There are probably no handmade books in the world more beautiful. The only models for Blake were, of course, the illuminated manuscripts of the Middle Ages. But Blake worked in an entirely different spirit. The medieval manuscripts, impressive as they are, remain pictorial and remote; they were created by copyists, ornamentalists and pious scribes who worked in a liturgical spirit. Blake's designs are the accessories of a single creative idea. His conception of the beautiful book, as Laurence Binyon said, was one of a complete unity, "in which the lettering, the decoration, the illustrations, the proportions of the page, the choice of paper, surpassed even the conceptions of the medieval scribes and miniaturists." Yet Blake was not aiming at a "beautiful book" for its own sake, or at the kind of isolated luxury product which we usually associate with book illustration by a master artist. To him all the arts were simultaneously necessary, in their highest creative use and inner proportion, to give us the ground essence of his vision and a stimulus to our own. What was most important to him was that he should get all his vision down, through all the arts open to him, in work done entirely in his own person.

Blake's search for unity began in his own hands, with

his sense of craft. The symbolic synthesis to be created by his imagination was an image of man pressing, with the full power of his aroused creativity, against the walls of natural appearances. Each page of "illuminated printing" for him was a little world, in which the structure of the poem, the designs on the border, the accompanying figures on the page, the tints of the color, the rhythm of the lettering, were joined together into the supreme metaphor.

The attempt to model some ideal unity in a single work is not unique in itself—it is the symbolic function of traditional religious art, and is to be found in the outer and inner architecture of the cathedrals, the structure of *The Divine Comedy*, and cruciformly printed poems of George Herbert. What is different in Blake is that he is not modeling after any symbols but his own. The symbols always have an inner relatedness that leads us from the outer world to the inner man. The symbols live in the ordered existence of his vision; the vision itself is entirely personal, in theme and in the logic that sustains it. What is before us, in one of his pages, has been created entirely by him in every sense, and the unimpeachable quality of his genius is shown in an order that is as great as his independence, and shows us how real both were. The characteristic of his genius is to lift his unexpected symbols for the inner world of the imagination into a world in which they stand apart from the natural world and defy it. When he designs illustrations to Gray's poems, the magnitude of his vision throws the lines he is illustrating off the page. But what impresses us in their magnitude is not their physical size, but the uncanny spiritual coherence which joins them together and gives them an effect of absolute force. Blake could never "illustrate" another man's work, even though it was pretty much the only way by which

he could earn a living. Even if he respected the other
man's work, as he did Milton and Dante, he created new
conceptions of their subject in his own designs. When
he did his twenty-one engravings to the Book of Job,
he reversed the pious maxims of the Bible story to show
a man destroyed by his own materialism and self-
righteousness. Fortunately, he did not set his Job de-
signs against a page reproduced from the Bible; he
selected passages, and wrote new ones, and put both
into the scroll-work of his border designs. His vision of
Job is entirely his own work, as the Job is indeed the
greatest of his "Prophetic Books." Where the words
were created by him, as in his poems, the love of the
word to the design is only one revelation of man's will
to wed the contraries—like the marriage of Heaven and
Hell. Blake's conception of union and of the infiniteness
of union has no physical status. For him infinity is in
man's passions and his will to know; it is a state of
being.

Yet what has been designed is bound, much as Blake
disliked all limits. So he carried the force and delicacy
of his longing for the infinite into the subtle inwardness
of everything he drew. In *Songs of Innocence and of
Experience,* he designed his poems in such a way that
the words on the line seem to grow like flowerheads out
of a thicket. Each hand-printed letter of script, each
vine trailing a border between the lines, each moving
figure above, beside, and below the page mounts and
unites to form some visible representation of the inner
life of man—seen in phases of the outward nature. Yet
Blake was not seeking to represent nature; he used it as
a book of symbols. When he put down something "nat-
ural" and visible on his page—a bramble, a tree, a leaf,
a figure moving mysteriously in its symbolic space—the
effort seemed to dissolve his need to believe in its sepa-

rate existence. The acid of the designer's imagination burned away the materials on which it worked. What he represented, for purposes of spiritual vision and imagery, dissolved its own exterior naturalness for him. The natural forms—from the arch of the sky to the stolid heroic figures he liked to draw—became a mold that would *contain* his symbolic ideas of them. This is what makes his gift so beautiful on one level, and often so unreachable on another. He brought a representation of the world into every conception; but he never drew an object for its own sake. He wrote and drew, as he lived, from a fathomless inner window, in an effort to make what was deepest and most invisible capturable by the mind of man. Then he used the thing created—the poem, the picture, joined in their double vision—as a window in itself, through which to look to what was still beyond. "I look through the eye," he said, "not with it."

In short, Blake was not looking for God. He shared in the mystic's quest, but he was not going the same way. But we can see at the same time that he was not interested in natural phenomena, in the indestructible actuality of what is not in ourselves but equally real. Spinoza once said that the greatest good is the knowledge of the union which the mind has with the whole nature. That is an exalted statement, but we can recognize its meaning through the work of naturalists of genius like Darwin, Marx, and Freud. The creative function of naturalism has been to establish, with some exactness, a measure of objective knowledge—whether in the description of matter and energy, man's own life as a biological organism, his economic society, or the life urges which civilization has pushed into a world below consciousness. Naturalism is a great and tragic way of looking at life, for with every advance in man's consciousness and in his ability to ascertain, to predict, and to control, he loses that view of his supreme importance which is at the center of religious myth. Naturalism helps to postpone death, but never denies it; it cannot distort objective truth for the sake of personal assurance; it finds assurance in man's ability to know something of what lies outside him. There flows from its positive insights an advance in man's consciousness of his own power that is more fertile and resourceful than any anthropocentric myth can inspire. Naturalism declares limits, and discovers new worlds of actuality between them. It is tragic, for by showing that man's experience is limited it gives him a sense of his permanent and unremitting struggle in a world he did not make. But the struggle is the image of his true life in the world, and one he deepens by art, knowledge, and love. The quality of tragedy is not sadness but grave exhilaration; it defines the possible.

Blake is not a naturalist; he believes in apprehension, not in being; in certainty at the price of reality. He does not believe that anything is finally real except the imagination of man. He grasped one horn of the classic dilemma—"how do I know that anything is real, since I know of reality only through my own mind?"—and pronounced that the problem was settled. He refused to believe the evidence of his senses that the human mind —however it may qualify or misread reality—is bombarded by something outside itself. We are eternally subjective; but there are objects. Indeed, it would seem to follow from our very ability to correct ourselves that we do measure our knowledge by some source. Our backs in Plato's cave are to the fire; but we know that the shadows on the wall before us are shadows, and not the fire itself. Blake assumed that what is partial is in error, and that what is limited is non-existent. But the truth is that he was not trying to prove anything phil-

osophically at all; his greatness depends not on his con-
ception of the world but on what he created through it.
In defense of his own personality, and in defiance of his
age, he imagined a world equal to his heart's desire. He
refused to admit objective reality only because he was
afraid man would have to share the creation.

It is here that Blake has perplexed his readers even
more than he has delighted them. The reason lies in his
refusal to concede a distance between what is real and
what is ideal; in his desperate need to claim them as
one. Blake is difficult not because he invented symbols
of his own; he created his symbols to show that the ex-
istence of any natural object and the value man's mind
places on it were one and the same. He was fighting the
acceptance of reality in the light of science as much as
he was fighting the suppression of human nature by ethi-
cal dogmas. He fought on two fronts, and shifted his
arms from one to the other without letting us know—
more exactly, he did not let himself know. He created
for himself a personality, in life and in art, that was the
image of the thing he sought.

Like all the great enlighteners of the eighteenth cen-
tury, Blake is against the *ancien régime* in all its mani-
festations—autocracy, feudalism, superstition. Though
he loathed the destructive reason of the Deists, he
sometimes praised it in the fight against "holy mystery."
He was fighting for free thought. Yet he is not only
a confederate of Diderot and Voltaire, Jefferson and
Tom Paine; he is a herald of the "heroic vitalism"
of Nietzsche and D. H. Lawrence, of Dostoevsky's
scorn for nineteenth-century utilitarianism and self-
contentment. Where the Encyclopedists were concerned
with the investigation, on "natural principles," of man's
place in society and his order in the universe, Blake—

who hated the Church as much as Voltaire and was as republican as Jefferson—was concerned with the freedom of man from all restrictions—whether imposed by the morality of the Church or the narrowness of positivism. Like Nietzsche, he considered himself an enemy of Socrates and of the Platonic dualism that became a permanent basis of Christian thought. What Blake said in so many of his early poems Nietzsche was to say in his autobiography: "All history is the experimental refutation of the theory of the so-called moral order of the world." Zarathustra, dancing mysteriously to the bacchanal of Nietzsche's imagined self-fulfillment, is prefigured in Blake's Los, the crusading imagination with the hammer in his hand. And like Nietzsche, Blake writes in his masterpiece, *The Marriage of Heaven and Hell*, with the playful daemonism of those who league themselves with the "Devil" because his opposite number restricts human rights:

The reason Milton wrote in fetters when he wrote of Angels & God, and at liberty when of Devils & Hell, is because he was a true poet and of the Devil's party without knowing it.

With it there is the stress on heroic energy, on the rights of the superior that cannot be claimed under what Nietzsche called the "slave-morality":

The eagle never lost so much time as when he submitted to learn of the crow.

Damn braces. Bless relaxes.

Improvement makes strait roads; but the crooked roads without Improvement are the roads of genius.

Destroy, Blake says, all that binds man to decayed institutions. But destroy as well man's obedience to moral precepts that hinder the full power of his creative

will to assert, to love and to build. Desire is never vicious
in itself; it is only turned to vicious ends when driven
out of its real channel. Restraint in the name of the
moral code is alone evil, for it distorts man's real nature.
It is a device of the rulers of this world to keep us
chained. For life is holy. Energy is eternal delight. Jesus
is dear to us not because he was divine, but because he
was a rebel against false Law, and the friend of man's
desire. He defied the Kings and Priests. He was against
punishment. He was the herald of man's joy, not of his
imaginary redemption. Joy is the only redemption and
all suppression is a little death. Humility is an imposture
born of cunning. Better wrath than pity. "The tygers of
wrath are wiser than the horses of instruction."

> If he had been Antichrist, Creeping Jesus,
> He'd have done anything to please us:
> Gone sneaking into the Synagogues
> And not used the Elders & Priests like Dogs,
> But humble as a Lamb or an Ass,
> Obey himself to Caiaphas.
> God wants not man to humble himself.
> . . . . . .
> For he acts with honest, triumphant Pride,
> And this is the cause that Jesus died.

In *The Marriage of Heaven and Hell*, Blake writes:
"Opposition is true friendship." His drive is always to-
ward creative self-assertion, toward man as a free crea-
tor. In *A Song of Liberty*, his vision of the old world
burning in the fires of the French Revolution leads him
to cry: "Empire is No More!"

> Let the Priests of the Raven of dawn no longer, in deadly
> black, with hoarse note curse the sons of joy. Nor his ac-
> cepted brethren—whom, tyrant, he calls free—lay the
> bound or build the roof. Nor pale religious letchery call
> that virginity that wishes but acts not!

So far Blake is a libertarian, an eighteenth-century radical more vehement, daring and imaginative in his conception of freedom than others, but sharing in a revolutionary tradition. Where he becomes truly prophetic and difficult is in his rejection of materialism. He denounces the Priest, in his "deadly black"; but he warns us not to "lay the bound or build the roof" with our anti-clerical freedom. He sets his thought absolutely against rationalism, scepticism, and experimentalism. He is with the Deists so long as they attack supernaturalism—detestable to Blake not because it is disprovable by reason, but because it implies obedience. He is against the Deists so long as they seek to submit the imagination to reason. Rationalism is dangerous because it leaves man in doubt. When the time-serving Bishop Watson wrote, at the request of the English Tory government, an attack on Tom Paine's *The Age of Reason*, Blake scrawled vehement attacks on the Bishop all over the margin of his *Apology for the Bible*.

It appears to me Now that Tom Paine is a better Christian than the Bishop.

I have read this Book with attention & find that the Bishop has only hurt Paine's heel while Paine has broken his head. The Bishop has not answer'd one of Paine's grand objections.

But in one of his most famous poems, he denounced Voltaire and Rousseau as the arch-Deists seeking to destroy man's capacity for visionary wonder:

Mock on, mock on, Voltaire! Rousseau!
Mock on, mock on: 'tis all in vain!
You throw the sand against the wind,
And the wind blows it back again.

The sand is the dead particles separated by reason from the true unity of the human vision. Man under the domination of reason is to Blake a creature who has lost his integral nature and has become a dead fragment in himself. Separateness is death; doubt is the child of separateness; the portions which man separates by his reason, in the analysis of natural objects, or by thinking of himself as a natural object, are the mocking ghosts of his dead imagination.

This impassioned rejection of all that is analytical and self-limiting in modern thought is central to Blake. It underlies all his conceptions, is the psychological background of his life, and falls, sometimes with a dead absoluteness, between his revolutionary thought and the modern world. It is only when we have understood that doubt and uncertainty stand to Blake's mind as the prime danger of modern life that we can see the main drives of his work, of his personal "queerness," and what led him to the artistic wreckage and incoherence of the later Prophetic Books. Blake's whole pattern, as man and artist, is that of one for whom life is meaningless without an absolute belief. He is like the nihilist Verkhovensky, in Dostoevsky's *The Possessed*, who "when he was excited preferred to risk anything rather than to remain in uncertainty." Freud spoke out of what is deepest and most courageous in the modern tradition when he said that "Man must learn to bear a certain portion of uncertainty." That is a great injunction which it is hard to follow: much harder than the authoritarian faiths of our time, the secular, sadistic religions, the phony ecstasy with which a Hitler's self-mortification is lost in vision of eternal conquest. But Blake is very much a man of our time: one who speaks to us with prophetic insight of our nihilism and insensibility. He was so frightened by what he could already see of it that he found his security only in an absolute personal myth. It is a trait that has become universal politics in our own time. Insecurity has become so endemic, in a society increasingly unresponsive to basic human needs, that men will apparently distort and destroy anything to find their way back to the mystical faith of the child in his parents, the medieval man in his God, and the Nordic in the pagan forest. Blake is peculiarly contemporary in his anxiety, his longing for a faith that will be absolute and yet insurgent, his fear of evidence that will destroy the fantasy of man as the *raison d'être* of the universe. He is as great as Dostoevsky in his understanding of our modern deficiencies; he is as self-deluding as Dostoevsky, who was so afraid of his own nihilism that he allied himself with all that was most obscurantist in Czarist Russia.

This does not make what is central in Blake's work any less prophetic and beautiful. He is not the enemy of society, any more than Dostoevsky was, or the D. H. Lawrence who succumbed to a silly literary Fascism. The very excesses of Blake's myth, like the golden quality in his best work, spring from his impassioned defense of human dignity. Far less than Blake have we solved the problem of restoring to modern man some basic assurance, of giving him a human role to play again. It is the mark of a genius like Blake, or Dostoevsky, or Lawrence, that what is purest and most consistent in his thought burns away his own suffering and fanaticism, while his art speaks to what is most deeply human in us. The distortions and flatulence of Blake's myth spring in part from the very abundance of his gifts—turned in on themselves, with the "fire seeking its own form," as he wrote in *The French Revolution*. Those who distrust reason are usually those who have not enough capacity for it to know why it is beautiful, and slander in advance what they are afraid will destroy their prestige. But there are also those, like Blake and Dostoevsky, who are supremely intelligent, and in whom the audacity and loneliness of genius, not to say social frustration, have led to the distrust of all that will not lead to personal security. Blake had one of the greatest minds in the history of our culture; and more fear of the mind than we can easily believe. He was a genius who from childhood on felt in himself such absolute personal gifts that, anticipating the devaluation of them by a materialistic society, made sure that society's values did not exist for him. Yet one of his most distinguishable personal traits, weaving through his vehement self-assertion, is his need to defend himself against society.

This is not the view of many people who have written on Blake's life; but with the exception of writers like Alexander Gilchrist and Mona Wilson, who at least sought the basic facts about him, most of his biographers have had no understanding of him. The usual view is that he was a happy mystic, who sat like a gloriously content martyr before his work, eating bread and locusts with an idiotic smile on his face. Blake evidently did enjoy great happiness in many periods, for he was a man for whom life consisted in exploring his own gifts. But there is even more in Blake's total revelation of himself, a rage against society, a deeply ingrained personal misery, that underlies his creative exuberance and gives it a melancholy and over-assertive personal force. He defends himself in so many secret ways that when he speaks of himself, at abrupt moments, his utterances have the heart-breaking appeal of someone who cries out: "I am really different from what you know!" To a Reverend Trusler, for example, who complained after commissioning some drawings that inspiration had led Blake too far, he wrote:

I feel that a man may be happy in This World. And I know that This World is a World of Imagination & Vision. I see Every thing I paint in This world, but Every body does not see alike. To the Eyes of a Miser a Guinea is far more beautiful than the Sun, & a bag worn with the use of Money has more beautiful proportions than a Vine filled with Grapes. The tree which moves some to tears of joy is in the Eyes of others only a Green thing which stands in the way. Some see Nature all Ridicule & Deformity, and by these I shall not regulate my proportions; & some scarce see Nature at all. But to the Eyes of the Man of Imagination, Nature is Imagination itself. As a man is, so he sees. As the Eye is formed, such are its Powers.

This is beautiful; as many of Blake's personal notes, in letters, marginalia, notebook jottings, and recorded conversation, are beautiful. But they are beautiful in the same way, just as most of *The Four Zoas, Milton,* and *Jerusalem* is ugly in the same way—as a series of passionately eloquent self-assertions, so burning in their exaltation that they seem to spring out of deep gulfs of private misery and doubt. That last word is always Blake's enemy. Just as he believed that

> He who doubts from what he sees
> Will ne'er Believe, do what you Please.
> If the Sun & Moon should doubt,
> They'd immediately Go out

so he felt the antagonism of the age to his vision to be such a burden that he exceeded what is normal in the human longing for certainty and made his kind of certainty the supreme test of a man. Reading a contemporary work on mental disorder, he suddenly scrawled in the margin:

Cowper came to me and said: "O that I were insane always. I will never rest. Can you not make me truly insane? I will never rest till I am so. O that in the bosom of God I was hid. You retain health and yet are as mad as any of us all—over us all—mad as a refuge from unbelief—from Bacon, Newton and Locke."

Blake never wrote anything more important to himself. If he was mad, it was as *a refuge from unbelief*, and thus with the satisfaction of being firmly placed in the sense of his own value. His terrible isolation spoke in the need to defend his identity; if madness was the cost of this, it at least placed him "over us all." And he was higher than his age and over most of those who lived in it—higher not in a fantasy of superiority, but in the imaginative subtlety and resolution of his gifts; his faith that

> we are put on earth a little space,
> That we may learn to bear the beams of love.

Yet what is so marked in his history is his need to prove to himself that his genius could survive. For he was struggling with his own temperament in a time when society threatened his right to exist.

Blake's need of certainty, whatever its personal roots, is also one of the great tragedies of modern capitalist society; particularly of that loss of personal status that was the immediate fate of millions in the industrial England of the "dark satanic mills." Blake was only one of many Englishmen who felt himself being slowly ground to death, in a world of such brutal exploitation and amid such inhuman ugliness, that the fires of the new industrial furnaces and the cries of the child laborers are always in his work. His poems and designs are meant to afford us spiritual vision; a vision beyond the factory system, the hideous new cities, the degradation of children for the sake of profit, the petty crimes for which children could still be hanged. "England," a man said to me in London on V-E day, "has never recovered from its industrial revolution"; Blake was afraid it could not survive it; the human cost was already too great.

He never saw the North of Britain, but the gray squalor
of the Clydebank, the great industrial maw of Man-
chester and Liverpool, the slums, the broken families
are remembered even in the apocalyptic rant of *Jeru-
salem*, where

> Scotland pours out his Sons to labour at the Furnaces;
> Wales gives his Daughters to the Loom.

The lovely poem at the head of *Milton*, beginning

> And did those feet in ancient time
> Walk upon England's mountains green?

is so intense a vision of a world other than the real in-
dustrial England that it has long been a Socialist hymn
of millions of its working people.

Blake was an artisan; an independent journeyman liv-
ing entirely on the labor of his hands, dependent on
patrons in a luxury trade that was being narrowed down
to those who could please most quickly. He lived as
near the bottom of the English social pyramid as was
possible to someone not sucked into the factories. His
London is the London of the small tradesmen, the
barely respectable artisans and shopkeepers who were
caught between the decline of handicrafts and the rise
of mass industry. He had to live by hackwork for pub-
lishers, but was so independent in his designs that he
was forced more and more to engrave after others. One
of the reasons why he delighted to make his own books
is that he enjoyed complete liberty as an artist-engraver;
they certainly would not have been printed by a com-
mercial publisher. But his own prints went largely un-
bought. The stray copies of *Songs of Innocence and of
Experience* and *The Marriage of Heaven and Hell* that
now belong only to the wealthiest collectors were of-
fered, often unsuccessfully, for a pittance. In 1809 he

held an exhibition of his pictures, featuring his design of the Canterbury Pilgrims, and offering with it "a descriptive catalogue" that is one of his most personal documents. The exhibition, held under the grudging hospitality of his brother James, was a complete failure.

To measure the full depth of Blake's alienation from his age is impossible. Like Tharmas in *The Four Zoas*, he felt himself "a famish'd Eagle, raging in the vast expanse." But it may help us to see his predicament when we realize that he was an impoverished engraver, without any real class to which he could belong; a libertarian without continuing faith in politics—"something else besides human life"; an unknown Romantic poet and artist who felt suffocated by the formalized tastes of the age; a visionary without religion; an engraver after artists he often despised; a poet whose works were unprocurable. Even in his own trade, engraving, he seemed outmoded in competition with sophisticated craftsmen, especially from the Continent, who advanced beyond Blake's stiff techniques. Blake learned to engrave in a rigid and rather lifeless tradition; all his early training was under the direction of a master, James Basire, who set him to copy Gothic monuments. What makes his art so unique is his ability to design, with great formal inventiveness, his own intellectual visions; technically he was an anachronism even in his own day. He never resolved the twin influences upon his work of Gothic and Michelangelo's heroic grandeur. His human figures are always distinguished by a somnambulistic quality: they are mechanical actors in the spell of a tyrannical stage director. Their look on the page is always one of watchful waiting; they are symbols of ideas and states of being. Blake satisfied his own conception of design, but he very rarely satisfied anyone else. Naturally he resented more successful fellow-artists; particularly in oil portrait, for which he had no skill and which symbolized to him the effort of society artists to paint with ingratiating "realism."

It is no wonder that Blake's writing so often sputters out into furious protest against a world that would give him neither a living nor a hearing. In his own mind he lived in "a city of assassinations." He was a man who could be easily cheated; when defrauded by a shrewd "art-publisher" of the day named Cromek, he took out his revenge, after Cromek had brazenly hinted that it was easy to take advantage of him, since he was "one living in the wilderness," by writing in his notebook:

> A Petty Sneaking Knave I knew—
> O Mr. Cr(omek), how do ye do?

But his ability to hit back ended in his notebook. He hated Sir Joshua Reynolds—the ruling light of the Royal Academy from which engravers were excluded; the genial and obliging portraitist of the ruling aristocracy, the complacent Augustan mind counseling artists to follow the rules. But all he could do about it was to note his hatred of Reynolds and his intense opposition to the latter's theories in the margins of Sir Joshua's *Discourses*.

> Having spent the Vigour of my Youth & Genius under the Opression of Sr Joshua & his Gang of Cunning Hired Knaves Without Employment & as much as could possibly be without Bread, The Reader must Expect to read in all my remarks on these Books Nothing but Indignation & Resentment. While Sr Joshua was rolling in Riches . . . (he) & Gainsborough Blotted & Blurred one against the other & Divided all the English World between them. Fuseli, Indignant, almost hid himself. I am hid.

Henry Fuseli was a Swiss-born artist, famous in London, who liked Blake and was one of his few friends. He was successful, as Blake was not, and Blake seems to have exaggerated Fuseli's artistic solidarity in his joy at having found a friend in his own craft. Fuseli once said that he found Blake "damned good to steal from."

The vehement marginalia that contain so many of Blake's deepest resentments—against Bacon, against Reynolds, against Bishop Watson and Wordsworth's "atheistic" love of nature—are an obvious symbol of his protest against society. Not being part of it, he put his dissent into the margins. What is not so obvious, however, is that much of his vehement struggle to assert his independence was based on his marriage. The dissenting and small tradesman's class into which Blake was born was one tributary of our Puritan culture; on Blake it imposed poverty made drearier by genteel conformity. Nietzsche, the lonely professor of Greek, became drunk on the vision of the all-conquering male, but the fantasy was his basic sex experience. Lawrence dreamed all his life of a sun-filled Mediterranean world, full of literary Indians and impossibly hospitable women, whose chief virtue was that they lacked the self-righteousness of Presbyterian miners and school-teachers in Nottingham. Blake in most accounts of his life is portrayed as the ideal husband, who taught his illiterate Catherine how to read, and even to see visions when he did. There is little doubt that he was the ideal husband; and apparently he could not stand it. Catherine Blake became the perfect amanuensis, to the man even more than to the artist. She even learned to write and draw so much in his style that her known contributions to his work would otherwise be indistinguishable from his own. She was the ideal wife of his artistic and intellectual alienation; she was the perfect helpmeet in his social and economic desperation. She starved with him, believed in him, and even saw visions for company. If visitors were shocked by the lack of soap in the Blake

household, she explained that "Mr. Blake's skin don't
dirt!" If Blake became completely indifferent to the
lack of funds, she would gently remind him of the state
of things by putting an empty plate before him for din-
ner.

Catherine Blake was an ideal wife; her only fault,
apparently, was that she was not a person in her own
right. The fault was most assuredly not in her but in
Blake's annihilating need of her. He made an adoring
servant out of her, and then evidently found that he
longed for a woman. All the stories we have of them add
up to very little, and those who drew upon her and
Blake's friends for reminiscences after his death felt
such veneration and excitement before their recovery of
a neglected genius that they prettied up his domestic
life as much as possible. But we do know that he pro-
posed to her at their first meeting when, complaining
that a girl had spurned him, she said: "Then I pity
you." "Do you truly pity me?" he asked, in pleasure.
Whereupon he found that he loved her. Yeats, who
helped to doctor up the truth about Blake's life as much
as anyone, thought this a lovely story and that they
lived happily ever after. Unfortunately, Blake's own
writing shows that he was tormented by her jealousy
and that he thought marriage was the devil.

It is not necessary to find malicious confirmation of
this in the famous story that he wanted Mary Wollstone-
craft to join his household for a *ménage à trois*. Mary
Wollstonecraft was a noble and deeply intelligent
woman, more than a century ahead of her time, who
believed in women's rights and took them. She was a
tragic and courageous woman, far more attractive than
the complacent bluestockings of London highbrow so-
ciety, and much more interesting than her husband,
William Godwin, or their daughter Mary, who became

Shelley's second wife. She was the English type of the great Continental heroines of feminism, from George Sand to Alexandra Kollontai. But though Blake was a member of the same intellectual radical group, headed by Johnson the bookseller, it is not hard to imagine how incongruous she must have looked at his side—Blake, who was the imperial visionary of his meager household, but in the London world a curious and threadbare crank. A liaison between John Wesley and Isadora Duncan would not have been more strange—indeed, Wesley was a worldly and aristocratic figure; Blake was a lower middle-class drudge, more of a Wesleyan than Wesley himself. But he seems to have been of the type that makes history, partly because he is not very happy at home.

Blake's "immoralism" (a silly word made necessary by the fact that *moral* lies like a fallen giant across our discourse) is of two kinds: lyrical and poignant expressions of human longing, and a dark obsession in the "Prophetic Books" with sex as the battleground of human struggle and revolt. And however narrow and pitiful the experience from which his own search for fulfillment sprang, there is no doubt that in its psychological truth, its tenderness and passionate support of human dignity, Blake's writing is one of the great prophecies of the love that is possible between man and woman. He is not a writer of "erotica"—the honeyed crumbs of those who have no bread; he rages in his notebooks, but he is never sly. The very status of the dirty story in our society reveals a conception of sex as something one puts over on the conventions. It is the great betrayal of human sincerity. Blake's fight is against secrecy, unnatural restraint, the fear of life—the distortions in the personality that follow from deception and resignation to it. There is implicit in all his attacks on the "moral code" an understanding that gratification is impossible without true union. In this, as in so much else of his thought, Blake painted not only the immediate consequences of a reactionary morality based on outward conformity—the anxieties, the subtle hostilities, the habit of lying. He also foresaw the danger that is exactly present in our modern eroticism, which has the same relation to the failure of love that totalitarian solutions have to the failure of society. When we compare Blake with an artist like D. H. Lawrence, or an oratorical rebel like Henry Miller, we can see how much the obsessiveness, the cringing over-emphasis on sex in the most advanced modern writing is due to the inability of these writers to treat sex naturally in the whole frame of the human organization. As the dirty story pays homage to puritanism, so our modern eroticism wearily proclaims that the part which has been dislodged from the whole shall now be the key to all experience. The limitations of eroticism have exactly the same character, in life and in art: it divorces sex from human culture. As medieval men despised the body for the sake of the spirit, and perhaps lost both, so we tend to forget that the body is above all a person. Every reaction in favor of some suppressed truth overshoots the mark. Hence, too, the dreary primitivism of so much advanced writing —as great a lie about our human nature as the genteel writing of the past.

Blake is not free of the characteristic modern obsessiveness; he was no more free than we are. But he always knows exactly what he is. His theme is always the defense of the integral human personality. His principal virtue is that he does not make a virtue of "frankness"; he is concerned with basic human desire, fear, longing, resentment; with the innermost movements of a human being in the world. He describes, in his great song cycle, the gulf between Innocence and Experience; he feels an inexpressible solidarity with those who are forever in it. For he knows that innocence and experience are not the faces of youth and age, but "the two contrary states of the human soul." He writes as a man, not as an "immoralist." One of the reasons why he is so supreme among those who have written of childhood is that he sees it as the nucleus of the whole human story, rather than as a state that precedes adult "wisdom." If he is afraid for the child, he pities the adult. In experience there is always the longing for "unorganized innocence: an impossibility"; in innocence there is the poignant foretelling of experience, which is death without the return to confidence and vision. Blake is utterly without cynicism. He never makes the characteristic modern mistake of devaluating a prime experience; he never throws out love with the love-affair. We may not agree with him that desire is infinite; we can never be sufficiently grateful to him for insisting that it is never cheap.

Blake is serious about sex, as he is serious about the child; and for the same reason. For he knows that as sex is the buried part of our civilization, so the child is the buried part of the man. His faith in the creative richness of love has the same source as his feeling for the secret richness of childhood: his ability to see through the dead skin of adulthood. He would have understood very well that our "child-psychology" shows the same guardedness toward the child that modern love and marriage reveal between men and women. The same guardedness and the same fear: for we "handle" children from the same negative fears and out of the same lack of positive participation and sympathy. Blake would have seen in our pedagogic carefulness the effort of caution to do the work of the imagination. In his own

time, when children were regarded as miniature adults,
or as slaves or pets to those who ruled by their maturity,
he showed that a child is not an abbreviated version of
the adult, but a different being. In our time he would
have seen that the distance between a parent and a
child is usually the distance between the parents as
lovers. For him sex meant enjoyment framed in wonder:
the full play of our life-striving beyond all the distor-
tions inflicted by respectable society and cynical experi-
ence. By the same token childhood was also a lost world
—calling to us from our buried life.

> Piping down the valleys wild,
> Piping songs of pleasant glee,
> On a cloud I saw a child,
> And he laughing said to me:
>
> "Pipe a song about a Lamb!"
> So I piped with merry chear.
> "Piper, pipe that song again;"
> So I piped; he wept to hear.

Innocence is belief and experience is doubt. The
tragedy of experience is that we become incapable of
love. The tragedy of childhood is that we inflict our
lovelessness upon it. Blake's thinking is always organic;
it is always directed to the hidden fountains of our hu-
manity. Having never lost the creative freshness of
childhood, he challenged experience with it. Having,
as I believe, no real love-affair of his own, he had it with
childhood. In any event, he had no children of his own.
He was a man who had to believe fully, at the highest
pitch of being, to live at all; and he loved childhood
because it was native in its certainty. Human sensibility
was so precious to him that he was ready to discard all
its natural trappings to preserve it. Blake never deals
with history, with the process and its reality; his search

is only for the central and forgotten sources of human feeling, imagination, solidarity. To be certain of them, he conceived the world over again in the image of his desire. But it is like our desire, even if it is nothing like our real world. And our desire is always a portion of the reality we have, as it is always a shadow on the reality we have not. That is why Blake at his best is enchanting even in the smallest proportions—in fact, it is difficult to read him with the usual continuity, so much does he fill our minds at each step.

The central subject of *Songs of Innocence and of Experience* is that of the child who is lost and found. In its symbolism, it is the great theme of all Blake's work—the "real man, the imagination," that has been lost and will be found again through human vision. In Innocence, the little boy loses his father in the night, and God the Father leads him back to his weeping mother. The child is lost to its guardians, for in Blake's mind the child's nature is beyond the parents' comprehension, and is alone in a world the parents cannot enter. The grief of the child is also the loneliness of the soul in its sudden prison of earth; he is protected by God the Father. In Experience, however, the little boy who demands of the priest the right to assert his own thoughts and desires is "burn'd in a holy place." The little girl who enjoys love, without shame or fear, is suddenly confronted with the earthly father whose "loving look, like the holy book," drives her into terror. One little girl is lost and yet found in Experience, however; for she enters lovingly into the world of the passions, where she lives in freedom from the "wolvish howl" and the "lions' growl."

Experience is the "contrary" of innocence, not its negation. Contraries are phases of the doubleness of all existence in the mind of man; they reflect the unalterable condition of the human struggle. As hell can be married to heaven, the body seen by the soul, so experience lifts innocence into a higher synthesis based on vision. But vision is impossible without truth to one's deepest feelings. A lie is "the negation of passion." Life is thought and creation; it is to be had only in its fullness, for the "want of thought" is death. To enter fully into life we must go through the flame of disbelief, kill the fiction that man's desire is lawless and evil. In Innocence

Mercy has a human heart, pity a human face

In Experience

Cruelty has a Human Heart
And jealousy a Human Face;
Terror the Human Form Divine,
And Secrecy the Human Dress.

The Human Dress is forged Iron,
The Human Form a fiery Forge,
The Human Face a Furnace seal'd,
The Human Heart its hungry Gorge.

That is what experience is for: to bring us from God the Father to the God that man alone creates. Experience is not evil; it merely shows us the face of evil as a human face, so that we shall learn that the world is exactly what man makes it, and that its ultimate triumphs occur within his understanding.

In the world of Innocence the child speaks to the lamb and marvels in its soft and bright goodness, over which stands the Jesus who is himself a lamb. In Experience we stare into the fiery eyes of the Tyger and think ourselves lost in the "forests of the night." But the Tyger is the face of the creation, marvelous and ambiguous; he is not evil. When Blake cries, in the most moving single expression in his work,

When the stars threw down their spears,
And water'd heaven with their tears,
Did he smile his work to see?
Did he who made the Lamb make thee?

he does not find the thought abhorrent. But he does not answer the question; he keeps it as one, where a religious man would answer it consolingly. Never is he more heretical than in this most famous of his poems, where he glories in the hammer and the fire out of which are struck the "deadly terrors" of the Tyger. Blake does not believe in a war between good and evil; he sees only the creative tension presented by the struggle of man to resolve the contraries. What has been created, by some unknown hand, is a fiery furnace into which our hands must go to seize the fire. "The Tyger" is a poem of triumphant human awareness; it is a hymn to pure being. And what gives it its power is Blake's ability to fuse two aspects of the same human drama: the movement with which a great thing is created, and the joy and wonderment with which we join ourselves to it. The opening and closing stanzas are the same, for as we begin with our wonder before the creation, so we can only end on it. It is the living eternal existence; the fire is, so long as we are. That is why Blake begins on the four great beats of "Tyger! Tyger!", which call the creation by a name and bring us in apprehension before it.

The poem is hammered together with alliterative strokes. *Frame* is there,

What immortal hand or eye
Could frame thy fearful symmetry?

because he wants *fearful* as well.

In what distant deeps or skies
Burnt the fire of thine eyes?
On what wings dare he aspire?
What the hand dare seize the fire?

begins the questioning. Blake goes straight to the poles:
we are in the presence of a creation that can be traced
from distant deeps to skies. What sustains the verse in
our ear is the long single tone in which are blended the
related sounds of *burnt, fire, thine, eyes*. By natural as-
sociation—from the burning fire to the topmost eyes of
the Tyger—and through the swell of the line, these
words also form a natural little scale of four notes—a
scale that ends in the crash of the question-mark. Blake's
mind is darting between the mysterious unseen *he*, the
maker of the Tyger, and the fire in its eyes. The fire is
central to his thought, so much so that it eclipses the
maker as a person and turns him into the force and
daring with which he creates. Blake does not write
"He"; he is far more interested in the creation than in
the creator. But so great is this creation that the creator
grows mysterious and powerful in its light. What is so
beautiful in the second stanza is the leap from the Tyger
to the creator. Blake goes from the fire to the creator's
wings. This is not because he has an image of a celestial
being with great wings, but because the fire could be
created only by someone lifted on topmost wings. Blake
is as astounded by the creator as he is by the Tyger—
and in the same way, for both are such revelations of
absolute energy. The emphasis on the creator, in the last
line of the second stanza, is thus on *dare*.

We are now in the midst of the creation—or rather,
of the great *thing* being created. The hammering, twist-
ing, laughing strokes with which the creator works are
not more decisive than Blake's own verse hammer. As
usual, he has leaped ahead of us, and begins on a new

question; a question that begins with *And* because it is
like a man taking breath between hammer strokes:

> And what shoulder, & what art,
> Could twist the sinews of thy heart?
> And when thy heart began to beat,
> What dread hand? & what dread feet?

The creator's shoulder, with terrible force, twists the
sinews to make the Tyger's heart. *Twists* is powerful
enough; but there is joined to it in Blake's mind what is
"crooked" and off the main path for the genius-creator.
The shoulder twisting the heart together has turned the
creator's back away from us, even as we imagine him at
his work. The hammer strokes now go faster and faster;
the creation is so swift and final with each blow that
Blake's mind rushes after the fall of the hammer, the
movements of the creating hands and feet, the beats of
the new heart. The poem now moves to the rhythm of
the great work. Yet the poet must know whose dread
hands and feet, working together before the anvil, could
create this. Where does the creator's body and tools end
and the Tyger begin?

> What the hammer? What the chain?
> In what furnace was thy brain?
> What the anvil? what dread grasp
> Dare its deadly terrors clasp?

The chains ring in the sorcerer's workshop. The ques-
tions now dart from the heart to the brain with the
same instantaneous force with which brain and heart
are being made. But *where* is this being done? Where is
the furnace in which the fire of consciousness is being
poured out into the Tyger's brain? What, in space and
time, could even hold the Tyger as it is being created?
Blake never answers, for the wonder with which he asks
them is the wonder with which he beholds the Tyger.

But he leaps ahead, in the last phrase of the third line and the whole fourth line after it, to create the image of so dread a power that it can grasp the terrors of the Tyger. It is the long courageous movement with which the clasp is made—a great hand moving into the furnace to bring the Tyger to us—that gives the creation its final awesomeness. Blake creates this by the length of his question. Between the dread grasp and the clasp that holds the terrors in its hand is the movement between the creation and our being witness to it. Technically the thing is done by leaving a distance, a moment's suspense, between the end of the third line on *grasp* and the hard closing of the stanza on *clasp*. The assonance of those two words, like bones rasping together, joins us to the thing. The terror is in our hands.

But when Blake asks,

> When the stars threw down their spears
> And water'd heaven with their tears,
> Did he smile his work to see?
> Did he who made the Lamb make thee?

he has no answer—least of all the comforting religious explanation of the division between the Lamb and the Tyger. The stars throwing down their "spears" join in the generation. But did he smile his work to see? *Did he?* Blake's answer is to bring us right back to the Tyger. He has no moral, and he will not let us off with anything less than our return to the fact that the Tyger exists—a fact that includes all its ambiguity and all our wonder and fear before it. The poem ends on the upbeat of man's eternal question of the world: where is its moral order? Blake offers no answer; he asks his question with the "fearful symmetry" of the creation straight before us.

Blake does not let us off with any conventional religious consolation; *nor does he let the creator off*. Had he believed in God, the contraries which are presented to man's mind by experience would have been easy to explain. The Christian explains them by the Fall—by that "happy guilt," as Augustine put it, which left man with a sense of original sin which only religion can cleanse away. Blake is utterly opposed to this: man never fell, and there is no prime evil in him to redeem. For him the contraries exist not because God willed it so in his punishment of man's transgression—could a just God punish man for "following his energies" and for showing curiosity? They exist because man's gift of vision is blocked up in himself by materialism and rationalism. Every man, by the very nature of life, is engaged in a struggle, against the false materialism of the age, to find his way back to perfect human sight. Man is not a sinner—he is a weary traveler lost under the hill, a material "spectre" looking for his "spiritual emanation." He is looking for his human center. Man cannot help getting lost when he deludes himself that he is a natural body subject to a natural society, obeying the laws of a natural God.

> Do what you will, this life's a fiction
> And is made up of contradiction.

But vision restores his human identity. With the aid of vision, and through the practice of art, man bursts through the contraries and weds them together by his own creativity.

Blake's Prophetic Books are his attempt to explain how the contraries arose. They are his Greek mythology, his Genesis, his Book of Revelations. Blake is not Diderot or Stendhal; he does not take man as he finds him.

He is a Bible-haunted English dissenter who has taken
on himself the burden of proving that man is an inde-
pendent spiritual being. This required the refutation of
all existing literature. The tortured rhetoric of the Pro-
phetic Books is not a lapse from taste; it is the awful
wilderness into which Blake had to enter by the nature
of his staggering task. This was to give man a new Bible,
and with it a new natural history; a new cosmogony,
and with it his own version, supplanting Hebrew and
Greek literature of man's first self-consciousness in the
universe. But this is not all he tried to do in the Pro-
phetic Books. No one in his time, after all, could escape
the influence of realism. To Blake the myth-maker the
age required a new Bible. As a contemporary he could
hardly escape the inspiration of neo-classical drama, of
the historical chronicle, and even of the psychological
novel. His Prophetic Books are in fact an attempt to
create, on the basis of a private myth, a new epic litera-
ture that would ride the currents of the age. His chief
model was *Paradise Lost*, and *Milton*, he tells us, was
written because Milton came back to earth and begged
him to refute the errors of his own epic. But Blake had
an eye on Greek tragedy as well, and the Book of Job,
and *The Divine Comedy*.

Blake was not a *"naif,"* a "wild man" piecing his
philosophy together from "odds and ends" around the
house. He was a very learned man who felt challenged
and uneasy by what he had learned. One of the reasons
why he labored so hard to create a new literature equal
to his own vision is that he could never free himself of
the models others had created. When we look at his first
poems in *Poetical Sketches*, we can see solemn imita-
tions of Shakespeare, Ossian, Gray, and Spenser; his first
beautiful songs move slowly away from neo-classic
form. His tracts, *There Is No Natural Religion* and *All*

Religions Are One, imitate the geometrical order of philosophic propositions that was the carry-over from mathematics to natural philosophy. *The Marriage of Heaven and Hell* is a parody of sources to which Blake was deeply indebted for his form: Genesis, the Proverbs, the Apocalypse, and Swedenborg. The Prophetic Books are an attempt to create a new classical literature, after all the sources. Nothing shows so clearly the tremendous inner conflicts in Blake as the ghosts of other men's books in his own. It is impossible, for anyone who has studied the Prophetic Books carefully, to see him as an enraptured scribe singing above the clouds. His visions in these books were an attempt to force down his own uneasiness. He could find his peace only by creating an epic world so singularly his own that it would supplant every other. He never succeeded. His task was beyond all human strength and all art. He created myths endlessly and represented them as human beings in endlessly energetic and turgid postures of struggle, oppression, and liberation. *But he never gave up the myth.* The "mad" Blake, whose wildest sayings furnish so much biographical chit-chat about him, was the man who still believed the myth long after suffering and alienation had dulled in his mind the objects it represented. Without the myth he would have been entirely lost, intolerably isolated. So he went even further—John Milton believed in it, too; and—the significant last chapter of Blake's thought—Jesus was above all a Blakean.

The last Prophetic Books are a jungle, but it is possible—if you have nothing else to do—to get through them. What Joyce said so lightly Blake would have repeated with absolute assurance—he demanded nothing less of his readers than that they should devote their lives to the elucidation of his works. Yet there are whole areas of the first Prophetic Books that represent Blake's art and thought at their purest; the illuminated designs, even to a fantastic jumble like *Jerusalem*, are overwhelming in their beauty and power. To labor over works like *The Four Zoas, Milton,* and *Jerusalem* for the sake of intellectual exegesis is against the whole spirit of art. Where Blake does not write poetry, he orates; and when he orates it is "the will trying to do the work cf the imagination." Yet his rhetorical resources were so overwhelming that they flow like hot lava over the stereotypes of the myth. He obviously felt so little the consecutiveness of his "argument" that in at least one copy of *Jerusalem* he allowed misplaced pages to remain where they were. His concern is not with the coherence of his theme, but with his need to get everything in. Even within the assumed order of the myth the characters lose their symbolic references when they do not transfer them among each other. They came to represent so much of Blake's private life as well as his public vision that he interrupted himself at regular intervals to preach against jealousy and the domination of man by woman.

Blake was never jarred by the tumult of all the conflicts he revealed in his Prophetic Books. His loneliness as a man and thinker was so overwhelming that he took his gifts as the measure of human insight. He was a lyric poet of genius and a very bad dramatic poet; but he suffered from the illusion that his poetic gift was also a dramatic and representational one. The gift of creating character is inseparable from an interest in history. Just as the novel owes its principal development to the modern consciousness that society is man-made, so the ability to create character is impossible without an understanding of men in relation to other men; in short, of man as a creature of process and conflict. Blake's characters are names attached arbitrarily to absolute human faculties and states of being. The name of the character may have a punning or derived relation to the faculty he represents, as Urizen is the god of this world and its sterility who is "your reason," or Orc, Blake's first hero, came into his mind from Norse mythology. So Albion is the central figure of man, "the eternal man," and Enitharmon is the "universal" woman. But when Blake sets them to orating against each other, their nominal identity is only the line which he must desperately hold on to to bring up the deep-sea fish of human passions, errors, lamentations. The figure of Urizen is an oppressor; Oric is the spirit of visionary emancipation; Los, who comes in later, is the spirit of time working to rejoin man to his lost unity, and the "Eternal Prophet." Through them, and many other characters, Blake is seeking to explain how man lost the gift of vision. Urizen is the false God, the Satan who separated himself from the prime unity and set in motion the divisions in man, the search after the analytical and the inhuman.

Blake is not interested in character. His figures are the human faculties at war with each other. He is trying to explain, in the form of a new Genesis, how the split in man occurred, and to show the necessary present struggle of man to unify himself back to an integral and imaginative human nature. He is also raging against all those who would hold him in—from the analytical God of Newton to the scepticism of Voltaire, from the successful painters of the day to "the shadowy female," who torments man by jealousy. But since he has no interest in history, the beginning, the present, and the future dissolve into each other. What was begun in error is suffered through error now. He is fighting his own sorrows even as he is trying to impose the massive structure of his hazardously built myth onto the contemporary world: to bring himself to us, and the England he actually lived in. Hence the bewildering jump from Old Testament names to English streets, cities, and counties, in which Blake's own cries were never heard:

O dreadful Loom of death! O piteous Female forms, compell'd
To weave the Woof of Death! On Camberwell Tirzah's courts,
Malah's on Blackheath; Rahab & Noah dwell on Windsor's heights,
Where once the Cherubs of Jesusalem spread to Lambeth's Vale.
Milcah's Pillars shine from Harrow to Hampstead, where Hoglah
On Highgate's heights magnificent Weaves over trembling Thames
To Shooter's Hill and thence to Blackheath, the dark Woof. Loud,
Loud roll the Weights & Spindles over the whole Earth, let down
On all sides round to the Four Quarters of the World, eastward on
Europe to Euphrates & Hindu, to Nile & back in Clouds
Of Death across the Atlantic to America North & South.

Hence, too, the poetic atrocities:

> In torrents of mud settling thick
> With Eggs of unnatural production

Which is dreadful, but only a paraphrase of the noble rant which deafens and dulls us all through the later books:

But in the Optic vegetative Nerves Sleep was transformed
To Death in old time by Satan, the father of Sin & Death:
And Satan is the Spectre of Orc, &. Orc is the generate Luvah.

Blake cannot get away from the materialist trappings, the naturalistic "spectre"; no one can, and his collapse as an artist in the later Prophetic Books is due to his effort to *dispel* the natural forms by a mythological explanation of them. He created his myth to contain his defiance, as it were; when he found it insufficient, he let it supplant life itself. On the subject of God, he even borrowed a thought from the Gnostic heresy, as he was indebted to the Jewish Cabala for his vision of the man who anciently contained all things of heaven and earth in himself. The Gnostic heresy is one the Catholic Church understandably rooted out in furious alarm— for it held that the world was dominated by Satan. It is not hard to understand how comforting this thought must have been to Blake. If this world is a mere deception, and all its natural appearances a masquerade through which man must look for spiritual vision, it is because the "real" God has been supplanted by Satan. So all spiritual vision leads us back to the "real" God, who is now Jesus. Blake's Jesus is the defiant iconoclast, the friend of artists and revolutionaries. When one reads *Jerusalem,* one thinks of Nietzsche, who when he went mad signed himself "The Crucified One," and of that old cry from the defeated—"Thou has conquered, O Galilean!"

Blake does not "yield" to Jesus; he creates Jesus in his own image.

The Son, O how unlike the Father! First God Almighty comes with a Thump on the head. Then Jesus Christ comes with a balm to heal it.

But not before he has shown us the inner thread in his snarled Prophetic Books—which is the lament against his own "selfhood" and the appeal against the Accuser, "who is the God of this World." It is impossible to read Blake's vehement and repeated cries against the "Accuser" without being moved by the tremendous burden

of guilt he carried despite his revolt and independence.
The "Accuser" is Satan, who rules this world, which is
"the Empire of nothing." It is he who tormented man
with a sense of sin; who made men and women look
upon their own human nature as evil; who plunged us
into the cardinal human heresy, which is the heresy
against man's own right and capacity to live. The "Ac-
cuser" is the age in which Blake lived and it is the false
god whose spectre mocks our thirst for life. It is the
spirit, to Blake, of all that limits man, shames man, and
drives him in fear. The Accuser is the spirit of the ma-
chine, which leads man himself into "machination." He
is jealousy, unbelief, and cynicism. But his dominion is
only in you; and he is only a specter.

The Accuser is the prime enemy, yet he is a fiction; he
need not exist. But Blake fought him so bitterly that he
acknowledged how great a price he had paid for his
own audacity. What was it that made him long at the
end, above everything else, for "forgiveness?" What was
it he had to be "forgiven" for?

And now let me finish with assuring you that, Tho' I
have been very unhappy, I am so no longer. I am again
Emerged into the light of day; I still & shall to Eternity
Embrace Christianity and Adore him who is the Express
image of God; but I have travel'd thro' Perils & Darkness
not unlike a Champion. I have Conquer'd, and shall go on
Conquering. Nothing can withstand the fury of my course
among the Stars of God & in the Abysses of the Accuser.
My enthusiasm is still what it was, only Enlarged and con-
firmed.

We do not know—his only name for his "guilt" re-
mains "selfhood"—that is, the full force of his individual
claim to self-assertion. Blake was a prophet who was not
delivered by his own prophecy. But if he succumbed at
all to the "Accuser," he did more than anyone else to

expose him. If he failed at the complete harmony to which all his own thought is directed, it is because man, though he is a little world in himself, is little indeed when measured against the whole of a creation that was not made for him alone—or for him to know everlasting certainty in it. Blake's tragedy was the human tragedy, made more difficult because his own fierce will to a better life prevented him from accepting any part of it. Laboring after the infinite, he felt himself shadowed by the Accuser. That is the personal cost he paid for his vision, as it helps us to understand his need of a myth that would do away with tragedy. But as there is something deeper than tragedy in Blake's life, so at the heart of his work there is always the call to us to recover our lost sight. Blake was a man who had all the contraries of human existence in his hands, and he never forgot that it is the function of man to resolve them.

Men are admitted into Heaven not because they have curbed & govern'd their Passions, or have no Passions, but because they have cultivated their Understandings.

ALFRED KAZIN

THE PORTABLE

WILLIAM BLAKE

PROSPECTUS

October 10, 1793.

TO THE PUBLIC

The Labours of the Artist, the Poet, the Musician, have been proverbially attended by poverty and obscurity; this was never the fault of the Public, but was owing to a neglect of means to propagate such works as have wholly absorbed the Man of Genius. Even Milton and Shakespeare could not publish their own works.

This difficulty has been obviated by the Author of the following productions now presented to the Public; who has invented a method of Printing both Letter-Press and Engraving in a style more ornamental, uniform, and grand, than any before discovered, while it produces works at less than one fourth of the expense.

If a method of Printing which combines the Painter and the Poet is a phenomenon worthy of public attention, provided that it exceeds in elegance all former methods, the Author is sure of his reward.

Mr. Blake's powers of invention very early engaged the attention of many persons of eminence and fortune; by whose means he has been regularly enabled to bring before the Public works (he is not afraid to say) of equal magnitude and consequence with the productions of any age or country: among which are two large highly finished engravings (and two more are nearly ready) which will commence a Series of subjects from the Bible, and another from the History of England.

The following are the Subjects of the several Works now published and on Sale at Mr. Blake's, No. 13, Hercules Buildings, Lambeth.

1. Job, a Historical Engraving. Size 1 ft. 7½ in. by 1 ft 2 in.: price 12s.
2. Edward and Elinor, a Historical Engraving. Size 1 ft. 6½ in. by 1 ft.: price 10s. 6d.
3. America, a Prophecy, in Illuminated Printing. Folio, with 18 designs: price 10s. 6d.
4. Visions of the Daughters of Albion, in Illuminated Printing. Folio, with 8 designs, price 7s. 6d.
5. The Book of Thel, a Poem in Illuminated Printing. Quarto, with 6 designs, price 3s.
6. The Marriage of Heaven and Hell, in Illuminated Printing. Quarto, with 14 designs, price 7s. 6d.
7. Songs of Innocence, in Illuminated Printing. Octavo, with 25 designs, price 5s.
8. Songs of Experience, in Illuminated Printing. Octavo, with 25 designs, price 5s.
9. The History of England, a small book of Engravings. Price 3s.
10. The Gates of Paradise, a small book of Engravings. Price 3s.

The Illuminated Books are Printed in Colours, and on the most beautiful wove paper that could be procured.

No Subscriptions for the numerous great works now in hand are asked, for none are wanted; but the Author will produce his works, and offer them to sale at a fair price.

I.

THE YOUNG BLAKE

From POETICAL SKETCHES

(1783)

TO THE MUSES

Whether on Ida's shady brow,
  Or in the chambers of the East,
The chambers of the sun, that now
  From antient melody have ceas'd;

Whether in Heav'n ye wander fair,
  Or the green corners of the earth,
Or the blue regions of the air,
  Where the melodious winds have birth;

Whether on chrystal rocks ye rove,
  Beneath the bosom of the sea
Wand'ring in many a coral grove,
  Fair Nine, forsaking Poetry!

How have you left the antient love
  That bards of old enjoy'd in you!
The languid strings do scarcely move!
  The sound is forc'd, the notes are few!

TO THE EVENING STAR

Thou fair-hair'd angel of the evening,
Now, whilst the sun rests on the mountains, light

Thy bright torch of love; thy radiant crown
Put on, and smile upon our evening bed!
Smile on our loves, and, while thou drawest the
Blue curtains of the sky, scatter thy silver dew

On every flower that shuts its sweet eyes
In timely sleep. Let thy west wind sleep on
The lake; speak silence with thy glimmering eyes,
And wash the dusk with silver. Soon, full soon,
Dost thou withdraw; then the wolf rages wide,
And the lion glares thro' the dun forest:
The fleeces of our flocks are cover'd with
Thy sacred dew: protect them with thine influence.

TO MORNING

O holy virgin! clad in purest white,
Unlock heav'n's golden gates, and issue forth;
Awake the dawn that sleeps in heaven; let light
Rise from the chambers of the east, and bring
The honied dew that cometh on waking day.
O radiant morning, salute the sun,
Rouz'd like a huntsman to the chace, and, with
Thy buskin'd feet, appear upon our hills.

SONG

How sweet I roam'd from field to field,
　　And tasted all the summer's pride,
'Till I the prince of love beheld,
　　Who in the sunny beams did glide!

He shew'd me lilies for my hair,
  And blushing roses for my brow;
He led me through his gardens fair,
  Where all his golden pleasures grow.

With sweet May dews my wings were wet,
  And Phœbus fir'd by vocal rage;
He caught me in his silken net,
  And shut me in his golden cage.

He loves to sit and hear me sing,
  Then, laughing, sports and plays with me;
Then stretches out my golden wing,
  And mocks my loss of liberty.

SONG

My silks and fine array,
  My smiles and languish'd air,
By love are driv'n away;
  And mournful lean Despair
Brings me yew to deck my grave:
Such end true lovers have.

His face is fair as heav'n,
  When springing buds unfold;
O why to him was't giv'n,
  Whose heart is wintry cold?
His breast is love's all worship'd tomb,
Where all love's pilgrims come.

Bring me an axe and spade,
  Bring me a winding sheet;

When I my grave have made,
  Let winds and tempests beat:
Then down I'll lie, as cold as clay.
True love doth pass away!

SONG

Love and harmony combine,
And around our souls intwine,
While thy branches mix with mine,
And our roots together join.

Joys upon our branches sit,
Chirping loud, and singing sweet;
Like gentle streams beneath our feet
Innocence and virtue meet.

Thou the golden fruit dost bear,
I am clad in flowers fair;
Thy sweet boughs perfume the air,
And the turtle buildeth there.

There she sits and feeds her young,
Sweet I hear her mournful song;
And thy lovely leaves among,
There is love: I hear his tongue.

There his charming nest doth lay,
There he sleeps the night away;
There he sports along the day,
And doth among our branches play.

SONG

I love the jocund dance,
　The softly-breathing song,
Where innocent eyes do glance,
　And where lisps the maiden's tongue.

I love the laughing vale,
　I love the echoing hill,
Where mirth does never fail,
　And the jolly swain laughs his fill.

I love the pleasant cot,
　I love the innocent bow'r,
Where white and brown is our lot,
　Or fruit in the mid-day hour.

I love the oaken seat,
　Beneath the oaken tree,
Where all the old villagers meet,
　And laugh our sports to see.

I love our neighbours all,
　But, Kitty, I better love thee;
And love them I ever shall;
　But thou art all to me.

SONG

Memory, hither come,
　And tune your merry notes;
And, while upon the wind
　Your music floats,

I'll pore upon the stream,
Where sighing lovers dream,
And fish for fancies as they pass
Within the watery glass.

I'll drink of the clear stream,·
  And hear the linnet's song;
And there I'll lie and dream
  The day along:
And, when night comes, I'll go
  To places fit for woe,
Walking along the darken'd valley
  With silent Melancholy.

MAD SONG

The wild winds weep,
  And the night is a-cold;
Come hither, Sleep,
  And my griefs unfold:
But lo! the morning peeps
  Over the eastern steeps,
And the rustling birds of dawn
The earth do scorn.

Lo! to the vault
  Of paved heaven,
With sorrow fraught
  My notes are driven:
They strike the ear of night,
  Make weep the eyes of day;
They make mad the roaring winds,
  And with tempests play.

Like a fiend in a cloud,
  With howling woe,
After night I do croud,
  And with night will go;
I turn my back to the east,
From whence comforts have increas'd;
For light doth seize my brain
With frantic pain.

SONG

Fresh from the dewy hill, the merry year
Smiles on my head, and mounts his flaming car;
Round my young brows the laurel wreathes a shade,
And rising glories beam around my head.

My feet are wing'd, while o'er the dewy lawn
I meet my maiden, risen like the morn:
Oh bless those holy feet, like angels' feet;
Oh bless those limbs, beaming with heav'nly light!

Like as an angel glitt'ring in the sky
In times of innocence and holy joy;
The joyful shepherd stops his grateful song
To hear the music of an angel's tongue.

So when she speaks, the voice of Heaven I hear:
So when we walk, nothing impure comes near;
Each field seems Eden, and each calm retreat;
Each village seems the haunt of holy feet.

But that sweet village, where my black-ey'd maid
Closes her eyes in sleep beneath night's shade,

Whene'er I enter, more than mortal fire
Burns in my soul, and does my song inspire.

SONG

When early morn walks forth in sober grey,
Then to my black ey'd maid I haste away;
When evening sits beneath her dusky bow'r,
And gently sighs away the silent hour,
The village bell alarms, away I go,
And the vale darkens at my pensive woe.

To that sweet village, where my black ey'd maid
Doth drop a tear beneath the silent shade,
I turn my eyes; and, pensive as I go,
Curse my black stars, and bless my pleasing woe.

Oft when the summer sleeps among the trees,
Whisp'ring faint murmurs to the scanty breeze,
I walk the village round; if at her side
A youth doth walk in stolen joy and pride,
I curse my stars in bitter grief and woe,
That made my love so high, and me so low.

O should she e'er prove false, his limbs I'd tear,
And throw all pity on the burning air;
I'd curse bright fortune for my mixed lot,
And then I'd die in peace, and be forgot.

TO SPRING

O thou with dewy locks, who lookest down
Thro' the clear windows of the morning, turn

Thine angel eyes upon our western isle,
Which in full choir hails thy approach, O Spring!

The hills tell each other, and the list'ning
Vallies hear; all our longing eyes are turned
Up to thy bright pavillions: issue forth,
And let thy holy feet visit our clime.

Come o'er the eastern hills, and let our winds
Kiss thy perfumed garments; let us taste
Thy morn and evening breath; scatter thy pearls
Upon our love-sick land that mourns for thee.

O deck her forth with thy fair fingers; pour
Thy soft kisses on her bosom; and put
Thy golden crown upon her languish'd head,
Whose modest tresses were bound up for thee!

TO SUMMER

O thou, who passest thro' our vallies in
Thy strength, curb thy fierce steeds, allay the heat
That flames from their large nostrils! thou, O Summer,
Oft pitched'st here thy golden tent, and oft
Beneath our oaks hast slept, while we beheld
With joy thy ruddy limbs and flourishing hair.

Beneath our thickest shades we oft have heard
Thy voice, when noon upon his fervid car
Rode o'er the deep of heaven; beside our spring
Sit down, and in our mossy vallies, on
Some bank beside a river clear, throw thy
Silk draperies off, and rush into the stream:
Our vallies love the Summer in his pride.

Our bards are fam'd who strike the silver wire:
Our youth are bolder than the southern swains:
Our maidens fairer in the sprightly dance:
We lack not songs, nor instruments of joy,
Nor echoes sweet, nor waters clear as heaven,
Nor laurel wreaths against the sultry heat.

TO AUTUMN

O Autumn, laden with fruit, and stained
With the blood of the grape, pass not, but sit
Beneath my shady roof; there thou may'st rest,
And tune thy jolly voice to my fresh pipe;
And all the daughters of the year shall dance!
Sing now the lusty song of fruits and flowers.

"The narrow bud opens her beauties to
The sun, and love runs in her thrilling veins;
Blossoms hang round the brows of morning, and
Flourish down the bright cheek of modest eve,
Till clust'ring Summer breaks forth into singing,
And feather'd clouds strew flowers round her head.

The spirits of the air live on the smells
Of fruit; and joy, with pinions light, roves round
The gardens, or sits singing in the trees."
Thus sang the jolly Autumn as he sat;
Then rose, girded himself, and o'er the bleak
Hills fled from our sight; but left his golden load.

TO WINTER

O Winter! bar thine adamantine doors:
The north is thine; there hast thou built thy dark

Deep-founded habitation. Shake not thy roofs,
Nor bend thy pillars with thine iron car.

He hears me not, but o'er the yawning deep
Rides heavy; his storms are unchain'd, sheathed
In ribbed steel; I dare not lift mine eyes,
For he hath rear'd his sceptre o'er the world.

Lo! now the direful monster, whose skin clings
To his strong bones, strides o'er the groaning rocks:
He withers all in silence, and his hand
Unclothes the earth, and freezes up frail life.

He takes his seat upon the cliffs; the mariner
Cries in vain. Poor little wretch! that deal'st
With storms, till heaven smiles, and the monster
Is driv'n yelling to his caves beneath mount Hecla.

II.

THERE IS
NO NATURAL RELIGION
and
ALL RELIGIONS
ARE ONE

THERE IS NO NATURAL RELIGION

FIRST SERIES

(1788)

The *Argument*. Man has no notion of moral fitness but from Education. Naturally he is only a natural organ subject to Sense.

I. Man cannot naturally Perceive but through his natural or bodily organs.

II. Man by his reasoning power can only compare & judge of what he has already perciev'd.

III. From a perception of only 3 senses or 3 elements none could deduce a fourth or fifth.

IV. None could have other than natural or organic thoughts if he had none but organic perceptions.

V. Man's desires are limited by his perceptions, none can desire what he has not perciev'd.

VI. The desires & perceptions of man, untaught by any thing but organs of sense, must be limited to objects of sense.

Conclusion. If it were not for the Poetic or Prophetic character the Philosophic & Experimental would soon be at the ratio of all things, & stand still, unable to do other than repeat the same dull round over again.

77

SECOND SERIES

(1788)

i. Man's perceptions are not bounded by organs of perception; he perceives more than sense (tho' ever so acute) can discover.

ii. Reason, or the ratio of all we have already known, is not the same that it shall be when we know more.

iii. [*This proposition has been lost.*]

iv. The bounded is loathed by its possessor. The same dull round, even of a universe, would soon become a mill with complicated wheels.

v. If the many become the same as the few when possess'd, More! More! is the cry of a mistaken soul; less than All cannot satisfy Man.

vi. If any could desire what he is incapable of possessing, despair must be his eternal lot.

vii. The desire of Man being Infinite, the possession is Infinite & himself Infinite.

Application. He who sees the Infinite in all things, sees God. He who sees the Ratio only, sees himself only.

Therefore God becomes as we are, that we may be as he is.

ALL RELIGIONS ARE ONE

The Voice of one crying in the Wilderness

The *Argument*. As the true method of knowledge is experiment, the true faculty of knowing must be the faculty which experiences. This faculty I treat of.

PRINCIPLE 1st. That the Poetic Genius is the true Man, and that the body or outward form of Man is derived from the Poetic Genius. Likewise that the forms of all things are derived from their Genius, which by the Ancients was call'd an Angel & Spirit & Demon.

PRINCIPLE 2d. As all men are alike in outward form, So (and with the same infinite variety) all are alike in the Poetic Genius.

PRINCIPLE 3d. No man can think, write, or speak from his heart, but he must intend truth. Thus all sects of Philosophy are from the Poetic Genius adapted to the weaknesses of every individual.

PRINCIPLE 4th. As none by traveling over known lands can find out the unknown, So from already acquired knowledge Man could not acquire more: therefore an universal Poetic Genius exists.

PRINCIPLE 5th. The Religions of all Nations are derived from each Nation's different reception of the Po-

etic Genius, which is every where call'd the Spirit of
Prophecy.

PRINCIPLE 6th. The Jewish & Christian Testaments
are An original derivation from the Poetic Genius; this
is necessary from the confined nature of bodily sensa-
tion.

PRINCIPLE 7th. As all men are alike (tho' infinitely
various), So all Religions &, as all similars, have one
source.

The true Man is the source, he being the Poetic Gen-
ius.

III.

SONGS
OF INNOCENCE
AND
OF EXPERIENCE

SHEWING THE TWO CONTRARY
STATES OF THE HUMAN SOUL

SONGS OF INNOCENCE

(1788–1794)

INTRODUCTION

Piping down the valleys wild,
Piping songs of pleasant glee,
On a cloud I saw a child,
And he laughing said to me:

"Pipe a song about a Lamb!"
So I piped with merry chear.
"Piper, pipe that song again;"
So I piped: he wept to hear.

"Drop thy pipe, thy happy pipe;
Sing thy songs of happy chear:"
So I sung the same again,
While he wept with joy to hear.

"Piper, sit thee down and write
In a book, that all may read."
So he vanish'd from my sight,
And I pluck'd a hollow reed,

And I made a rural pen,
And I stain'd the water clear,
And I wrote my happy songs
Every child may joy to hear.

THE SHEPHERD

How sweet is the Shepherd's sweet lot!
From the morn to the evening he strays;
He shall follow his sheep all the day,
And his tongue shall be filled with praise.

For he hears the lamb's innocent call,
And he hears the ewe's tender reply;
He is watchful while they are in peace,
For they know when their Shepherd is nigh.

THE ECCHOING GREEN

The Sun does arise,
And make happy the skies;
The merry bells ring
To welcome the Spring;
The skylark and thrush,
The birds of the bush,
Sing louder around
To the bells' chearful sound,
While our sports shall be seen
On the Ecchoing Green.

Old John, with white hair,
Does laugh away care,
Sitting under the oak,
Among the old folk.
They laugh at our play,
And soon they all say:
"Such, such were the joys

When we all, girls & boys,
In our youth time were seen
On the Ecchoing Green."

Till the little ones, weary,
No more can be merry;
The sun does descend,
And our sports have an end.
Round the laps of their mothers
Many sisters and brothers,
Like birds in their nest,
Are ready for rest,
And sport no more seen
On the darkening Green.

THE LAMB

Little Lamb, who made thee?
Dost thou know who made thee?
Gave thee life, & bid thee feed
By the stream & o'er the mead;
Gave thee clothing of delight,
Softest clothing, wooly, bright;
Gave thee such a tender voice,
Making all the vales rejoice?
Little Lamb, who made thee?
Dost thou know who made thee?

Little Lamb, I'll tell thee,
Little Lamb, I'll tell thee:
He is called by thy name,
For he calls himself a Lamb.
He is meek, & he is mild;
He became a little child.

I a child, & thou a lamb,
We are called by his name.
 Little Lamb, God bless thee!
 Little Lamb, God bless thee!

THE LITTLE BLACK BOY

My mother bore me in the southern wild,
And I am black, but O! my soul is white;
White as an angel is the English child,
But I am black, as if bereav'd of light.

My mother taught me underneath a tree,
And sitting down before the heat of day,
She took me on her lap and kissed me,
And pointing to the east, began to say:

"Look on the rising sun: there God does live,
And gives his light, and gives his heat away;
And flowers and trees and beasts and man receive
Comfort in morning, joy in the noonday.

"And we are put on earth a little space,
That we may learn to bear the beams of love;
And these black bodies and this sunburnt face
Is but a cloud, and like a shady grove.

"For when our souls have learn'd that heat to bear,
The cloud will vanish; we shall hear his voice,
Saying: 'Come out from the grove, my love & care,
And round my golden tent like lambs rejoice.'"

Thus did my mother say, and kissed me;
And thus I say to little English boy:

When I from black and he from white cloud free,
And round the tent of God like lambs we joy,

I'll shade him from the heat, till he can bear
To lean in joy upon our father's knee;
And then I'll stand and stroke his silver hair,
And be like him, and he will then love me.

THE BLOSSOM

Merry, Merry Sparrow!
Under leaves so green
A happy Blossom
Sees you swift as arrow
Seek your cradle narrow
Near my Bosom.

Pretty, Pretty Robin!
Under leaves so green
A happy Blossom
Hears you sobbing, sobbing,
Pretty, Pretty Robin,
Near my Bosom.

THE CHIMNEY SWEEPER

When my mother died I was very young,
And my father sold me while yet my tongue
Could scarcely cry " 'weep! 'weep! 'weep! 'weep!"
So your chimneys I sweep, & in soot I sleep.

There's little Tom Dacre, who cried when his head,
That curl'd like a lamb's back, was shav'd: so I said

"Hush, Tom! never mind it, for when your head's bare
You know that the soot cannot spoil your white hair."

And so he was quiet, & that very night,
As Tom was a-sleeping, he had such a sight!
That thousands of sweepers, Dick, Joe, Ned, & Jack,
Were all of them lock'd up in coffins of black.

And by came an Angel who had a bright key,
And he open'd the coffins & set them all free;
Then down a green plain leaping, laughing, they run,
And wash in a river, and shine in the Sun.

Then naked & white, all their bags left behind,
They rise upon clouds and sport in the wind;
And the Angel told Tom, if he'd be a good boy,
He'd have God for his father, & never want joy.

And so Tom awoke; and we rose in the dark,
And got with our bags & our brushes to work.
Tho' the morning was cold, Tom was happy & warm;
So if all do their duty they need not fear harm.

THE LITTLE BOY LOST

"Father! father! where are you going?
O do not walk so fast.
Speak, father, speak to your little boy,
Or else I shall be lost."

The night was dark, no father was there;
The child was wet with dew;
The mire was deep, & the child did weep,
And away the vapour flew.

THE LITTLE BOY FOUND

The little boy lost in the lonely fen,
Led by the wand'ring light,
Began to cry; but God, ever nigh,
Appear'd like his father in white.

He kissed the child & by the hand led
And to his mother brought,
Who in sorrow pale, thro' the lonely dale,
Her little boy weeping sought.

LAUGHING SONG

When the green woods laugh with the voice of joy,
And the dimpling stream runs laughing by;
When the air does laugh with our merry wit,
And the green hill laughs with the noise of it;

When the meadows laugh with lively green,
And the grasshopper laughs in the merry scene,
When Mary and Susan and Emily
With their sweet round mouths sing "Ha, Ha, He!"

When the painted birds laugh in the shade,
Where our table with cherries and nuts is spread,
Come live & be merry, and join with me,
To sing the sweet chorus of "Ha, Ha, He!"

A CRADLE SONG

Sweet dreams, form a shade
O'er my lovely infant's head;
Sweet dreams of pleasant streams
By happy, silent, moony beams.

Sweet sleep, with soft down
Weave thy brows an infant crown
Sweet sleep, Angel mild,
Hover o'er my happy child.

Sweet smiles, in the night
Hover over my delight;
Sweet smiles, Mother's smiles,
All the livelong night beguiles.

Sweet moans, dovelike sighs,
Chase not slumber from thy eyes.
Sweet moans, sweeter smiles,
All the dovelike moans beguiles.

Sleep, sleep, happy child,
All creation slept and smil'd;
Sleep, sleep, happy sleep,
While o'er thee thy mother weep.

Sweet babe, in thy face
Holy image I can trace.
Sweet babe, once like thee,
Thy maker lay and wept for me,

Wept for me, for thee, for all,
When he was an infant small

Thou his image ever see,
Heavenly face that smiles on thee,

Smiles on thee, on me, on all;
Who became an infant small.
Infant smiles are his own smiles;
Heaven & earth to peace beguiles.

THE DIVINE IMAGE

To Mercy, Pity, Peace, and Love
All pray in their distress;
And to these virtues of delight
Return their thankfulness.

For Mercy, Pity, Peace, and Love
Is God, our father dear,
And Mercy, Pity, Peace, and Love
Is Man, his child and care.

For Mercy has a human heart,
Pity a human face,
And Love, the human form divine,
And Peace, the human dress.

Then every man, of every clime,
That prays in his distress,
Prays to the human form divine,
Love, Mercy, Pity, Peace.

And all must love the human form,
In heathen, turk, or jew;
Where Mercy, Love, & Pity dwell
There God is dwelling too.

HOLY THURSDAY

'Twas on a Holy Thursday, their innocent faces clean,
The children walking two & two, in red & blue & green,
Grey-headed beadles walk'd before, with wands as
  white as snow,
Till into the high dome of Paul's they like Thames'
  waters flow.

O what a multitude they seem'd, these flowers of Lon-
  don town!
Seated in companies they sit with radiance all their own.
The hum of multitudes was there, but multitudes of
  lambs,
Thousands of little boys & girls raising their innocent
  hands.

Now like a mighty wind they raise to heaven the voice
  of song,
Or like harmonious thunderings the seats of Heaven
  among.
Beneath them sit the aged men, wise guardians of the
  poor;
Then cherish pity, lest you drive an angel from your
  door.

NIGHT

The sun descending in the west,
The evening star does shine;
The birds are silent in their nest,
And I must seek for mine.

The moon like a flower
In heaven's high bower,
With silent delight
Sits and smiles on the night.

Farewell, green fields and happy groves,
Where flocks have took delight.
Where lambs have nibbled, silent moves
The feet of angels bright;
Unseen they pour blessing
And joy without ceasing,
On each bud and blossom,
And each sleeping bosom.

They look in every thoughtless nest,
Where birds are cover'd warm;
They visit caves of every beast,
To keep them all from harm.
If they see any weeping
That should have been sleeping,
They pour sleep on their head,
And sit down by their bed.

When wolves and tygers howl for prey,
They pitying stand and weep;
Seeking to drive their thirst away,
And keep them from the sheep;
But if they rush dreadful,
The angels, most heedful,
Receive each mild spirit,
New worlds to inherit.

And there the lion's ruddy eyes
Shall flow with tears of gold,
And pitying the tender cries,

And walking round the fold,
Saying "Wrath, by his meekness,
And by his health, sickness
Is driven away
From our immortal day.

"And now beside thee, bleating lamb,
I can lie down and sleep;
Or think on him who bore thy name,
Graze after thee and weep.
For, wash'd in life's river,
My bright mane for ever
Shall shine like the gold
As I guard o'er the fold."

SPRING

Sound the Flute!
Now it's mute.
Birds delight
Day and Night;
Nightingale
In the dale,
Lark in Sky,
Merrily,
Merrily, Merrily, to welcome in the Year.

Little Boy,
Full of joy;
Little Girl,
Sweet and small;
Cock does crow,
So do you;
Merry voice,

Infant noise,
Merrily, Merrily, to welcome in the Year.

Little Lamb,
Here I am;
Come and lick
My white neck;
Let me pull
Your soft Wool;
Let me kiss
Your soft face:
Merrily, Merrily, we welcome in the Year.

NURSE'S SONG

When the voices of children are heard on the green
And laughing is heard on the hill,
My heart is at rest within my breast
    And everything else is still.

"Then come home, my children, the sun is gone down
And the dews of night arise;
Come, come, leave off play, and let us away
Till the morning appears in the skies."

"No, no, let us play, for it is yet day
And we cannot go to sleep;
Besides, in the sky the little birds fly
And the hills are all cover'd with sheep."

"Well, well, go & play till the light fades away
And then go home to bed."
The little ones leaped & shouted & laugh'd
    And all the hills ecchoed.

INFANT JOY

"I have no name:
I am but two days old."
What shall I call thee?
"I happy am,
Joy is my name."
Sweet joy befall thee!

Pretty joy!
Sweet joy but two days old,
Sweet joy I call thee:
Thou dost smile,
I sing the while,
Sweet joy befall thee!

A DREAM

Once a dream did weave a shade
O'er my Angel-guarded bed,
That an Emmet lost its way
Where on grass methought I lay.

Troubled, 'wilder'd, and forlorn,
Dark, benighted, travel-worn,
Over many a tangled spray,
All heart-broke I heard her say:

"O, my children! do they cry?
Do they hear their father sigh?
Now they look abroad to see:
Now return and weep for me."

Pitying, I drop'd a tear;
But I saw a glow-worm near,
Who replied: "What wailing wight
Calls the watchman of the night?

"I am set to light the ground,
While the beetle goes his round:
Follow now the beetle's hum;
Little wanderer, hie thee home."

ON ANOTHER'S SORROW

Can I see another's woe,
And not be in sorrow too?
Can I see another's grief,
And not seek for kind relief?

Can I see a falling tear,
And not feel my sorrow's share?
Can a father see his child
Weep, nor be with sorrow fill'd?

Can a mother sit and hear
An infant groan an infant fear?
No, no! never can it be!
Never, never can it be!

And can he who smiles on all
Hear the wren with sorrows small,
Hear the small bird's grief & care,
Hear the woes that infants bear,

And not sit beside the nest,
Pouring pity in their breast;

And not sit the cradle near,
Weeping tear on infant's tear;

And not sit both night & day,
Wiping all our tears away?
O, no! never can it be!
Never, never can it be!

He doth give his joy to all;
He becomes an infant small;
He becomes a man of woe;
He doth feel the sorrow too.

Think not thou canst sigh a sigh
And thy maker is not by;
Think not thou canst weep a tear
And thy maker is not near.

O! he gives to us his joy
That our grief he may destroy;
Till our grief is fled & gone
He doth sit by us and moan.

SONGS OF EXPERIENCE

INTRODUCTION

Hear the voice of the Bard!
Who Present, Past, & Future, sees;
Whose ears have heard
The Holy Word
That walk'd among the ancient trees,

Calling the lapsed Soul,
And weeping in the evening dew;
That might controll
The starry pole,
And fallen, fallen light renew!

"O Earth, O Earth, return!
Arise from out the dewy grass;
Night is worn,
And the morn
Rises from the slumberous mass.

"Turn away no more;
Why wilt thou turn away?
The starry floor,
The wat'ry shore,
Is giv'n thee till the break of day."

EARTH'S ANSWER

Earth rais'd up her head
From the darkness dread & drear.
Her light fled,
Stony dread!
And her locks cover'd with grey despair.

"Prison'd on wat'ry shore,
Starry Jealousy does keep my den:
Cold and hoar,
Weeping o'er,
I hear the father of the ancient men.

"Selfish father of men!
Cruel, jealous, selfish fear!
Can delight,
Chain'd in night,
The virgins of youth and morning bear?

"Does spring hide its joy
When buds and blossoms grow?
Does the sower
Sow by night,
Or the plowman in darkness plow?

"Break this heavy chain
That does freeze my bones around.
Selfish! vain!
Eternal bane!
That free Love with bondage bound."

THE CLOD AND THE PEBBLE

"Love seeketh not Itself to please,
Nor for itself hath any care,
But for another gives its ease,
And builds a Heaven in Hell's despair."

So sung a little Clod of Clay
Trodden with the cattle's feet,
But a Pebble of the brook
Warbled out these metres meet:

"Love seeketh only Self to please,
To bind another to Its delight,
Joys in another's loss of ease,
And builds a Hell in Heaven's despite."

HOLY THURSDAY

Is this a holy thing to see
In a rich and fruitful land,
Babes reduc'd to misery,
Fed with cold and usurous hand?

Is that trembling cry a song?
Can it be a song of joy?
And so many children poor?
It is a land of poverty!

And their sun does never shine,
And their fields are bleak & bare,

And their ways are fill'd with thorns:
It is eternal winter there.

For where-e'er the sun does shine,
And where-e'er the rain does fall,
Babe can never hunger there,
Nor poverty the mind appall.

THE LITTLE GIRL LOST

In futurity
I prophetic see
That the earth from sleep
(Grave the sentence deep)

Shall arise and seek
For her maker meek;
And the desart wild
Become a garden mild.

* * *

In the southern clime,
Where the summer's prime
Never fades away,
Lovely Lyca lay.

Seven summers old
Lovely Lyca told;
She had wander'd long
Hearing wild birds' song.

"Sweet sleep, come to me
Underneath this tree.

Do father, mother weep,
Where can Lyca sleep?

"Lost in desart wild
Is your little child.
How can Lyca sleep
If her mother weep?

"If her heart does ake
Then let Lyca wake;
If my mother sleep,
Lyca shall not weep.

"Frowning, frowning night,
O'er this desart bright
Let thy moon arise
While I close my eyes."

Sleeping Lyca lay
While the beasts of prey,
Come from caverns deep,
View'd the maid asleep.

The kingly lion stood
And the virgin view'd,
Then he gamboll'd round
O'er the hallow'd ground.

Leopards, tygers, play
Round her as she lay,
While the lion old
Bow'd his mane of gold

And her bosom lick,
And upon her neck

From his eyes of flame
Ruby tears there came;

While the lioness
Loos'd her slender dress,
And naked they convey'd
To caves the sleeping maid.

THE LITTLE GIRL FOUND

All the night in woe
Lyca's parents go
Over vallies deep,
While the desarts weep.

Tired and woe-begone,
Hoarse with making moan,
Arm in arm seven days
They trac'd the desart ways.

Seven nights they sleep
Among shadows deep,
And dream they see their child
Starv'd in desart wild.

Pale, thro' pathless ways
The fancied image strays
Famish'd, weeping, weak,
With hollow piteous shriek.

Rising from unrest,
The trembling woman prest
With feet of weary woe:
She could no further go.

In his arms he bore
Her, arm'd with sorrow sore;
Till before their way
A couching lion lay.

Turning back was vain:
Soon his heavy mane
Bore them to the ground.
Then he stalk'd around,

Smelling to his prey;
But their fears allay
When he licks their hands,
And silent by them stands.

They look upon his eyes
Fill'd with deep surprise,
And wondering behold
A spirit arm'd in gold.

On his head a crown,
On his shoulders down
Flow'd his golden hair.
Gone was all their care.

"Follow me," he said;
"Weep not for the maid;
In my palace deep
Lyca lies asleep."

Then they followed
Where the vision led,
And saw their sleeping child
Among tygers wild.

To this day they dwell
In a lonely dell;
Nor fear the wolvish howl
Nor the lions' growl.

THE CHIMNEY SWEEPER

A little black thing among the snow,
Crying ''weep! 'weep!' in notes of woe!
"Where are thy father & mother? say?"
"They are both gone up to the church to pray.

"Because I was happy upon the heath,
And smil'd among the winter's snow,
They clothed me in the clothes of death,
And taught me to sing the notes of woe.

"And because I am happy & dance & sing,
They think they have done me no injury,
And are gone to praise God & his Priest & King,
Who make up a heaven of our misery."

NURSE'S SONG

When the voices of children are heard on the green
And whisp'rings are in the dale:
The days of my youth rise fresh in my mind,
My face turns green and pale.

Then come home, my children, the sun is gone down,
And the dews of night arise;
Your spring & your day are wasted in play,
And your winter and night in disguise.

THE SICK ROSE

O rose, thou art sick!
The invisible worm
That flies in the night,
In the howling storm,

Has found out thy bed
Of crimson joy,
And his dark secret love
Does thy life destroy.

THE FLY

Little Fly,
Thy summer's play
My thoughtless hand
Has brush'd away.

Am not I
A fly like thee?
Or art not thou
A man like me?

For I dance,
And drink, & sing,
Till some blind hand
Shall brush my wing.

If thought is life
And strength & breath,

And the want
Of thought is death;

Then am I
A happy fly,
If I live
Or if I die.

THE ANGEL

I dreamt a Dream! what can it mean?
And that I was a maiden Queen,
Guarded by an Angel mild:
Witless woe was ne'er beguil'd!

And I wept both night and day,
And he wip'd my tears away,
And I wept both day and night,
And hid from him my heart's delight.

So he took his wings and fled;
Then the morn blush'd rosy red;
I dried my tears, & arm'd my fears
With ten thousand shields and spears.

Soon my Angel came again:
I was arm'd, he came in vain;
For the time of youth was fled,
And grey hairs were on my head.

THE TYGER

Tyger! Tyger! burning bright
In the forests of the night,
What immortal hand or eye
Could frame thy fearful symmetry?

In what distant deeps or skies
Burnt the fire of thine eyes?
On what wings dare he aspire?
What the hand dare sieze the fire?

And what shoulder, & what art,
Could twist the sinews of thy heart?
And when thy heart began to beat,
What dread hand? & what dread feet?

What the hammer? what the chain?
In what furnace was thy brain?
What the anvil? what dread grasp
Dare its deadly terrors clasp?

When the stars threw down their spears,
And water'd heaven with their tears,
Did he smile his work to see?
Did he who made the Lamb make thee?

Tyger! Tyger! burning bright
In the forests of the night,
What immortal hand or eye,
Dare frame thy fearful symmetry?

MY PRETTY ROSE-TREE

A flower was offer'd to me,
Such a flower as May never bore;
But I said "I've a Pretty Rose-tree,"
And I passed the sweet flower o'er.

Then I went to my Pretty Rose-tree,
To tend her by day and by night;
But my Rose turn'd away with jealousy,
And her thorns were my only delight.

AH! SUN-FLOWER

Ah, Sun-flower! weary of time,
Who countest the steps of the Sun,
Seeking after that sweet golden clime
Where the traveller's journey is done:

Where the Youth pined away with desire,
And the pale Virgin shrouded in snow
Arise from their graves, and aspire
Where my Sun-flower wishes to go.

THE LILLY

The modest Rose puts forth a thorn,
The humble Sheep a threat'ning horn;
While the Lilly white shall in Love delight,
Nor a thorn, nor a threat, stain her beauty bright.

THE GARDEN OF LOVE

I went to the Garden of Love,
And saw what I never had seen:
A Chapel was built in the midst,
Where I used to play on the green.

And the gates of this Chapel were shut,
And "Thou shalt not" writ over the door;
So I turn'd to the Garden of Love
That so many sweet flowers bore;

And I saw it was filled with graves,
And tomb-stones where flowers should be;
And Priests in black gowns were walking their rounds,
And binding with briars my joys & desires.

THE LITTLE VAGABOND

Dear Mother, dear Mother, the Church is cold,
But the Ale-house is healthy & pleasant & warm;
Besides I can tell where I am used well,
Such usage in Heaven will never do well.

But if at the Church they would give us some Ale,
And a pleasant fire our souls to regale,
We'd sing and we'd pray all the live-long day,
Nor ever once wish from the Church to stray.

Then the Parson might preach, & drink, & sing,
And we'd be as happy as birds in the spring;

And modest Dame Lurch, who is always at Church,
Would not have bandy children, nor fasting, nor birch.

And God, like a father rejoicing to see
His children as pleasant and happy as he,
Would have no more quarrel with the Devil or the
Barrel,
But kiss him, & give him both drink and apparel.

LONDON

I wander thro' each charter'd street,
Near where the charter'd Thames does flow,
And mark in every face I meet
Marks of weakness, marks of woe.

In every cry of every Man,
In every Infant's cry of fear,
In every voice, in every ban,
The mind-forg'd manacles I hear.

How the Chimney-sweeper's cry
Every black'ning Church appalls;
And the hapless Soldier's sigh
Runs in blood down Palace walls.

But most thro' midnight streets I hear
How the youthful Harlot's curse
Blasts the new born Infant's tear,
And blights with plagues the Marriage hearse.

THE HUMAN ABSTRACT

Pity would be no more
If we did not make somebody Poor;
And Mercy no more could be
If all were as happy as we.

And mutual fear brings peace,
Till the selfish loves increase:
Then Cruelty knits a snare,
And spreads his baits with care.

He sits down with holy fears,
And waters the ground with tears;
Then Humility takes its root
Underneath his foot.

Soon spreads the dismal shade
Of Mystery over his head;
And the Catterpiller and Fly
Feed on the Mystery.

And it bears the fruit of Deceit,
Ruddy and sweet to eat;
And the Raven his nest has made
In its thickest shade.

The Gods of the earth and sea
Sought thro' Nature to find this Tree;
But their search was all in vain:
There grows one in the Human Brain.

INFANT SORROW

My mother groan'd! my father wept.
Into the dangerous world I leapt:
Helpless, naked, piping loud:
Like a fiend hid in a cloud.

Struggling in my father's hands,
Striving against my swadling bands,
Bound and weary I thought best
To sulk upon my mother's breast.

A POISON TREE

I was angry with my friend:
I told my wrath, my wrath did end.
I was angry with my foe:
I told it not, my wrath did grow.

And I water'd it in fears,
Night & morning with my tears;
And I sunned it with smiles,
And with soft deceitful wiles.

And it grew both day and night,
Till it bore an apple bright;
And my foe beheld it shine,
And he knew that it was mine,

And into my garden stole
When the night had veil'd the pole:

In the morning glad I see
My foe outstretch'd beneath the tree.

A LITTLE BOY LOST

'Nought loves another as itself,
Nor venerates another so,
Nor is it possible to Thought
A greater than itself to know:

"And Father, how can I love you
Or any of my brothers more?
I love you like the little bird
That picks up crumbs around the door."

The Priest sat by and heard the child,
In trembling zeal he siez'd his hair:
He led him by his little coat,
And all admir'd the Priestly care.

And standing on the altar high,
"Lo! what a fiend is here!" said he,
"One who sets reason up for judge
Of our most holy Mystery."

The weeping child could not be heard,
The weeping parents wept in vain;
They strip'd him to his little shirt,
And bound him in an iron chain;

And burn'd him in a holy place,
Where many had been burn'd before:
The weeping parents wept in vain.
Are such things done on Albion's shore?

A LITTLE GIRL LOST

Children of the future Age
Reading this indignant page,
Know that in a former time
Love! sweet Love! was thought a crime.

In the Age of Gold,
Free from winter's cold,
Youth and maiden bright
To the holy light,
Naked in the sunny beams delight.

Once a youthful pair,
Fill'd with softest care,
Met in garden bright
Where the holy light
Had just remov'd the curtains of the night.

There, in rising day,
On the grass they play;
Parents were afar,
Strangers came not near,
And the maiden soon forgot her fear.

Tired with kisses sweet,
They agree to meet
When the silent sleep
Waves o'er heaven's deep,
And the weary tired wanderers weep.

To her father white
Came the maiden bright;

But his loving look,
Like the holy book,
All her tender limbs with terror shook.

"Ona! pale and weak!
To thy father speak:
O, the trembling fear!
O, the dismal care!
That shakes the blossoms of my hoary hair."

ADDITIONAL POEMS

(1794–1801)

TO TIRZAH

Whate'er is Born of Mortal Birth
Must be consumed with the Earth
To rise from Generation free:
Then what have I to do with thee?

The Sexes sprung from Shame & Pride,
Blow'd in the morn; in evening died;
But Mercy chang'd Death into Sleep;
The Sexes rose to work & weep.

Thou, Mother of my Mortal part,
With cruelty didst mould my Heart,
And with false self-decieving tears
Didst bind my Nostrils, Eyes, & Ears:

Didst close my Tongue in senseless clay,
And me to Mortal Life betray.
The Death of Jesus set me free:
Then what have I to do with thee?

THE SCHOOLBOY

I love to rise in a summer morn
When the birds sing on every tree;

The distant huntsman winds his horn,
And the sky-lark sings with me.
O! what sweet company.

But to go to school in a summer morn,
O! it drives all joy away;
Under a cruel eye outworn,
The little ones spend the day
In sighing and dismay.

Ah! then at times I drooping sit,
And spend many an anxious hour,
Nor in my book can I take delight,
Nor sit in learning's bower,
Worn thro' with the dreary shower.

How can the bird that is born for joy
Sit in a cage and sing?
How can a child, when fears annoy,
But droop his tender wing,
And forget his youthful spring?

O! father & mother, if buds are nip'd
And blossoms blown away,
And if the tender plants are strip'd
Of their joy in the springing day,
By sorrow and care's dismay,

How shall the summer arise in joy,
Or the summer fruits appear?
Or how shall we gather what griefs destroy,
Or bless the mellowing year,
When the blasts of winter appear?

THE VOICE OF THE ANCIENT BARD

Youth of delight, come hither,
And see the opening morn,
Image of truth new born.
Doubt is fled, & clouds of reason,
Dark disputes & artful teazing.
Folly is an endless maze,
Tangled roots perplex her ways.
How many have fallen there!
They stumble all night over bones of the dead,
And feel they know not what but care,
And wish to lead others, when they should be led.

A DIVINE IMAGE

Cruelty has a Human Heart,
And Jealousy a Human Face;
Terror the Human Form Divine,
And Secrecy the Human Dress.

The Human Dress is forged Iron,
The Human Form a fiery Forge,
The Human Face a Furnace seal'd,
The Human Heart its hungry Gorge.

IV.

VERSES
AND
FRAGMENTS

FROM THE
ROSSETTI AND PICKERING
MANUSCRIPTS

FIRST SERIES

(1793–1799)

§

Never seek to tell thy love
Love that never told can be;
For the gentle wind does move
Silently, invisibly.

I told my love, I told my love,
I told her all my heart,
Trembling, cold, in ghastly fears—
Ah, she doth depart.

Soon as she was gone from me
A traveller came by
Silently, invisibly—
O, was no deny.

§

I laid me down upon a bank
Where love lay sleeping.
I heard among the rushes dank
Weeping, Weeping.

Then I went to the heath & the wild
To the thistles & thorns of the waste

And they told me how they were beguil'd,
Driven out, & compel'd to be chaste.

§

I saw a chapel all of gold
That none did dare to enter in,
And many weeping stood without,
Weeping, mourning, worshipping.

I saw a serpent rise between
The white pillars of the door,
And he forc'd & forc'd & forc'd,
Down the golden hinges tore.

And along the pavement sweet,
Set with pearls & rubies bright,
All his slimy length he drew,
Till upon the altar white

Vomiting his poison out
On the bread & on the wine.
So I turn'd into a sty
And laid me down among the swine.

§

I asked a thief to steal me a peach:
He turned up his eyes.
I ask'd a lithe lady to lie her down:
Holy & meek she cries.

As soon as I went an angel came:
He wink'd at the thief
And smil'd at the dame,
And without one word spoke
Had a peach from the tree,
And 'twixt earnest & joke
Enjoy'd the Lady.

§

I heard an Angel singing
When the day was springing,
"Mercy, Pity, Peace
Is the world's release."

Thus he sung all day
Over the new mown hay,
Till the sun went down
And haycocks looked brown.

I heard a Devil curse
Over the heath & the furze,
"Mercy could be no more,
If there was nobody poor,

"And pity no more could be,
If all were as happy as we."
At his curse the sun went down,
And the heavens gave a frown.

Down pour'd the heavy rain
Over the new reap'd grain,
And Miseries' increase
Is Mercy, Pity, Peace.

A CRADLE SONG

Sleep, Sleep, beauty bright
Dreaming o'er the joys of night.
Sleep, Sleep: in thy sleep
Little sorrows sit & weep.

Sweet Babe, in thy face
Soft desires I can trace
Secret joys & secret smiles
Little pretty infant wiles.

As thy softest limbs I feel
Smiles as of the morning steal
O'er thy cheek & o'er thy breast
Where thy little heart does rest.

O, the cunning wiles that creep
In thy little heart asleep.
When thy little heart does wake,
Then the dreadful lightnings break.

From thy cheek & from thy eye
O'er the youthful harvests nigh
Infant wiles & infant smiles
Heaven & Earth of peace beguiles.

§

I fear'd the fury of my wind
Would blight all blossoms fair & true;

And my sun it shin'd & shin'd
And my wind it never blew.

But a blossom fair or true
Was not found on any tree;
For all blossoms grew & grew
Fruitless, false, tho' fair to see.

§

Why should I care for the men of thames,
Or the cheating waves of charter'd streams,
Or shrink at the little blasts of fear
That the hireling blows into my ear?

Tho' born on the cheating banks of Thames,
Tho' his waters bathed my infant limbs,
The Ohio shall wash his stains from me:
I was born a slave, but I go to be free.

INFANT SORROW

My mother groan'd, my father wept;
Into the dangerous world I leapt,
Helpless, naked, piping loud,
Like a fiend hid in a cloud.

Struggling in my father's hands
Striving against my swaddling bands,
Bound & weary, I thought best
To sulk upon my mother's breast.

When I saw that rage was vain,
And to sulk would nothing gain,
Turning many a trick & wile,
I began to soothe & smile.

And I sooth'd day after day
Till upon the ground I stray;
And I smil'd night after night,
Seeking only for delight.

And I saw before me shine
Clusters of the wand'ring vine,
And many a lovely flower & tree
Stretch'd their blossoms out to me.

My father then with holy look,
In his hands a holy book,
Pronounc'd curses on my head
And bound me in a mirtle shade.

IN A MIRTLE SHADE

Why should I be bound to thee,
O my lovely mirtle tree?
Love, free love, cannot be bound
To any tree that grows on ground.

O, how sick & weary I
Underneath my mirtle lie,
Like to dung upon the ground
Underneath my mirtle bound.

Oft my mirtle sigh'd in vain
To behold my heavy chain;

Oft my father saw us sigh,
And laugh'd at our simplicity.

So I smote him & his gore
Stain'd the roots my mirtle bore.
But the time of youth is fled,
And grey hairs are on my head.

§

Silent, Silent Night
Quench the holy light
Of thy torches bright.

For possess'd of Day
Thousand spirits stray
That sweet joys betray

Why should joys be sweet
Used with deceit
Nor with sorrows meet?

But an honest joy
Does itself destroy
For a harlot coy.

§

O lapwing, thou fliest around the heath,
Nor seest the net that is spread beneath.
Why dost thou not fly among the corn fields?
They cannot spread nets where a harvest yields.

§

Thou hast a lap full of seed,
And this is a fine country.
Why dost thou not cast thy seed
And live in it merrily?

Shall I cast it on the sand
And turn it into fruitful land?
For on no other ground
Can I sow my seed
Without tearing up
Some stinking weed.

TO NOBODADDY

Why art thou silent & invisible,
Father of Jealousy?
Why dost thou hide thy self in clouds
From every searching Eye?

Why darkness & obscurity
In all thy words & laws,
That none dare eat the fruit but from
The wily serpent's jaws?
Or is it because Secresy gains females' loud applause?

§

Are not the joys of morning sweeter
Than the joys of night?

And are the vig'rous joys of youth
Ashamed of the light?

Let age & sickness silent rob
The vineyards in the night;
But those who burn with vig'rous youth
Pluck fruits before the light.

§

Love to faults is always blind,
Always is to joy inclin'd,
Lawless, wing'd, & unconfin'd,
And breaks all chains from every mind.

Deceit to secresy confin'd,
Lawful, cautious, & refin'd;
To every thing but interest blind,
And forges fetters for the mind.

THE WILD FLOWER'S SONG

As I wander'd the forest,
The green leaves among,
I heard a wild flower
Singing a song:

"I slept in the dark
In the silent night,
I murmur'd my fears
And I felt delight.

"In the morning I went
As rosy as morn

To seek for new Joy,
But I met with scorn."

SOFT SNOW

I walked abroad in a snowy day:
I ask'd the soft snow with me to play:
She play'd & she melted in all her prime,
And the winter call'd it a dreadful crime.

AN ANCIENT PROVERB

Remove away that black'ning church:
Remove away that marriage hearse:
Remove away that place of blood:
You'll quite remove the ancient curse.

TO MY MIRTLE

To a lovely mirtle bound,
Blossoms show'ring all around,
O, how sick & weary I
Underneath my mirtle lie.
Why should I be bound to thee,
O, my lovely mirtle tree?

MERLIN'S PROPHECY

The harvest shall flourish in wintry weather
When two virginities meet together:

The King & the Priest must be tied in a tether
Before two virgins can meet together.

DAY

The Sun arises in the East,
Cloth'd in robes of blood & gold;
Swords & spears & wrath increast
All around his bosom roll'd,
Crown'd with warlike fires & raging desires.

THE MARRIAGE RING

"Come hither my sparrows,
My little arrows.
If a tear or a smile
Will a man beguile,
If an amorous delay
Clouds a sunshiny day,
If the step of a foot
Smites the heart to its root,
'Tis the marriage ring
Makes each fairy a king."

So a fairy sung.
From the leaves I sprung.
He leap'd from the spray
To flee away.
But in my hat caught
He soon shall be taught.
Let him laugh, let him cry,
He's my butterfly;

For I've pull'd out the sting
Of the marriage ring.

§

The sword sung on the barren heath,
The sickle in the fruitful field:
The sword he sung a song of death,
But could not make the sickle yield.

§

Abstinence sows sand all over
The ruddy limbs & flaming hair,
But Desire Gratified
Plants fruits of life & beauty there.

§

In a wife I would desire
What in whores is always found—
The lineaments of Gratified desire.

§

If you trap the moment before it's ripe,
The tears of repentence you'll certainly wipe;
But if once you let the ripe moment go
You can never wipe off the tears of woe.

ETERNITY

He who binds to himself a joy
Does the winged life destroy;
But he who kisses the joy as it flies
Lives in eternity's sun rise.

THE QUESTION ANSWER'D

What is it men in women do require?
The lineaments of Gratified Desire.
What is it women do in men require?
The lineaments of Gratified Desire.

LACEDEMONIAN INSTRUCTION

"Come hither, my boy, tell me what thou seest there."
"A fool tangled in a religious snare."

RICHES

The countless gold of a merry heart,
The rubies & pearls of a loving eye,
The indolent never can bring to the mart,
Nor the secret hoard up in his treasury.

AN ANSWER TO THE PARSON

"Why of the sheep do you not learn peace?"
"Because I don't want you to shear my fleece."

§

The look of love alarms
Because 'tis fill'd with fire;
But the look of soft deceit
Shall win the lover's hire.

§

Which are beauties sweetest dress?
Soft deceit & idleness,
These are beauties sweetest dress.

MOTTO TO THE SONGS OF INNOCENCE & OF EXPERIENCE

The Good are attracted by Men's perceptions,
And think not for themselves;
Till Experience teaches them to catch
And to cage the Fairies & Elves.

And then the Knave begins to snarl
And the Hypocrite to howl;
And all his good Friends shew their private ends,
And the Eagle is known from the Owl.

§

Her whole Life is an Epigram, smart, smooth, & neatly
    pen'd,
Platted quite neat to catch applause with a sliding noose
    at the end.

§

An old maid early—e'er I knew
Ought but the love that on me grew;
And now I'm cover'd o'er & o'er
And wish that I had been a whore.

O, I cannot, cannot find
The undaunted courage of a Virgin Mind,
For Early I in love was crost,
Before my flower of love was lost.

§

"Let the Brothels of Paris be opened
With many an alluring dance
To awake the Pestilence thro' the city,"
Said the beautiful Queen of France.

The King awoke on his couch of gold,
As soon as he heard these tidings told:
"Arise & come, both fife & drum,
And the Famine shall eat both crust & crumb."

Then he swore a great & solemn Oath:
"To kill the people I am loth,
But If they rebel, they must go to hell:
They shall have a Priest & a passing bell."

Then old Nobodaddy aloft
Farted & belch'd & cough'd,

And said, "I love hanging & drawing & quartering
Every bit as well as war & slaughtering.
Damn praying & singing,
Unless they will bring in
The blood of ten thousand by fighting ~~or swinging~~."

The Queen of France just touched this Globe,
And the Pestilence darted from her robe;
But our good Queen quite grows to the ground,
And a great many suckers grow all around.

Fayette beside King Lewis stood;
He saw him sign his hand;
And soon he saw the famine rage
About the fruitful land.

Fayette beheld the Queen to smile
And wink her lovely eye;
And soon he saw the pestilence
From street to street to fly.

Fayette beheld the King & Queen
In tears & iron bound;
But mute Fayette wept tear for tear,
And guarded them around.

Fayette, Fayette, thou'rt bought & sold,
And sold is thy happy morrow;
Thou gavest the tears of Pity away
In exchange for the tears of sorrow.

Who will exchange his own fire side
For the steps of another's door?
Who will exchange his wheaten loaf
For the links of a dungeon floor?

O, who would smile on the wintry seas,
& Pity the stormy roar?
Or who will exchange his new born child
For the dog at the wintry door?

§

A fairy leapt upon my knee
Singing & dancing merrily;
I said, "Thou thing of patches, rings,
Pins, Necklaces, & such like things,
Disguiser of the Female Form,
Thou paltry, gilded, poisonous worm!"
Weeping, he fell upon my thigh,
And thus in tears did soft reply:
"Knowest thou not, O Fairies' Lord!
How much by us Contemn'd, Abhorr'd,
Whatever hides the Female form
That cannot bear the Mental storm?
Therefore in Pity still we give
Our lives to make the Female live;
And what would turn into disease
We turn to what will joy & please."

LINES FOR THE ILLUSTRATIONS
TO GRAY'S POEMS

Around the Springs of Gray my wild root weaves.
Traveller repose & Dream among my leaves.

TO MRS. ANNA FLAXMAN

A little Flower grew in a lonely Vale.
Its form was lovely but its colours pale.
One standing in the Porches of the Sun,
When his Meridian Glories were begun,
Leap'd from the steps of fire & on the grass
Alighted where this little flower was.
With hands divine he mov'd the gentle Sod
And took the Flower up in its native Clod;
Then planting it upon a Mountain's brow—
" 'Tis your own fault if you don't flourish now."

SECOND SERIES

(1800–1810)

§

The Angel that presided o'er my birth
Said, "Little creature, form'd of Joy & Mirth,
Go love without the help of any Thing on Earth."

MORNING

To find the Western path
Right thro' the Gates of Wrath
I urge my way;
Sweet Mercy leads me on:
With soft repentant moan
I see the break of day.

The war of swords & spears
Melted by dewy tears
Exhales on high;
The Sun is freed from fears
And with soft grateful tears
Ascends the sky.

§

Terror in the house does roar,
But Pity stands before the door.

141

§

Mock on, Mock on, Voltaire, Rousseau:
Mock on, Mock on; 'tis all in vain!
You throw the sand against the wind,
And the wind blows it back again.

And every sand becomes a Gem
Reflected in the beams divine;
Blown back they blind the mocking Eye,
But still in Israel's paths they shine.

The Atoms of Democritus
And Newton's Particles of light
Are sands upon the Red sea shore,
Where Israel's tents do shine so bright.

§

My Spectre around me night & day
Like a Wild beast guards my way.
My Emanation far within
Weeps incessantly for my Sin.

A Fathomless & boundless deep,
There we wander, there we weep;
On the hungry craving wind
My Spectre follows thee behind.

He scents thy footsteps in the snow,
Wheresoever thou dost go

Thro' the wintry hail & rain.
When wilt thou return again?

Dost thou not in Pride & scorn
Fill with tempests all my morn,
And with jealousies & fears
Fill my pleasant nights with tears?

Seven of my sweet loves thy knife
Has bereaved of their life.
Their marble tombs I built with tears
And with cold & shuddering fears.

Seven more loves weep night & day
Round the tombs where my loves lay,
And seven more loves attend each night
Around my couch with torches bright.

And seven more Loves in my bed
Crown with wine my mournful head,
Pitying & forgiving all
Thy transgressions, great & small.

When wilt thou return & view
My loves, & them to life renew?
When wilt thou return & live?
When wilt thou pity as I forgive?

"Never, Never, I return:
Still for Victory I burn.
Living, thee alone I'll have
And when dead I'll be thy Grave.

"Thro' the Heaven & Earth & Hell
Thou shalt never never quell:

I will fly & thou pursue,
Night & Morn the flight renew."

Till I turn from Female Love,
And root up the Infernal Grove,
I shall never worthy be
To Step into Eternity.

And, to end thy cruel mocks,
Annihilate thee on the rocks,
And another form create
To be subservient to my Fate.

Let us agree to give up Love,
And root up the infernal grove;
Then shall we return & see
The worlds of happy Eternity.

& Throughout all Eternity
I forgive you, you forgive me.
As our dear Redeemer said:
"This the Wine & this the Bread."

[Additional stanzas]

O'er my Sins thou sit & moan:
Hast thou no sins of thy own?
O'er my Sins thou sit & weep,
And lull thy own Sins fast asleep.

What Transgressions I commit
Are for thy Transgressions fit.
They thy Harlots, thou their slave,
And my Bed becomes their Grave.

Poor pale pitiable form
That I follow in a Storm,
Iron tears & groans of lead
Bind around my aking head.

THE MENTAL TRAVELLER

I travel'd thro' a Land of Men,
A Land of Men & Women too,
And heard & saw such dreadful things
As cold Earth wanderers never knew.

For there the Babe is born in joy
That was begotten in dire woe;
Just as we Reap in joy the fruit
Which we in bitter tears did sow.

And if the Babe is born a Boy
He's given to a Woman Old,
Who nails him down upon a rock,
Catches his shrieks in cups of gold.

She binds iron thorns around his head,
She pierces both his hands & feet,
She cuts his heart out at his side
To make it feel both cold & heat.

Her fingers number every Nerve,
Just as a Miser counts his gold;
She lives upon his shrieks & cries,
And she grows young as he grows old.

Till he becomes a bleeding youth,
And she becomes a Virgin bright;

Then he rends up his Manacles
And binds her down for his delight.

He plants himself in all her Nerves,
Just as a Husbandman his mould;
And she becomes his dwelling place
And Garden fruitful seventy fold.

An aged Shadow, soon he fades,
Wand'ring round an Earthly Cot,
Full filled all with gems & gold
Which he by industry had got.

And these are the gems of the Human Soul,
The rubies & pearls of a lovesick eye,
The countless gold of the akeing heart,
The martyr's groan & the lover's sigh.

They are his meat, they are his drink;
He feeds the Beggar & the Poor
And the wayfaring Traveller:
For ever open is his door.

His grief is their eternal joy;
They make the roofs & walls to ring;
Till from the fire on the hearth
A little Female Babe does spring.

And she is all of solid fire
And gems & gold, that none his hand
Dares stretch to touch her Baby form,
Or wrap her in his swaddling-band.

But She comes to the Man she loves,
If young or old, or rich or poor;

They soon drive out the aged Host,
A Beggar at another's door.

He wanders weeping far away,
Until some other take him in;
Oft blind & age-bent, sore distrest,
Untill he can a Maiden win.

And to allay his freezing Age
The Poor Man takes her in his arms;
The Cottage fades before his sight,
The Garden & its lovely Charms.

The Guests are scatter'd thro' the land,
For the Eye altering alters all;
The Senses roll themselves in fear,
And the flat Earth becomes a Ball;

The stars, sun, Moon, all shrink away,
A desart vast without a bound,
And nothing left to eat or drink,
And a dark desart all around.

The honey of her Infant lips,
The bread & wine of her sweet smile,
The wild game of her roving Eye,
Does him to Infancy beguile;

For as he eats & drinks he grows
Younger & younger every day;
And on the desart wild they both
Wander in terror & dismay.

Like the wild Stag she flees away,
Her fear plants many a thicket wild;

While he pursues her night & day,
By various arts of Love beguil'd,

By various arts of Love & Hate,
Till the wide desart planted o'er
With Labyrinths of wayward Love,
Where roam the Lion, Wolf & Boar,

Till he becomes a wayward Babe,
And she a weeping Woman Old.
Then many a Lover wanders here;
The Sun & Stars are nearer roll'd.

The trees bring forth sweet Extacy
To all who in the desart roam;
Till many a City there is Built,
And many a pleasant Shepherd's home.

But when they find the frowning Babe,
Terror strikes thro' the region wide:
They cry "The Babe! the Babe is Born!"
And flee away on Every side.

For who dare touch the frowning form,
His arm is wither'd to its root;
Lions, Boars, Wolves, all howling flee,
And every Tree does shed its fruit.

And none can touch that frowning form,
Except it be a Woman Old;
She nails him down upon the Rock,
And all is done as I have told.

THE CRYSTAL CABINET

The Maiden caught me in the Wild,
Where I was dancing merrily;
She put me into her Cabinet
And Lock'd me up with a golden Key.

This Cabinet is form'd of Gold
And Pearl & Crystal shining bright,
And within it opens into a World
And a little lovely Moony Night.

Another England there I saw,
Another London with its Tower,
Another Thames & other Hills,
And another pleasant Surrey Bower,

Another Maiden like herself,
Translucent, lovely, shining clear,
Threefold each in the other clos'd—
O, what a pleasant trembling fear!

O, what a smile! a threefold Smile
Fill'd me, that like a flame I burn'd;
I bent to Kiss the lovely Maid,
And found a Threefold Kiss return'd.

I strove to sieze the inmost Form
With ardor fierce & hands of flame,
But burst the Crystal Cabinet,
And like a Weeping Babe became—

A weeping Babe upon the wild,
And Weeping Woman pale reclin'd,
And in the outward air again
I fill'd with woes the passing Wind.

AUGURIES OF INNOCENCE

To see a World in a Grain of Sand
And a Heaven in a Wild Flower,
Hold Infinity in the palm of your hand
And Eternity in an hour.

A Robin Red breast in a Cage
Puts all Heaven in a Rage.
A dove house fill'd with doves & Pigeons
Shudders Hell thro' all its regions.
A dog starv'd at his Master's Gate
Predicts the ruin of the State.
A Horse misus'd upon the Road
Calls to Heaven for Human blood.
Each outcry of the hunted Hare
A fibre from the Brain does tear.
A Skylark wounded in the wing,
A Cherubim does cease to sing.
The Game Cock clip'd & arm'd for fight
Does the Rising Sun affright.
Every Wolf's & Lion's howl
Raises from Hell a Human Soul.
The wild deer, wand'ring here & there,
Keeps the Human Soul from Care.
The Lamb misus'd breeds Public strife
And yet forgives the Butcher's Knife.
The Bat that flits at close of Eve
Has left the Brain that won't Believe.

The Owl that calls upon the Night
Speaks the Unbeliever's fright.
He who shall hurt the little Wren
Shall never be belov'd by Men.
He who the Ox to wrath has mov'd
Shall never be by Woman lov'd.
The wanton Boy that kills the Fly
Shall feel the Spider's enmity.
He who torments the Chafer's sprite
Weaves a Bower in endless Night.
The Catterpiller on the Leaf
Repeats to thee thy Mother's grief.
Kill not the Moth nor Butterfly,
For the Last Judgment draweth nigh.
He who shall train the Horse to War
Shall never pass the Polar Bar.
The Beggar's Dog & Widow's Cat,
Feed them & thou wilt grow fat.
The Gnat that sings his Summer's song
Poison gets from Slander's tongue.
The poison of the Snake & Newt
Is the sweat of Envy's Foot.
The Poison of the Honey Bee
Is the Artist's Jealousy.
The Prince's Robes & Beggar's Rags
Are Toadstools on the Miser's Bags.
A truth that's told with bad intent
Beats all the Lies you can invent.
It is right it should be so;
Man was made for Joy & Woe;
And when this we rightly know
Thro' the World we safely go,
Joy & Woe are woven fine,
A Clothing for the Soul divine;
Under every grief & pine

Runs a joy with silken twine.
The Babe is more than swadling Bands;
Throughout all these Human Lands
Tools were made, & Born were hands,
Every Farmer Understands.
Every Tear from Every Eye
Becomes a Babe in Eternity;
This is caught by Females bright
And return'd to its own delight.
The Bleat, the Bark, Bellow & Roar
Are Waves that Beat on Heaven's Shore.
The Babe that weeps the Rod beneath
Writes Revenge in realms of death.
The Beggar's Rags, fluttering in Air,
Does to Rags the Heavens tear.
The Soldier, arm'd with Sword & Gun,
Palsied strikes the Summer's Sun.
The poor Man's Farthing is worth more
Than all the Gold on Afric's Shore.
One Mite wrung from the Labrer's hands
Shall buy & sell the Miser's Lands:
Or, if protected from on high,
Does that whole Nation sell & buy.
He who mocks the Infant's Faith
Shall be mock'd in Age & Death.
He who shall teach the Child to Doubt
The rotting Grave shall ne'er get out.
He who respects the Infant's faith
Triumphs over Hell & Death.
The Child's Toys & the Old Man's Reasons
Are the Fruits of the Two seasons.
The Questioner, who sits so sly,
Shall never know how to Reply.
He who replies to words of Doubt

Doth put the Light of Knowledge out.
The Strongest Poison ever known
Came from Caesar's Laurel Crown.
Nought can deform the Human Race
Like to the Armour's iron brace.
When Gold & Gems adorn the Plow
To peaceful Arts shall Envy Bow.
A Riddle or the Cricket's Cry
Is to Doubt a fit Reply.
The Emmet's Inch & Eagle's Mile
Make Lame Philosophy to smile.
He who Doubts from what he sees
Will ne'er Believe, do what you Please.
If the Sun & Moon should doubt,
They'd immediately Go out.
To be in a Passion you Good may do,
But no Good if a Passion is in you.
The Whore & Gambler, by the State
Licenc'd, build that Nation's Fate.
The Harlot's cry from Street to Street
Shall weave Old England's winding Sheet.
The Winner's Shout, the Loser's Curse,
Dance before dead England's Hearse.
Every Night & every Morn
Some to Misery are Born.
Every Morn & every Night
Some are Born to sweet delight.
Some are Born to sweet delight,
Some are Born to Endless Night.
We are led to Believe a Lie
When we see not Thro' the Eye
Which was Born in a Night to perish in a Night
When the Soul Slept in Beams of Light.
God Appears & God is Light

To those poor Souls who dwell in Night,
But does a Human Form Display
To those who Dwell in Realms of day.

THE GREY MONK

"I die, I die!" the Mother said,
"My Children die for lack of Bread.
What more has the merciless Tyrant said?"
The Monk sat down on the Stony Bed.

The blood red ran from the Grey Monk's side,
His hands & feet were wounded wide,
His Body bent, his arms & knees
Like to the roots of ancient trees.

His eye was dry; no tear could flow:
A hollow groan first spoke his woe.
He trembled & shudder'd upon the Bed;
At length with a feeble cry he said:

"When God commanded this hand to write
In the studious hours of deep midnight,
He told me the writing I wrote should prove
The Bane of all that on Earth I lov'd.

"My Brother starv'd between two Walls,
His Children's Cry my Soul appalls;
I mock'd at the wrack & griding chain,
My bent body mocks their torturing pain.

"Thy Father drew his sword in the North,
With his thousands strong he marched forth;

Thy Brother has arm'd himself in Steel
To avenge the wrongs thy Children feel.

"But vain the Sword & vain the Bow,
They never can work War's overthrow.
The Hermit's Prayer & the Widow's tear
Alone can free the World from fear.

"For a Tear is an Intellectual Thing,
And a Sigh is the Sword of an Angel King,
And the bitter groan of the Martyr's woe
Is an Arrow from the Almightie's Bow.

"The hand of Vengeance found the Bed
To which the Purple Tyrant fled;
The iron hand crush'd the Tyrant's head
And became a Tyrant in his stead."

LONG JOHN BROWN AND LITTLE MARY BELL

Little Mary Bell had a Fairy in a Nut,
Long John Brown had the Devil in his Gut;
Long John Brown lov'd Little Mary Bell,
And the Fairy drew the Devil into the Nut-shell.

Her Fairy skip'd out & her Fairy Skip'd in;
He laugh'd at the Devil saying "Love is a Sin."
The Devil he raged & the Devil he was wroth,
And the Devil enter'd into the Young Man's broth.

He was soon in the Gut of the loving Young Swain,
For John eat & drank to drive away Love's pain;

But all he could do he grew thinner & thinner,
Tho' he eat & drank as much as ten Men for his dinner.

Some said he had a Wolf in his stomach day & night,
Some said he had the Devil & they guess'd right;
The Fairy skip'd about in his Glory, Joy & Pride,
And he laugh'd at the Devil till poor John Brown died.

Then the Fairy skip'd out of the old Nut shell,
And woe & alack for Pretty Mary Bell!
For the Devil crept in when the Fairy skip'd out,
And there goes Miss Bell with her fusty old Nut.

WILLIAM BOND

I wonder whether the Girls are mad,
And I wonder whether they mean to kill,
And I wonder if William Bond will die,
For assuredly he is very ill.

He went to Church in a May morning
Attended by Fairies, one, two & three;
But the Angels of Providence drove them away,
And he return'd home in Misery.

He went not out to the Field nor Fold,
He went not out to the Village nor Town,
But he came home in a black, black cloud,
And took to his Bed & there lay down.

And an Angel of Providence at his Feet,
And an Angel of Providence at his Head,
And in the midst a Black, Black Cloud,
And in the midst the Sick Man on his Bed.

And on his Right hand was Mary Green,
And on his Left hand was his Sister Jane,
And their tears fell thro' the black, black Cloud
To drive away the sick man's pain.

"O William, if thou dost another Love,
Dost another Love better than poor Mary,
Go & take that other to be thy Wife,
And Mary Green shall her servant be."

"Yes, Mary, I do another Love,
Another I Love far better than thee,
And Another I will have for my Wife;
Then what have I to do with thee?

"For thou art Melancholy Pale,
And on thy Head is the cold Moon's shine,
But she is ruddy & bright as day,
And the sun beams dazzle from her eyne."

Mary trembled & Mary chill'd
And Mary fell down on the right hand floor,
That William Bond & his Sister Jane
Scarce could recover Mary more.

When Mary woke & found her Laid
On the Right hand of her William dear,
On the Right hand of his loved Bed,
And saw her William Bond so near,

The Fairies that fled from William Bond
Danced around her Shining Head;
They danced over the Pillow white,
And the Angels of Providence left the Bed.

I thought Love liv'd in the hot sun shine,
But O, he lives in the Moony light!
I thought to find Love in the heat of day,
But sweet Love is the Comforter of Night.

Seek Love in the Pity of others' Woe,
In the gentle relief of another's care,
In the darkness of night & the winter's snow,
In the naked & outcast, Seek Love there!

THE SMILE

There is a Smile of Love,
And there is a Smile of Deceit,
And there is a Smile of Smiles
In which these two Smiles meet.

And there is a Frown of Hate,
And there is a Frown of Disdain,
And there is a Frown of Frowns
Which you strive to forget in vain,

For it sticks in the Heart's deep core
And it sticks in the deep Back bone;
And no Smile that ever was smil'd,
But only one Smile alone,

That betwixt the Cradle & Grave
It only once Smil'd can be;
But, when it once is Smil'd,
There's an end to all Misery.

THE GOLDEN NET

Three Virgins at the break of day:
"Whither, young Man, whither away?
Alas for woe! alas for woe!"
They cry, & tears for ever flow.
The one was Cloth'd in flames of fire,
The other Cloth'd in iron wire,
The other Cloth'd in tears & sighs
Dazling bright before my Eyes.
They bore a Net of golden twine
To hang upon the branches fine.
Pitying I wept to see the woe
That Love & Beauty undergo,
To be consum'd in burning Fires
And in ungratified desires,
And in tears cloth'd Night & day
Melted all my Soul away.
When they saw my Tears, a Smile
That did Heaven itself beguile,
Bore the Golden Net aloft
As on downy Pinions soft
Over the Morning of my day.
Underneath the Net I stray,
Now intreating Burning Fire,
Now intreating Iron Wire,
Now intreating Tears & Sighs.
O when will the morning rise?

MARY

Sweet Mary, the first time she ever was there,
Came into the Ball room among the Fair;
The young Men & Maidens around her throng,
And these are the words upon every tongue:

"An Angel is here from the heavenly climes,
Or again does return the golden times;
Her eyes outshine every brilliant ray,
She opens her lips—'tis the Month of May."

Mary moves in soft beauty & conscious delight
To augment with sweet smiles all the joys of the Night,
Nor once blushes to own to the rest of the Fair
That sweet Love & Beauty are worthy our care.

In the Morning the Villagers rose with delight
And repeated with pleasure the joys of the night,
And Mary arose among Friends to be free,
But no Friend from henceforward thou, Mary, shalt see.

Some said she was proud, some call'd her a whore,
And some, when she passed by, shut to the door;
A damp cold came o'er her, her blushes all fled;
Her lillies & roses are blighted & shed.

"O, why was I born with a different Face?
Why was I not born like this Envious Race?
Why did Heaven adorn me with bountiful hand,
And then set me down in an envious Land?

"To be weak as a Lamb & smooth as a dove,
And not to raise Envy, is call'd Christian Love;
But if you raise Envy your Merit's to blame
For planting such spite in the weak & the tame.

"I will humble my Beauty, I will not dress fine,
I will keep from the Ball, & my Eyes shall not shine;
And if any Girl's Lover forsakes her for me,
I'll refuse him my hand & from Envy be free."

She went out in Morning attir'd plain & neat;
"Proud Mary's gone Mad," said the Child in the Street;
She went out in Morning in plain neat attire,
And came home in Evening bespatter'd with mire.

She trembled & wept, sitting on the Bed side;
She forgot it was Night, & she trembled & cried;
She forgot it was Night, she forgot it was Morn,
Her soft Memory imprinted with Faces of Scorn,

With Faces of Scorn & with Eyes of disdain
Like foul Fiends inhabiting Mary's mild Brain;
She remembers no Face like the Human Divine.
All Faces have Envy, sweet Mary, but thine;

And thine is a Face of sweet Love in despair,
And thine is a Face of mild sorrow & care,
And thine is a Face of wild terror & fear
That shall never be quiet till laid on its bier.

THE LAND OF DREAMS

Awake, awake, my little Boy!
Thou wast thy Mother's only joy;

Why dost thou weep in thy gentle sleep?
Awake! thy Father does thee keep.

"O, what Land is the Land of Dreams?
What are its Mountains & what are its Streams?
O Father, I saw my Mother there,
Among the Lillies by waters fair.

"Among the Lambs, clothed in white,
She walk'd with her Thomas in sweet delight.
I wept for joy, like a dove I mourn;
O! when shall I again return?"

Dear Child, I also by pleasant Streams
Have wander'd all Night in the Land of Dreams;
But tho' calm & warm the waters wide,
I could not get to the other side.

"Father, O Father! what do we here
In this Land of unbelief & fear?
The Land of Dreams is better far,
Above the light of the Morning Star."

DEDICATION OF THE ILLUSTRATIONS
TO BLAIR'S GRAVE

TO THE QUEEN

The Door of Death is made of Gold,
That Mortal Eyes cannot behold;
But, when the Mortal Eyes are clos'd,
And cold and pale the Limbs repos'd,
The Soul awakes; and, wond'ring, sees
In her mild Hand the golden Keys:

The Grave is Heaven's golden Gate,
And rich and poor around it wait;
O Shepherdess of England's Fold,
Behold this Gate of Pearl and Gold!

To dedicate to England's Queen
The Visions that my Soul has seen,
And, by Her kind permission, bring
What I have borne on solemn Wing
From the vast regions of the Grave,
Before Her Throne my Wings I wave;
Bowing before my Sov'reign's Feet,
"The Grave produc'd these Blossoms sweet
In mild repose from Earthly strife;
The Blossoms of Eternal Life!"

§

If it is True, what the Prophets write,
That the heathen Gods are all stocks & stones,
Shall we, for the sake of being Polite,
Feed them with the juice of our marrow bones?

And if Bezaleel & Aholiab drew
What the Finger of God pointed to their View,
Shall we suffer the Roman & Grecian Rods
To compell us to worship them as Gods?

They stole them from the Temple of the Lord,
And Worshipp'd them that they might make
                              Inspired Art Abhorr'd.

The Wood & Stone were call'd The Holy Things
And their Sublime Intent given to their Kings,

All the Atonements of Jehovah spurn'd,
And Criminals to Sacrifices Turn'd.

§

Why was Cupid a Boy
And why a boy was he?
He should have been a Girl
For ought that I can see.

For he shoots with his bow,
And the Girl shoots with her Eye,
And they both are merry & glad
And laugh when we do cry.

And to make Cupid a Boy
Was the Cupid Girl's mocking plan;
For a boy can't interpret the thing
Till he is become a man.

And then he's so pierc'd with cares
And wounded with arrowy smarts,
That the whole business of his life
Is to pick out the heads of the darts.

'Twas the Greeks' love of war
Turn'd Love into a Boy,
And Woman into a Statue of Stone—
And away flew every Joy.

§

When a Man has Married a Wife, he finds out whether
Her knees & elbows are only glewed together.

ON THE VIRGINITY OF THE VIRGIN MARY & JOHANNA SOUTHCOTT

Whate'er is done to her she cannot know,
And if you'll ask her she will swear it so.
Whether 'tis good or evil none's to blame:
No one can take the pride, no one the shame.

§

Grown old in Love from Seven till Seven times Seven,
I oft have wish'd for Hell for Ease from Heaven.

§

Since all the Riches of this World
May be gifts from the Devil & Earthly Kings,
I should suspect that I worship'd the Devil
If I thank'd my God for Worldly things.

§

Nail his neck to the Cross: nail it with a nail.
Nail his neck to the Cross: ye all have power over his
tail.

§

The Caverns of the Grave I've seen,
And these I shew'd to England's Queen.

But now the Caves of Hell I view:
Who shall I dare to shew them to?
What mighty Soul in Beauty's form
Shall dauntless View the Infernal Storm?
Egremont's Countess can controll
The flames of Hell that round me roll.
If she refuse, I still go on
Till the Heavens & Earth are gone,
Still admir'd by Noble minds,
Follow'd by Envy on the winds,
Re-engrav'd Time after Time,
Ever in their youthful prime,
My designs unchang'd remain.
Time may rage but rage in vain.
Far above Time's troubled Fountains
On the Great Atlantic Mountains,
In my Golden House on high,
There they Shine Eternally.

§

I rose up at the dawn of day—
Get thee away! get thee away!
Pray'st thou for Riches? away! away!
This is the Throne of Mammon grey.

Said I, "This sure is very odd.
I took it to be the Throne of God.
For every Thing besides I have:
It is only for Riches that I can crave.

"I have Mental Joy & Mental Health
And Mental Friends & Mental wealth;

I've a Wife I love & that loves me;
I've all but Riches Bodily.

"I am in God's presence night & day,
And he never turns his face away.
The accuser of sins by my side does stand
"And he holds my money bag in his hand.

"For my worldly things God makes him pay,
And he'd pay more if to him I would pray;
And so you may do the worst you can do:
Be assur'd Mr. devil I won't pray to you.

"Then If for Riches I must not Pray,
God knows I little of Prayers need say.
So as a Church is known by its Steeple,
If I pray it must be for other People.

"He says, if I do not worship him for a God,
I shall eat coarser food & go worse shod;
So as I don't value such things as these,
You must do, Mr. devil, just as God please."

V.

SELECTIONS
FROM
THE LETTERS

LETTERS

Blake's letters are no more personal than his other writing; he threw the full power of his personality, and its unwaking dream, into everything he did. But unlike so much of his other work, the letters show his encounter with the world. Here he is *in* the society he usually defied; it is one of the few glimpses we have of him in relation to others. Here Blake is not the lord of his own creations, a man always ready to console himself for the uniqueness of his thoughts by his own pleasure in them. He is a man talking to other men—reporting on the progress of work in hand, giving technical advice to interested craftsmen, inquiring after the health of a patron, hinting at the possibility of a sale. On occasion he is even ready to have a mutual conversation about his work, as from one man of good sense to another. He never adjusts his views to the correspondent's measure, but with the stiff and old-fashioned courtesy of his class, and out of his abundant good nature, shows himself a man ready for friendship.

Yet Blake had almost no friends; he had only admirers and enemies, patrons and colleagues. At the end, thanks to his young admirer John Linnell, there were even disciples. Friendship to him meant tolerance and encouragement of his work. The friends of his visions were his friends, and he was always ready to believe in another's

171

friendship where the usual skepticism or indifference was missing. He was touchingly grateful to anyone who took him seriously. "As to Myself, about whom you are so kindly interested, I live by miracle." When he is happy at a favor, he puts a poem into a letter. "Happiness stretch'd forth across the hills." It is not hard to believe that his happiness often did, when he felt the world would receive him. Yet these are primarily business letters. Blake was a man who never stopped thinking and working. A letter to him was the sixth finger of the hand which gave his message to the world.

Most of the letters are either to artists who befriended him—George Cumberland, John Flaxman the sculptor, Ozias Humphry, John Linnell; or to patrons like William Hayley and Thomas Butts. What is perhaps the greatest single letter, Blake's defense and exposition of his imagination to the Reverend John Trusler, beginning "I really am sorry that you are fallen out with the spiritual world," was written after the Reverend had expressed dissatisfaction with illustrations he had commissioned Blake to do for him. The nature of the Reverend Trusler's work may be guessed from the titles of two of his books—*Hogarth Moralized* and *The Way To Be Rich and Respectable*. When he received the letter he added, *Blake, dim'd with superstition*.

Thomas Butts (1759-1846), the great patron of Blake's middle period, was a wealthy and genial official who filled his house in Fitzroy Square with Blake's pictures. For many years he bought Blake's work regularly, sometimes taking a drawing a week, until he did not have room on his walls for more. Butts, though he was sometimes made uneasy by Blake's radicalism, thought well of him and tried in many ways to help him. At one period he engaged Blake to teach drawing to his son, Thomas, Junior. The Butts and Blake families got on amiably, and Butts became one of the great supports of the artist's life. The son, however, thought so little of Blake's work that he sold the original "inventions" to *The Book of Job,* as well as many other pictures.

William Hayley (1745-1820), who seems in the end to have exasperated Blake more than anyone he ever knew, was a sentimental and interminable versifier, author of the popular *The Triumphs of Temper,* lives of Cowper and Romney, and endless memorials to himself and his illegitimate son, Thomas Alphonso. Hayley, from all reports, seems to have been one of the most notorious bores of the age: a sententious squire who delivered himself of poetic epistles on all subjects. Byron said that his work was "for ever feeble and for ever tame"; Blake's account of their relations portrays a sentimental and stubborn mediocrity who employed him for a variety of jobs but seems never to have understood the talent he exploited. It was Hayley who made possible Blake's three-year stay at the Felpham cottage, in Sussex. There Blake worked, with pathetic gratitude for a chance to live in the country, at illustrations to Hayley's life of Cowper and Hayley's *Ballads* ("Founded on Anecdotes Relating to Animals"), as well as many other tasks which he could finally no longer endure. One of his first commissions for Hayley was to decorate the library of the "Bard" with eighteen heads, nearly of life size, of the great poets—among them the bewept image of the son, Thomas Alphonso, encircled by doves. In the end Hayley's complacency and interference got so on Blake's nerves that he thought it better to return to London.

John Flaxman (1755-1826), one of the earliest and most important of Blake's artist friends, was one of the most important of eighteenth-century sculptors and designers, and as important to the art of his day as Blake was generally ignored by it. His delicate and "classical" illustrations to Homer are probably his best work, but the churches of England are full of his memorials and monuments.

George Cumberland (the elder), was the author of *Thoughts on Outline,* which Blake helped to illustrate and one of the first proponents of the National Gallery. He was a devoted friend to Blake, and may have suggested the engraving technique that Blake developed into his unique method of "illuminated printing." The last engraving Blake ever did was a message card, or bookplate, for Cumberland.

Ozias Humphry (1742-1810), was one of the most famous of English miniature painters, and despite his own respectability, a great admirer of Blake's. Humphry obtained the commission from the Countess of Egremont that led to the tempera of *The Last Judgment,* described here in his letter of thanks to Humphry.

Richard Phillips, to whom Blake wrote a defense of his friend Fuseli's painting that became a characteristic attack on the painters of the period, was the editor of *The Monthly Magazine* and a bookseller.

John Linnell (1792-1882), a portrait and landscape painter, became the great support of Blake's old age, and introduced him to many young painters in the 1820's who admired and copied Blake. Linnell was one of Blake's most understanding and affectionate friends. He commissioned the illustrations to *The Book of Job* and the designs from *The Divine Comedy,* as well as a series of water-color drawings to *Paradise Regained* and other work. Linnell was so devoted to Blake that he wanted to name one of his sons after him. There is a fine letter by Linnell, written in 1830 to the Quaker poet, Bernard Barton, who had dedicated a sonnet to Linnell in gratitude for his kindness to Blake. Linnell declined to accept the dedication, saying that he did not deserve it, and added of Blake: "I never in all my conversations with him could for a moment feel that there was the least justice in calling him insane; he could always explain his paradoxes satisfactorily when he pleased, but to many he spoke so that 'hearing they might *not* hear.' He was more like the ancient patterns of virtue than I ever expected to see in this world; he feared nothing so much as being rich, lest he should lose his spiritual riches."

TO GEORGE CUMBERLAND

Lambeth
6 Decembr. 1795

DEAR SIR,

I congratulate you, not on any atchievement, because I know that the Genius that produces the Designs can execute them in any manner, notwithstanding the pretended Philosophy which teaches that Execution is the power of One & Invention of Another—Locke says it is the same faculty that Invents Judges, & I say he who can Invent can Execute.

As to laying on the Wax, it is as follows:

Take a cake of Virgin's Wax (I don't know what animal produces it) & stroke it regularly over the surface of a warm plate (the Plate must be warm enough to melt the Wax as it passes over), then immediately draw a feather over it & you will get an even surface which, when cold, will receive any impression minutely.

NOTE: The danger is in not covering the plate *all over*.

Now you will, I hope, shew all the family of Antique Borers that Peace & Plenty & Domestic Happiness is the Source of Sublime Art, & prove to the Abstract Philosophers that Enjoyment & not Abstinence is the food of Intellect.

Yours sincerely,
WILL BLAKE.

Health to Mrs. Cumberland & family.

The pressure necessary to roll off the lines is the same as when you print, or not quite so great. I have not been able to send a proof of the bath tho' I have done the corrections, my paper not being in order.

TO THE REVD. DR. TRUSLER

Hercules Buildgs., Lambeth,
Augst. 16, 1799.

REVD. SIR,

I find more & more that my Style of Designing is a Species by itself, & in this which I send you have been compell'd by my Genius or Angel to follow where he led; if I were to act otherwise it would not fulfil the purpose for which alone I live, which is, in conjunction with such men as my friend Cumberland, to renew the lost art of the Greeks.

I attempted every morning for a fortnight together to follow your Dictate, but when I found my attempts were in vain, resolv'd to shew an independence which I know will please an Author better than slavishly following the track of another, however admirable that track may be. At any rate, my Excuse must be: I could not do otherwise; it was out of my power!

I know I begged of you to give me your Ideas, &
promised to build on them; here I counted without my
host. I now find my mistake.

The Design I have sent Is:

A Father, taking leave of his Wife & Child, Is watch'd
by Two Fiends incarnate, with intention that when his
back is turned they will murder the mother & her in-
fant. If this is not Malevolence with a vengeance, I have
never seen it on Earth; & if you approve of this, I have
no doubt of giving you Benevolence with Equal Vigor,
as also Pride & Humility, but cannot previously describe
in words what I mean to Design, for fear I should Evap-
orate the spirit of my Invention. But I hope that none of
my Designs will be destitute of Infinite Particulars
which will present themselves to the Contemplator. And
tho' I call them Mine, I know that they are not Mine,
being of the same opinion with Milton when he says
That the Muse visits his slumbers & awakes & governs
his song when Morn purples the East, & being also in
the predicament of that prophet who says: "I cannot go
beyond the command of "the Lord, to speak good or
bad."

If you approve of my Manner, & it is agreeable to you,
I would rather Paint Pictures in oil of the same dimen-
sions than make Drawings, & on the same terms; by this
means you will have a number of Cabinet pictures,
which I flatter myself will not be unworthy of a scholar
of Rembrandt & Teniers, whom I have studied no less
than Rafael & Michaelangelo. Please to send me your
orders respecting this, & In my next Effort I promise
more Expedition.

> I am, Revd. Sir,
> 'Your very humble servt.
> WILLM. BLAKE.

TO THE REVD. DR. TRUSLER

13 Hercules Buildings,
Lambeth,
August 23, 1799.

REVD. SIR,

I really am sorry that you are fall'n out with the Spiritual World, Especially if I should have to answer for it. I feel very sorry that your Ideas & Mine on Moral Painting differ so much as to have made you angry with my method of study. If I am wrong, I am wrong in good company. I had hoped your plan comprehended All Species of this Art, & Expecially that you would not regret that Species which gives Existence to Every other, namely, Visions of Eternity. You say that I want somebody to Elucidate my Ideas. But you ought to know that What is Grand is necessarily obscure to Weak men. That which can be made Explicit to the Idiot is not worth my care. The wisest of the Ancients consider'd what is not too Explicit as the fittest for Instruction, becauses it rouzes the faculties to act. I name Moses, Solomon, Esop, Homer, Plato.

But as you have favor'd me with your remarks on my Design, permit me in return to defend it against a mistaken one, which is, That I have supposed Malevolence without a Cause. Is not Merit in one a Cause of Envy in another, & Serenity & Happiness & Beauty a Cause of Malevolence? But Want of Money & the Distress of A Thief can never be alleged as the Cause of his Thieving, for many honest people endure greater hardships with Fortitude. We must therefore seek the Cause elsewhere than in want of Money, for that is the Miser's passion, not the Thief's.

I have therefore proved your Reasonings Ill proportion'd, which you can never prove my figures to be; they are those of Michael Angelo, Rafael & the Antique, & of the best living Models. I percieve that your Eye is perveted by Caricature Prints, which ought not to abound so much as they do. Fun I love, but too much Fun is of all things the most loathsom. Mirth is better than Fun, & Happiness is better than Mirth. I feel that a Man may be happy in This World. And I know that This World Is a World of Imagination & Vision. I see Every thing I paint In This World, but Every body does not see alike. To the Eyes of a Miser a Guinea is far more beautiful than the Sun, & a bag worn with the use of Money has more beautiful proportions than a Vine filled with Grapes. The tree which moves some to tears of joy is in the Eyes of others only a Green thing which stands in the way. Some see Nature all Ridicule & Deformity, & by these I shall not regulate my proportions; & some scarce see Nature at all. But to the Eyes of the Man of Imagination, Nature is Imagination itself. As a man is, so he sees. As the Eye is formed, such are its Powers. You certainly Mistake, when you say that the Visions of Fancy are not to be found in This World. To Me This World is all One continued Vision of Fancy or Imagination, & I feel Flatter'd when I am told so. What is it sets Homer, Virgil & Milton in so high a rank of Art? Why is the Bible more Entertaining & Instructive than any other book? Is it not because they are addressed to the Imagination, which is Spiritual Sensation, & but mediately to the Understanding or Reason? Such is True Painting, and such was alone valued by the Greeks & the best modern Artists. Consider what Lord Bacon says: "Sense sends over to Imagination before Reason have judged, & Reason sends over to Imagination before the Decree can be acted." See Advancemt. of Learning, Part 2, P. 47 of first Edition.

But I am happy to find a Great Majority of Fellow Mortals who can Elucidate My Visions, & Particularly they have been Elucidated by Children, who have taken a greater delight in contemplating my Pictures than I even hoped. Neither Youth nor Childhood is Folly or Incapacity. Some Children are Fools & so are some Old Men. But There is a vast Majority on the side of Imagination or Spiritual Sensation.

To Engrave after another Painter is infinitely more laborious than to Engrave one's own Inventions. And of the size you require my price has been Thirty Guineas, & I cannot afford to do it for less. I had Twelve for the Head I sent you as a specimen; but after my own designs I could do at least Six times the quantity of labour in the same time, which will account for the difference of price as also that Chalk Engraving is at least six times as laborious as Aqua tinta. I have no objection to Engraving after another Artist. Engraving is the profession I was apprenticed to, & should never have attempted to live by anything else, If orders had not come in for my Designs & Paintings, which I have the pleasure to tell you are Increasing Every Day. Thus If I am a Painter it is not to be attributed to seeking after. But I am contented whether I live by Painting or Engraving.

I am, Revd. Sir, your very obedient servant,

WILLIAM BLAKE.

TO GEORGE CUMBERLAND

Hercules Buildings,
Lambeth,
Augst. 26, 1799.

DEAR CUMBERLAND,

I ought long ago to have written to you to thank you for your kind recommendation to Dr. Trusler, which, tho' it has fail'd of success, is not the less to be remember'd by me with Gratitude.

I have made him a Drawing in my best manner; he has sent it back with a Letter full of Criticisms, in which he says It accords not with his Intentions, which are to Reject all Fancy from his Work. How far he Expects to please, I cannot tell. But as I cannot paint Dirty rags & old shoes where I ought to place Naked Beauty or simple ornament, I despair of Ever pleasing one Class of Men. Unfortunately our authors of books are among this Class; how soon we shall have a change for the better I cannot Prophecy. Dr. Trusler says: "*Your Fancy,* from what I have seen of it, & I have seen variety at Mr. Cumberland's, seems to be in the other world, or the World of Spirits, which accords not with my Intentions, which, whilst living in This World, Wish to follow *the Nature of it.*" I could not help smiling at the difference between the doctrines of Dr. Trusler & those of Christ. But, however, for his own sake I am sorry that a Man should be so enamour'd of Rowlandson's caricatures as to call them copies from life & manners, or fit Things for a Clergyman to write upon.

Pray let me intreat you to persevere in your Designing; it is the only source of Pleasure. All your other pleasures depend upon It. It is the Tree; your Pleasures are the Fruit. Your Inventions of Intellectual Visions are the Stamina of every thing you value. Go on, if not for your own sake, yet for ours, who love & admire your works; but, above all, For the Sake of the Arts. Do not throw aside for any long time the honour intended you by Nature to revive the Greek workmanship. I study your outlines as usual, just as if they were antiques.

As to Myself, about whom you are so kindly Interested, I live by Miracle. I am Painting small Pictures from the Bible. For as to Engraving, in which art I cannot reproach myself with any neglect, yet I am laid by in a corner as if I did not Exist, & since my Young's Night Thoughts have been publish'd, Even Johnson & Fuseli have discarded my Graver. But as I know that he who Works & has his health cannot starve, I laugh at Fortune & Go on & on. I think I foresee better Things than I have ever seen. My Work pleases my employer, & I have an order for Fifty small Pictures at one Guinea each, which is something better than mere copying after another artist. But above all, I feel myself happy & contented let what will come; having passed now near twenty years in ups & downs, I am used to them, & perhaps a little practise in them may turn out to benefit. It is now Exactly Twenty years since I was upon the ocean of business, & tho' [I] laugh at Fortune, I am perswaded that She Alone is the Governor of Worldly Riches, & when it is Fit she will call on me; till then I wait with Patience, in hopes that She is busied among my Friends.

With Mine & My Wife's best compliments to Mrs. Cumberland, I remain,

Yours sincerely,

WILLM. BLAKE.

TO WILLIAM HAYLEY

Lambeth,
May 6, 1800.

DEAR SIR,

I am very sorry for your immense loss, which is a repetition of what all feel in this valley of misery and happiness mixed. I send the shadow of the departed angel, and hope the likeness is improved. The lips I have again lessened as you advise, and done a good many other softenings to the whole. I know that our deceased friends are more really with us than when they were apparent to our mortal part. Thirteen years ago I lost a brother, and with his spirit I converse daily and hourly in the spirit, and see him in my remembrance, in the regions of my imagination. I hear his advice, and even now write from his dictate. Forgive me for expressing to you my enthusiasm, which I wish all to partake of, since it is to me a source of immortal joy, even in this world. By it I am the companion of angels. May you continue to be so more and more; and to be more and more persuaded that every mortal loss is an immortal gain. The ruins of Time build mansions in Eternity.

I have also sent a proof of Pericles for your remarks, thanking you for the kindness with which you express them, and feeling heartily your grief with a brother's sympathy.

I remain,
Dear Sir,
Your humble servant,
WILLIAM BLAKE.

TO GEORGE CUMBERLAND

13, Hercules Buildings, Lambeth.
2, July, 1800.

DEAR CUMBERLAND,

I have to congratulate you on your plan for a National Gallery being put into Execution. All your wishes shall in due time be fulfilled; the immense flood of Grecian light & glory which is coming on Europe will more than realize our warmest wishes. Your honours will be unbounded when your plan shall be carried into Execution as it must be if England continues a Nation. I hear that it is now in the hands of Ministers, That the King shews it great Countenance & Encouragement, that it will soon be before Parliament, & that it *must* be extended & enlarged to take in Originals both of Painting & Sculpture by considering every valuable original that is brought into England or can be purchased Abroad as its objects of Acquisition. Such is the Plan as I am told & such must be the plan if England wishes to continue at all worth notice; as you have yourself observ'd only now, we must possess Originals as well as France or be Nothing.

Excuse, I intreat you, my not returning Thanks at the proper moment for your kind present. No perswasion could make my stupid head believe that it was proper for me to trouble you with a letter of meer compliment & Expression of thanks. I begin to Emerge from a deep pit of Melancholy, Melancholy without any real reason for it, a Disease which God keep you from & all good men. Our artists of all ranks praise your outlines &

wish for more. Flaxman is very warm in your commendation & more and more of A Grecian. Mr. Hayley has lately mentioned your work on outline in Notes to an Essay on Sculpture in Six Epistles to John Flaxman. I have been too little among friends which I fear they will not Excuse & I know not how to apologize for. Poor Fuseli, sore from the lash of Envious tongues, praises you & dispraises with the same breath; he is not naturally good natured, but he is artificially very ill natured, yet even from him I learn the Estimation you are held in among artists & connoisseurs.

I am still Employ'd in making Designs & little Pictures with now & then an Engraving & find that in future to live will not be so difficult as it has been. It is very Extraordinary that London in so few years from a city of meer Necessaries or at l[e]ast a commerce of the lowest order of luxuries should have become a City of Elegance in some degree & that its once stupid inhabitants should enter into an Emulation of Grecian manners. There are now, I believe, as many Booksellers as there are Butchers & as many Printshops as of any other trade. We remember when a Print shop was a rare bird in London & I myself remember when I thought my pursuits of Art a kind of criminal dissipation & neglect of the main chance, which I hid my face for not being able to abandon as a Passion which is forbidden by Law & Religion, but now it appears to be Law & Gospel too, at least I hear so from the few friends I have dared to visit in my stupid Melancholy. Excuse this communication of sentiments which I felt necessary to my repose at this time. I feel very strongly that I neglect my Duty to my Friends but It is not want of Gratitude or Friendship but perhaps an Excess of both.

Let me hear of your welfare. Remember My & My

Wife's Respectful Compliments to Mrs. Cumberland &
Family

    & believe me to be for Ever
Yours
WILLIAM BLAKE.

TO JOHN FLAXMAN

MY DEAREST FRIEND,

    It is to you I owe All my present Happiness. It is to
you I owe perhaps the Principal Happiness of my life.
I have presum'd on your friendship in staying so long
away & not calling to know of your welfare, but hope
now every thing is nearly completed for our removal to
Felpham, that I shall see you on Sunday, as we have ap-
pointed Sunday afternoon to call on Mrs. Flaxman at
Hampstead. I send you a few lines, which I hope you
will Excuse. And As the time is arriv'd when Men shall
again converse in Heaven & walk with Angels, I know
you will be pleased with the Intention, & hope you will
forgive the Poetry.

    To My Dearest Friend, John Flaxman, these lines:

I bless thee, O Father of Heaven & Earth, that ever I saw
    Flaxman's face.
Angels stand round my Spirit in Heaven, the blessed of
    Heaven are my friends upon Earth.
When Flaxman was taken to Italy, Fuseli was given to me
    for a season,
And now Flaxman hath given me Hayley his friend to be
    mine, such my lot upon Earth.
Now my lot in the Heavens is this, Milton lov'd me in child-
    hood & shew'd me his face.
Ezra came with Isaiah the Prophet, but Shakespeare in riper
    years gave me his hand;

Paracelsus & Behmen appear'd to me, terrors appear'd in
 the Heavens above
And in Hell beneath, & a mighty & awful change threatened
 the Earth.
The American War began. All its dark horrors passed before
 my face
Across the Atlantic to France. Then the French Revolution
 commenc'd in thick clouds,
And My Angels have told me that seeing such visions I
 could not subsist on the Earth,
But by my conjunction with Flaxman, who knows to for-
 give Nervous Fear.

I remain, for Ever Yours,   WILLIAM BLAKE.

Be so kind as to Read & then seal the Inclosed & send
it on its much beloved Mission.

TO MRS. FLAXMAN[1]

H B, Lambeth,
14 Septr. 1800.

MY DEAREST FRIEND,

 I hope you will not think we could forget your Serv-
ices to us, or any way neglect to love & remember with
affection even the hem of your garment; we indeed pre-
sume on your kindness in neglecting to have call'd on
you since my Husband's first return from Felpham. We
have been incessantly busy in our great removal; but
can never think of going without first paying our proper
duty to you & Mr. Flaxman. We intend to call on Sun-
day afternoon in Hampstead, to take farewell, All things
being now nearly completed for our setting forth on
Tuesday Morning; it is only Sixty Miles, & Lambeth
was One Hundred, for the terrible desart of London

---

[1] *Written by Catherine Blake.*

was between. My husband has been obliged to finish several things necessary to be finished before our migration; the Swallows call us, fleeting past our window at this moment. O how we delight in talking of the pleasure we shall have in preparing you a summer bower at Felpham, & we not only talk, but behold! the Angels of our journey have inspired a song to you:

To My Dear Friend, Mrs. Anna Flaxman.

This Song to the flower of Flaxman's joy,
To the blossom of hope, for a sweet decoy:
Do all that you can or all that you may,
To entice him to Felpham & far away:

Away to Sweet Felpham, for Heaven is there;
The Ladder of Angels descends thro' the air;
On the Turret its spiral does softly descend,
Thro' the village then winds, at My Cot it does end.

You stand in the village & look up to heaven;
The precious stones glitter on flights seventy seven;
And My Brother is there, & My Friend & Thine
Descend & ascend with the Bread & the Wine.

The Bread of sweet Thought & the Wine of Delight
Feeds the Village of Felpham by day & by night;
And at his own door the bless'd Hermit does stand,
Dispensing, Unceasing, to all the whole Land.

W. BLAKE.

Recieve my & my husband's love & affection, & believe me to be Yours affectionately,

CATHERINE BLAKE.

TO JOHN FLAXMAN

Felpham,
Septr. 21, 1800, Sunday Morning.

DEAR SCULPTOR OF ETERNITY,

We are safe arrived at our Cottage, which is more beautiful than I thought it, & more convenient. It is a perfect Model for Cottages &, I think, for Palaces of Magnificence, only Enlarging, not altering its proportions, & adding ornaments & not principals. Nothing can be more Grand than its Simplicity & Usefulness. Simple without Intricacy, it seems to be the Spontaneous Effusion of Humanity, congenial to the wants of Man. No other formed House can ever please me so well; nor shall I ever be perswaded, I believe, that it can be improved either in Beauty or Use.

Mr. Hayley recieved us with his usual brotherly affection. I have begun to work. Felpham is a sweet place for Study, because it is more Spiritual than London. Heaven opens here on all sides her golden Gates; her windows are not obstructed by vapours; voices of Celestial inhabitants are more distinctly heard, & their forms more distinctly seen; & my Cottage is also a Shadow of their houses. My Wife & Sister are both well, courting Neptune for an embrace.

Our Journey was very pleasant; & tho' we had a great deal of Luggage, No Grumbling; All was Chearfulness & Good Humour on the Road, & yet we could not arrive at our Cottage before half past Eleven at night, owing to the necessary shifting of our Luggage from one Chaise to another; for we had Seven Different Chaises, & as many different drivers. We set out between Six & Seven in the Morning of Thursday, with Sixteen heavy boxes & portfolios full of prints. And Now Begins a New life, because another covering of Earth is shaken off. I am more famed in Heaven for my works than I could well concieve. In my Brain are studies & Chambers filled with books & pictures of old, which I wrote & painted in ages of Eternity before my mortal life; & those works are the delight & Study of Archangels. Why, then, should I be anxious about the riches or fame of mortality? The Lord our father will do for us & with us according to his divine will for our Good.

You, O dear Flaxman, are a Sublime Archangel, My Friend & Companion from Eternity; in the Divine bosom is our dwelling place. I look back into the regions of Reminiscence & behold our ancient days before this Earth appear'd in its vegetated mortality to my mortal vegetated Eyes. I see our houses of Eternity, which can never be separated, tho' our Mortal vehicles should stand at the remotest corners of heaven from each other.

Farewell, My Best Friend! Remember Me & My Wife in Love & Friendship to our Dear Mrs. Flaxman, whom we ardently desire to Entertain beneath our thatched roof of rusted gold, & believe me for ever to remain

Your Grateful & Affectionate,

WILLIAM BLAKE.

TO THOMAS BUTTS

DEAR FRIEND OF MY ANGELS,

We are safe arrived at our Cottage without accident or hindrance, tho' it was between Eleven & Twelve o'clock at night before we could get home, owing to the necessary shifting of our boxes & portfolios from one Chaise to another. We had Seven different Chaises & as many different drivers. All upon the road was chearful-

ness & welcome; tho' our luggage was very heavy there
was no grumbling at all. We travel'd thro' a most beauti-
ful country on a most glorious day. Our Cottage is more
beautiful than I thought it, & also more convenient, for
tho' small it is well proportion'd, & if I should ever build
a Palace it would be only My Cottage Enlarged. Please
to tell Mrs. Butts that we have dedicated a Chamber
for her service, & that it has a very fine view of the Sea.
Mr. Hayley reciev'd me with his usual brotherly affec-
tion. My Wife & Sister are both very well, & courting
Neptune for an Embrace, whose terrors this morning
made them afraid, but whose mildness is often Equal
to his terrors. The villagers of Felpham are not meer
Rustics; they are polite & modest. Meat is cheaper than
in London, but the sweet air & the voices of winds,
trees & birds, & the odours of the happy ground, makes
it a dwelling for immortals. Work will go on here with
God speed.—A roller & two harrows lie before my win-
dow. I met a plow on my first going out at my gate the
first morning after my arrival, & the Plowboy said to
the Plowman, "Father, The Gate is Open." I have begun
to Work, & find that I can work with greater pleasure
than ever. Hope soon to give you a proof that Felpham
is propitious to the Arts.

God bless you! I shall wish for you on Tuesday Eve-
ning as usual. Pray give My & My wife & sister's love &
respects to Mrs. Butts; accept them yourself, & believe
me, for ever,

Your affectionate & obliged Friend,

WILLIAM BLAKE.

My Sister will be in town in a week, & bring with her
your account & whatever else I can finish.

Direct to Me:

Blake, Felpham, near Chichester, Sussex.

TO THOMAS BUTTS

Felpham, *Octr. 2d 1800.*

FRIEND OF RELIGION & ORDER,

I thank you for your very beautiful & encouraging Verses, which I account a Crown of Laurels, & I also thank you for your reprehension of follies by me foster'd. Your prediction will, I hope, be fulfilled in me, & in future I am the determined advocate of Religion & Humility, the two bands of Society. Having been so full of the Business of Settling the sticks & feathers of my nest, I have not got any forwarder with "the three Marys" or with any other of your commissions; but hope, now I have commenced a new life of industry, to do credit to that new life by Improved Works. Recieve from me a return of verses, such as Felpham produces by me, tho' not such as she produces by her Eldest Son; however, such as they are, I cannot resist the temptation to send them to you.

> To my Friend Butts I write
> My first Vision of Light,
> On the yellow sands sitting.
> The Sun was Emitting
> His Glorious beams
> From Heaven's high Streams.
> Over Sea, over Land
> My Eyes did Expand
> Into regions of air
> Away from all Care,
> Into regions of fire
> Remote from Desire;
> The Light of the Morning
> Heaven's Mountains adorning:
> In particles bright
> The jewels of Light

Distinct shone & clear.
Amaz'd & in fear
I each particle gazed,
Astonish'd, Amazed;
For each was a Man
Human-form'd. Swift I ran,
For they beckon'd to me
Remote by the Sea,
Saying: "Each grain of Sand,
Every Stone on the Land,
Each rock & each hill,
Each fountain & rill,
Each herb & each tree,
Mountain, hill, earth & sea,
Cloud, Meteor & Star,
Are Men seen Afar."
I stood in the Streams
Of Heaven's bright beams,
And Saw Felpham sweet
Beneath my bright feet
In soft Female charms;
And in her fair arms
My Shadow I knew
And my wife's shadow too,
And My Sister & Friend.
We like Infants descend
In our Shadows on Earth,
Like a weak mortal birth.
My Eyes more and more
Like a Sea without shore
Continue Expanding,
The Heavens commanding,
Till the Jewels of Light,
Heavenly Men beaming bright,
Appear'd as One Man,
Who complacent began
My limbs to infold
In his beams of bright gold;
Like dross purg'd away
All my mire & my clay.
Soft consum'd in delight
In his bosom Sun bright
I remain'd. Soft he smil'd,

And I heard his voice Mild
Saying: "This is My Fold,
O thou Ram horn'd with gold,
Who awakest from Sleep
On the Sides of the Deep.
On the Mountains around
The roarings resound
Of the lion & wolf,
The loud Sea & deep gulf.
These are guards of My Fold,
O thou Ram horn'd with gold!"
And the voice faded mild.
I remain'd as a Child;
All I ever had known
Before me bright Shone.
I saw you & your wife
By the fountains of Life.
Such the Vision to me
Appear'd on the sea.

Mrs. Butts will, I hope, Excuse my not having finish'd the Portrait. I wait for less hurried moments. Our Cottage looks more & more beautiful. And tho' the weather is wet, the Air is very Mild, much Milder than it was in London when we came away. Chichester is a very handsome City, Seven miles from us; we can get most Conveniences there. The Country is not so destitute of accomodations to our wants as I expected it would be. We have had but little time for viewing the Country, but what we have seen is Most Beautiful, & the People are Genuine Saxons, handsomer than the people about London. Mrs. Butts will Excuse the following lines:

To Mrs. Butts.

Wife of the Friend of those I most revere,
Receive this tribute from a Harp sincere;
Go on in Virtuous Seed sowing on Mold
Of Human Vegetation, & Behold

Your Harvest Springing to Eternal Life,
Parent of Youthful Minds, & happy Wife!
W.B.
I am for Ever Yours,
WILLIAM BLAKE.

TO WILLIAM HAYLEY

Felpham, 26th November 1800.

DEAR SIR,

Absorbed by the poets Milton, Homer, Camoens, Er-
cilla, Ariosto, and Spenser, whose physiognomies have
been my delightful study, *Little Tom* has been of late
unattended to, and my wife's illness not being quite
gone off, she has not printed any more since you went to
London. But we can muster a few in colours and some
in black, which I hope will be no less favour'd, tho' they
are rough like rough sailors. We mean to begin printing
again to-morrow. Time flies very fast and very merrily.
I sometimes try to be miserable that I may do more
work, but find it is a foolish experiment. Happinesses
have wings and wheels; miseries are leaden legged, and
their whole employment is to clip the wings and to take
off the wheels of our chariots. We determine, therefore,
to be happy and do all that we can, tho' not all that we
would. Our dear friend Flaxman is the theme of my
emulation in this of industry, as well as in other virtues
and merits. Gladly I hear of his full health and spirits.
Happy son of the immortal Phidias, his lot is truly glori-
ous, and mine no less happy in his friendship and in that
of his friends. Our cottage is surrounded by the same
guardians you left with us; they keep off every wind.
We hear the west howl at a distance, the south bounds
on high over our thatch, and smiling on our cottage say:

"You lay too low for my anger to injure." As to the east and north, I believe they cannot get past the Turret.

My wife joins with me in duty and affection to you. Please to remember us both in love to Mr. and Mrs. Flaxman, and

> believe me to be your affectionate,
>> Enthusiastic, hope fostered visionary,
>>> WILLIAM BLAKE.

TO THOMAS BUTTS

> Felpham Cottage, of Cottages the prettiest,
>> *September 11, 1801.*

MY DEAR SIR,

I hope you will continue to excuse my want of steady perseverance, by which want I am still so much your debtor & you so much my Credit-er; but such as I can be, I will. I can be grateful, & I can soon Send you some of your designs which I have nearly completed. In the mean time by my Sister's hands I transmit to Mrs. Butts an attempt at your likeness, which I hope she, who is the best judge, will think like. Time flies faster (as seems to me) here than in London. I labour incessantly & accomplish not one half of what I intend, because my Abstract folly hurries me often away while I am at work, carrying me over Mountains & Valleys, which are not Real, in a Land of Abstraction where Spectres of the Dead wander. This I endeavour to prevent & with my whole might chain my feet to the world of Duty & Reality; but in vain! the faster I bind, the better is the Ballast, for I, so far from being bound down, take the world with me in my flights, & often it seems lighter than a ball of wool rolled by the wind. Bacon & Newton would prescribe ways of making the world heavier to me, &

Pitt would prescribe distress for a medicinal potion; but as none on Earth can give me Mental Distress, & I know that all Distress inflicted by Heaven is a Mercy, a Fig for all Corporeal! Such Distress is My mock & scorn. Alas! wretched, happy, ineffectual labourer of time's moments that I am! who shall deliver me from this Spirit of Abstraction & Improvidence? Such, my Dear Sir, Is the truth of my state, & I tell it you in palliation of my seeming neglect of your most pleasant orders; but I have not neglected them; & yet a Year is rolled over, & only now I approach the prospect of sending you some, which you may expect soon. I should have sent them by My Sister, but, as the Coach goes three times a week to London & they will arrive as safe as with her, I shall have the opportunity of inclosing several together which are not yet completed. I thank you again & again for your generous forbearance, of which I have need—& now I must express my wishes to see you at Felpham & to shew you Mr. Hayley's Library, which is still un-finish'd, but is in a finishing way & looks well. I ought also to mention my Extreme disappointment at Mr. Johnson's forgetfulness, who appointed to call on you but did Not. He is also a happy Abstract, known by all his Friends as the most innocent forgetter of his own Interests. He is nephew to the late Mr. Cowper the Poet; you would like him much. I continue painting Minia-tures & Improve more & more, as all my friends tell me; but my Principal labour at this time is Engraving Plates for Cowper's Life, a Work of Magnitude, which Mr. Hayley is now labouring with all his matchless industry, & which will be a most valuable acquisition to Litera-ture, not only on account of Mr. Hayley's composition, but also as it will contain Letters of Cowper to his friends, Perhaps, or rather Certainly, the very best let-ters that ever were published.

My wife joins with me in Love to you & Mrs. Butts, hoping that her joy is now increased, & yours also, in an increase of family & of health & happiness.

I remain, Dear Sir,

Ever Yours Sincerely,

WILLIAM BLAKE.

Next time I have the happiness to see you, I am determined to paint another Portrait of you from Life in my best manner, for Memory will not do in such minute operations; for I have now discover'd that without Nature before the painter's Eye, he can never produce any thing in the walks of Natural Painting. Historical Designing is one thing & Portrait Painting another, & they are as Distinct as any two Arts can be. Happy would that Man be who could unite them!

P.S. Please to Remember our best respects to Mr. Birch, & tell him that Felpham Men are the mildest of the human race; if it is the will of Providence, they shall be the wisest. We hope that he will, next summer, joke us face to face.—God bless you all!

TO   JOHN   FLAXMAN

Oct 19, 1801.

DEAR FLAXMAN,

I rejoice to hear that your Great Work is accomplished. Peace opens the way to greater still. The Kingdoms of this World are now become the Kingdoms of God & His Christ, & we shall reign with him for ever & ever. The Reign of Literature & the Arts commences. Blessed are those who are found studious of Literature & Humane & polite accomplishments. Such have their lamps burning & such shall shine as the stars.

Mr. Thomas, your friend to whom you was so kind as to make honourable mention of me, has been at Felpham & did me the favor to call on me. I have promis'd him to send my designs for Comus when I have done them, directed to you.

Now I hope to see the Great Works of Art, as they are so near to Felpham: Paris being scarce further off than London. But I hope that France & England will henceforth be as One Country and their Arts One, & that you will ere long be erecting Monuments In Paris— Emblems of Peace.

My wife joins with me in love to You & Mrs. Flaxman.

I remain, Yours Sincerely

WILLIAM BLAKE.

I have just seen Weller.—all y'r friends in the North are willing to await y'r leisure for Works of Marble, but Weller says it would soothe & comfort the good sister of the upright Mr. D. to see a little sketch from y'r hand. Adio.

TO THOMAS BUTTS

Felpham,
Jany. 10, 1802.

DEAR SIR,

Your very kind & affectionate Letter & the many kind things you have said in it, call'd upon me for an immediate answer; but it found My Wife & Myself so Ill, & My wife so very ill, that till now I have not been able to do this duty. The Ague & Rheumatism have been almost her constant Enemies, which she has combated in vain ever since we have been here; & her sickness is always my sorrow, of course. But what you tell me about your sight afflicted me not a little, & that about your health, in another part of your letter, makes me intreat you to take due care of both; it is a part of our duty to God & man to take due care of his Gifts; & tho' we ought not [to] think *more* highly of ourselves, yet we ought to think *As* highly of ourselves as immortals ought to think.

When I came down here, I was more sanguine than I am at present; but it was because I was ignorant of many things which have since occurred, & chiefly the unhealthiness of the place. Yet I do not repent of coming on a thousand accounts; & Mr. H., I doubt not, will do ultimately all that both he & I wish—that is, to lift me out of difficulty; but this is no easy matter to a man who, having Spiritual Enemies of such formidable magnitude, cannot expect to want natural hidden ones.

Your approbation of my pictures is a Multitude to Me, & I doubt not that all your kind wishes in my behalf shall in due time be fulfilled. Your kind offer of pecuniary assistance I can only thank you for at present, because I have enough to serve my present purpose here; our expenses are small, & our income, from our incessant labour, fully adequate to them at present. I am now engaged in Engraving 6 small plates for a New Edition of Mr. Hayley's Triumphs of Temper, from drawings by Maria Flaxman, sister to my friend the Sculptor, and it seems that other things will follow in course, if I do but Copy these well; but Patience! if Great things do not turn out, it is because such things depend on the Spiritual & not on the Natural World; & if it was fit for me, I doubt not that I should be Employ'd in Greater things; & when it is proper, my Talents shall be properly exercised in Public, as I hope they are now in private; for, till then, I leave no stone unturn'd & no path unexplor'd that lends to improvement in my beloved Arts. One thing of real consequence I have accomplish'd by com-

ing into the country, which is to me consolation enough:
namely, I have recollected all my scatter'd thoughts on
Art & resumed my primitive & original ways of Execu-
tion in both painting & engraving, which in the confu-
sion of London I had very much lost & obliterated from
my mind. But whatever becomes of my labours, I would
rather that they should be preserv'd in your Green
House (not, as you mistakenly call it, dunghill) than in
the cold gallery of fashion.—The Sun may yet shine, &
then they will be brought into open air.

But you have so generously & openly desired that I
will divide my griefs with you, that I cannot hide what
it is now become my duty to explain.—My unhappiness
has arisen from a source which, if explor'd too narrowly,
might hurt my pecuniary circumstances, As my depend-
ence is on Engraving at present, & particularly on the
Engravings I have in hand for Mr. H.: & I find on all
hands great objections to my doing anything but the
meer drudgery of business, & intimations that if I do not
confine myself to this, I shall not live; this has always
pursu'd me. You will understand by this the source of
all my uneasiness. This from Johnson & Fuseli brought
me down here, & this from Mr. H. will bring me back
again; for that I cannot live without doing my duty to
lay up treasures in heaven is Certain & Determined, &
to this I have long made up my mind, & why this should
be made an objection to Me, while Drunkenness, Lewd-
ness, Gluttony & even Idleness itself, does not hurt other
men, let Satan himself Explain. The Thing I have most
at Heart—more than life, or all that seems to make life
comfortable without—Is the Interest of True Religion
& Science, & whenever any thing appears to affect that
Interest (Especially if I myself omit any duty to my Sta-
tion as a Soldier of Christ), It gives me the greatest of
torments. I am not ashamed, afraid, or averse to tell you

what Ought to be Told: That I am under the direction
of Messengers from Heaven, Daily & Nightly; but the
nature of such things is not, as some suppose, without
trouble or care. Temptations are on the right hand &
left; behind, the sea of time & space roars & follows
swiftly; he who keeps not right onward is lost, & if our
footsteps slide in clay, how can we do otherwise than
fear & tremble? but I should not have troubled You with
this account of my spiritual state, unless it had been
necessary in explaining the actual cause of my uneasi-
ness, into which you are so kind as to Enquire; for I
never obtrude such things on others unless question'd,
& then I never disguise the truth.—But if we fear to do
the dictates of our Angels, & tremble at the Tasks set
before us; if we refuse to do Spiritual Acts because of
Natural Fears or Natural Desires! Who can describe the
dismal torments of such a state!—I too well remember
the Threats I heard!—"If you, who are organised by
Divine Providence for spiritual communion, Refuse, &
bury your Talent in the Earth, even tho' you should
want Natural Bread, Sorrow & Desperation pursues you
thro' life, & after death shame & confusion of face to
eternity. Every one in Eternity will leave you, aghast at
the Man who was crown'd with glory & honour by his
brethren, & betray'd their cause to their enemies. You
will be call'd the base Judas who betray'd his Friend!"
—Such words would make any stout man tremble, &
how then could I be at ease? But I am now no longer in
That State, & now go on again with my Task, Fearless,
and tho' my path is difficult, I have no fear of stumbling
while I keep it.

My wife desires her kindest Love to Mrs. Butts, & I
have permitted her to send it to you also; we often wish
that we could unite again in Society, & hope that the

time is not distant when we shall do so, being determin'd not to remain another winter here, but to return to London.

"I hear a voice you cannot hear, that says I must not stay,
I see a hand you cannot see, that beckons me away."

Naked we came here, naked of Natural things, & naked we shall return; but while cloth'd with the Divine Mercy, we are richly cloth'd in Spiritual & suffer all the rest gladly. Pray give my Love to Mrs. Butts & your family. I am, Yours Sincerely,

WILLIAM BLAKE.

P.S. Your Obliging proposal of Exhibiting my two Pictures likewise calls for my thanks; I will finish the other, & then we shall judge of the matter with certainty.

TO THOMAS BUTTS

Felpham, *Novr. 22, 1802.*

DEAR SIR,

My Brother tells me that he fears you are offended with me. I fear so too, because there appears some reason why you might be so. But when you have heard me out, you will not be so.

I have now given two years to the intense study of those parts of the art which relate to light & shade & colour, & am Convinc'd that either my understanding is incapable of comprehending the beauties of Colouring, or the Pictures which I painted for you Are Equal in Every part of the Art, & superior in One, to any thing that has been done since the age of Rafael.—All Sr. J. Reynolds's discourses to the Royal Academy will shew that the Venetian finesse in Art can never be united with the Majesty of Colouring necessary to Historical beauty; & in a letter to the Revd. Mr. Gilpin, author of a work on Picturesque Scenery, he says Thus: "It may be worth consideration whether the epithet Picturesque is not applicable to the excellencies of the inferior Schools rather than to the higher. The works of Michael Angelo, Rafael, &c., appear to me to have nothing of it: whereas Rubens & the Venetian Painters may also be said to have Nothing Else.—Perhaps Picturesque is somewhat synonymous to the word Taste, which we should think improperly applied to Homer or Milton, but very well to Prior or Pope. I suspect that the application of these words are to Excellencies of an inferior order, & which are incompatible with the Grand Style. You are certainly right in saying that variety of Tints & Forms is Picturesque; but it must be remember'd, on the other hand, that the reverse of this (*uniformity of Colour & a long continuation of lines*) produces Grandeur."—So says Sir Joshua, and so say I; for I have now proved that the parts of the art which I neglected to display in those little pictures & drawings which I had the pleasure & profit to do for you, are incompatible with the designs. —There is nothing in the Art which our Painters do that I can confess myself ignorant of. I also Know & Understand & can assuredly affirm, that the works I have done for you are Equal to Carrache or Rafael (and I am now seven years older than Rafael was when he died), I say they are Equal to Carrache or Rafael, or Else I am Blind, Stupid, Ignorant and Incapable in two years' Study to understand those things which a Boarding school Miss can comprehend in a fortnight. Be assured,

My dear Friend, that there is not one touch in those Drawings & Pictures but what came from my Head & my Heart in Unison; That I am Proud of being their Author and Grateful to you my Employer; & that I look upon you as the Chief of my Friends, whom I would endeavour to please, because you, among all men, have enabled me to produce these things. I would not send you a Drawing or a Picture till I had again reconsider'd my notions of Art, & had put myself back as if I was a learner. I have proved that I am Right, & shall now Go on with the Vigour I was in my Childhood famous for.

But I do not pretend to be Perfect: but, if my Works have faults, Carrache, Corregio, & Rafael's have faults also; let me observe that the yellow leather flesh of old men, the ill drawn & ugly young women, &, above all, the dawbed black & yellow shadows that are found in most fine, ay, & the finest pictures, I altogether reject as ruinous to Effect, tho' Connoisseurs may think otherwise.

Let me also notice that Carrache's Pictures are not like Correggio's, nor Correggio's like Rafael's; &, if neither of them was to be encouraged till he did like any of the others, he must die without Encouragement. My Pictures are unlike any of these Painters, & I would have them to be so. I think the manner I adopt More Perfect than any other; no doubt They thought the same of theirs.

You will be tempted to think that, as I improve, The Pictures, &c., that I did for you are not what I would now wish them to be. On this I beg to say That they are what I intended them, & that I know I never shall do better; for, if I were to do them over again, they would lose as much as they gain'd, because they were done in the heat of my Spirits.

But you will justly enquire why I have not written all this time to you? I answer I have been very Unhappy, & could not think of troubling you about it, or any of my real Friends. (I have written many letters to you which I burn'd & did not send) & why I have not before now finish'd the Miniature I promiss'd to Mrs. Butts? I answer I have not, till now, in any degree pleased myself, & now I must intreat you to Excuse faults, for Portrait Painting is the direct contrary to Designing & Historical Painting, in every respect. If you have not Nature before you for Every Touch, you cannot Paint Portrait; & if you have Nature before you at all, you cannot Paint History; it was Michael Angelo's opinion & is Mine. Pray Give My Wife's love with mine to Mrs. Butts; assure her that it cannot be long before I have the pleasure of Painting from you in Person, & then that she may Expect a likeness, but now I have done All I could, & know she will forgive any failure in consideration of the Endeavour.

And now let me finish with assuring you that, Tho' I have been very unhappy, I am so no longer. I am again Emerged into the light of day; I still & shall to Eternity Embrace Christianity and Adore him who is the Express image of God; but I have travel'd thro' Perils & Darkness not unlike a Champion. I have Conquer'd, and shall Go on Conquering. Nothing can withstand the fury of my Course among the Stars of God & in the Abysses of the Accuser. My Enthusiasm is still what it was, only Enlarged and confirm'd.

I now Send Two Pictures & hope you will approve of them. I have enclosed the Account of Money receiv'd & Work done, which I ought long ago to have sent you; pray forgive Errors in omissions of this kind. I am incapable of many attentions which it is my Duty to observe towards you, thro' multitude of employment & thro' hope of soon seeing you again. I often omit to

Enquire of you. But pray let me now hear how you do
& of the welfare of your family.

Accept my Sincere love & respect.

I remain Yours Sincerely,

WILLM. BLAKE.

A Piece of Sea Weed serves for a Barometer; it gets
wet & dry as the weather gets so.

TO THOMAS BUTTS

DEAR SIR,

After I had finish'd my Letter, I found that I had not
said half what I intended to say, & in particular I wish to
ask you what subject you choose to be painted on the
remaining Canvas which I brought down with me (for
there were three), and to tell you that several of the
Drawings were in great forwardness; you will see by the
Inclosed Account that the remaining Number of Draw-
ings which you gave me orders for is Eighteen. I will
finish these with all possible Expedition, if indeed I
have not tired you, or, as it is politely call'd, Bored you
too much already; or, if you would rather cry out
"Enough, Off, Off!", tell me in a Letter of forgiveness if
you were offended, & of accustom'd friendship if you
were not. But I will bore you more with some Verses
which My Wife desires me to Copy out & send you with
her kind love & Respect; they were Composed above a
twelvemonth ago, while walking from Felpham to La-
vant to meet my Sister:

With happiness stretch'd across the hills
In a cloud that dewy sweetness distills,
With a blue sky spread over with wings

And a mild sun that mounts & sings,
With trees & fields full of Fairy elves
And little devils who fight for themselves—
Rememb'ring the Verses that Hayley sung
When my heart knock'd against the root of my tongue—
With Angels planted in Hawthorn bowers
And God himself in the passing hours,
With Silver Angels across my way
And Golden Demons that none can stay,
With my Father hovering upon the wind
And my Brother Robert just behind
And my Brother John, the evil one,
In a black cloud making his mone;
Tho' dead, they appear upon my path,
Notwithstanding my terrible wrath:
They beg, they intreat, they drop their tears,
Fill'd full of hopes, fill'd full of fears—
With a thousand Angels upon the Wind
Pouring disconsolate from behind
To drive them off, & before my way
A frowning Thistle implores my stay.
What to others a trifle appears
Fills me full of smiles or tears;
For double the vision my Eyes do see,
And a double vision is always with me.
With my inward Eye 'tis an old Man grey;
With my outward, a Thistle across my way.
"If thou goest back," the thistle said,
"Thou art to endless woe betray'd;
For here does Theotormon lower
And here is Enitharmon's bower
And Los the terrible thus hath sworn,
Because thou backward dost return,
Poverty, Envy, old age & fear
Shall bring thy Wife upon a bier;
And Butts shall give what Fuseli gave,
A dark black Rock & a gloomy Cave."

I struck the Thistle with my foot,
And broke him up from his delving root:
"Must the duties of life each other cross?
Must every joy be dung & dross?
Must my dear Butts feel cold neglect

Because I give Hayley his due respect?
Must Flaxman look upon me as wild,
And all my friends be with doubts beguil'd?
Must my Wife live in my Sister's bane,
Or my Sister survive on my Love's pain?
The curses of Los, the terrible shade,
And his dismal terrors make me afraid."

So I spoke & struck in my wrath
The old man weltering upon my path.
Then Los appear'd in all his power:
In the Sun he appear'd, descending before
My face in fierce flames; in my double sight
'Twas outward a Sun, inward Los in his might.

"My hands are labour'd day & night,
And Ease comes never in my sight.
My Wife has no indulgence given
Except what comes to her from heaven.
We eat little, we drink less;
This Earth breeds not our happiness.
Another Sun feeds our life's streams,
We are not warmed with thy beams;
Thou measurest not the Time to me,
Nor yet the Space that I do see;
My Mind is not with thy light array'd
Thy terrors shall not make me afraid."

When I had my Defiance given,
The Sun stood trembling in heaven;
The Moon that glow'd remote below,
Became leprous & white as snow;
And every soul of men on the Earth
Felt affliction & sorrow & sickness & dearth.
Los flam'd in my path, & the Sun was hot
With the bows of my Mind & the Arrows of Thought—
My bowstring fierce with Ardour breathes,
My arrows glow in their golden sheaves;
My brother & father march before;
The heavens drop with human gore.

Now I a fourfold vision see,
And a fourfold vision is given to me;

'Tis fourfold in my supreme delight
And threefold in soft Beulah's night
And twofold Always. May God us keep
From Single vision & Newton's sleep!

I also inclose you some Ballads by Mr. Hayley, with prints to them by your Hble. Servt. I should have sent them before now, but could not get any thing done for you to please myself; for I do assure you that I have truly studied the two little pictures I now send, & do not repent of the time I have spent upon them.

God bless you.

Yours,

W. B.

P.S. I have taken the liberty to trouble you with a letter to my Brother, which you will be so kind as to send or give him, & oblige yours,

W. B.

TO THOMAS BUTTS

Felpham,
April 25, 1803.

My DEAR SIR,

I write in haste, having reciev'd a pressing Letter from my Brother. I intended to have sent the Picture of the Riposo, which is nearly finish'd much to my satisfaction, but not quite; you shall have it soon. I now send the 4 Numbers for Mr. Birch, with best Respects to him. The Reason the Ballads have been suspended is the pressure of other business, but they will go on again soon.

Accept of my thanks for your kind & heartening Letter. You have Faith in the Endeavours of Me, your

weak brother and fellow Disciple; how great must be
your faith in our Divine Master! You are to me a Lesson
of Humility, while you Exalt me by such distinguishing
commendations. I know that you see certain merits in
me, which, by God's Grace, shall be made fully ap-
parent & perfect in Eternity; in the mean time I must
not bury the Talents in the Earth, but do my endeavour
to live to the Glory of our Lord & Saviour; & I am also
grateful to the kind hand that endeavours to lift me out
of despondency, even if it lifts me too high.

And now, My Dear Sir, Congratulate me on my re-
turn to London, with the full approbation of Mr. Hayley
& with Promise—But, Alas!

Now I may say to you, what perhaps I should not
dare to say to anyone else: That I can alone carry on my
visionary studies in London unannoy'd, & that I may
converse with my friends in Eternity, See Visions,
Dream Dreams & prophecy & speak Parables unobserv'd
& at liberty from the Doubts of other Mortals; perhaps
Doubts proceeding from Kindness, but Doubts are al-
ways pernicious, Especially when we Doubt our
Friends. Christ is very decided on this Point: "He who is
Not With Me is Against Me." There is no Medium or
Middle state; & if a Man is the Enemy of my Spiritual
Life while he pretends tc be the Friend of my Cor-
poreal, he is a Real Enemy—but the Man may be the
friend of my Spiritual Life while he seems the Enemy
of my Corporeal, but Not Vice Versa.

What is very pleasant, Every one who hears of my
going to London again Applauds it as the only course
for the interest of all concern'd in My Works, Observing
that I ought not to be away from the opportunities Lon-
don affords of seeing fine Pictures, and the various im-
provements in Works of Art going on in London.

But none can know the Spiritual Acts of my three

years' Slumber on the banks of the Ocean, unless he has seen them in the Spirit, or unless he should read My long Poem descriptive of those Acts; for I have in these three years composed an immense number of verses on One Grand Theme, Similar to Homer's Iliad or Milton's Paradise Lost, the Persons & Machinery intirely new to the Inhabitants of Earth (some of the Persons Excepted). I have written this Poem from immediate Dictation, twelve or sometimes twenty or thirty lines at a time, without Premeditation & even against my Will; the Time it has taken in writing was thus render'd Non Existent, & an immense Poem Exists which seems to be the Labour of a long Life, all produc'd without Labour or Study. I mention this to shew you what I think the Grand Reason of my being brought down here.

I have a thousand & ten thousand things to say to you. My heart is full of futurity. I percieve that the sore travel which has been given me these three years leads to Glory & Honour. I rejoice & I tremble: "I am fearfully & wonderfully made." I had been reading the cxxxix Psalm a little before your Letter arrived. I take your advice. I see the face of my Heavenly Father; he lays his Hand upon my Head & gives a blessing to all my works; why should I be troubled? why should my heart & flesh cry out? I will go on in the Strength of the Lord; through Hell will I sing forth his Praises, that the Dragons of the Deep may praise him, & that those who dwell in darkness & in the Sea coasts may be gather'd into his Kingdom. Excuse my, perhaps, too great Enthusiasm. Please to accept of & give our Loves to Mrs. Butts & your amiable Family, & believe me to be,

Ever Yours Affectionately,

WILL BLAKE.

TO THOMAS BUTTS

Felpham,
July 6, 1803.

DEAR SIR,

I send you the Riposo, which I hope you will think my best Picture in many respects. It represents the Holy Family in Egypt, Guarded in their Repose from those Fiends, the Egyptian Gods, and tho' not directly taken from a Poem of Milton's (for till I had design'd it Milton's Poem did not come into my Thoughts), Yet it is very similar to his Hymn on the Nativity, which you will find among his smaller Poems, & will read with great delight. I have given, in the background a building, which may be supposed the ruin of a Part of Nimrod's tower, which I conjecture to have spread over many Countries; for he ought to be reckon'd of the Giant brood.

I have now on the Stocks the following drawings for you: 1. Jephthah sacrificing his Daughter; 2. Ruth & her mother in Law & Sister; 3. The three Maries at the Sepulcher; 4. The Death of Joseph; 5. The Death of the Virgin Mary; 6. St. Paul Preaching; & 7. The Angel of the Divine Presence clothing Adam & Eve with Coats of Skins.

These are all in great forwardness, & I am satisfied that I improve very much & shall continue to do so while I live, which is a blessing I can never be too thankful for both to God & Man.

We look forward every day with pleasure toward our meeting again in London with those whom we have learn'd to value by absence no less perhaps than we did by presence; for recollection often surpasses every thing, indeed, the prospect of returning to our friends is supremely delightful—Then, I am determined that Mrs. Butts shall have a good likeness of You, if I have hands & eyes left; for I am become a likeness taker & succeed admirably well; but this is not to be atchiev'd without the original sitting before you for Every touch, all likenesses from memory being necessarily very, very defective; But Nature & Fancy are Two Things & can Never be join'd; neither ought any one to attempt it, for it is Idolatry & destroys the Soul.

I ought to tell you that Mr. H is quite agreeable to our return, & that there is all the appearance in the world of our being fully employ'd in Engraving for his projected Works, Particularly Cowper's Milton, a Work now on foot by Subscription, & I understand that the Subscription goes on briskly. This work is to be a very Elegant one & to consist of All Milton's Poems, with Cowper's Notes and translations by Cowper from Milton's Latin & Italian Poems. These works will be ornamented with Engravings from Designs from Romney, Flaxman & Yr. hble Servt., & to be Engrav'd also by the last mention'd. The Profits of the work are intended to be appropriated to Erect a Monument to the Memory of Cowper in St. Paul's or Westminster Abbey. Such is the Project—& Mr. Addington & Mr. Pitt are both among the Subscribers, which are already numerous & of the first rank; the price of the Work is Six Guineas—Thus I hope that all our three years' trouble Ends in Good Luck at last & shall be forgot by my affections & only remember'd by my Understanding; to be a Memento in time to come, & to speak to future generations by a Sublime Allegory, which is now perfectly completed into a Grand Poem. I may praise it, since I dare not pretend to be any other than the Secretary; the Authors are in Eternity. I consider it as the Grandest Poem that this World Contains.

Allegory addressed to the Intellectual powers, while it is altogether hidden from the Corporeal Understanding, is My Definition of the Most Sublime Poetry; it is also somewhat in the same manner defin'd by Plato. This Poem shall, by Divine Assistance, be progressively Printed & Ornamented with Prints & given to the Public. But of this work I take care to say little to Mr. H., since he is as much averse to my poetry as he is to a Chapter in the Bible. He knows that I have writ it, for I have shewn it to him, & he has read Part by his own desire & has looked with sufficient contempt to enhance my opinion of it. But I do not wish to irritate by seeming too obstinate in Poetic pursuits. But if all the World should set their faces against This, I have Orders to set my face like a flint (Ezekiel iiiC, 9v) against their faces, & my forehead against their foreheads.

As to Mr. H., I feel myself at liberty to say as follows upon this ticklish subject: I regard Fashion in Poetry as little as I do in Painting; so, if both Poets & Painters should alternately dislike (but I know the majority of them will not), I am not to regard it at all, but Mr. H. approves of My Designs as little as he does of my Poems, and I have been forced to insist on his leaving me in both to my own Self Will; for I am determin'd to be no longer Pester'd with his Genteel Ignorance & Polite Disapprobation. I know myself both Poet & Painter, & it is not his affected Contempt that can move me to any thing but a more assiduous pursuit of both Arts. Indeed, by my late Firmness I have brought down his affected Loftiness, & he begins to think I have some Genius: as if Genius & Assurance were the same thing! but his imbecile attempts to depress Me only deserve laughter. I say thus much to you, knowing that you will not make a bad use of it. But it is a Fact too true That, if I had only depended on Mortal Things, both myself

& my wife must have been Lost. I shall leave every one in This Country astonish'd at my Patience & Forbearance of Injuries upon Injuries; & I do assure you that, if I could have return'd to London a Month after my arrival here, I should have done so, but I was commanded by my Spiritual friends to bear all, to be silent, & to go thro' all without murmuring, &, in fine, hope, till my three years should be almost accomplish'd; at which time I was set at liberty to remonstrate against former conduct & to demand Justice & Truth; which I have done in so effectual a manner that my antagonist is silenc'd completely, & I have compell'd what should have been of freedom—My Just Right as an Artist & as a Man; & if any attempt should be made to refuse me this, I am inflexible & will relinquish any engagement of Designing at all, unless altogether left to my own Judgment, As you, My dear Friend, have always left me; for which I shall never cease to honour & respect you.

When we meet, I will perfectly describe to you my Conduct & the Conduct of others toward me, & you will see that I have labour'd hard indeed, & have been borne on angel's wings. Till we meet I beg of God our Saviour to be with you & me, & yours & mine. Pray give my & my wife's love to Mrs. Butts & Family, & believe me to remain,

Yours in truth & sincerity,
WILL BLAKE.

TO THOMAS BUTTS

Felpham,
August 16, 1803.

Dear Sir,

I send 7 Drawings, which I hope will please you; this, I believe, about balances our account. Our return to London draws on apace; our Expectation of meeting again with you is one of our greatest pleasures. Pray tell me how your Eyes do. I never sit down to work but I think of you, & feel anxious for the sight of that friend whose Eyes have done me so much good. I omitted (very unaccountably) to copy out in my last Letter that passage in my rough sketch which related to your kindness in offering to Exhibit my 2 last Pictures in the Gallery in Berners Street; it was in these Words: "I sincerely thank you for your kind offer of Exhibiting my 2 Pictures; the trouble you take on my account, I trust, will be recompensed to you by him who seeth in secret; if you should find it convenient to do so, it will be gratefully remember'd by me among the other numerous kindnesses I have received from you."

I go on with the remaining Subjects which you gave me commission to Execute for you, but shall not be able to send any more before my return, tho' perhaps I may bring some with me finish'd. I am at Present in a Bustle to defend myself against a very unwarrantable warrant from a Justice of Peace in Chichester, which was taken out against me by a Private in Captn. Leathes's troop of 1st or Royal Dragoons, for an assault & seditious words. The wretched Man has terribly Perjur'd himself, as has his Comrade; for, as to Sedition, not one Word relating to the King or Government was spoken by either him or me. His Enmity arises from my having turned him out of my Garden, into which he was invited as an assistant by a Gardener at work therein, without my knowledge that he was so invited. I desired him, as politely as was possible, to go out of the Garden; he made me an impertinent answer. I insisted on his leaving the Garden; he refused. I still persisted in desiring his departure; he then threaten'd to knock out my Eyes, with many abominable imprecations & with some contempt for my Person; it affronted my foolish Pride. I therefore took him by the Elbows & pushed him before me till I had got him out; there I intended to have left him, but he, turning about, put himself into a Posture of Defiance, threatening & swearing at me. I, perhaps foolishly & perhaps not, stepped out at the Gate, &, putting aside his blows, took him again by the Elbows, &, keeping his back to me, pushed him forwards down the road about fifty yards—he all the while endeavouring to turn round & strike me, & raging & cursing, which drew out several neighbours; at length, when I had got him to where he was Quarter'd, which was very quickly done, we were met at the Gate by the Master of the house, The Fox Inn (who is the proprietor of my Cottage), & his wife & Daughter & the Man's Comrade & several other people. My Landlord compell'd the Soldiers to go in doors, after many abusive threats against me & my wife from the two Soldiers; but not one word of threat on account of Sedition was utter'd at that time. This method of Revenge was Plann'd between them after they had got together into the stable. This is the whole outline. I have for witnesses: The Gardener, who is Hostler at the Fox & who Evidences that, to his knowledge, no word of the remotest tendency to Government or Sedition was utter'd: Our next door Neighbour, a Miller's wife, who saw me turn him before me down the road, & saw & heard all that happen'd at the Gate of the Inn, who Evidences that no Expression of threatening on account of Sedition was utter'd in the heat of their fury by either of the Dragoons; this was the woman's own remark, & does high honour to her good sense, as she observes that, whenever a quarrel happens, the offence is always repeated. The Landlord of the Inn & his Wife & daughter will Evidence the same, & will evidently prove the Comrade perjur'd, who swore that he heard me, while at the Gate, utter Seditious words & D— the K—, without which perjury I could not have been committed; & I had no witness with me before the Justices who could combat his assertion, as the Gardener remain'd in my Garden all the while, & he was the only person I thought necessary to take with me. I have been before a Bench of Justices at Chichester this morning; but they, as the Lawyer who wrote down the Accusation told me in private, are compell'd by the Military to suffer a prosecution to be enter'd into: altho' they must know, & it is manifest, that the whole is a Fabricated Perjury. I have been forced to find Bail. Mr. Hayley was kind enough to come forwards, & Mr. Seagrave, printer at Chichester; Mr. H. in £100, & Mr. S. in £50; & myself am bound in £100 for my appearance at the Quarter Sessions, which is after Michaelmas. So I shall have the satisfaction to see my friends in Town before this Contemptible business comes on. I say Contemptible, for it must be manifest to every one that the whole accusation is a wilful Perjury. Thus, you see, my dear Friend, that I cannot leave this place without some adventure; it has struck a consternation thro' all the Villages round. Every Man is now afraid of speaking to, or looking at, a Soldier; for the peaceable Villagers have always been forward in expressing their kindness for us, & they express their sorrow at our departure as soon as

they hear of it. Every one here is my Evidence for Peace
& Good Neighbourhood; & yet, such is the present state
of things, this foolish accusation must be tried in Public.
Well, I am content, I murmur not & doubt not that I
shall recieve Justice, & am only sorry for the trouble &
expense. I have heard that my Accuser is a disgraced
Sergeant; his name is John Scholfield; perhaps it will be
in your power to learn somewhat about the Man. I am
very ignorant of what I am requesting of you; I only
suggest what I know you will be kind enough to Ex-
cuse if you can learn nothing about him, & what, I as
well know, if it is possible, you will be kind enough to
do in this matter.

Dear Sir, This perhaps was suffer'd to Clear up some
doubts, & to give opportunity to those whom I doubted
to clear themselves of all imputation. If a Man offends
me ignorantly & not designedly, surely I ought to con-
sider him with favour & affection. Perhaps the simplicity
of myself is the origin of all offences committed against
me. If I have found this, I shall have learned a most
valuable thing, well worth three years' perseverance. I
have found it. It is certain that a too passive manner, in-
consistent with my active physiognomy, had done me
much mischief. I must now express to you my conviction
that all is come from the spiritual World for Good, & not
for Evil.

Give me your advice in my perilous adventure; burn
what I have peevishly written about any friend. I have
been very much degraded & injuriously treated; but if
it all arise from my own fault, I ought to blame myself.

O why was I born with a different face?
Why was I not born like the rest of my race?
When I look, each one starts! when I speak, I offend;
Then I'm silent & passive & lose every Friend.

Then my verse I dishonour, My pictures despise,
My person degrade & my temper chastise;
And the pen is my terror, the pencil my shame;
All my Talents I bury, and dead is my Fame.

I am either too low or too highly priz'd;
When Elate I am Envy'd, When Meek I'm despis'd.

This is but too just a Picture of my Present state. I pray God to keep you & all men from it, & to deliver me in his own good time. Pray write to me, & tell me how you & your family enjoy health. My much terrified Wife joins me in love to you & Mrs. Butts & all your family. I again take the liberty to beg of you to cause the Enclos'd Letter to be deliver'd to my Brother, & remain Sincerely & Affectionately Yours,

WILLIAM BLAKE.

TO WILLIAM HAYLEY

London,
7 October, 1803.

DEAR SIR,

Your generous & tender solicitude about your devoted rebel makes it absolutely necessary that he should trouble you with an account of his safe arrival, which will excuse his begging the favor of a few lines to inform him how you escaped the contagion of the Court of Justice— I fear that you have & must suffer more on my account than I shall ever be worth—Arrived safe in London, my wife in very poor health, still I resolve not to lose hope of seeing better days.

Art in London flourishes. Engravers in particular are wanted. Every Engraver turns away work that he cannot execute from his superabundant Employment. Yet no one brings work to me. I am content that it shall be so as long as God pleases. I know that many works of a lucrative nature are in want of hands; other Engravers are courted. I suppose that I must go a Courting, which I shall do awkwardly; in the meantime I lose no moment to complete Romney to satisfaction.

How is it possible that a Man almost 50 years of Age, who has not lost any of his life since he was five years old without incessant labour & study, how is it possible that such a one with ordinary common sense can be inferior to a boy of twenty, who scarcely has taken or deigns to take pencil in hand, but who rides about the Parks or saunters about the Playhouses, who Eats & drinks for business not for need, how is it possible that such a fop can be superior to the studious lover of Art can scarcely be imagin'd. Yet such is somewhat like my fate & such it is likely to remain. Yet I laugh & sing, for if on Earth neglected I am in heaven a Prince among Princes, & even on Earth beloved by the Good as a Good Man; this I should be perfectly contented with, but at certain periods a blaze of reputation arises round me in which I am consider'd as one distinguish'd by some mental perfection, but the flame soon dies again & I am left stupified and astonish'd. O that I could live as others do in a regular succession of Employment, this wish I fear is not to be accomplish'd to me—Forgive this Dirge-like lamentation over a dead horse, & now I have lamented over the dead horse let me laugh & be merry with my friends till Christmas, for as Man liveth not by bread alone, I shall live altho I should want bread—nothing is necessary to me but to do my Duty & to rejoice in the exceeding joy that is always poured out on my Spirit, to pray that my friends & you above the rest may be made partakers of the joy that the world cannot concieve, that you may still be replenish'd with the same

& be as you always have been, a glorious & triumphant
Dweller in immortality. Please to pay for me my best
thanks to Miss Poole: tell her that I wish her a continued
Excess of Happiness—some say that Happiness is not
Good for Mortals, & they ought to be answer'd that Sor-
row is not fit for Immortals & is utterly useless to any
one; a blight never does good to a tree, & if a blight kill
not a tree but it still bear fruit, let none say that the fruit
was in consequence of the blight. When this Soldier-
like danger is over I will do double the work I do now,
for it will hang heavy on my Devil who terribly resents
it; but I soothe him to peace, & indeed he is a good na-
tur'd Devil after all & certainly does not lead me into
scrapes—he is not in the least to be blamed for the pres-
ent scrape, as he was out of the way all the time on
other employment seeking amusement in making Verses,
to which he constantly leads me very much to my hurt
& sometimes to the annoyance of my friends; as I per-
cieve he is now doing the same work by my letter, I will
finish it, wishing you health & joy in God our Saviour.

To Eternity yours,
WILL^M. BLAKE.

TO WILLIAM HAYLEY

24 May, 1804.

DEAR SIR,

I thank you heartily for your kind offer of reading, &c.
I have read the book thro' attentively and was much en-
tertain'd and instructed, but have not yet come to the
Life of Washington. I suppose an American would tell
me that Washington did all that was done before he was
born, as the French now adore Buonaparte and the Eng-
lish our poor George; so the Americans will consider

Washington as their god. This is only Grecian, or rather Trojan, worship, and perhaps will be revised [?] in an age or two. In the meantime I have the happiness of seeing the Divine countenance in such men as Cowper and Milton more distinctly than in any prince or hero. Mr. Phillips has sent a small poem; he would not tell the author's name, but desired me to inclose it for you with Washington's *Life*. . . .

Mr. Johnson has, at times, written such letters to me as would have called for the sceptre of Agamemnon rather than the tongue of Ulysses, and I will venture to give it as my settled opinion that if you suffer yourself to be persuaded to print in London you will be cheated every way; but, however, as some little excuse, I must say that in London every calumny and falsehood utter'd against another of the same trade is thought fair play. Engravers, Painters, Statuaries, Printers, Poets, we are not in a field of battle, but in a City of Assassinations. This makes your lot truly enviable, and the country is not only more beautiful on account of its expanded meadows, but also on account of its benevolent minds. My wife joins with me in the hearty wish that you may long enjoy your beautiful retirement.

I am, with best respects to Miss Poole, for whose health we constantly send wishes to our spiritual friends,

Yours sincerely,
WILLIAM BLAKE.

TO WILLIAM HAYLEY

23 October, 1804.

DEAR SIR,

I received your kind letter with the note to Mr. Payne, and have had the cash from him. I should have returned my thanks immediately on receipt of it, but hoped to be able to send, before now, proofs of the two plates, the Head of R[omney] and The Shipwreck, which you shall soon see in a much more perfect state. I write immediately because you wish I should do so, to satisfy you that I have received your kind favour.

I take the extreme pleasure of expressing my joy at our good Lady of Lavant's continued recovery: but with a mixture of sincere sorrow on account of the beloved Counsellor. My wife returns her heartfelt thanks for your kind inquiry concerning her health. She is surprisingly recovered. Electricity is the wonderful cause; the swelling of her legs and knees is entirely reduced. She is very near as free from rheumatism as she was five years ago, and we have the greatest confidence in her perfect recovery.

The pleasure of seeing another poem from your hands has truly set me longing (my wife says I ought to have said us) with desire and curiosity; but, however, "Christmas is a-coming."

Our good and kind friend Hawkins is not yet in town —hope soon to have the pleasure of seeing him, with the courage of conscious industry, worthy of his former kindness to me. For now! O Glory! and O Delight! I have entirely reduced that spectrous fiend to his station, whose annoyance has been the ruin of my labours for the last passed twenty years of my life. He is the enemy of conjugal love and is the Jupiter of the Greeks, an iron-hearted tyrant, the ruiner of ancient Greece. I speak with perfect confidence and certainty of the fact which has passed upon me. Nebuchadnezzar had seven times passed over him; I have had twenty; thank God I was not altogether a beast as he was; but I was a slave bound in a mill among beasts and devils; these beasts and these devils are now, together with myself, become children of light and liberty, and my feet and my wife's feet are free from fetters. O lovely Felpham, parent of Immortal Friendship, to thee I am eternally indebted for my three years' rest from perturbation and the strength I now enjoy. Suddenly, on the day after visiting the Truchsessian Gallery of pictures, I was again enlightened with the light I enjoyed in my youth, and which has for exactly twenty years been closed from me as by a door and by window-shutters. Consequently I can, with confidence, promise you ocular demonstration of my altered state on the plates I am now engraving after Romney, whose spiritual aid has not a little conduced to my restoration to the light of Art. O the distress I have undergone, and my poor wife with me: incessantly labouring and incessantly spoiling what I had done well. Every one of my friends was astonished at my faults, and could not assign a reason; they knew my industry and abstinence from every pleasure for the sake of study, and yet—and yet—and yet there wanted the proofs of industry in my works. I thank God with entire confidence that it shall be so no longer—he is become my servant who domineered over me, he is even as a brother who was my enemy. Dear Sir, excuse my enthusiasm or rather madness, for I am really drunk with intellectual vision whenever I take a pencil or graver into my hand, even as I used to be in my youth, and as I have not been for twenty dark, but very profitable, years. I thank God that I courageously pursued my course through darkness. In a short time I shall make my assertion good that I am become suddenly as I was at first, by producing the Head of Romney and The Shipwreck quite another thing from what you or I ever expected them to be. In short, I am now satisfied and proud of my work, which I have not been for the above long period.

If our excellent and manly friend Meyer is yet with

you, please to make my wife's and my own most respect-
ful and affectionate compliments to him, also to our kind
friend at Lavant.

I remain, with my wife's joint affection,

Your sincere and obliged servant,

WILL BLAKE.

TO WILLIAM HAYLEY

4 December, 1804.

"Proofs of my plates will wait on you in a few days.
I have mentioned your proposals to our noble Flaxman,
whose high & generous spirit relinquishes the whole to
me—but that he will overlook and advise. . . . I have
indeed fought thro' a Hell of terrors and horrors (which
none could know but myself) in a divided existence;
now no longer divided nor at war with myself, I shall
travel on in the strength of the Lord God, as Poor Pil-
grim "says." [*Extracts from sale catalogue.*]

TO WILLIAM HAYLEY

South Molton Street,
28 Dec^r., 1804.

DEAR SIR,

The Death of so Excellent a Man as my Generous Ad-
vocate is a Public Loss, which those who knew him can
best Estimate, & to those who have an affection for him
like Yours, is a Loss that only can be repair'd in Eter-
nity, where it will indeed with such abundant felicity, in
the meeting Him a Glorified Saint who was a suffering
Mortal, that our Sorrow is swallow'd up in Hope. Such
Consolations are alone to be found in Religion, the Sun

& the Moon of our Journey; & such sweet Verses as yours in your last beautiful Poem must now afford you their full reward.

Farewell, Sweet Rose! thou hast got before me into the Celestial City. I also have but a few more Mountains to pass: for I hear the bells ring & the trumpets sound to welcome thy arrival among Cowper's Glorified Band of Spirits of Just Men made Perfect.

Now, My Dear Sir, I will thank you for the transmission of ten Pounds to the Dreamer over his own Fortunes: for I certainly am that Dreamer; but tho' I dream over my own Fortunes, I ought not to Dream over those of other Men, & accordingly have given a look over my account Book, in which I have regularly written down Every Sum I have receiv'd from you; & tho' I never can balance the account of obligations with you, I ought to do my best at all times & in all circumstances. I find that you was right in supposing that I had been paid for all I have done; but when I wrote last requesting ten pounds, I thought it was Due on the Shipwreck (which it was), but I did not advert to the Twelve Guineas which you Lent Me when I made up 30 Pounds to pay our worthy Seagrave in part of his Account. I am therefore that 12 Guineas in your Debt: Which If I had consider'd, I should have used more consideration, & more ceremony also, in so serious an affair as the calling on you for more Money; but, however, your kind answer to my Request makes me Doubly Thank you.

The two Cartoons which I have of Hecate & Pliny are very unequal in point of finishing: the Pliny is a Sketch, tho' admirably contrived for an Effect equal to Rembrandt. But the Hecate is a finish'd Production, which will call for all the Engraver's nicest attention; indeed it is more finish'd than the Shipwreck; it is everybody['s] favourite who have seen it, & they regularly prefer it to the Shipwreck as a work of Genius. As to the Price of the Plates, Flaxman declares to me that he will not pretend to set a price upon Engraving. I think it can only be done by some Engraver. I consulted Mr. Parker on the subject, before I decided on the Shipwreck, & it was his opinion, & he says it still is so, that a Print of that size cannot be done under 30 Guineas, if finish'd, &, if a Sketch, 15 Guineas; as, therefore, Hecate must be a Finish'd Plate, I consider 30 Guineas as its Price, & the Pliny 15 Guineas.

Our Dear Friend Hawkins is out of Town, & will not return till April. I have sent to him, by a parcel from Col. Sibthorpe's, your Desirable Poetical Present for Mrs. Hawkins. His address is this—To John Hawkins, Esqr., Dallington, near Northampton. Mr. Edwards is out of Town likewise.

I am very far from shewing the Portrait of Romney as a finish'd Proof; be assured that with our Good Flaxman's good help, & with your remarks on it in addition, I hope to make it a Supernaculum. The Shipwreck, also, will be infinitely better the next proof. I feel very much gratified at your approval of my Queen Catherine: beg to observe that the Print of Romeo & the Apothecary annex'd to your copy is a shamefully worn-out impression, but it was the only one I could get at Johnson's. I left a good impression of it when I left Felpham last in one of Heath's Shakespeare: you will see that it is not like the same Plate with the worn-out Impression. My wife joins me in love & in rejoicing in Miss Poole's continued health. I am, dear Sir,

Yours sincerely,
WILL BLAKE.

P.S. I made a very high finish'd Drawing of Romney as a companion to my drawing of the head of Cowper (you remember), with which Flaxman is very much satisfied, & says that when my Print is like that I need wish it no better, & I am determin'd to make it so at least.

W.B.

TO WILLIAM HAYLEY

Sth. Molton Street,
11 December, 1805.

DEAR SIR,

I cannot omit to Return you my sincere & Grateful Acknowledgments for the kind Reception you have given my New Projected Work. It bids fair to set me above the difficulties I have hitherto encountered. But my Fate has been so uncommon that I expect Nothing. I was alive and in health and with the same Talents I now have all the time of Boydell's, Machlin's, Bowyer's, & other great works. I was known to them and was look'd upon by them as Incapable of Employment in those Works; it may turn out so again, notwithstanding appearances. I am prepared for it, but at the same time sincerely Grateful to Those whose Kindness & Good opinion has supported me thro' all hitherto. You, Dear Sir, are one who has my Particular Gratitude, having conducted me thro' Three that would have been the Darkest Years that ever Mortal Suffer'd, which were render'd thro' your means a Mild and Pleasant Slumber. I speak of Spiritual Things, Not of Natural; of Things known only to Myself and to Spirits Good and Evil, but Not known to Men on Earth. It is the passage thro' these Three Years that has brought me into my Present State, and I *know* that if I had not been with You I must have Perish'd. Those Dangers are now passed and I can see them beneath my feet. It will not be long before I shall be able to present the full history of my Spiritual Sufferings to the dwellers upon Earth and of the Spiritual Victories obtained for me by my Friends. Excuse this Effusion of the Spirit from One who cares little for this World, which passes away, whose happiness is Secure in Jesus our Lord, and who looks for suffering till the time of complete deliverance. In the meanwhile I am kept Happy, as I used to be, because I throw Myself and all that I have on our Saviour's Divine Providence. O what wonders are the Children of Men! Would to God that they would consider it,—that they would consider their Spiritual Life, regardless of that faint Shadow called Natural Life, and that they would Promote Each other's Spiritual labours, each according to its Rank, & that they would know that Receiving a Prophet as a Prophet is a Duty which If omitted is more Severely Avenged than Every Sin and Wickedness beside. It is the Greatest of Crimes to Depress True Art and Science. I know that those who are dead from the Earth, & who mocked and Despised the Meekness of True Art (and such, I find, have been the situation of our Beautiful, Affectionate Ballads), I know that such Mockers are Most Severely Punished in Eternity. I know it, for I see it & dare not help. The Mocker of Art is the Mocker of Jesus. Let us go on, Dear Sir, following his Cross: let us take it up daily, Persisting in Spiritual Labours & the Use of that Talent which it is Death to Bury, and of that Spirit to which we are called.

Pray Present My Sincerest Thanks to our Good Paulina, whose kindness to Me shall receive recompense in the Presence of Jesus. Present also my Thanks to the generous Seagrave, In whose debt I have been too long, but perceive that I shall be able to settle with him soon what is between us. I have delivered to Mr. Sanders the 3 works of Romney, as Mrs. Lambert told me you wished to have them. A very few touches will finish the

Shipwreck; those few I have added upon a Proof before I parted with the Picture. It is a Print that I feel proud of, on a New inspection. Wishing you and All Friends in Sussex a Merry & Happy Christmas,

I remain, Ever Your Affectionate,

WILL BLAKE and his Wife CATHERINE BLAKE.

TO RICHARD PHILLIPS

[June, 1806.]

SIR,

My indignation was exceedingly moved at reading a criticism in *Bell's Weekly Messenger* (25th May) on the picture of Count Ugolino, by Mr. Fuseli, in the Royal Academy Exhibition; and your Magazine being as extensive in its circulation as that Paper, and as it also must from its nature be more permanent, I take the advantageous opportunity to counteract the widely diffused malice which has for many years, under the pretence of admiration of the arts, been assiduously sown and planted among the English public against true art, such as it existed in the days of Michael Angelo and Raphael. Under pretence of fair criticism and candour, the most wretched taste ever produced has been upheld for many, very many years; but now, I say, now its end is come. Such an artist as Fuseli is invulnerable, he needs not my defence; but I should be ashamed not to set my hand and shoulder, and whole strength, against those wretches who, under pretence of criticism, use the dagger and the poison.

My criticism on this picture is as follows: Mr. Fuseli's Count Ugolino is the father of sons of feeling and dignity, who would not sit looking in their parent's face in the moment of his agony, but would rather retire and die in secret, while they suffer him to indulge his passionate and innocent grief, his innocent and venerable madness and insanity and fury, and whatever paltry, cold-hearted critics cannot, because they dare not, look upon. Fuseli's Count Ugolino is a man of wonder and admiration, of resentment against man and devil, and of humiliation before God; prayer and parental affection fill the figure from head to foot. The child in his arms, whether boy or girl signifies not (but the critic must be a fool who has not read Dante, and who does not know a boy from a girl), I say, the child is as beautifully drawn as it is coloured—in both, inimitable! and the effect of the whole is truly sublime, on account of that very colouring which our critic calls black and heavy. The German flute colour, which was used by the Flemings (they call it burnt bone), has possessed the eye of certain connoisseurs, that they cannot see appropriate colouring, and are blind to the gloom of a real terror.

The taste of English amateurs has been too much formed upon pictures imported from Flanders and Holland; consequently our countrymen are easily brow-beat on the subject of painting; and hence it is so common to hear a man say: "I am no judge of pictures." But O Englishmen! know that every man ought to be a judge of pictures, and every man is so who has not been connoisseured out of his senses.

A gentleman who visited me the other day, said, "I am very much surprised at the dislike that some connoisseurs shew on viewing the pictures of Mr. Fuseli; but the truth is, he is a hundred years beyond the present generation." Though I am startled at such an assertion, I hope the contemporary taste will shorten the hundred years into as many hours; for I am sure that any person consulting his own eyes must prefer what is so supereminent; and I am sure that any person consulting his own reputation, or the reputation of his country, will refrain from disgracing either by such ill-judged criticisms in future.

Yours,
WM. BLAKE.

TO RICHARD PHILLIPS

17 Sth Molton St.
Oct 14 [1807]

SIR

A circumstance has occurred which has again raised my Indignation.

I read in the "Oracle & True Briton" of Octr. 13, 1807, that a Mr. Blair, a Surgeon, has, with *the Cold fury of Robespierre*, caused the Police to sieze upon the Person & Goods or Property of an Astrologer & to commit him to Prison. The Man who can Read the Stars often is opressed by their Influence, no less than the Newtonian who reads Not & cannot Read is opressed by his own Reasonings & Experiments. We are all subject to Error: Who shall say, except the National Religionists, that we are not all subject to Crime?

My desire is that you would Enquire into this Affair & that you would publish this in your Monthly Magazine. I do not pay the postage of this Letter, because you, as Sheriff, are bound to attend to it.

WILLIAM BLAKE.

TO OZIAS HUMPHRY

18 January, 1808.

The design of The Last Judgment, which I have completed, by your recommendation, for the Countess of

Egremont, it is necessary to give some account of; and its various parts ought to be described, for the accommodation of those who give it the honour of their attention.

Christ seated on the Throne of Judgment: before His feet and around Him the Heavens, in clouds, are rolling like a scroll, ready to be consumed in the fires of Angels, who descend with the four trumpets sounding to the four winds.

Beneath, the earth is convulsed with the labours of the Resurrection. In the caverns of the earth is the Dragon with seven heads and ten horns, chained by two Angels; and above his cavern, on the earth's surface, is the Harlot, seized and bound by two Angels with chains, while her palaces are falling into ruins, and her counsellors and warriors are descending into the abyss, in wailing and despair.

Hell opens beneath the Harlot's seat on the left hand, into which the wicked are descending.

The right hand of the design is appropriated to the Resurrection of the Just; the left hand of the design is appropriated to the Resurrection and Fall of the Wicked.

Immediately before the Throne of Christ are Adam and Eve, kneeling in humiliation, as representatives of the whole human race. Abraham and Moses kneel on each side beneath them; from the cloud on which Eve kneels, is seen Satan, wound round by the Serpent, and falling headlong; the Pharisees appear on the left hand, pleading their own Righteousness before the Throne of Christ and before the Book of Death, which is opened on clouds by two Angels; many groups of figures are falling from before the throne, and from the sea of fire which flows before the steps of the throne, on which are seen the seven Lamps of the Almighty, burning before the throne. Many figures, chained and bound together, and in various attitudes of despair and horror, fall through the air, and some are scourged by Spirits with flames of fire into the abyss of Hell which opens beneath, on the left hand of the Harlot's seat; where others are howling and descending into the flames, and in the act of dragging each other into Hell, and of contending and fighting with each other on the brink of perdition.

Before the Throne of Christ on the right hand, the Just, in humiliation and in exultation, rise through the air with their children and families, some of whom are bowing before the Book of Life, which is opened on clouds by two Angels; many groups arise in exultation; among them is a figure crowned with stars, and the moon beneath her feet, with six infants around her— she represents the Christian Church. Green hills appear beneath with the graves of the blessed, which are seen bursting with their births of immortality; parents and children, wives and husbands, embrace and arise together, and in exulting attitudes tell each other that the New Jerusalem is ready to descend upon earth; they arise upon the air rejoicing; others, newly awaked from the grave, stand upon the earth embracing and shouting to the Lamb, who cometh in the clouds with power and great glory.

The whole upper part of the design is a view of Heaven opened, around the Throne of Christ. In the clouds, which roll away, are the four living creatures filled with eyes, attended by seven Angels with seven vials of the wrath of God, and above these, seven Angels with the seven trumpets; these compose the cloud which, by its rolling away, displays the opening seats of the Blessed; on the right and the left of which are seen the four-and-twenty Elders seated on thrones to judge the Dead.

Behind the seat and Throne of Christ appear the

Tabernacle with its veil opened, the Candlestick on the right, the Table with Shewbread on the left, and, in the midst, the Cross in place of the Ark, the Cherubim bowing over it.

On the right hand of the Throne of Christ is Baptism, on His left is the Lord's Supper—the two introducers into Eternal Life. Women with infants approach the figure of an Apostle, which represents Baptism; and on the left hand the Lord's Supper is administered by Angels, from the hands of another aged Apostle; these kneel on each side of the throne, which is surrounded by a glory: in the glory many infants appear, representing Eternal Creation flowing from the Divine Humanity in Jesus, who opens the Scroll of Judgment, upon His knees, before the Living and the Dead.

Such is the Design which you, my dear Sir, have been the cause of my producing, and which, but for you, might have slept till the Last Judgment.

WILLIAM BLAKE.

TO GEORGE CUMBERLAND

19 Decr., 1808.

DEAR CUMBERLAND,

I am very much obliged by your kind ardour in my cause, & should immediately Engage in reviewing my former pursuits of painting if I had not so long been turned out of the old channel into a new one, that it is impossible for me to return to it without destroying my present course. New Vanities, or rather new pleasures, occupy my thoughts. New profits seem to arise before me so tempting that I have already involved myself in engagements that preclude all possibility of promising anything. I have, however, the satisfaction to inform you that I have Myself begun to print an account of my various Inventions in Art, for which I have procured a Publisher, & am determin'd to pursue the plan of publishing what I may get printed without disarranging my time, which in future must alone be devoted to Designing & Painting. When I have got my work printed I will send it you first of any body; in the mean time, believe me to be

Your sincere friend,
WILL BLAKE.

TO OZIAS HUMPHRY

[1809]

DEAR SIR,

You will see in this little work the cause of difference between you & me. You demand of me to Mix two things that Reynolds has confess'd cannot be mixed. You will perceive that I not only detest False Art, but have the Courage to say so Publickly & to dare all the Power on Earth to oppose—Florentine & Venetian Art cannot exist together. Till the Venetian & Flemish are destroy'd, the Florentine & Roman cannot Exist; this will be shortly accomplish'd; till then I remain your Grateful, altho' Seemingly otherwise, I say your Grateful & Sincere

WILLIAM BLAKE.

I inclose a ticket of admission if you should honour my Exhibition with a Visit.

TO DAWSON TURNER

17 South Molton Street,
9 June, 1818.

SIR,

I send you a List of the different Works you have done me the honour to enquire after—unprofitable enough to me, tho' Expensive to the Buyer. Those I Printed for Mr. Humphry are a selection from the different Books of such as could be Printed without the Writing, tho' to the Loss of some of the best things. For they, when Printed perfect, accompany Poetical Personifications & Acts, without which Poems they never could have been Executed.

								£	s.	d.
America	-	-	-	-	18 Prints	folio	-	5	5	0
Europe		-	-	-	17 do.	folio	-	5	5	0
Visions, &c.	-	-	-		8 do.	folio	-	3	3	0
Thel	-	-	-		6 do.	Quarto	-	2	2	0
Songs of Innocence	-				28 do.	Octavo	-	3	3	0
Songs of Experience	-				26 do.	Octavo	-	3	3	0
Urizen	-	-	-		28 Prints	Quarto	-	5	5	0
Milton	-	-	-		50 do.	Quarto	-	10	10	0

12 Large Prints, Size of Each about 2 feet by 1 & ½, Historical & Poetical, Printed in Colours
each 5 5 0

These last 12 Prints are unaccompanied by any writing.

The few I have Printed & Sold are sufficient to have gained me great reputation as an Artist, which was the chief thing Intended. But I have never been able to produce a Sufficient number for a general Sale by means of a regular Publisher. It is therefore necessary to me that any Person wishing to have any or all of them should send me their Order to Print them on the above terms, &

I will take care that they shall be done at least as well as any I have yet Produced.

I am, Sir, with many thanks for your very Polite approbation of my works,

Your most obedient Servant,
WILLIAM BLAKE.

TO JOHN LINNELL

Feby. 1, 1826.

DEAR SIR,

I am forced to write, because I cannot come to you, & this on two accounts. First, I omitted to desire you would come & take a Mutton chop with us the day you go to Cheltenham, & I will go with you to the Coach; also, I will go to Hampstead to see Mrs. Linnell on Sunday, but will return before dinner (I mean if you set off before that), & Second, I wish to have a Copy of Job to shew to Mr. Chantry.

For I am again laid up by a cold in my stomach; the Hampstead Air, as it always did, so I fear it always will do this, Except it be the Morning air; & That, in my Cousin's time, I found I could bear with safety & perhaps benefit. I believe my Constitution to be a good one, but it has many peculiarities that no one but myself can know. When I was young, Hampstead, Highgate, Hornsea, Muswell Hill, & even Islington & all places North of London, always laid me up the day after, & sometimes two or three days, with precisely the same Complaint & the same torment of the Stomach, Easily removed, but excruciating while it lasts & enfeebling for some time after. Sr. Francis Bacon would say, it is want of discipline in Mountainous Places. Sr. Francis Bacon is a Liar. No discipline will turn one Man into another, even in the least particle, & such discipline I call Presumption & Folly. I have tried it too much not to know this, & am very sorry for all such who may be led to such ostentatious Exertion against their Eternal Existence itself, because it is Mental Rebellion against the Holy Spirit, & fit only for a Soldier of Satan to perform.

Though I hope in a morning or two to call on you in Cirencester Place, I feared you might be gone, or I might be too ill to let you know how I am, & what I wish.

I am, dear Sir,
Yours sincerely,
WILLIAM BLAKE.

TO JOHN LINNELL

Tuesday Night [? 1826].

DEAR SIR,

I return you thanks for The Two Pounds you now send me. As to Sr. T. Lawrence, I have not heard from him as yet, & hope that he has a good opinion of my willingness to appear grateful, tho' not able, on account of this abominable Ague, or whatever it is. I am in Bed & at work; my health I cannot speak of, for if it was not for the Cold weather I think I should soon get about again. Great Men die equally with the little. I am sorry for Ld. Ls.; he is a man of very singular abilities, as also for the D. of C.; but perhaps, & I verily believe it, Every death is an improvement of the State of the Departed. I can draw as well a-Bed as Up, & perhaps better; but I cannot Engrave. I am going on with Dante, & please myself.

I am, dr. Sir, yours sincerely,
WILLIAM BLAKE.

TO JOHN LINNELL

Friday Evening.
May 19, 1826.

Dear Sir,

I have had another desperate shivering Fit; it came on yesterday afternoon after as good a morning as I ever experienced. It began by a gnawing Pain in the Stomach, & soon spread a deathly feel all over the limbs, which brings on the shivering fit, when I am forced to go to bed, where I contrive to get into a little perspiration, which takes it quite away. It was night when it left me, so I did not get up, but just as I was going to rise this morning, the shivering fit attacked me again & the pain, with its accompanying deathly feel. I got again into a perspiration, & was well, but so much weaken'd that I am still in bed. This entirely prevents me from the pleasure of seeing you on Sunday at Hampstead, as I fear the attack again when I am away from home.

I am, dr. Sir,
Yours sincerely,
William Blake.

TO JOHN LINNELL

5 July, 1826.

Dear Sir,

I thank you for the Receit of Five Pounds this Morning, & Congratulate you on the receit of another fine Boy; am glad to hear of Mrs. Linnell's health & safety.

I am getting better every hour; my Plan is diet only; & if the Machine is capable of it, shall make an old man yet. I go on just as if perfectly well, which indeed I am, except in those paroxysms which I now believe will never more return. Pray let your own health & convenience put all solicitude concerning me at rest. You have a Family, I have none; there is no comparison between our necessary avocations.

> Believe me to be, dr. Sir,
> Yours sincerely,
> WILLIAM BLAKE.

TO JOHN LINNELL

February, 1827.

DEAR SIR,

I thank you for the five pounds received to-day. Am getting better every morning, but slowly, as I am still feeble and tottering, though all the symptoms of my complaint seem almost gone. The fine weather is very beneficial and comfortable to me. I go on, as I think, improving my engravings of Dante more and more, and shall soon get proofs of these four which I have, and beg the favour of you to send me the two plates of Dante which you have, that I may finish them sufficiently to make show of colour and strength.

I have thought and thought of the removal. I cannot get my mind out of a state of terrible fear at such a step. The more I think, the more I feel terror at what I wished at first and thought a thing of benefit and good hope. You will attribute it to its right cause—intellectual peculiarity, that must be myself alone shut up in myself, or reduced to nothing. I could tell you of visions and dreams upon the subject. I have asked and entreated Divine help, but fear continues upon me, and I must relinquish the step that I had wished to take, and still wish, but in vain.

Your success in your profession is, above all things to me, most gratifying. May it go on to the perfection you wish, and more. So wishes also

Yours sincerely,
WILLIAM BLAKE.

TO GEORGE CUMBERLAND

N 3, FOUNTAIN COURT, STRAND.
12 April, 1827.

I have been very near the gates of death, and have returned very weak and an old man, feeble and tottering, but not in spirit and life, not in the real man, the imagination, which liveth for ever. In that I am stronger and stronger, as this foolish body decays. I thank you for the pains you have taken with poor Job. I know too well that the great majority of Englishmen are fond of the indefinite, which they measure by Newton's doctrine of the fluxions of an atom, a thing which does not exist. These are politicians, and think that Republican art is inimical to their atom, for a line or a lineament is not formed by chance. A line is a line in its minutest subdivisions, straight or crooked. It is itself, not intermeasurable by anything else. Such is Job. But since the French Revolution Englishmen are all intermeasurable by one another: certainly a happy state of agreement, in which I for one do not agree. God keep you and me from the divinity of yes and no too—the yea, nay, creeping Jesus—from supposing up and down to be the same thing, as all experimentalists must suppose.

You are desirous, I know, to dispose of some of my works, but having none remaining of all I have printed, I cannot print more except at a great loss. I am now painting a set of the Songs of Innocence and Experience for a friend at ten guineas. The last work I produced is a poem entitled Jerusalem, the Emanation of the Giant Albion, but find that to print it will cost my time the amount of Twenty Guineas. One I have Finish'd. It contains 100 Plates, but it is not likely I shall get a Customer for it.

As you wish me to send you a list with the Prices of these things, they are as follows:

	£	s.	d.
America	6	6	0
Europe	6	6	0
Visions, &c.	5	5	0
Thel	3	3	0
Songs of Inn. & Exp.	10	10	0
Urizen	6	6	0

The Little Card I will do as soon as Possible, but when you Consider that I have been reduced to a Skeleton, from which I am slowly recovering, you will, I hope, have Patience with me.

Flaxman is Gone, & we must All soon follow, every one to his Own Eternal House, Leaving the delusive Goddess Nature & her Laws, to get into Freedom from all Law of the Members, into The Mind, in which every one is King & Priest in his own House. God send it so on Earth, as it is in Heaven.

I am, dear Sir, Yours affectionately,
WILLIAM BLAKE.

TO JOHN LINNELL

25 April, 1827.

DEAR SIR,

I am going on better Every day, as I think, both in health & in work. I thank you for The Ten Pounds which

I recieved from you this day, which shall be put to the best use; as also for the prospect of Mr. Ottley's advantageous acquaintance. I go on without daring to count on Futurity, which I cannot do without doubt & Fear that ruins Activity, & are the greatest hurt to an artist such as I am. As to Ugolino, &c., I never supposed that I should sell them; my Wife alone is answerable for their having Existed in any finish'd State. I am too much attach'd to Dante to think much of anything else. I have Proved the Six Plates, & reduced the Fighting devils ready for the Copper. I count myself sufficiently Paid If I live as I now do, & only fear that I may be Unlucky to my friends, & especially that I may not be so to you.

> I am, sincerely yours,
> WILLIAM BLAKE.

TO JOHN LINNELL

3 July, 1827.

DEAR SIR,

I thank you for the Ten Pounds you are so kind as to send me at this time. My journey to Hampstead on Sunday brought on a relapse which is lasted till now. I find I am not so well as I thought. I must not go on in a youthful Style; however, I am upon the mending hand to-day, & hope soon to look as I did; for I have been yellow, accompanied by all the old Symptoms.

> I am, dear Sir,
> Yours sincerely,
> WILLIAM BLAKE.

VI.

THE
PROPHETIC
BOOKS

THE MARRIAGE OF
HEAVEN AND HELL

(1793)

THE ARGUMENT

Rintrah roars & shakes his fires in the burden'd air;
Hungry clouds swag on the deep.

Once meek, and in a perilous path,
The just man kept his course along
The vale of death.
Roses are planted where thorns grow,
And on the barren heath
Sing the honey bees.

Then the perilous path was planted,
And a river and a spring
On every cliff and tomb,
And on the bleached bones
Red clay brought forth;

Till the villain left the paths of ease,
To walk in perilous paths, and drive
The just man into barren climes.

Now the sneaking serpent walks
In mild humility,
And the just man rages in the wilds
Where lions roam.

Rintrah roars & shakes his fires in the burden'd air;
Hungry clouds swag on the deep.

As a new heaven is begun, and it is now thirty-three
years since its advent, the Eternal Hell revives. And lo!
Swedenborg is the Angel sitting at the tomb: his writ-
ings are the linen clothes folded up. Now is the domin-
ion of Edom, & the return of Adam into Paradise. See
Isaiah xxxiv & xxxv Chap.

Without Contraries is no progression. Attraction and
Repulsion, Reason and Energy, Love and Hate, are
necessary to Human existence.

From these contraries spring what the religious call
Good & Evil. Good is the passive that obeys Reason.
Evil is the active springing from Energy.

Good is Heaven. Evil is Hell.

THE VOICE OF THE DEVIL

All Bibles or sacred codes have been the causes of the
following Errors:

1. That Man has two real existing principles: Viz: a
Body & a Soul.

2. That Energy, call'd Evil, is alone from the Body;
& that Reason, call'd Good, is alone from the Soul.

3. That God will torment Man in Eternity for follow-
ing his Energies.

But the following Contraries to these are True:

1. Man has no Body distinct from his Soul; for that
call'd Body is a portion of Soul discern'd by the five
Senses, the chief inlets of Soul in this age.

2. Energy is the only life, and is from the Body; and

Reason is the bound or outward circumference of Energy.

3. Energy is Eternal Delight.

Those who restrain desire, do so because theirs is weak enough to be restrained; and the restrainer or reason usurps its place & governs the unwilling.

And being restrain'd, it by degrees becomes passive, till it is only the shadow of desire.

The history of this is written in Paradise Lost, & the Governor or Reason is call'd Messiah.

And the original Archangel, or possessor of the command of the heavenly host, is call'd the Devil or Satan, and his children are call'd Sin & Death.

But in the Book of Job, Milton's Messiah is call'd Satan.

For this history has been adopted by both parties.

It indeed appear'd to Reason as if Desire was cast out; but the Devil's account is, that the Messiah fell, & formed a heaven of what he stole from the Abyss.

This is shewn in the Gospel, where he prays to the Father to send the comforter, or Desire, that Reason may have Ideas to build on; the Jehovah of the Bible being no other than he who dwells in flaming fire.

Know that after Christ's death, he became Jehovah.

But in Milton, the Father is Destiny, the Son a Ratio of the five senses, & the Holy-ghost Vacuum!

NOTE: The reason Milton wrote in fetters when he wrote of Angels & God, and at liberty when of Devils & Hell, is because he was a true Poet and of the Devil's party without knowing it.

A MEMORABLE FANCY

As I was walking among the fires of hell, delighted
with the enjoyments of Genius, which to Angels look
like torment and insanity, I collected some of their
Proverbs; thinking that as the sayings used in a nation
mark its character, so the Proverbs of Hell show the
nature of Infernal wisdom better than any description of
buildings or garments.

When I came home: on the abyss of the five senses,
where a flat sided steep frowns over the present world, I
saw a mighty Devil folded in black clouds, hovering
on the sides of the rock: with corroding fires he wrote
the following sentence now percieved by the minds of
men, & read by them on earth:

How do you know but ev'ry Bird that cuts the airy way,
Is an immense world of delight, clos'd by your senses
    five?

PROVERBS OF HELL

In seed time learn, in harvest teach, in winter enjoy.

Drive your cart and your plow over the bones of the
dead.

The road of excess leads to the palace of wisdom.

Prudence is a rich, ugly old maid courted by In-
capacity.

He who desires but acts not, breeds pestilence.

The cut worm forgives the plow.

Dip him in the river who loves water.

A fool sees not the same tree that a wise man sees.

He whose face gives no light, shall never become a star.

Eternity is in love with the productions of time.

The busy bee has no time for sorrow.

The hours of folly are measur'd by the clock; but of wisdom, no clock can measure.

All wholesome food is caught without a net or a trap.

Bring out number, weight & measure in a year of dearth.

No bird soars too high, if he soars with his own wings.

A dead body revenges not injuries.

The most sublime act is to set another before you.

If the fool would persist in his folly he would become wise.

Folly is the cloke of knavery.

Shame is Pride's cloke.

Prisons are built with stones of Law, Brothels with bricks of Religion.

The pride of the peacock is the glory of God.

The lust of the goat is the bounty of God.

The wrath of the lion is the wisdom of God.

The nakedness of woman is the work of God.

Excess of sorrow laughs. Excess of joy weeps.

The roaring of lions, the howling of wolves, the raging of the stormy sea, and the destructive sword, are portions of eternity, too great for the eye of man.

The fox condemns the trap, not himself.

Joys impregnate. Sorrows bring forth.

Let man wear the fell of the lion, woman the fleece of the sheep.

The bird a nest, the spider a web, man friendship.

The selfish, smiling fool, & the sullen, frowning fool shall be both thought wise, that they may be a rod.

What is now proved was once only imagin'd.

The rat, the mouse, the fox, the rabbet watch the

roots; the lion, the tyger, the horse, the elephant watch the fruits.

The cistern contains: the fountain overflows.

One thought fills immensity.

Always be ready to speak your mind, and a base man will avoid you.

Every thing possible to be believ'd is an image of truth.

The eagle never lost so much time as when he submitted to learn of the crow.

The fox provides for himself, but God provides for the lion.

Think in the morning. Act in the noon. Eat in the evening. Sleep in the night.

He who has suffer'd you to impose on him, knows you.

As the plow follows words, so God rewards prayers.

The tygers of wrath are wiser than the horses of instruction.

Expect poison from the standing water.

You never know what is enough unless you know what is more than enough.

Listen to the fool's reproach! it is a kingly title!

The eyes of fire, the nostrils of air, the mouth of water, the beard of earth.

The weak in courage is strong in cunning.

The apple tree never asks the beech how he shall grow; nor the lion, the horse, how he shall take his prey.

The thankful reciever bears a plentiful harvest.

If others had not been foolish, we should be so.

The soul of sweet delight can never be defil'd.

When thou seest an Eagle, thou seest a portion of Genius; lift up thy head!

As the caterpiller chooses the fairest leaves to lay her eggs on, so the priest lays his curse on the fairest joys.

To create a little flower is the labour of ages.

Damn braces. Bless relaxes.

The best wine is the oldest, the best water the newest.

Prayers plow not! Praises reap not!

Joys laugh not! Sorrows weep not!

The head Sublime, the heart Pathos, the genitals Beauty, the hands & feet Proportion.

As the air to a bird or the sea to a fish, so is contempt to the contemptible.

The crow wish'd every thing was black, the owl that every thing was white.

Exuberance is Beauty.

If the lion was advised by the fox, he would be cunning.

Improvement makes strait roads; but the crooked roads without Improvement are roads of Genius.

Sooner murder an infant in its cradle than nurse unacted desires.

Where man is not, nature is barren.

Truth can never be told so as to be understood, and not be believ'd.

Enough! or Too much.

The ancient Poets animated all sensible objects with Gods or Geniuses, calling them by the names and adorning them with the properties of woods, rivers, mountains, lakes, cities, nations, and whatever their enlarged & numerous senses could percieve.

And particularly they studied the genius of each city & country, placing it under its mental deity;

Till a system was formed, which some took advantage of, & enslav'd the vulgar by attempting to realize or abstract the mental deities from their objects: thus began Priesthood;

Choosing forms of worship from poetic tales.

And at length they pronounc'd that the Gods had order'd such things.

Thus men forgot that All deities reside in the human breast.

A MEMORABLE FANCY

The Prophets Isaiah and Ezekiel dined with me, and I asked them how they dared so roundly to assert that God spoke to them; and whether they did not think at the time that they would be misunderstood, & so be the cause of imposition.

Isaiah answer'd: "I saw no God, nor heard any, in a finite organical perception; but my senses discover'd the infinite in everything, and as I was then perswaded, & remain confirm'd, that the voice of honest indignation is the voice of God, I cared not for consequences, but wrote."

Then I asked: "Does a firm perswasion that a thing is so, make it so?"

He replied: "All poets believe that it does, & in ages of imagination this firm perswasion removed mountains; but many are not capable of a firm perswasion of any thing."

Then Ezekiel said: "The philosophy of the east taught the first principles of human perception: some nations held one principle for the origin, and some another: we of Israel taught that the Poetic Genius (as you now call it) was the first principle and all the others merely derivative, which was the cause of our despising the Priests & Philosophers of other countries, and prophecy-ing that all Gods would at last be proved to originate in ours & to be the tributaries of the Poetic Genius; it was this that our great poet, King David, desired so fervently & invokes so pathetic'ly, saying by this he conquers enemies & governs kingdoms; and we so loved our God, that we cursed in his name all the deities of surrounding nations, and asserted that they had rebelled: from these opinions the vulgar came to think that all nations would at last be subject to the jews."

"This," said he, "like all firm perswasions, is come to pass; for all nations believe the jews' code and worship the jews' god, and what greater subjection can be?"

I heard this with some wonder, & must confess my own conviction. After dinner I ask'd Isaiah to favour the world with his lost works; he said none of equal value was lost. Ezekiel said the same of his.

I also asked Isaiah what made him go naked and barefoot three years? he answer'd: "the same that made our friend Diogenes, the Grecian."

I then asked Ezekiel why he eat dung, & lay so long on his right & left side? he answer'd, "the desire of raising other men into a perception of the infinite: this the North American tribes practise, & is he honest who resists his genius or conscience only for the sake of present ease or gratification?"

The ancient tradition that the world will be consumed in fire at the end of six thousand years is true, as I have heard from Hell.

For the cherub with his flaming sword is hereby commanded to leave his guard at tree of life; and when he does, the whole creation will be consumed and appear infinite and holy, whereas it now appears finite & corrupt.

This will come to pass by an improvement of sensual enjoyment.

But first the notion that man has a body distinct from

his soul is to be expunged; this I shall do by printing in the infernal method, by corrosives, which in Hell are salutary and medicinal, melting apparent surfaces away, and displaying the infinite which was hid.

If the doors of perception were cleansed every thing would appear to man as it is, infinite.

For man has closed himself up, till he sees all things thro' narrow chinks of his cavern.

A MEMORABLE FANCY

I was in a Printing house in Hell, & saw the method in which knowledge is transmitted from generation to generation.

In the first chamber was a Dragon-Man, clearing away the rubbish from a cave's mouth; within, a number of Dragons were hollowing the cave.

In the second chamber was a Viper folding round the rock & the cave, and others adorning it with gold, silver and precious stones.

In the third chamber was an Eagle with wings and feathers of air: he caused the inside of the cave to be infinite; around were numbers of Eagle-like men who built palaces in the immense cliffs.

In the fourth chamber were Lions of flaming fire, raging around & melting the metals into living fluids.

In the fifth chamber were Unnam'd forms, which cast the metals into the expanse.

There they were reciev'd by Men who occupied the sixth chamber, and took the forms of books & were arranged in libraries.

The Giants who formed this world into its sensual existence, and now seem to live in it in chains, are in truth the causes of its life & the sources of all activity; but the chains are the cunning of weak and tame minds which have power to resist energy; according to the proverb, the weak in courage is strong in cunning.

Thus one portion of being is the Prolific, the other the Devouring: to the Devourer it seems as if the producer was in his chains; but it is not so, he only takes portions of existence and fancies that the whole.

But the Prolific would cease to be Prolific unless the Devourer, as a sea, received the excess of his delights.

Some will say: "Is not God alone the Prolific?" I answer: "God only Acts & Is, in existing beings or Men."

These two classes of men are always upon earth, & they should be enemies: whoever tries to reconcile them seeks to destroy existence.

Religion is an endeavour to reconcile the two.

NOTE: Jesus Christ did not wish to unite, but to separate them, as in the Parable of sheep and goats! & he says: "I came not to send Peace, but a Sword."

Messiah or Satan or Tempter was formerly thougnt to be one of the Antediluvians who are our Energies.

A MEMORABLE FANCY

An Angel came to me and said: "O pitiable foolish young man! O horrible! O dreadful state! consider the hot burning dungeon thou art preparing for thyself to all eternity, to which thou art going in such career."

I said: "Perhaps you will be willing to shew me my eternal lot, & we will contemplate together upon it, and see whether your lot or mine is most desirable."

So he took me thro' a stable & thro' a church & down

into the church vault, at the end of which was a mill: thro' the mill we went, and came to a cave: down the winding cavern we groped our tedious way, till a void boundless as a nether sky appear'd beneath us, & we held by the roots of trees and hung over this immensity; but I said: "if you please, we will commit ourselves to this void, and see whether providence is here also: if you will not, I will:" but he answer'd: "do not presume, O young man, but as we here remain, behold thy lot which will soon appear when the darkness passes away."

So I remain'd with him, sitting in the twisted roof of an oak; he was suspended in a fungus, which hung with the head downward into the deep.

By degrees we beheld the infinite Abyss, fiery as the smoke of a burning city; beneath us, at an immense distance, was the sun, black but shining; round it were fiery tracks on which revolv'd vast spiders, crawling after their prey, which flew, or rather swum, in the infinite deep, in the most terrific shapes of animals sprung from corruption; & the air was full of them, & seem'd composed of them: these are Devils, and are called Powers of the air. I now asked my companion which was my eternal lot? he said: "between the black & white spiders."

But now, from between the black & white spiders, a cloud and fire burst and rolled thro' the deep, black'ning all beneath, so that the nether deep grew black as a sea, & rolled with a terrible noise; beneath us was nothing now to be seen but a black tempest, till looking east between the clouds & the waves, we saw a cataract of blood mixed with fire, and not many stones' throw from us appear'd and sunk again the scaly fold of a monstrous serpent; at last, to the east, distant about three degrees, appear'd a fiery crest above the waves; slowly it reared like a ridge of golden rocks, till we discover'd two globes of crimson fire, from which the sea fled away in clouds of smoke; and now we saw it was the head of Leviathan; his forehead was divided into streaks of green & purple like those on a tyger's forehead: soon we saw his mouth & red gills hang just above the raging foam, tinging the black deep with beams of blood, advancing toward us with all the fury of a spiritual existence.

My friend the Angel climb'd up from his station into the mill: I remain'd alone; & then this appearance was no more, but I found myself sitting on a pleasant bank beside a river by moonlight, hearing a harper, who sung to the harp; & his theme was: "The man who never alters his opinion is like standing water, & breeds reptiles of the mind."

But I arose and sought for the mill, & there I found my Angel, who, surprised, asked me how I escaped?

I answer'd: "All that we saw was owing to your metaphysics; for when you ran away, I found myself on a bank by moonlight hearing a harper. But now we have seen my eternal lot, shall I shew you yours?" he laugh'd at my proposal; but I by force suddenly caught him in my arms, & flew westerly thro' the night, till we were elevated above the earth's shadow; then I flung myself with him directly into the body of the sun; here I clothed myself in white, & taking in my hand Swedenborg's volumes, sunk from the glorious clime, and passed all the planets till we came to saturn: here I stay'd to rest, & then leap'd into the void between saturn & the fixed stars.

"Here," said I, "is your lot, in this space—if space it may be call'd." Soon we saw the stable and the church, & I took him to the altar and open'd the Bible, and lo! it was a deep pit, into which I descended, driving the Angel before me; soon we saw seven houses of brick; one we enter'd; in it were a number of monkeys, baboons, & all of that species, chain'd by the middle, grinning and snatching at one another, but withheld by the shortness of their chains: however, I saw that they sometimes grew numerous, and then the weak were caught by the strong, and with a grinning aspect, first coupled with, & then devour'd, by plucking off first one limb and then another, till the body was left a helpless trunk; this, after grinning & kissing it with seeming fondness, they devour'd too; and here & there I saw one savourily picking the flesh off his own tail; as the stench terribly annoy'd us both, we went into the mill, & I in my hand brought the skeleton of a body, which in the mill was Aristotle's Analytics.

So the Angel said: "thy phantasy has imposed upon me, & thou oughtest to be ashamed."

I answer'd: "we impose on one another, & it is but lost time to converse with you whose works are only Analytics."

Opposition is true Friendship.

I have always found that Angels have the vanity to speak of themselves as the only wise; this they do with a confident insolence sprouting from systematic reasoning.

Thus Swedenborg boasts that what he writes is new: tho' it is only the Contents or Index of already publish'd books.

A man carried a monkey about for a shew, & because he was a little wiser than the monkey, grew vain, and conciev'd himself as much wiser than seven men. It is so with Swedenborg: he shews the folly of churches, & exposes hypocrites, till he imagines that all are religious,

& himself the single one on earth that ever broke a net.

Now hear a plain fact: Swedenborg has not written one new truth. Now hear another: he has written all the old falsehoods.

And now hear the reason. He conversed with Angels who are all religious, & conversed not with Devils who all hate religion, for he was incapable thro' his conceited notions.

Thus Swedenborg's writings are a recapitulation of all superficial opinions, and an analysis of the more sublime—but no further.

Have now another plain fact. Any man of mechanical talents may, from the writings of Paracelsus or Jacob Behmen, produce ten thousand volumes of equal value with Swedenborg's, and from those of Dante or Shakespear an infinite number.

But when he has done this, let him not say that he knows better than his master, for he only holds a candle in sunshine.

A MEMORABLE FANCY

Once I saw a Devil in a flame of fire, who arose before an Angel that sat on a cloud, and the Devil utter'd these words:

"The worship of God is: Honouring his gifts in other men, each according to his genius, and loving the greatest men best: those who envy or calumniate great men hate God; for there is no other God."

The Angel hearing this became almost blue; but mastering himself he grew yellow, & at last white, pink, & smiling, and then replied:

"Thou Idolater! is not God One? & is not he visible in Jesus Christ? and has not Jesus Christ given his sanction to the law of ten commandments? and are not all other men fools, sinners, & nothings?"

The Devil answer'd: "Bray a fool in a morter with wheat, yet shall not his folly be beaten out of him; if Jesus Christ is the greatest man, you ought to love him in the greatest degree; now hear how he has given his sanction to the law of ten commandments: did he not mock at the sabbath and so mock the sabbath's God? murder those who were murder'd because of him? turn away the law from the woman taken in adultery? steal the labor of others to support him? bear false witness when he omitted making a defence before Pilate? covet when he pray'd for his disciples, and when he bid them shake off the dust of their feet against such as refused to lodge them? I tell you, no virtue can exist without breaking these ten commandments. Jesus was all virtue, and acted from impulse, not from rules."

When he had so spoken, I beheld the Angel, who stretched out his arms, embracing the flame of fire, & he was consumed and arose as Elijah.

NOTE: This Angel, who is now become a Devil, is my particular friend; we often read the Bible together in its infernal or diabolical sense, which the world shall have if they behave well.

I have also The Bible of Hell, which the world shall have whether they will or no.

One Law for the Lion & Ox is Oppression.

A SONG OF LIBERTY

1. The Eternal Female groan'd! it was heard over all the Earth.

2. Albion's coast is sick, silent; the American meadows faint!

3. Shadows of Prophecy shiver along by the lakes and the rivers, and mutter across the ocean: France, rend down thy dungeon!

4. Golden Spain, burst the barriers of old Rome!

5. Cast thy keys, O Rome, into the deep down falling, even to eternity down falling,

6. And weep.

7. In her trembling hand she took the new born terror, howling.

8. On those infinite mountains of light, now barr'd out by the atlantic sea, the new born fire stood before the starry king!

9. Flag'd with grey brow'd snows and thunderous visages, the jealous wings wav'd over the deep.

10. The speary hand burned aloft, unbuckled was the shield; forth went the hand of jealousy among the flaming hair, and hurl'd the new born wonder thro' the starry night.

11. The fire, the fire is falling!

12. Look up! look up! O citizen of London, enlarge thy countenance! O Jew, leave counting gold! return to thy oil and wine. O African! black African! (go, winged thought, widen his forehead.)

13. The fiery limbs, the flaming hair, shot like the sinking sun into the western sea.

14. Wak'd from his eternal sleep, the hoary element roaring fled away.

15. Down rush'd, beating his wings in vain, the jealous king; his grey brow'd councellors, thunderous warriors, curl'd veterans, among helms, and shields, and chariots, horses, elephants, banners, castles, slings, and rocks.

16. Falling, rushing, ruining! buried in the ruins, on Urthona's dens;

17. All night beneath the ruins; then, their sullen flames faded, emerge round the gloomy king.

18. With thunder and fire, leading his starry hosts thro' the waste wilderness, he promulgates his ten commands, glancing his beamy eyelids over the deep in dark dismay,

19. Where the son of fire in his eastern cloud, while the morning plumes her golden breast,

20. Spurning the clouds written with curses, stamps the stony law to dust, loosing the eternal horses from the dens of night, crying:

EMPIRE IS NO MORE! AND NOW THE LION & WOLF SHALL
CEASE

CHORUS

Let the Priests of the Raven of dawn no longer, in deadly black, with hoarse note curse the sons of joy. Nor his accepted brethren—whom, tyrant, he calls free— lay the bound or build the roof. Nor pale religious letchery call that virginity that wishes but acts not!

For every thing that lives is Holy.

FOR THE SEXES:
THE GATES OF PARADISE

(1793–1818)

FRONTISPIECE

WHAT IS MAN?

The Sun's Light when he unfolds it
Depends on the Organ that beholds it.

[PROLOGUE]

Mutual Forgiveness of each Vice,
Such are the Gates of Paradise.
Against the Accuser's chief desire,
Who walk'd among the Stones of Fire,
Jehovah's Finger Wrote the Law:
Then Wept! then rose in Zeal & Awe,
And the Dead Corpse from Sinai's heat
Buried beneath his Mercy Seat.
O Christians, Christians! tell me Why
You rear it on your Altars high.

I found him beneath a Tree.

[2]

WATER
Thou Waterest him with Tears:

[3]

EARTH
He struggles into Life

AIR
On Cloudy Doubts & Reasoning Cares

[5]

FIRE
That end in endless Strife.

[6]

At length for hatching ripe he breaks the shell.

[7]

What are these? ALAS! the Female Martyr,
Is She also the Divine Image?

[8]

MY SON! MY SON!

[9]

I WANT! I WANT!

[10]

HELP! HELP!

[11]

AGED IGNORANCE
Perceptive Organs closed, their Objects close.

[12]

Does thy God, O Priest, take such vengeance as this?

[13]

Fear & Hope are—Vision.

[14]

The Traveller hasteth in the Evening.

[15]

DEATH'S DOOR

[16]

I have said to the Worm:
Thou art my Mother &-my sister.

THE KEYS

The Catterpiller on the Leaf
Reminds thee of thy Mother's Grief.

OF THE GATES

1 My Eternal Man set in Repose,
  The Female from his darkness rose
  And she found me beneath a Tree,
  A Mandrake, & in her Veil hid me.
  Serpent Reasonings us entice
  Of Good & Evil, Virtue & Vice.
2 Doubt Self Jealous, Wat'ry folly,
3 Struggling thro' Earth's Melancholy.
4 Naked in Air, in Shame & Fear,
5 Blind in Fire with shield & spear,

Two Horn'd Reasoning, Cloven Fiction,
In Doubt, which is Self contradiction,
A dark Hermaphrodite We stood,
Rational Truth, Root of Evil & Good.
Round me flew the Flaming Sword;
Round her snowy Whirlwinds roar'd,
Freezing her Veil, the Mundane Shell.
6 I rent the Veil where the Dead dwell:
When weary Man enters his Cave
He meets his Saviour in the Grave.
Some find a Female Garment there,
And some a Male, woven with care,
Lest the Sexual Garments sweet
Should grow a devouring Winding sheet.
7 One Dies! Alas! the Living & Dead,
One is slain & One is fled.
8 In Vain-glory hatcht & nurst,
By double Spectres Self Accurst,
My Son! my Son! thou treatest me
But as I have instructed thee.
9 On the shadows of the Moon
Climbing thro' Night's highest noon.
10 In Time's Ocean falling drown'd.
In Aged Ignorance profound,
11 Holy & cold, I clip'd the Wings
Of all Sublunary Things,
12 And in depths of my Dungeons
Closed the Father & the Sons.
13 But when once I did descry
The Immortal Man that cannot Die,
14 Thro' evening shades I haste away
To close the Labours of my Day.
15 The Door of Death I open found
And the Worm Weaving in the Ground:
16 Thou'rt my Mother from the Womb,

Wife, Sister, Daughter, to the Tomb,
Weaving to Dreams the Sexual strife
And weeping over the Web of Life.

TO THE ACCUSER WHO IS
THE GOD OF THIS WORLD

Truly, My Satan, thou art but a Dunce,
And dost not know the Garment from the Man.
Every Harlot was a Virgin once,
Nor can'st thou ever change Kate into Nan.

Tho' thou art Worship'd by the Names Divine
Of Jesus & Jehovah, thou art still
The Son of Morn in weary Night's decline,
The lost Traveller's Dream under the Hill.

THE BOOK OF THEL

(1789)

THEL'S MOTTO

Does the Eagle know what is in the pit?
Or wilt thou go ask the Mole?
Can Wisdom be put in a silver rod?
Or Love in a golden bowl?

I

The daughters of the Seraphim led round their sunny
flocks,
All but the youngest: she in paleness sought the secret
air,
To fade away like morning beauty from her mortal day:
Down by the river of Adona her soft voice is heard,
And thus her gentle lamentation falls like morning dew:

"O life of this our spring! why fades the lotus of the
water,
Why fade these children of the spring, born but to smile
& fall?
Ah! Thel is like a wat'ry bow, and like a parting cloud;
Like a reflection in a glass; like shadows in the water;
Like dreams of infants, like a smile upon an infant's
face;
Like the dove's voice; like transient day; like music in
the air.

279

Ah! gentle may I lay me down, and gentle rest my head,
And gentle sleep the sleep of death, and gentle hear the
voice
Of him that walketh in the garden in the evening time."

The Lilly of the valley, breathing in the humble grass,
Answer'd the lovely maid and said: "I am a wat'ry weed,
And I am very small and love to dwell in lowly vales;
So weak, the gilded butterfly scarce perches on my
head.
Yet I am visited from heaven, and he that smiles on all
Walks in the valley and each morn over me spreads his
hand,
Saying, 'Rejoice, thou humble grass, thou new-born lilly
flower,
Thou gentle maid of silent valleys and of modest brooks;
For thou shalt be clothed in light, and fed with morning
manna,
Till summer's heat melts thee beside the fountains and
the springs
To flourish in eternal vales.' Then why should Thel com-
plain?
Why should the mistress of the vales of Har utter a
sigh?"

She ceas'd & smil'd in tears, then sat down in her silver
shrine.

Thel answer'd: "O thou little virgin of the peaceful val-
ley,
Giving to those that cannot crave, the voiceless, the o'er-
tired;
Thy breath doth nourish the innocent lamb, he smells
thy milky garments,

He crops thy flowers while thou sittest smiling in his
face,
Wiping his mild and meekin mouth from all contagious
taints.
Thy wine doth purify the golden honey; thy perfume,
Which thou dost scatter on every little blade of grass
that springs,
Revives the milked cow, & tames the fire-breathing
steed.
But Thel is like a faint cloud kindled at the rising sun:
I vanish from my pearly throne, and who shall find my
place?"

"Queen of the vales," the Lilly answer'd, "ask the tender
cloud,
And it shall tell thee why it glitters in the morning sky,
And why it scatters its bright beauty thro' the humid air.
Descend, O little Cloud, & hover before the eyes of
Thel."

The Cloud descended, and the Lilly bow'd her modest
head
And went to mind her numerous charge among the ver-
dant grass.

II

"O little Cloud," the virgin said, "I charge thee tell to
me
Why thou complainest not when in one hour thou fade
away:
Then we shall seek thee, but not find. Ah! Thel is like to
thee:
I pass away: yet I complain, and no one hears my
voice."

The Cloud then shew'd his golden head & his bright
form emerg'd,
Hovering and glittering on the air before the face of
Thel.

"O virgin, know'st thou not our steeds drink of the
golden springs
Where Luvah doth renew his horses? Look'st thou on
my youth,
And fearest thou, because I vanish and am seen no
more,
Nothing remains? O maid, I tell thee, when I pass away
It is to tenfold life, to love, to peace and raptures holy:
Unseen descending, weigh my light wings upon balmy
flowers,
And court the fair-eyed dew to take me to her shining
tent:
The weeping virgin, trembling kneels before the risen
sun,
Till we arise link'd in a golden band and never part,
But walk united, bearing food to all our tender flowers."

"Dost thou, O little Cloud? I fear that I am not like thee,
For I walk thro' the vales of Har, and smell the sweetest
flowers,
But I feed not the little flowers; I hear the warbling
birds,
But I feed not the warbling birds; they fly and seek their
food:
But Thel delights in these no more, because I fade
away;
And all shall say, 'Without a use this shining woman
liv'd,
Or did she only live to be at death the food of worms?' "

The Cloud reclin'd upon his airy throne and answer'd
    thus:

"Then if thou art the food of worms, O virgin of the
    skies,
How great thy use, how great thy blessing! Every thing
    that lives
Lives not alone nor for itself. Fear not, and I will call
The weak worm from its lowly bed, and thou shalt hear
    its voice.
Come forth, worm of the silent valley, to thy pensive
    queen."

The helpless worm arose, and sat upon the Lilly's leaf,
And the bright Cloud sail'd on, to find his partner in the
    vale.

III

Then Thel astonish'd view'd the Worm upon its dewy
    bed.

"Art thou a Worm? Image of weakness, art thou but a
    Worm?
I see thee like an infant wrapped in the Lilly's leaf.
Ah! weep not, little voice, thou canst not speak, but thou
    canst weep.
Is this a Worm? I see thee lay helpless & naked, weep-
    ing,
And none to answer, none to cherish thee with mother's
    smiles."

The Clod of Clay heard the Worm's voice & rais'd her
    pitying head:
She bow'd over the weeping infant, and her life exhal'd

In milky fondness: then on Thel she fix'd her humble
  eyes.

"O beauty of the vales of Har! we live not for ourselves.
Thou seest me the meanest thing, and so I am indeed.
My bosom of itself is cold, and of itself is dark;
But he, that loves the lowly, pours his oil upon my head,
And kisses me, and binds his nuptial bands around my
  breast,
And says: 'Thou mother of my children, I have loved
  thee
And I have given thee a crown that none can take
  away.'
But how this is, sweet maid, I know not, and I cannot
  know;
I ponder, and I cannot ponder; yet I live and love."

The daughter of beauty wip'd her pitying tears with her
  white veil,
And said: "Alas! I knew not this, and therefore did I
  weep.
That God would love a Worm I knew, and punish the
  evil foot
That wilful bruis'd its helpless form; but that he cher-
  ish'd it
With milk and oil I never knew, and therefore did I
  weep;
And I complain'd in the mild air, because I fade away,
And lay me down in thy cold bed, and leave my shining
  lot."

"Queen of the vales," the matron Clay answer'd, "I
  heard thy sighs,

And all thy moans flew o'er my roof, but I have call'd
    them down.
Wilt thou, O Queen, enter my house? 'Tis given thee to
    enter
And to return: fear nothing, enter with thy virgin feet."

IV

The eternal gates' terrific porter lifted the northern bar:
Thel enter'd in & saw the secrets of the land unknown.
She saw the couches of the dead, & where the fibrous
    roots
Of every heart on earth infixes deep its restless twists:
A land of sorrows & of tears where never smile was seen.

She wander'd in the land of clouds thro' valleys dark,
    list'ning
Dolours & lamentations; waiting oft beside a dewy grave
She stood in silence, list'ning to the voices of the ground,
Till to her own grave plot she came, & there she sat
    down,
And heard this voice of sorrow breathed from the hollow
    pit.

"Why cannot the Ear be closed to its own destruction?
Or the glist'ning Eye to the poison of a smile?
Why are Eyelids stor'd with arrows ready drawn,
Where a thousand fighting men in ambush lie?
Or an Eye of gifts & graces show'ring fruits & coined
    gold?
Why a Tongue impress'd with honey from every wind?
Why an Ear, a whirlpool fierce to draw creations in?
Why a Nostril wide inhaling terror, trembling, & af-
    fright?

Why a tender curb upon the youthful burning boy?
Why a little curtain of flesh on the bed of our desire?"

The Virgin started from her seat, & with a shriek
Fled back unhinder'd till she came into the vales of Har.

THE END

VISIONS OF
THE DAUGHTERS OF ALBION

The Eye sees more than the Heart knows

(1793)

THE ARGUMENT

I loved Theotormon,
And I was not ashamed;
I trembled in my virgin fears,
And I hid in Leutha's vale!

I plucked Leutha's flower,
And I rose up from the vale;
But the terrible thunders tore
My virgin mantle in twain.

VISIONS

Enslav'd, the Daughters of Albion weep; a trembling
    lamentation
Upon their mountains; in their valleys, sighs toward
    America.

For the soft soul of America, Oothoon, wander'd in woe,
Along the vales of Leutha seeking flowers to comfort
    her;
And thus she spoke to the bright Marygold of Leutha's
    vale:

287

"Art thou a flower? art thou a nymph? I see thee now a
    flower,
Now a nymph! I dare not pluck thee from thy dewy
    bed!"

The Golden nymph replied: "Pluck thou my flower,
    Oothoon the mild!
Another flower shall spring, because the soul of sweet
    delight
Can never pass away." She ceas'd, & clos'd her golden
    shrine.

Then Oothoon pluck'd the flower, saying: "I pluck thee
    from thy bed,
Sweet flower, and put thee here to glow between my
    breasts,
And thus I turn my face to where my whole soul seeks."

Over the waves she went in wing'd exulting swift de-
    light,
And over Theotormon's reign took her impetuous course.

Bromion rent her with his thunders; on his stormy bed
Lay the faint maid, and soon her woes appall'd his thun-
    ders hoarse.

Bromion spoke: "Behold this harlot here on Bromion's
    bed,
And let the jealous dolphins sport around the lovely
    maid!
Thy soft American plains are mine, and mine thy north
    & south:
Stampt with my signet are the swarthy children of the
    sun;

They are obedient, they resist not, they obey the
  scourge;
Their daughters worship terrors and obey the violent.
Now thou maist marry Bromion's harlot, and protect the
  child
Of Bromion's rage, that Oothoon shall put forth in nine
  moons' time."

Then storms rent Theotormon's limbs: he roll'd his
  waves around
And folded his black jealous waters round the adulterate
  pair.
Bound back to back in Bromion's caves, terror & meek-
  ness dwell:

At entrance Theotormon sits, wearing the threshold
  hard
With secret tears; beneath him sound like waves on a
  desart shore
The voice of slaves beneath the sun, and children
  bought with money,
That shiver in religious caves beneath the burning fires
Of lust, that belch incessant from the summits of the
  earth.

Oothoon weeps not; she cannot weep! her tears are
  locked up;
But she can howl incessant writhing her soft snowy
  limbs
And calling Theotormon's Eagles to prey upon her flesh.

"I call with holy voice! Kings of the sounding air,
Rend away this defiled bosom that I may reflect
The image of Theotormon on my pure transparent
  breast."

The Eagles at her call descend & rend their bleeding
    prey:
Theotormon severely smiles; her soul reflects the smile,
As the clear spring, mudded with feet of beasts, grows
    pure & smiles.

The Daughters of Albion hear her woes, & eccho back
    her sighs.

"Why does my Theotormon sit weeping upon the thresh-
    old,
And Oothoon hovers by his side, perswading him in
    vain?
I cry: arise, O Theotormon! for the village dog
Barks at the breaking day; the nightingale has done
    lamenting;
The lark does rustle in the ripe corn, and the Eagle re-
    turns
From nightly prey and lifts his golden beak to the pure
    east,
Shaking the dust from his immortal pinions to awake
The sun that sleeps too long. Arise, my Theotormon, I
    am pure
Because the night is gone that clos'd me in its deadly
    black.

"They told me that the night & day were all that I could
    see;
They told me that I had five senses to inclose me up,
And they inclos'd my infinite brain into a narrow circle,
And sunk my heart into the Abyss, a red, round globe,
    hot burning,
Till all from life I was obliterated and erased.
Instead of morn arises a bright shadow, like an eye

In the eastern cloud; instead of night a sickly charnel
    house:
That Theotormon hears me not! to him the night and
    morn
Are both alike; a night of sighs, a morning of fresh tears,
And none but Bromion can hear my lamentations.

"With what sense is it that the chicken shuns the raven-
    ous hawk?
With what sense does the tame pigeon measure out the
    expanse?
With what sense does the bee form cells? have not the
    mouse & frog
Eyes and ears and sense of touch? yet are their habita-
    tions
And their pursuits as different as their forms and as their
    joys.
Ask the wild ass why he refuses burdens, and the meek
    camel
Why he loves man: is it because of eye, ear, mouth, or
    skin,
Or breathing nostrils? No, for these the wolf and tyger
    have.
Ask the blind worm the secrets of the grave, and why
    her spires
Love to curl round the bones of death; and ask the
    rav'nous snake
Where she gets poison, & the wing'd eagle why he loves
    the sun;
And then tell me the thoughts of man, that have been
    hid of old.

"Silent I hover all the night, and all day could be silent
If Theotormon once would turn his loved eyes upon me.

How can I be defil'd when I reflect thy image pure?
Sweetest the fruit that the worm feeds on, & the soul
    prey'd on by woe,
The new wash'd lamb ting'd with the village smoke, &
    the bright swan
By the red earth of our immortal river. I bathe my
    wings,
And I am white and pure to hover round Theotormon's
    breast."

Then Theotormon broke his silence, and he answered:
"Tell me what is the night or day to one o'erflow'd with
    woe?
Tell me what is a thought, & of what substance is it
    made?
Tell me what is a joy, & in what gardens do joys grow?
And in what rivers swim the sorrows? and upon what
    mountains
Wave shadows of discontent? and in what houses dwell
    the wretched,
Drunken with woe forgotten, and shut up from cold de-
    spair?
Tell me where dwell the thoughts forgotten till thou
    call them forth?
Tell me where dwell the joys of old? & where the ancient
    loves,
And when will they renew again, & the night of oblivion
    past,
That I might traverse times & spaces far remote, and
    bring
Comforts into a present sorrow and a night of pain?
Where goest thou, O thought? to what remote land is
    thy flight?
If thou returnest to the present moment of affliction

Wilt thou bring comforts on thy wings, and dews and
    honey and balm,
Or poison from the desart wilds, from the eyes of the
    envier?"

Then Bromion said, and shook the cavern with his lam-
    entation:

"Thou knowest that the ancient trees seen by thine eyes
    have fruit,
But knowest thou that trees and fruits flourish upon the
    earth
To gratify senses unknown? trees, beasts and birds un-
    known;
Unknown, not unperciev'd, spread in the infinite micro-
    scope,
In places yet unvisited by the voyager, and in worlds
Over another kind of seas, and in atmospheres un-
    known:
Ah! are there other wars beside the wars of sword and
    fire?
And are there other sorrows beside the sorrows of pov-
    erty?
And are there other joys beside the joys of riches and
    ease?
And is there not one law for both the lion and the ox?
And is there not eternal fire and eternal chains
To bind the phantoms of existence from eternal life?"

Then Oothoon waited silent all the day and all the
    night;
But when the morn arose, her lamentation renew'd.
The Daughters of Albion hear her woes, & eccho back
    her sighs.

"O Urizen! Creator of men! mistaken Demon of heaven!
Thy joys are tears, thy labour vain to form men to thine
　　image.
How can one joy absorb another? are not different joys
Holy, eternal, infinite? and each joy is a Love.

"Does not the great mouth laugh at a gift, & the narrow
　　eyelids mock
At the labour that is above payment? and wilt thou take
　　the ape
For thy councellor, or the dog for a schoolmaster to thy
　　children?
Does he who contemns poverty and he who turns with
　　abhorrence
From usury feel the same passion, or are they moved
　　alike?
How can the giver of gifts experience the delights of the
　　merchant?
How the industrious citizen the pains of the husband-
　　man?
How different far the fat fed hireling with hollow drum,
Who buys whole corn fields into wastes, and sings upon
　　the heath!
How different their eye and ear! how different the world
　　to them!
With what sense does the parson claim the labour of the
　　farmer?
What are his nets & gins & traps; & how does he sur-
　　round him
With cold floods of abstraction, and with forests of soli-
　　tude,
To build him castles and high spires, where kings &
　　priests may dwell;
Till she who burns with youth, and knows no fixed lot,
　　is bound

In spells of law to one she loaths? and must she drag the
    chain
Of life in weary lust? must chilling, murderous thoughts
    obscure
The clear heaven of her eternal spring; to bear the win-
    try rage
Of a harsh terror, driv'n to madness, bound to hold a rod
Over her shrinking shoulders all the day, & all the night
To turn the wheel of false desire, and longings that
    wake her womb
To the abhorred birth of cherubs in the human form,
That live a pestilence & die a meteor, & are no more;
Till the child dwell with one he hates, and do the deed
    he loaths,
And the impure scourge force his seed into its unripe
    birth
Ere yet his eyelids can behold the arrows of the day?

"Does the whale worship at thy footsteps as the hungry
    dog;
Or does he scent the mountain prey because his nostrils
    wide
Draw in the ocean? does his eye discern the flying cloud
As the raven's eye? or does he measure the expanse like
    the vulture?
Does the still spider view the cliffs where eagles hide
    their young;
Or does the fly rejoice because the harvest is brought in?
Does not the eagle scorn the earth & despise the treas-
    ures beneath?
But the mole knoweth what is there, & the worm shall
    tell it thee.
Does not the worm erect a pillar in the mouldering
    church yard

And a palace of eternity in the jaws of the hungry
    grave?
Over his porch these words are written: 'Take thy bliss,
    O Man!
And sweet shall be thy taste, & sweet thy infant joys re-
    new!'

"Infancy! fearless, lustful, happy, nestling for delight
In laps of pleasure: Innocence! honest, open, seeking
The vigorous joys of morning light; open to virgin bliss.
Who taught thee modesty, subtil modesty, child of night
    & sleep?
When thou awakest wilt thou dissemble all thy secret
    joys,
Or wert thou not awake when all this mystery was dis-
    clos'd?
Then com'st thou forth a modest virgin, knowing to dis-
    semble,
With nets found under thy night pillow, to catch virgin
    joy
And brand it with the name of whore, & sell it in the
    night,
In silence, ev'n without a whisper, and in seeming sleep.
Religious dreams and holy vespers light thy smoky fires:
Once were thy fires lighted by the eyes of honest morn.
And does my Theotormon seek this hypocrite modesty,
This knowing, artful, secret, fearful, cautious, trembling
    hypocrite?
Then is Oothoon a whore indeed! and all the virgin joys
Of life are harlots, and Theotormon is a sick man's
    dream;
And Oothoon is the crafty slave of selfish holiness.

"But Oothoon is not so: a virgin fill'd with virgin fancies,
Open to joy and to delight where ever beauty appears;

If in the morning sun I find it, there my eyes are fix'd
In happy copulation; if in evening mild, wearied with
   work,
Sit on a bank and draw the pleasures of this free born
   joy.

"The moment of desire! the moment of desire! The vir-
   gin
That pines for man shall awaken her womb to enormous
   joys
In the secret shadows of her chamber: the youth shut up
   from
The lustful joy shall forget to generate & create an amo-
   rous image
In the shadows of his curtains and in the folds of his si-
   lent pillow.
Are not these the places of religion, the rewards of con-
   tinence,
The self enjoyings of self denial? why dost thou seek re-
   ligion?
Is it because acts are not lovely that thou seekest soli-
   tude
Where the horrible darkness is impressed with reflec-
   tions of desire?

"Father of Jealousy, be thou accursed from the earth!
Why hast thou taught my Theotormon this accursed
   thing?
Till beauty fades from off my shoulders, darken'd and
   cast out,
A solitary shadow wailing on the margin of non-entity.

"I cry: Love! Love! Love! happy happy Love! free as
   the mountain wind!

Can that be Love that drinks another as a sponge drinks
    water,
That clouds with jealousy his nights, with weepings all
    the day,
To spin a web of age around him, grey and hoary, dark,
Till his eyes sicken at the fruit that hangs before his
    sight?
Such is self-love that envies all, a creeping skeleton
With lamplike eyes watching around the frozen mar-
    riage bed.

"But silken nets and traps of adamant will Oothoon
    spread,
And catch for thee girls of mild silver, or of furious gold.
I'll lie beside thee on a bank & view their wanton play
In lovely copulation, bliss on bliss, with Theotormon:
Red as the rosy morning, lustful as the first born beam,
Oothoon shall view his dear delight, nor e'er with jeal-
    ous cloud
Come in the heaven of generous love, nor selfish blight-
    ings bring.

"Does the sun walk in glorious raiment on the secret
    floor
Where the cold miser spreads his gold; or does the
    bright cloud drop
On his stone threshold? does his eye behold the beam
    that brings
Expansion to the eye of pity? or will he bind himself
Beside the ox to thy hard furrow? does not that mild
    beam blot
The bat, the owl, the glowing tyger, and the king of
    night?
The sea fowl takes the wintry blast for a cov'ring to her
    limbs,

And the wild snake the pestilence to adorn him with
gems & gold;
And trees & birds & beasts & men behold their eternal
joy.
Arise, you little glancing wings, and sing your infant
joy!
Arise, and drink your bliss, for every thing that lives is
holy!"

Thus every morning wails Oothoon; but Theotormon
sits
Upon the margin'd ocean conversing with shadows dire.

The Daughters of Albion hear her woes, & eccho back
her sighs.

THE END

AMERICA

A PROPHECY

(1793)

PRELUDIUM

The shadowy Daughter of Urthona stood before red Orc,
When fourteen suns had faintly journey'd o'er his dark
    abode:
His food she brought in iron baskets, his drink in cups
    of iron:
Crown'd with a helmet & dark hair the nameless female
    stood;
A quiver with its burning stores, a bow like that of
    night,
When pestilence is shot from heaven: no other arms she
    need!
Invulnerable tho' naked, save where clouds roll round
    her loins
Their awful folds in the dark air: silent she stood as
    night;
For never from her iron tongue could voice or sound
    arise,
But dumb till that dread day when Orc assay'd his fierce
    embrace.

"Dark Virgin," said the hairy youth, "thy father stern,
    abhorr'd,
Rivets my tenfold chains while still on high my spirit
    soars;

Sometimes an eagle screaming in the sky, sometimes a
  lion
Stalking upon the mountains, & sometimes a whale, I
  lash
The raging fathomless abyss; anon a serpent folding
Around the pillars of Urthona, and round thy dark limbs
On the Canadian wilds I fold; feeble my spirit folds,
For chain'd beneath I rend these caverns: when thou
  bringest food
I howl my joy, and my red eyes seek to behold thy
  face—
In vain! these clouds roll to & fro, & hide thee from my
  sight."

Silent as despairing love, and strong as jealousy,
The hairy shoulders rend the links; free are the wrists of
  fire;
Round the terrific loins he siez'd the panting, struggling
  womb;
It joy'd: she put aside her clouds & smiled her first-born
  smile,
As when a black cloud shews its lightnings to the silent
  deep.

Soon as she saw the terrible boy, then burst the virgin
  cry:

"I know thee, I have found thee, & I will not let thee go:
Thou art the image of God who dwells in darkness of
  Africa,
And thou art fall'n to give me life in regions of dark
  death.
On my American plains I feel the struggling afflictions
Endur'd by roots that writhe their arms into the nether
  deep.

I see a Serpent in Canada who courts me to his love,
In Mexico an Eagle, and a Lion in Peru;
I see a Whale in the South-sea, drinking my soul away.
O what limb rending pains I feel! thy fire & my frost
Mingle in howling pains, in furrows by thy lightnings
    rent.
This is eternal death, and this the torment long fore-
    told."

A PROPHECY

The Guardian Prince of Albion burns in his nightly tent:
Sullen fires across the Atlantic glow to America's shore,
Piercing the souls of warlike men who rise in silent
    night.
Washington, Franklin, Paine & Warren, Gates, Hancock
    & Green
Meet on the coast glowing with blood from Albion's
    fiery Prince.

Washington spoke: "Friends of America! look over the
    Atlantic sea;
A bended bow is lifted in heaven, & a heavy iron chain
Descends, link by link, from Albion's cliffs across the
    sea, to bind
Brothers & sons of America till our faces pale and yel-
    low,
Heads deprest, voices weak, eyes downcast, hands work-
    bruis'd,
Feet bleeding on the sultry sands, and the furrows of
    the whip
Descend to generations that in future times forget."

The strong voice ceas'd, for a terrible blast swept over
    the heaving sea:

The eastern cloud rent: on his cliffs stood Albion's
wrathful Prince,
A dragon form, clashing his scales: at midnight he arose,
And flam'd red meteors round the land of Albion be-
neath;
His voice, his locks, his awful shoulders, and his glow-
ing eyes
Appear to the Americans upon the cloudy night.
Solemn heave the Atlantic waves between the gloomy
nations,
Swelling, belching from its deeps red clouds & raging
fires.
Albion is sick! America faints! enrag'd the Zenith grew.
As human blood shooting its veins all round the orbed
heaven,
Red rose the clouds from the Atlantic in vast wheels of
blood,
And in the red clouds rose a Wonder o'er the Atlantic
sea,
Intense! naked! a Human fire, fierce glowing, as the
wedge
Of iron heated in the furnace: his terrible limbs were
fire
With myriads of cloudy terrors, banners dark & towers
Surrounded: heat but not light went thro' the murky
atmosphere.

The King of England looking westward trembles at the
vision.

Albion's Angel stood beside the Stone of night, and saw
The terror like a comet, or more like the planet red
That once enclos'd the terrible wandering comets in its
sphere.

Then, Mars, thou wast our center, & the planets three
    flew round
Thy crimson disk: so e'er the Sun was rent from thy red
    sphere.
The Spectre glow'd his horrid length staining the temple
    long
With beams of blood; & thus a voice came forth, and
    shook the temple:

"The morning comes, the night decays, the watchmen
    leave their stations;
The grave is burst, the spices shed, the linen wrapped
    up;
The bones of death, the cov'ring clay, the sinews shrunk
    & dry'd
Reviving shake, inspiring move, breathing, awakening,
Spring like redeemed captives when their bonds & bars
    are burst.
Let the slave grinding at the mill run out into the field,
Let him look up into the heavens & laugh in the bright
    air;
Let the inchained soul, shut up in darkness and in sigh-
    ing,
Whose face has never seen a smile in thirty weary years,
Rise and look out; his chains are loose, his dungeon
    doors are open;
And let his wife and children return from the oppres-
    sor's scourge.
They look behind at every step & believe it is a dream,
Singing: 'The Sun has left his blackness & has found a
    fresher morning,
And the fair Moon rejoices in the clear & cloudless night;
For Empire is no more, and now the Lion & Wolf shall
    cease.' "

In thunders ends the voice. Then Albion's Angel wrath-
    ful burnt
Beside the Stone of Night, and like the Eternal Lion's
    howl
In famine & war, reply'd: "Art thou not Orc, who
    serpent-form'd
Stands at the gate of Enitharmon to devour her chil-
    dren?
Blasphemous Demon, Antichrist, hater of Dignities,
Lover of wild rebellion, and transgressor of God's Law,
Why dost thou come to Angel's eyes in this terrific
    form?"

The Terror answer'd: "I am Orc, wreath'd round the
    accursed tree:
The times are ended; shadows pass, the morning 'gins to
    break;
The fiery joy, that Urizen perverted to ten commands,
What night he led the starry hosts thro' the wide wilder-
    ness,
That stony law I stamp to dust; and scatter religion
    abroad
To the four winds as a torn book, & none shall gather
    the leaves;
But they shall rot on desart sands, & consume in bottom-
    less deeps,
To make the desarts blossom, & the deeps shrink to their
    fountains,
And to renew the fiery joy, and burst the stony roof;
That pale religious letchery, seeking Virginity,
May find it in a harlot, and in coarse-clad honesty
The undefil'd, tho' ravish'd in her cradle night and
    morn;
For everything that lives is holy, life delights in life;

Because the soul of sweet delight can never be defil'd.

Fires inwrap the earthly globe, yet man is not consum'd;

Amidst the lustful fires he walks; his feet become like
　　brass,

His knees and thighs like silver, & his breast and head
　　like gold."

"Sound! sound! my loud war-trumpets, & alarm my Thir-
　　teen Angels!

Loud howls the eternal Wolf! the eternal Lion lashes
　　his tail!

America is darken'd; and my punishing Demons, ter-
　　rified,

Crouch howling before their caverns deep, like skins
　　dry'd in the wind.

They cannot smite the wheat, nor quench the fatness
　　of the earth;

They cannot smite with sorrows, nor subdue the plow
　　and spade;

They cannot wall the city, nor moat round the castle of
　　princes;

They cannot bring the stubbed oak to overgrow the
　　hills;

For terrible men stand on the shores, & in their robes I
　　see

Children take shelter from the lightnings: there stands
　　Washington

And Paine and Warren with their foreheads rear'd to-
　　ward the east.

But clouds obscure my aged sight. A vision from afar!

Sound! sound! my loud war-trumpets, & alarm my thir-
　　teen Angels!

Ah vision from afar! Ah rebel form that rent the ancient

Heavens! Eternal Viper, self-renew'd, rolling in clouds,

I see thee in thick clouds and darkness on America's shore,

Writhing in pangs of abhorred birth; red flames the crest rebellious

And eyes of death; the harlot womb, oft opened in vain,

Heaves in enormous circles: now the times are return'd upon thee,

Devourer of thy parent, now thy unutterable torment renews.

Sound! sound! my loud war-trumpets, & alarm my thirteen Angels!

Ah terrible birth! a young one bursting! where is the weeping mouth,

And where the mother's milk? instead, those ever-hissing jaws

And parched lips drop with fresh gore: now roll thou in the clouds;

Thy mother lays her length outstretch'd upon the shore beneath.

Sound! sound! my loud war-trumpets, & alarm my thirteen Angels!

Loud howls the eternal Wolf! the eternal Lion lashes his tail!"

Thus wept the Angel voice, & as he wept, the terrible blasts

Of trumpets blew a loud alarm across the Atlantic deep.

No trumpets answer; no reply of clarions or of fifes:

Silent the Colonies remain and refuse the loud alarm.

On those vast shady hills between America & Albion's shore,

Now barr'd out by the Atlantic sea, call'd Atlantean hills,

Because from their bright summits you may pass to the
    Golden world,
An ancient palace, archetype of mighty Emperies,
Rears its immortal pinnacles, built in the forest of God
By Ariston, the king of beauty, for his stolen bride.

Here on their magic seats the thirteen Angels sat per-
    turb'd,
For clouds from the Atlantic hover o'er the solemn roof.

Fiery the Angels rose, & as they rose deep thunder roll'd
Around their shores, indignant burning with the fires of
    Orc;
And Boston's Angel cried aloud as they flew thro' the
    dark night.

He cried: "Why trembles honesty, and like a murderer
Why seeks he refuge from the frowns of his immortal
    station?
Must the generous tremble & leave his joy to the idle, to
    the pestilence,
That mock him? who commanded this? what God? what
    Angel?
To keep the gen'rous from experience till the ungener-
    ous
Are unrestrain'd performers of the energies of nature;
Till pity is become a trade, and generosity a science
That men get rich by; & the sandy desart is giv'n to the
    strong?
What God is he writes laws of peace & clothes him in a
    tempest?
What pitying Angel lusts for tears and fans himself with
    sighs?
What crawling villain preaches abstinence & wraps him-
    self

In fat of lambs? no more I follow, no more obedience
pay!"

So cried he, rending off his robe & throwing down his
scepter
In sight of Albion's Guardian; and all the thirteen
Angels
Rent off their robes to the hungry wind, & threw their
golden scepters
Down on the land of America; indignant they descended
Headlong from out their heav'nly heights, descending
swift as fires
Over the land; naked & flaming are their lineaments seen
In the deep gloom; by Washington & Paine & Warren
they stood;
And the flame folded, roaring fietce within the pitchy
night
Before the Demon red, who burnt towards America,
In black smoke, thunders, and loud winds, rejoicing in
its terror,
Breaking in smoky wreaths from the wild deep, & gath'r-
ing thick
In flames as of a furnace on the land from North to
South,
What time the thirteen Governors that England sent,
convene
In Bernard's house; the flames cover'd the land, they
rouze, they cry;
Shaking their mental chains, they rush in fury to the
sea
To quench their anguish; at the feet of Washington
down fall'n
They grovel on the sand and writhing lie, while all
The British soldiers thro' the thirteen states sent up a
howl

Of anguish, threw their swords & muskets to the earth, & ran

From their encampments and dark castles, seeking where to hide

From the grim flames, and from the visions of Orc, in sight

Of Albion's Angel; who, enrag'd, his secret clouds open'd

From north to south and burnt outstretch'd on wings of wrath, cov'ring

The eastern sky, spreading his awful wings across the heavens.

Beneath him roll'd his num'rous hosts, all Albion's Angels camp'd

Darken'd the Atlantic mountains; & their trumpets shook the valleys,

Arm'd with diseases of the earth to cast upon the Abyss,

Their numbers forty millions, must'ring in the eastern sky.

In the flames stood & view'd the armies drawn out in the sky,

Washington, Franklin, Paine, & Warren, Allen, Gates, & Lee,

And heard the voice of Albion's Angel give the thunderous command;

His plagues, obedient to his voice, flew forth out of their clouds,

Falling upon America, as a storm to cut them off,

As a blight cuts the tender corn when it begins to appear.

Dark is the heaven above, & cold & hard the earth beneath:

And as a plague wind fill'd with insects cuts off man & beast,

And as a sea o'erwhelms a land in the day of an earth-
    quake,
Fury! rage! madness! in a wind swept through America;
And the red flames of Orc, that folded roaring, fierce,
    around
The angry shores; and the fierce rushing of th' inhabit-
    ants together!
The citizens of New York close their books & lock their
    chests;
The mariners of Boston drop their anchors and unlade;
The scribe of Pensylvania casts his pen upon the earth;
The builder of Virginia throws his hammer down in fear.

Then had America been lost, o'erwhelm'd by the Atlan-
    tic,
And Earth had lost another portion of the infinite,
But all rush together in the night in wrath and raging
    fire.
The red fires rag'd! the plagues recoil'd! then roll'd they
    back with fury
On Albion's Angels: then the Pestilence began in streaks
    of red
Across the limbs of Albion's Guardian; the spotted
    plague smote Bristol's
And the Leprosy London's Spirit, sickening all their
    bands:
The millions sent up a howl of anguish and threw off
    their hammer'd mail,
And cast their swords & spears to earth, & stood, a naked
    multitude:
Albion's Guardian writhed in torment on the eastern sky,
Pale, quiv'ring toward the brain his glimmering eyes,
    teeth chattering,
Howling & shuddering, his legs quivering, convuls'd
    each muscle & sinew:

Sick'ning lay London's Guardian, and the ancient miterd
     York,
Their heads on snowy hills, their ensigns sick'ning in the
     sky.
The plagues creep on the burning winds driven by
     flames of Orc,
And by the fierce Americans rushing together in the
     night,
Driven o'er the Guardians of Ireland, and Scotland and
     Wales.
They, spotted with plagues, forsook the frontiers; & their
     banners, sear'd
With fires of hell, deform their ancient heavens with
     shame & woe.
Hid in his caves the Bard of Albion felt the enormous
     plagues,
And a cowl of flesh grew o'er his head, & scales on his
     back & ribs;
And, rough with black scales, all his Angels fright their
     ancient heavens.
The doors of marriage are open, and the Priests in rus-
     tling scales
Rush into reptile coverts, hiding from the fires of Orc,
That play around the golden roofs in wreaths of fierce
     desire,
Leaving the females naked and glowing with the lusts of
     youth.

For the female spirits of the dead, pining in bonds of
     religion,
Run from their fetters reddening, & in long drawn
     arches sitting,
They feel the nerves of youth renew, and desires of an-
     cient times

Over their pale limbs, as a vine when the tender grape
appears.

Over the hills, the vales, the cities, rage the red flames
fierce:
The Heavens melted from north to south; and Urizen,
who sat
Above all heavens, in thunders wrap'd, emerg'd his lep-
rous head
From out his holy shrine, his tears in deluge piteous
Falling into the deep sublime; flag'd with grey-brow'd
snows
And thunderous visages, his jealous wings wav'd over
the deep;
Weeping in dismal howling woe, he dark descended,
howling
Around the smitten bands, clothed in tears & trembling,
shudd'ring cold.
His stored snows he poured forth, and his icy magazines
He open'd on the deep, and on the Atlantic sea white
shiv'ring
Leprous his limbs, all over white, and hoary was his
visage,
Weeping in dismal howlings before the stern Americans,
Hiding the Demon red with clouds & cold mists from the
earth;
Till Angels & weak men twelve years should govern o'er
the strong;
And then their end should come, when France receiv'd
the Demon's light.

Stiff shudderings shook the heav'nly thrones! France,
Spain, & Italy
In terror view'd the bands of Albion, and the ancient
Guardians,

Fainting upon the elements, smitten with their own
   plagues.
They slow advance to shut the five gates of their law-
   built heaven,
Filled with blasting fancies and with mildews of despair,
With fierce disease and lust, unable to stem the fires of
   Orc.
But the five gates were consum'd, & their bolts and
   hinges melted;
And the fierce flames burnt round the heavens & round
   the abodes of men.

FINIS

EUROPE

(1794)

A PROPHECY

"Five windows light the cavern'd Man: thro' one he
    breathes the air;
Thro' one hears music of the spheres; thro' one the eter-
    nal vine
Flourishes, that he may recieve the grapes; thro' one
    can look
And see small portions of the eternal world that ever
    groweth;
Thro' one himself pass out what time he please; but he
    will not,
For stolen joys are sweet & bread eaten in secret pleas-
    ant."

So sang a Fairy, mocking, as he sat on a streak'd Tulip,
Thinking none saw him: when he ceas'd I started from
    the trees
And caught him in my hat, as boys knock down a but-
    terfly.
"How know you this," said I, "small Sir? where did you
    learn this song?"
Seeing himself in my possession, thus he answer'd me:
"My master, I am yours! command me, for I must obey."

"Then tell me, what is the material world, and is it
    dead?"

He, laughing, answer'd: "I will write a book on leaves
  of flowers,
If you will feed me on love-thoughts & give me now and
  then
A cup of sparkling poetic fancies; so, when I am tipsie,
I'll sing to you to this soft lute, and shew you all alive
The world, where every particle of dust breathes forth
  its joy."

I took him home in my warm bosom: as we went along
Wild flowers I gather'd, & he shew'd me each eternal
  flower:
He laugh'd aloud to see them whimper because they
  were pluck'd.
They hover'd round me like a cloud of incense: when I
  came
Into my parlour and sat down and took my pen to write.
My Fairy sat upon the table and dictated EUROPE.

PRELUDIUM

The nameless shadowy female rose from out the breast
  of Orc,
Her snaky hair brandishing in the winds of Enitharmon;
And thus her voice arose:

"O mother Enitharmon, wilt thou bring forth other sons?
To cause my name to vanish, that my place may not be
  found,
For I am faint with travail,
Like the dark cloud disburden'd in the day of dismal
  thunder.

"My roots are brandish'd in the heavens, my fruits in
earth beneath
Surge, foam and labour into life, first born & first con-
sum'd!
Consumed and consuming!
Then why shouldst thou, accursed mother, bring me
into life?

"I wrap my turban of thick clouds around my lab'ring
head,
And fold the sheety waters as a mantle round my limbs;
Yet the red sun and moon
And all the overflowing stars rain down prolific pains.

"Unwilling I look up to heaven, unwilling count the
stars:
Sitting in fathomless abyss of my immortal shrine
I sieze their burning power
And bring forth howling terrors, all devouring fiery
kings,

"Devouring & devoured, roaming on dark and desolate
mountains,
In forests of eternal death, shrieking in hollow trees.
Ah mother Enitharmon!
Stamp not with solid form this vig'rous progeny of fires.

"I bring forth from my teeming bosom myriads of
flames,
And thou dost stamp them with a signet; then they roam
abroad
And leave me void as death.
Ah! I am drown'd in shady woe and visionary joy.

"And who shall bind the infinite with an eternal band?
To compass it with swaddling bands? and who shall
    cherish it
With milk and honey?
I see it smile, & I roll inward, & my voice is past."

       She ceast, & roll'd her shady clouds
       Into the secret place.

A PROPHECY

The deep of winter came,
What time the secret child
Descended thro' the orient gates of the eternal day:
War ceas'd, & all the troops like shadows fled to their
    abodes.

Then Enitharmon saw her sons & daughters rise around;
Like pearly clouds they meet together in the crystal
    house;
And Los, possessor of the moon, joy'd in the peaceful
    night,
Thus speaking, while his num'rous sons shook their
    bright fiery wings:

"Again the night is come
That strong Urthona takes his rest;
And Urizen, unloos'd from chains,
Glows like a meteor in the distant north.
Stretch forth your hands and strike the elemental
    strings!
Awake the thunders of the deep!

"The shrill winds wake,
Till all the sons of Urizen look out and envy Los.
Sieze all the spirits of life, and bind
Their warbling joys to our loud strings!
Bind all the nourishing sweets of earth
To give us bliss, that we may drink the sparkling wine of
     Los!
And let us laugh at war,
Despising toil and care,
Because the days and nights of joy in lucky hours renew.

"Arise, O Orc, from thy deep den!
First born of Enitharmon, rise!
And we will crown thy head with garlands of the ruddy
     vine;
For now thou art bound,
And I may see thee in the hour of bliss, my eldest born."

The horrent Demon rose surrounded with red stars of
     fire
Whirling about in furious circles round the immortal
     fiend.

Then Enitharmon down descended into his red light,
And thus her voice rose to her children: the distant
     heavens reply:

"Now comes the night of Enitharmon's joy!
Who shall I call? Who shall I send,
That Woman, lovely Woman, may have dominion?
Arise, O Rintrah, thee I call! & Palamabron, thee!
Go! tell the Human race that Woman's love is Sin;
That an Eternal life awaits the worms of sixty winters
In an allegorical abode where existence hath never come.

Forbid all Joy, & from her childhood shall the little fe-
　　male
Spread nets in every secret path.

"My weary eyelids draw towards the evening; my bliss
　　is yet but new.

"Arise, O Rintrah, eldest born, second to none but Orc!
O lion Rintrah, raise thy fury from thy forests black!
Bring Palamabron, horned priest, skipping upon the
　　mountains,
And silent Elynittria, the silver bowed queen.
Rintrah, where hast thou hid thy bride?
Weeps she in desart shades?
Alas! my Rintrah, bring the lovely jealous Ocalythron.

"Arise, my son! bring all thy brethren, O thou king of
　　fire!
Prince of the sun! I see thee with thy innumerable race,
Thick as the summer stars;
But each, ramping, his golden mane shakes,
And thine eyes rejoice because of strength, O Rintrah,
　　furious king!"

Enitharmon slept
Eighteen hundred years. Man was a Dream!
The night of Nature and their harps unstrung!
She slept in middle of her nightly song
Eighteen hundred years, a female dream.

Shadows of men in fleeting bands upon the winds
Divide the heavens of Europe
Till Albion's Angel, smitten with his own plagues, fled
　　with his bands.

The cloud bears hard on Albion's shore,
Fill'd with immortal demons of futurity:
In council gather the smitten Angels of Albion;
The cloud bears hard upon the council house, down
    rushing
On the heads of Albion's Angels.

One hour they lay buried beneath the ruins of that hall;
But as the stars rise from the salt lake, they arise in pain,
In troubled mists, o'erclouded by the terrors of strugling
    times.

In thoughts perturb'd they rose from the bright ruins,
    silent following
The fiery King, who sought his ancient temple, serpent-
    form'd,
That stretches out its shady length along the Island
    white.
Round him roll'd his clouds of war; silent the Angel
    went
Along the infinite shores of Thames to golden Verulam.
There stand the venerable porches that high-towering
    rear
Their oak-surrounded pillars, form'd of massy stones,
    uncut
With tool, stones precious, such eternal in the heavens,
Of colours twelve, few known on earth, give light in the
    opake,
Plac'd in the order of the stars, when the five senses
    whelm'd
In deluge o'er the earth-born man; then turn'd the fluxile
    eyes
Into two stationary orbs, concentrating all things:
The ever-varying spiral ascents to the heavens of heav-
    ens

Were bended downward, and the nostrils' golden gates
    shut,
Turn'd outward, barr'd and petrify'd against the infinite.

Thought chang'd the infinite to a serpent, that which
    pitieth
To a devouring flame; and man fled from its face and
    hid
In forests of night: then all the eternal forests were di-
    vided
Into earths rolling in circles of space, that like an ocean
    rush'd
And overwhelmed all except this finite wall of flesh.
Then was the serpent temple form'd, image of infinite
Shut up in finite revolutions, and man became an Angel,
Heaven a mighty circle turning, God a tyrant crown'd.

Now arriv'd the ancient Guardian at the southern porch
That planted thick with trees of blackest leaf & in a vale
Obscure enclos'd the Stone of Night; oblique it stood,
    o'erhung
With purple flowers and berries red, image of that sweet
    south
Once open to the heavens, and elevated on the human
    neck,
Now overgrown with hair and cover'd with a stony roof.
Downward 'tis sunk beneath th' attractive north, that
    round the feet,
A raging whirlpool, draws the dizzy enquirer to his
    grave.

    Albion's Angel rose upon the Stone of Night.
    He saw Urizen on the Atlantic;
    And his brazen Book

That Kings & Priests had copied on Earth,
Expanded from North to South.

And the clouds & fires pale roll'd round in the night of
    Enitharmon,
Round Albion's cliffs & London's walls: still Enitharmon
    slept.
Rolling volumes of grey mist involve Churches, Palaces,
    Towers;
For Urizen unclasp'd his Book, feeding his soul with
    pity.
The youth of England, hid in gloom, curse the pain'd
    heavens, compell'd
Into the deadly night to see the form of Albion's Angel.
Their parents brought them forth, & aged ignorance
    preaches, canting,
On a vast rock, perciev'd by those senses that are clos'd
    from thought:
Bleak, dark, abrupt it stands & overshadows London
    city.
They saw his boney feet on the rock, the flesh consum'd
    in flames;
They saw the Serpent temple lifted above, shadowing
    the Island white;
They heard the voice of Albion's Angel howling in
    flames of Orc,
Seeking the trump of the last doom.

Above the rest the howl was heard from Westminster
    louder & louder:
The Guardian of the secret codes forsook his ancient
    mansion,
Driven out by the flames of Orc; his furr'd robes & false
    locks

Adhered and grew one with his flesh, and nerves & veins
  shot thro' them.
With dismal torment sick, hanging upon the wind, he
  fled
Groveling along Great George Street thro' the Park gate:
  all the soldiers
Fled from his sight: he drag'd his torments to the wilder-
  ness.

Thus was the howl thro' Europe!
For Orc rejoic'd to hear the howling shadows;
But Palamabron shot his lightnings, trenching down his
  wide back;
And Rintrah hung with all his legions in the nether
  deep.

Enitharmon laugh'd in her sleep to see (O woman's tri-
  umph!)
Every house a den, every man bound: the shadows are
  fill'd
With spectres, and the windows wove over with curses
  of iron:
Over the doors "Thou shalt not," & over the chimneys
  "Fear" is written:
With bands of iron round their necks fasten'd into the
  walls
The citizens, in leaden gyves the inhabitants of suburbs
Walk heavy; soft and bent are the bones of villagers.

Between the clouds of Urizen the flames of Orc roll
  heavy
Around the limbs of Albion's Guardian, his flesh con-
  suming:
Howlings & hissings, shrieks & groans, & voices of de-
  spair

Arise around him in the cloudy heavens of Albion. Furi-
ous,
The red limb'd Angel siez'd in horror and torment
The Trump of the last doom; but he could not blow the
iron tube!
Thrice he assay'd presumptuous to awake the dead to
Judgment.

A mighty Spirit leap'd from the land of Albion,
Nam'd Newton: he siez'd the trump & blow'd the enor-
mous blast!
Yellow as leaves of Autumn, the myriads of Angelic
hosts
Fell thro' the wintry skies seeking their graves,
Rattling their hollow bones in howling and lamentation.

Then Enitharmon woke, nor knew that she had slept;
And eighteen hundred years were fled
As if they had not been.
She call'd her sons & daughters
To the sports of night
Within her crystal house,
And thus her song proceeds:

"Arise, Ethinthus! tho' the earth-worm call,
Let him call in vain,
Till the night of holy shadows
And human solitude is past!

"Ethinthus, queen of waters, how thou shinest in the
sky!
My daughter, how do I rejoice! for thy children flock
around
Like the gay fishes on the wave, when the cold moon
drinks the dew.

Ethinthus! thou art sweet as comforts to my fainting
    soul,
For now thy waters warble round the feet of Enithar-
mon.

"Manathu-Varcyon! I behold thee flaming in my halls,
Light of thy mother's soul! I see thy lovely eagles round;
Thy golden wings are my delight, & thy flames of soft
    delusion.

"Where is my lureing bird of Eden? Leutha, silent love!
Leutha, the many colour'd bow delights upon thy
    wings:
Soft soul of flowers, Leutha!
Sweet smiling pestilence! I see thy blushing light;
Thy daughters, many changing,
Revolve like sweet perfumes ascending, O Leutha,
    silken queen!

"Where is the youthful Antamon, prince of the pearly
    dew?
O Antamon! why wilt thou leave thy mother Enithar-
mon?
Alone I see thee, crystal form,
Floating upon the bosom'd air
With lineaments of gratified desire.
My Antamon, the seven churches of Leutha seek thy
    love.

"I hear the soft Oothoon in Enitharmon's tents;
Why wilt thou give up woman's secrecy, my melancholy
    child?
Between two moments bliss is ripe.
O Theotormon! robb'd of joy, I see thy salt tears flow
Down the steps of my crystal house.

"Sotha & Thiralatha! secret dwellers of dreamful caves,
Arise and please the horrent fiend with your melodious
 songs;
Still all your thunders, golden-hoof'd, & bind your horses
 black.
Orc! smile upon my children!
Smile, son of my afflictions.
Arise, O Orc, and give our mountains joy of thy red
 light!"

She ceas'd; for All were forth at sport beneath the sol-
 emn moon
Waking the stars of Urizen with their immortal songs,
That nature felt thro' all her pores the enormous revelry
Till morning oped the eastern gate;
Then every one fled to his station, & Enitharmon wept.

But terrible Orc, when he beheld the morning in the
 east,
Shot from the heights of Enitharmon,
And in the vineyards of red France appear'd the light of
 his fury.

The sun glow'd fiery red!
The furious terrors flew around
On golden chariots raging with red wheels dropping
 with blood!
The Lions lash their wrathful tails!
The Tigers couch upon the prey & suck the ruddy tide,
And Enitharmon groans & cries in anguish and dismay.

Then Los arose: his head he rear'd in snaky thunders
 clad;
And with a cry that shook all nature to the utmost pole,
Call'd all his sons to the strife of blood.

THE FIRST BOOK
OF URIZEN

(1794)

PRELUDIUM TO THE FIRST BOOK
OF URIZEN

Of the primeval Priest's assum'd power,
When Eternals spurn'd back his religion
And gave him a place in the north,
Obscure, shadowy, void, solitary.

Eternals! I hear your call gladly.
Dictate swift winged words & fear not
To unfold your dark visions of torment.

I

1. Lo, a shadow of horror is risen
In Eternity! Unknown, unprolific,
Self-clos'd, all-repelling: what Demon
Hath form'd this abominable void,
This soul-shudd'ring vacuum? Some said
"It is Urizen." But unknown, abstracted,
Brooding, secret, the dark power hid. '

328

2. Times on times he divided & measur'd
Space by space in his ninefold darkness,
Unseen, unknown; changes appear'd
Like desolate mountains, rifted furious
By the black winds of perturbation.

3. For he strove in battles dire,
In unseen conflictions with shapes
Bred from his forsaken wilderness
Of beast, bird, fish, serpent & element,
Combustion, blast, vapour and cloud.

4. Dark, revolving in silent activity:
Unseen in tormenting passions:
An activity unknown and horrible,
A self-contemplating shadow,
In enormous labours occupied.

5. But Eternals beheld his vast forests;
Age on ages he lay, clos'd, unknown,
Brooding shut in the deep; all avoid
The petrific, abominable chaos.

6. His cold horrors silent, dark Urizen
Prepar'd; his ten thousands of thunders,
Rang'd in gloom'd array, stretch out across
The dread world; & the rolling of wheels,
As of swelling seas, sound in his clouds,
In his hills of stor'd snows, in his mountains
Of hail & ice; voices of terror
Are heard, like thunders of autumn
When the cloud blazes over the harvests.

II

1. Earth was not: nor globes of attraction;
The will of the Immortal expanded
Or contracted his all flexible senses;
Death was not, but eternal life sprung.

2. The sound of a trumpet the heavens
Awoke, & vast clouds of blood roll'd
Round the dim rocks of Urizen, so nam'd
That solitary one in Immensity.

3. Shrill the trumpet: & myriads of Eternity
Muster around the bleak desarts,
Now fill'd with clouds, darkness, & waters,
That roll'd perplex'd, lab'ring; & utter'd
Words articulate bursting in thunders
That roll'd on the tops of his mountains:

4. "From the depths of dark solitude, From
The eternal abode in my holiness,
Hidden, set apart, in my stern counsels,
Reserv'd for the days of futurity,
I have sought for a joy without pain,
For a solid without fluctuation.
Why will you die, O Eternals?
Why live in unquenchable burnings?

5. "First I fought with the fire, consum'd
Inwards into a deep world within:
A void immense, wild, dark & deep,
Where nothing was: Nature's wide womb;

And self balanc'd, stretch'd o'er the void,
I alone, even I! the winds merciless
Bound; but condensing in torrents
They fall & fall; strong I repell'd
The vast waves, & arose on the waters
A wide world of solid obstruction.

6. "Here alone I, in books form'd of metals,
Have written the secrets of wisdom,
The secrets of dark contemplation,
By fightings and conflicts dire
With terrible monsters Sin-bred
Which the bosoms of all inhabit,
Seven deadly Sins of the soul.

7. "Lo! I unfold my darkness, and on
This rock place with strong hand the Book
Of eternal brass, written in my solitude:

8. "Laws of peace, of love, of unity,
Of pity, compassion, forgiveness;
Let each chuse one habitation,
His ancient infinite mansion,
One command, one joy, one desire,
One curse, one weight, one measure,
One King, one God, one Law."

III

1. The voice ended: they saw his pale visage
Emerge from the darkness, his hand
On the rock of eternity unclasping
The Book of brass. Rage siez'd the strong,

2. Rage, fury, intense indignation,
In cataracts of fire, blood, & gall,
In whirlwinds of sulphurous smoke,
And enormous forms of energy,
All the seven deadly sins of the soul
In living creations appear'd,
In the flames of eternal fury.

3. Sund'ring, dark'ning, thund'ring,
Rent away with a terrible crash,
Eternity roll'd wide apart,
Wide asunder rolling;
Mountainous all around
Departing, departing, departing,
Leaving ruinous fragments of life
Hanging, frowning cliffs & all between,
An ocean of voidness unfathomable.

4. The roaring fires ran o'er the heav'ns
In whirlwinds & cataracts of blood,
And o'er the dark desarts of Urizen
Fires pour thro' the void on all sides
On Urizen's self-begotten armies.

5. But no light from the fires: all was darkness
In the flames of Eternal fury.

6. In fierce anguish & quenchless flames
To the desarts and rocks he ran raging
To hide; but he could not: combining,
He dug mountains & hills in vast strength,
He piled them in incessant labour,
In howlings & pangs & fierce madness,
Long periods in burning fires labouring

Till hoary, and age-broke, and aged,
In despair and the shadows of death.

7. And a roof vast, petrific around
On all sides he fram'd, like a womb,
Where thousands of rivers in veins
Of blood pour down the mountains to cool
The eternal fires, beating without
From Eternals; & like a black globe,
View'd by sons of Eternity standing
On the shore of the infinite ocean,
Like a human heart, strugling & beating,
The vast world of Urizen appear'd.

8. And Los, round the dark globe of Urizen,
Kept watch for Eternals to confine
The obscure separation alone;
For Eternity stood wide apart,
As the stars are apart from the earth.

9. Los wept, howling around the dark Demon,
And cursing his lot; for in anguish
Urizen was rent from his side,
And a fathomless void for his feet,
And intense fires for his dwelling.

10. But Urizen laid in a stony sleep,
Unorganiz'd, rent from Eternity.

11. The Eternals said: "What is this? Death.
Urizen is a clod of clay."

12. Los howl'd in a dismal stupor,
Groaning, gnashing, groaning,
Till the wrenching apart was healed.

13. But the wrenching of Urizen heal'd not.
Cold, featureless, flesh or clay,
Rifted with direful changes,
He lay in a dreamless night,

14. Till Los rouz'd his fires, affrighted
At the formless, unmeasurable death.

IV [a]

1. Los, smitten with astonishment,
Frighten'd at the hurtling bones

2. And at the surging, sulphureous,
Perturbed Immortal, mad raging

3. In whirlwinds & pitch & nitre
Round the furious limbs of Los.

4. And Los formed nets & gins
And threw the nets round about.

5. He watch'd in shudd'ring fear
The dark changes, & bound every change
With rivets of iron & brass.

6. And these were the changes of Urizen:

IV [b]

1. Ages on ages roll'd over him;
In stony sleep ages roll'd over him,
Like a dark waste stretching, chang'able,

By earthquakes riv'n, belching sullen fires:
On ages roll'd ages in ghastly
Sick torment; around him in whirlwinds
Of darkness the eternal Prophet howl'd,
Beating still on his rivets of iron,
Pouring sodor of iron; dividing
The horrible night into watches.

2. And Urizen (so his eternal name)
His prolific delight obscur'd more & more
In dark secresy, hiding in surgeing
Sulphureous fluid his phantasies.
The Eternal Prophet heav'd the dark bellows,
And turn'd restless the tongs, and the hammer
Incessant beat, forging chains new & new,
Numb'ring with links hours, days & years.

3. The Eternal mind, bounded, began to roll
Eddies of wrath ceaseless round & round,
And the sulphureous foam, surgeing thick,
Settled, a lake, bright & shining clear,
White as the snow on the mountains cold.

4. Forgetfulness, dumbness, necessity,
In chains of the mind locked up,
Like fetters of ice shrinking together,
Disorganiz'd, rent from Eternity,
Los beat on his fetters of iron,
And heated his furnaces, & pour'd
Iron sodor and sodor of brass.

5. Restless turn'd the Immortal inchain'd,
Heaving dolorous, anguish'd unbearable;
Till a roof, shaggy wild, inclos'd
In an orb his fountain of thought.

6. In a horrible, dreamful slumber,
Like the linked infernal chain,
A vast Spine writh'd in torment
Upon the winds, shooting pain'd
Ribs, like a bending cavern;
And bones of solidness froze
Over all his nerves of joy.
And a first Age passed over,
And a state of dismal woe.

7. From the caverns of his jointed Spine
Down sunk with fright a red
Round Globe, hot burning, deep,
Deep down into the Abyss;
Panting, Conglobing, Trembling,
Shooting out ten thousand branches
Around his solid bones.
And a second Age passed over,
And a state of dismal woe.

8. In harrowing fear rolling round,
His nervous brain shot branches
Round the branches of his heart
On high into two little orbs,
And fixed in two little caves,
Hiding carefully from the wind,
His Eyes beheld the deep.
And a third Age passed over,
And a state of dismal woe.

9. The pangs of hope began.
In heavy pain, striving, struggling,
Two Ears in close volutions
From beneath his orbs of vision
Shot spiring out and petrified

As they grew. And a fourth Age passed,
And a state of dismal woe.

10. In ghastly torment sick,
Hanging upon the wind,
Two Nostrils bend down to the deep.
And a fifth Age passed over,
And a state of dismal woe.

11. In ghastly torment sick,
Within his ribs bloated round,
A craving Hungry Cavern;
Thence arose his channel'd Throat,
And, like a red flame, a Tongue
Of thirst & of hunger appear'd.
And a sixth Age passed over,
And a state of dismal woe.

12. Enraged & stifled with torment,
He threw his right Arm to the north,
His left Arm to the south
Shooting out in anguish deep,
And his feet stamp'd the nether Abyss
In trembling & howling & dismay.
And a seventh Age passed over,
And a state of dismal woe.

v

1. In terrors Los shrunk from his task:
His great hammer fell from his hand.
His fires beheld, and sickening
Hid their strong limbs in smoke;
For with noises, ruinous, loud,

With hurtlings & clashings & groans,
The Immortal endur'd his chains,
Tho' bound in a deadly sleep.

2. All the myriads of Eternity,
All the wisdom & joy of life
Roll like a sea around him,
Except what his little orbs
Of sight by degrees unfold.

3. And now his eternal life
Like a dream was obliterated.

4. Shudd'ring, the Eternal Prophet smote
With a stroke from his north to south region.
The bellows & hammer are silent now;
A nerveless silence his prophetic voice
Siez'd; a cold solitude & dark void
The Eternal Prophet & Urizen clos'd.

5. Ages on ages roll'd over them,
Cut off from life & light, frozen
Into horrible forms of deformity.
Los suffer'd his fires to decay;
Then he look'd back with anxious desire,
But the space, undivided by existence,
Struck horror into his soul.

6. Los wept obscur'd with mourning,
His bosom earthquak'd with sighs;
He saw Urizen deadly black
In his chains bound, & Pity began,

7. In anguish dividing & dividing,
For pity divides the soul

In pangs, eternity on eternity,
Life in cataracts pour'd down his cliffs.
The void shrunk the lymph into Nerves
Wand'ring wide on the bosom of night
And left a round globe of blood
Trembling upon the void.
Thus the Eternal Prophet was divided
Before the death image of Urizen;
For in changeable clouds and darkness.
In a winterly night beneath,
The Abyss of Los stretch'd immense;
And now seen, now obscur'd, to the eyes
Of Eternals the visions remote
Of the dark seperation appear'd:
As glasses discover Worlds
In the endless Abyss of space,
So the expanding eyes of Immortals
Beheld the dark visions of Los
And the globe of life blood trembling.

8. The globe of life blood trembled
Branching out into roots,
Fibrous, writhing upon the winds,
Fibres of blood, milk and tears,
In pangs, eternity on eternity.
At length in tears & cries imbodied,
A female form, trembling and pale,
Waves before his deathy face.

9. All Eternity shudder'd at sight
Of the first female now separate,
Pale as a cloud of snow
Waving before the face of Los.

10. Wonder, awe, fear, astonishment
Petrify the eternal myriads
At the first female form now separate.
They call'd her Pity, and fled.

11. "Spread a Tent with strong curtains around
   them.
Let cords & stakes bind in the Void,
That Eternals may no more behold them."

12. They began to weave curtains of darkness,
They erected large pillars round the Void,
With golden hooks fasten'd in the pillars;
With infinite labour the Eternals
A woof wove, and called it Science.

VI

1. But Los saw the Female & pitied;
He embrac'd her; she wept, she refus'd;
In perverse and cruel delight
She fled from his arms, yet he follow'd.

2. Eternity shudder'd when they saw
Man begetting his likeness
On his own divided image.

3. A time passed over: the Eternals
Began to erect the tent,
When Enitharmon, sick,
Felt a Worm within her Womb.

4. Yet helpless it lay like a Worm
In the trembling womb
To be moulded into existence.

5. All day the worm lay on her bosom;
All night within her womb
The worm lay till it grew to a serpent,
With dolorous hissings & poisons
Round Enitharmon's loins folding.

6. Coil'd within Enitharmon's womb
The serpent grew, casting its scales;
With sharp pangs the hissings began
To change to a grating cry:
Many sorrows and dismal throes,
Many forms of fish, bird & beast
Brought forth an Infant form
Where was a worm before.

7. The Eternals their tent finished
Alarm'd with these gloomy visions,
When Enitharmon groaning
Produc'd a man Child to the light.

8. A shriek ran thro' Eternity,
And a paralytic stroke,
At the birth of the Human shadow.

9. Delving earth in his resistless way,
Howling, the Child with fierce flames
Issu'd from Enitharmon.

10. The Eternals closed the tent;
They beat down the stakes, the cords

Stretch'd for a work of eternity.
No more Los beheld Eternity.

11. In his hands he siez'd the infant,
He bathed him in springs of sorrow,
He gave him to Enitharmon.

VII

1. They named the child Orc; he grew,
Fed with milk of Enitharmon.

2. Los awoke her. O sorrow & pain!
A tight'ning girdle grew
Around his bosom. In sobbings
He burst the girdle in twain;
But still another girdle
Oppress'd his bosom. In sobbings
Again he burst it. Again
Another girdle succeeds.
The girdle was form'd by day,
By night was burst in twain.

3. These falling down on the rock
Into an iron Chain
In each other link by link lock'd.

4. They took Orc to the top of a mountain.
O how Enitharmon wept!
They chain'd his young limbs to the rock
With the Chain of Jealousy
Beneath Urizen's deathful shadow.

5. The dead heard the voice of the child
And began to awake from sleep;
All things heard the voice of the child
And began to awake to life.

6. And Urizen, craving with hunger,
Stung with the odours of Nature,
Explor'd his dens around.

7. He form'd a line & a plummet
To divide the Abyss beneath;
He form'd a dividing rule;

8. He formed scales to weigh,
He formed massy weights;
He formed a brazen quadrant;
He formed golden compasses,
And began to explore the Abyss;
And he planted a garden of fruits.

9. But Los encircled Enitharmon
With fires of Prophecy
From the sight of Urizen & Orc.

10. And she bore an enormous race.

VIII

1. Urizen explor'd his dens,
Mountain, moor & wilderness,
With a globe of fire lighting his journey,
A fearful journey, annoy'd
By cruel enormities, forms
Of life on his forsaken mountains.

2. And his world teem'd vast enormities,
Fright'ning, faithless, fawning
Portions of life, similitudes
Of a foot, or a hand, or a head,
Or a heart, or an eye; they swam mischevous,
Dread terrors, delighting in blood.

3. Most Urizen sicken'd to see
His eternal creations appear,
Sons & daughters of sorrow on mountains
Weeping, wailing. First Thiriel appear'd,
Astonish'd at his own existence,
Like a man from a cloud born; & Utha,
From the waters emerging, laments;
Grodna rent the deep earth, howling
Amaz'd; his heavens immense cracks
Like the ground parch'd with heat, then Fuzon
Flam'd out, first begotten, last born;
All his Eternal sons in like manner;
His daughters from green herbs & cattle,
From monsters & worms of the pit.

4. He in darkness clos'd view'd all his race,
And his soul sicken'd! he curs'd
Both sons & daughters; for he saw
That no flesh nor spirit could keep
His iron laws one moment.

5. For he saw that life liv'd upon death:
The Ox in the slaughter house moans,
The Dog at the wintry door;
And he wept & he called it Pity,
And his tears flowed down on the winds.

6. Cold he wander'd on high, over their cities
In weeping & pain & woe;
And wherever he wander'd, in sorrows
Upon the aged heavens,
A cold shadow follow'd behind him
Like a spider's web, moist, cold & dim,
Drawing out from his sorrowing soul,
The dungeon-like heaven dividing,
Where ever the footsteps of Urizen
Walked over the cities in sorrow;

7. Till a Web, dark & cold, throughout all
The tormented element stretch'd
From the sorrows of Urizen's soul.
And the Web is a Female in embrio.
None could break the Web, no wings of fire,

8. So twisted the cords, & so knotted
The meshes, twisted like to the human brain.

9. And all call'd it The Net of Religion.

IX

1. Then the Inhabitants of those Cities
Felt their Nerves change into Marrow,
And hardening Bones began
In swift diseases and torments,
In throbbings & shootings & grindings
Thro' all the coasts; till weaken'd
The Senses inward rush'd, shrinking
Beneath the dark net of infection;

2. Till the shrunken eyes, clouded over,
Discern'd not the woven hipocrisy;
But the streaky slime in their heavens,
Brought together by narrowing perceptions,
Appear'd transparent air; for their eyes
Grew small like the eyes of a man,
And in reptile forms shrinking together,
Of seven feet stature they remain'd.

3. Six days they shrunk up from existence,
And on the seventh day they rested,
And they bless'd the seventh day, in sick hope,
And forgot their eternal life.

4. And their thirty cities divided
In form of a human heart.
No more could they rise at will
In the infinite void, but bound down
To earth by their narrowing perceptions
They lived a period of years;
Then left a noisom body
To the jaws of devouring darkness.

5. And their children wept, & built
Tombs in the desolate places,
And form'd laws of prudence, and call'd them
The eternal laws of God.

6. And the thirty cities remain'd,
Surrounded by salt floods, now call'd
Africa: its name was then Egypt.

7. The remaining sons of Urizen
Beheld their brethren shrink together
Beneath the Net of Urizen.

Perswasion was in vain;
For the ears of the inhabitants
Were wither'd & deafen'd & cold,
And their eyes could not discern
Their brethren of other cities.

8. So Fuzon call'd all together
The remaining children of Urizen,
And they left the pendulous earth.
They called it Egypt, & left it.

9. And the salt Ocean rolled englob'd.

THE END OF THE FIRST BOOK OF URIZEN

THE BOOK OF AHANIA

(1795)

I

1. Fuzon on a chariot iron-wing'd
On spiked flames rose; his hot visage
Flam'd furious; sparkles his hair & beard
Shot down his wide bosom and shoulders.
On clouds of smoke rages his chariot
And his right hand burns red in its cloud
Moulding into a vast Globe his wrath,
As the thunder-stone is moulded.
Son of Urizen's silent burnings:

2. "Shall we worship this Demon of smoke,'
Said Fuzon, "this abstract non-entity,
"This cloudy God seated on waters,
"Now seen, now obscur'd, King of sorrow?"

3. So he spoke in a fiery flame,
On Urizen frowning indignant,
The Globe of wrath shaking on high;
Roaring with fury he threw
The howling Globe; burning it flew
Length'ning into a hungry beam. Swiftly

4. Oppos'd to the exulting flam'd beam,
The broad Disk of Urizen upheav'd
Across the Void many a mile.

5. It was forg'd in mills where the winter
Beats incessant: ten winters the disk
Unremitting endur'd the cold hammer.

6. But the strong arm that sent it remember'd
The sounding beam: laughing, it tore through
That beaten mass, keeping its direction,
The cold loins of Urizen dividing.

7. Dire shriek'd his invisible Lust;
Deep groan'd Urizen! stretching his awful hand,
Ahania (so name his parted soul)
He siez'd on his mountains of Jealousy.
He groan'd anguish'd, & called her Sin,
Kissing her and weeping over her;
Then hid her in darkness, in silence,
Jealous, tho' she was invisible.

8. She fell down a faint shadow wand'ring
In chaos and circling dark Urizen,
As the moon anguish'd circles the earth,
Hopeless! abhorr'd! a death-shadow,
Unseen, unbodied, unknown,
The mother of Pestilence.

9. But the fiery beam of Fuzon
Was a pillar of fire to Egypt
Five hundred years wand'ring on earth,
Till Los siez'd it and beat in a mass
With the body of the sun.

II

1. But the forehead of Urizen gathering,
And his eyes pale with anguish, his lips

Blue & changing, in tears and bitter
Contrition he prepar'd his Bow,

2. Form'd of Ribs, that in his dark solitude,
When obscur'd in his forests, fell monsters
Arose. For his dire Contemplations
Rush'd down like floods from his mountains,
In torrents of mud settling thick,
With Eggs of unnatural production:
Forthwith hatching, some howl'd on his hills,
Some in vales, some aloft flew in air.

3. Of these, an enormous dread Serpent,
Scaled and poisonous horned,
Approach'd Urizen, even to his knees,
As he sat on his dark rooted Oak.

4. With his horns he push'd furious:
Great the conflict & great the jealousy
In cold poisons, but Urizen smote him.

5. First he poison'd the rocks with his blood,
Then polish'd his ribs, and his sinews
Dried, laid them apart till winter;
Then a Bow black prepar'd: on this Bow
A poisoned rock plac'd in silence.
He utter'd these words to the Bow:

6. "O Bow of the clouds of secresy!
O nerve of that lust-form'd monster!
Send this rock swift, invisible thro'
The black clouds on the bosom of Fuzon."

7. So saying, In torment of his wounds
He bent the enormous ribs slowly,

A circle of darkness! then fixed
The sinew in its rest; then the Rock,
Poisonous source, plac'd with art, lifting difficult
Its weighty bulk; silent the rock lay,

8. While Fuzon, his tygers unloosing,
Thought Urizen slain by his wrath.
"I am God!" said he, "eldest of things."

9. Sudden sings the rock; swift & invisible
On Fuzon flew, enter'd his bosom;
His beautiful visage, his tresses
That gave light to the mornings of heaven,
Were smitten with darkness, deform'd
And outstretch'd on the edge of the forest.

10. But the Rock fell upon the Earth,
Mount Sinai in Arabia.

III

1. The Globe shook, and Urizen seated
On black clouds his sore wound anointed;
The ointment flow'd down on the void
Mix'd with blood—here the snake gets her poison.

2. With difficulty & great pain Urizen
Lifted on high the dead corse:
On his shoulders he bore it to where
A Tree hung over the Immensity.

3. For when Urizen shrunk away
From Eternals, he sat on a rock
Barren: a rock which himself

From redounding fancies had petrified.
Many tears fell on the rock,
Many sparks of vegetation.
Soon shot the pained root
Of Mystery under his heel:
It grew a thick tree: he wrote
In silence his book of iron,
Till the horrid plant bending its boughs
Grew to roots when it felt the earth,
And again sprung to many a tree.

4. Amaz'd started Urizen when
He beheld himself compassed round
And high roofed over with trees.
He arose, but the stems stood so thick
He with difficulty and great pain
Brought his Books, all but the Book
Of iron, from the dismal shade.

5. The Tree still grows over the Void
Enrooting itself all around,
An endless labyrinth of woe!

6. The corse of his first begotten
On the accursed Tree of Mystery,
On the topmost stem of this Tree,
Urizen nail'd Fuzon's corse.

IV

1. Forth flew the arrows of pestilence
Round the pale living Corse on the tree.

2. For in Urizen's slumbers of abstraction
In the infinite ages of Eternity,
When his Nerves of Joy melted & flow'd,
A white Lake on the dark blue air
In perturb'd pain and dismal torment
Now stretching out, now swift conglobing,

3. Effluvia vapor'd above
In noxious clouds; these hover'd thick
Over the disorganiz'd Immortal,
Till petrific pain scurf'd o'er the Lakes
As the bones of man, solid & dark.

4. The clouds of disease hover'd wide
Around the Immortal in torment,
Perching around the hurtling bones,
Disease on disease, shape on shape
Winged screaming in blood & torment.

5. The Eternal Prophet beat on his anvils;
Enrag'd in the desolate darkness
He forg'd nets of iron around
And Los threw them around the bones.

6. The shapes screaming flutter'd vain:
Some combin'd into muscles & glands,
Some organs for craving and lust;
Most remain'd on the tormented void,
Urizen's army of horrors.

7. Round the pale living Corse on the Tree
Forty years flew the arrows of pestilence.

8. Wailing and terror and woe
Ran thro' all his dismal world;

Forty years all his sons & daughters
Felt their skulls harden; then Asia
Arose in the pendulous deep.

9. They reptilize upon the Earth.

10. Fuzon groan'd on the Tree.

V

1. The lamenting voice of Ahania
Weeping upon the void!
And round the Tree of Fuzon,
Distant in solitary night,
Her voice was heard, but no form
Had she; but her tears from clouds
Eternal fell round the Tree.

2. And the voice cried: "Ah, Urizen! Love!
Flower of morning! I weep on the verge
Of Non-entity; how wide the Abyss
Between Ahania and thee!

3. "I lie on the verge of the deep;
I see thy dark clouds ascend;
I see thy black forests and floods,
A horrible waste to my eyes!

4. "Weeping I walk over rocks,
Over dens & thro' valleys of death.
Why didst thou despise Ahania
To cast me from thy bright presence
Into the World of Loneness?

5. "I cannot touch his hand,
Nor weep on his knees, nor hear
His voice & bow, nor see his eyes
And joy, nor hear his footsteps and
My heart leap at the lovely sound!
I cannot kiss the place
Whereon his bright feet have trod,
But I wander on the rocks
With hard necessity.

6. "Where is my golden palace?
Where my ivory bed?
Where the joy of my morning hour?
Where the sons of eternity singing

7. "To awake bright Urizen, my king,
To arise to the mountain sport,
To the bliss of eternal valleys;

8. "To awake my king in the morn,
To embrace Ahania's joy
On the bredth of his open bosom?
From my soft cloud of dew to fall
In showers of life on his harvests,

9. "When he gave my happy soul
To the sons of eternal joy,
When he took the daughters of life
Into my chambers of love,

10. "When I found babes of bliss on my beds
And bosoms of milk in my chambers
Fill'd with eternal seed.
O eternal births sung round Ahania
In interchange sweet of their joys!

11. "Swell'd with ripeness & fat with fatness,
Bursting on winds, my odors,
My ripe figs and rich pomegranates
In infant joy at thy feet,
O Urizen, sported and sang.

12. "Then thou with thy lap full of seed,
With thy hand full of generous fire
Walked forth from the clouds of morning,
On the virgins of springing joy,
On the human soul to cast
The seed of eternal science.

13. "The sweat poured down thy temples;
To Ahania return'd in evening,
The moisture awoke to birth
My mothers-joys, sleeping in bliss.

14. "But now alone over rocks, mountains,
Cast out from thy lovely bosom,
Cruel jealousy! selfish fear!
Self-destroying, how can delight
Renew in these chains of darkness,
Where bones of beasts are strown
On the bleak and snowy mountains,
Where bones from the birth are buried
Before they see the light?"

FINIS

THE BOOK OF LOS

(1795)

I

1. Eno, aged Mother,
Who the chariot of Leutha guides
Since the day of thunders in old time,

2. Sitting beneath the eternal Oak
Trembled and shook the steadfast Earth,
And thus her speech broke forth:

3. "O Times remote!
When Love & Joy were adoration,
And none impure were deem'd:
Not Eyeless Covet,
Nor Thin-lip'd Envy,
Nor Bristled Wrath,
Nor Curled Wantonness;

4. "But Covet was poured full,
Envy fed with fat of lambs,
Wrath with lion's gore,
Wantonness lull'd to sleep
With the virgin's lute
Or sated with her love;

5. "Till Covet broke his locks & bars
And slept with open doors;

357

Envy sung at the rich man's feast;
Wrath was follow'd up and down
By a little ewe lamb,
And Wantonness on his own true love
Begot a giant race."

6. Raging furious, the flames of desire
Ran thro' heaven & earth, living flames
Intelligent, organiz'd, arm'd
With destruction & plagues. In the midst
The Eternal Prophet, bound in a chain,
Compell'd to watch Urizen's shadow,

7. Rag'd with curses & sparkles of fury:
Round the flames roll, as Los hurls his chains,
Mounting up from his fury, condens'd,
Rolling round & round, mounting on high
Into vacuum, into non-entity
Where nothing was; dashed wide apart,
His feet stamp the eternal fierce-raging
Rivers of wide flame; they roll round
And round on all sides, making their way
Into darkness and shadowy obscurity.

8. Wide apart stood the fires: Los remain'd
In the void between fire and fire:
In trembling and horror they beheld him;
They stood wide apart, driv'n by his hands
And his feet, which the nether abyss
Stamp'd in fury and hot indignation.

9. But no light from the fires! all was
Darkness round Los: heat was not; for bound up

Into fiery spheres from his fury,
The gigantic flames trembled and hid.

10. Coldness, darkness, obstruction, a Solid
Without fluctuation, hard as adamant,
Black as marble of Egypt, impenetrable,
Bound in the fierce raging Immortal;
And the seperated fires froze in:
A vast solid without fluctuation
Bound in his expanding clear senses.

II

1. The Immortal stood frozen amidst
The vast rock of eternity times
And times, a night of vast durance,
Impatient, stifled, stiffen'd, hard'ned;

2. Till impatience no longer could bear
The hard bondage: rent, rent, the vast solid,
With a crash from immense to immense,

3. Cracked across into numberless fragments.
The Prophetic wrath, strugling for vent,
Hurls apart, stamping furious to dust
And crumbling with bursting sobs, heaves
The black marble on high into fragments.

4. Hurl'd apart on all sides as a falling
Rock, the innumerable fragments away
Fell asunder; and horrible vacuum
Beneath him, & on all sides round,

5. Falling, falling, Los fell & fell,
Sunk precipitant, heavy, down, down,
Times on times, night on night, day on day—
Truth has bounds, Error none—falling, falling,
Years on years, and ages on ages
Still he fell thro' the void, still a void
Found for falling, day & night without end;
For tho' day or night was not, their spaces
Were measur'd by his incessant whirls
In the horrid vacuity bottomless.

6. The Immortal revolving, indignant,
First in wrath threw his limbs like the babe
New born into our world: wrath subsided,
And contemplative thoughts first arose;
Then aloft his head rear'd in the Abyss
And his downward-borne fall chang'd oblique

7. Many ages of groans, till there grew
Branchy forms organizing the Human
Into finite inflexible organs;

8. Till in process from falling he bore
Sidelong on the purple air, wafting
The weak breeze in efforts o'erwearied.

9. Incessant the falling Mind labour'd,
Organizing itself, till the Vacuum
Became element, pliant to rise
Or to fall or to swim or to fly,
With ease searching the dire vacuity.

III

1. The Lungs heave incessant, dull, and heavy;
For as yet were all other parts formless,
Shiv'ring, clinging around like a cloud,
Dim & glutinous as the white Polypus
Driv'n by waves & englob'd on the tide.

2. And the unformed part crav'd repose;
Sleep began; the Lungs heave on the wave:
Weary, overweigh'd, sinking beneath
In a stifling black fluid, he woke.

3. He arose on the waters; but soon
Heavy falling, his organs like roots
Shooting out from the seed, shot beneath,
And a vast world of waters around him
In furious torrents began.

4. Then he sunk, & around his spent Lungs
Began intricate pipes that drew in
The spawn of the waters, Outbranching
An immense Fibrous Form, stretching out
Thro' the bottoms of immensity raging.

5. He rose on the floods; then he smote
The wild deep with his terrible wrath,
Seperating the heavy and thin.

6. Down the heavy sunk, cleaving around
To the fragments of solid: up rose
The thin, flowing round the fierce fires
That glow'd furious in the expanse.

IV

1. Then Light first began: from the fires,
Beams, conducted by fluid so pure,
Flow'd around the Immense. Los beheld
Forthwith, writhing upon the dark void,
The Back bone of Urizen appear
Hurtling upon the wind
Like a serpent! like an iron chain
Whirling about in the Deep.

2. Upfolding his Fibres together
To a Form of impregnable strength,
Los, astonish'd and terrified, built
Furnaces; he formed an Anvil,
A Hammer of adamant: then began
The binding of Urizen day and night.

3. Circling round the dark Demon with howlings,
Dismay & sharp blightings, the Prophet
Of Eternity beat on his iron links.

4. And first from those infinite fires,
The light that flow'd down on the winds
He siez'd, beating incessant, condensing
The subtil particles in an Orb.

5. Roaring indignant, the bright sparks
Endur'd the vast Hammer; but unwearied
Los beat on the Anvil, till glorious
An immense Orb of fire he fram'd.

6. Oft he quench'd it beneath in the Deeps,
Then survey'd the all bright mass, Again
Siezing fires from the terrific Orbs,
He heated the round Globe, then beat,
While, roaring, his Furnaces endur'd
The chain'd Orb in their infinite wombs.

7. Nine ages completed their circles
When Los heated the glowing mass, casting
It down into the Deeps: the Deeps fled
Away in redounding smoke: the Sun
Stood self-balanc'd. And Los smil'd with joy.
He the vast Spine of Urizen siez'd,
And bound down to the glowing illusion.

8. But no light! for the Deep fled away
On all sides, and left an unform'd
Dark vacuity: here Urizen lay
In fierce torments on his glowing bed;

9. Till his Brain in a rock & his Heart
In a fleshy slough formed four rivers
Obscuring the immense Orb of fire
Flowing down into night: till a Form
Was completed, a Human Illusion
In darkness and deep clouds involv'd.

THE END OF THE BOOK OF LOS

THE SONG OF LOS

(1795)

AFRICA

I will sing you a song of Los, the Eternal Prophet:
He sung it to four harps at the tables of Eternity.
>>>*In heart-formed Africa*
Urizen faded! Ariston shudder'd!
>>>*And thus the Song began:*

Adam stood in the garden of Eden
And Noah on the mountains of Ararat;
They saw Urizen give his Laws to the Nations
By the hands of the children of Los.

Adam shudder'd! Noah faded! black grew the sunny
>>>African
When Rintrah gave Abstract Philosophy to Brama in the
>>>East.
(Night spoke to the Cloud:
"Lo these Human form'd spirits, in smiling hipocrisy,
>>>War
Against one another; so let them War on, slaves to the
>>>eternal Elements.")
Noah shrunk beneath the waters;
Abram fled in fires from Chaldea;
Moses beheld upon Mount Sinai forms of dark delusion.

To Trismegistus, Palamabron gave an abstract Law:
To Pythagoras, Socrates & Plato.

Times rolled on o'er all the sons of Har: time after time
Orc on Mount Atlas howl'd, chain'd down with the
     Chain of Jealousy;
Then Oothoon hover'd over Judah & Jerusalem,
And Jesus heard her voice (a man of sorrows) he re-
     ciev'd
A Gospel from wretched Theotormon.

The human race began to wither, for the healthy built
Secluded places, fearing the joys of Love,
And the diseased only propagated.
So Antamon call'd up Leutha from her valleys of delight
And to Mahomet a loose Bible gave.
But in the North, to Odin, Sotha gave a Code of War,
Because of Diralada, thinking to reclaim his joy.

These were the Churches, Hospitals, Castles, Palaces,
Like nets & gins & traps to catch the joys of Eternity,
          And all the rest a desart;
Till, like a dream, Eternity was obliterated & erased.

Since that dread day when Har and Heva fled
Because their brethren & sisters liv'd in War & Lust;
And as they fled they shrunk
Into two narrow doleful forms
Creeping in reptile flesh upon
The bosom of the ground;
And all the vast of Nature shrunk
Before their shrunken eyes.

Thus the terrible race of Los & Enitharmon gave
Laws & Religions to the sons of Har, binding them more

And more to Earth, closing and restraining,
Till a Philosophy of Five Senses was complete.
Urizen wept & gave it into the hands of Newton &
    Locke.

Clouds roll heavy upon the Alps round Rousseau & Vol-
    taire,
And on the mountains of Lebanon round the deceased
    Gods
Of Asia, & on the desarts of Africa round the Fallen An-
    gels
The Guardian Prince of Albion burns in his nightly tent.

ASIA

The Kings of Asia heard
The howl rise up from Europe,
And each ran out from his Web,
From his ancient woven Den;
For the darkness of Asia was startled
At the thick-flaming, thought-creating fires of Orc.

And the Kings of Asia stood
And cried in bitterness of soul:

"Shall not the King call for Famine from the heath,
Nor the Priest for Pestilence from the fen,
To restrain, to dismay, to thin
The inhabitants of mountain and plain,
In the day of full-feeding prosperity
And the night of delicious songs?

"Shall not the Councellor throw his curb
Of Poverty on the laborious,

To fix the price of labour,
To invent allegoric riches?

"And the privy admonishers of men
Call for fires in the City,
For heaps of smoking ruins
In the night of prosperity & wantonness?

"To turn man from his path,
To restrain the child from the womb,
To cut off the bread from the city,
That the remnant may learn to obey,

"That the pride of the heart may fail,
That the lust of the eyes may be quench'd,
That the delicate ear in its infancy
May be dull'd, and the nostrils clos'd up,
To teach mortal worms the path
That leads from the gates of the Grave?"

Urizen heard them cry,
And his shudd'ring, waving wings
Went enormous above the red flames,
Drawing clouds of despair thro' the heavens
Of Europe as he went.
And his Books of brass, iron & gold
Melted over the land as he flew,
Heavy-waving, howling, weeping.

And he stood over Judea,
And stay'd in his ancient place,
And stretch'd his clouds over Jerusalem;

For Adam, a mouldering skeleton,
Lay bleach'd on the garden of Eden;

And Noah, as white as snow,
On the mountains of Ararat.

Then the thunders of Urizen bellow'd aloud
From his woven darkness above.

Orc, raging in European darkness,
Arose like a pillar of fire above the Alps,
Like a serpent of fiery flame!
    The sullen Earth
    Shrunk!

Forth from the dead dust, rattling bones to bones
Join; shaking convuls'd, the shiv'ring clay breathes,
And all flesh naked stands: Fathers and Friends,
Mothers & Infants, Kings & Warriors.

The Grave shrieks with delight & shakes
Her hollow womb & clasps the solid stem:
Her bosom swells with wild desire,
And milk & blood & glandous wine
In rivers rush & shout & dance,
On mountain, dale and plain.

The SONG of LOS is Ended.

Urizen Wept.

From THE FOUR ZOAS

(1797)

THE TORMENTS OF LOVE & JEALOUSY IN
THE DEATH AND JUDGEMENT
OF ALBION THE ANCIENT MAN

VALA

[INTRODUCTION TO NIGHT THE FIRST]

The Song of the Aged Mother which shook the heavens
    with wrath,
Hearing the march of long resounding, strong heroic
    Verse
Marshall'd in order for the day of Intellectual Battle.
The heavens quake, the earth was moved & shudder'd,
    & the mountains
With all their woods, the streams & valleys wail'd in dis-
    mal fear.
Four Mighty Ones are in every Man; a Perfect Unity
Cannot Exist but from the Universal Brotherhood of
    Eden,
The Universal Man, To Whom be Glory Evermore.
    Amen.
What are the Natures of those Living Creatures the
    Heav'nly Father only
Knoweth. No Individual knoweth, nor can know in all
    Eternity.

[ENION AND THARMAS]

Enion said: "Thy fear has made me tremble, thy terrors
    have surrounded me.
All Love is lost: Terror succeeds, & Hatred instead of
    Love,
And stern demands of Right & Duty instead of Liberty.
Once thou wast to Me the loveliest son of heaven—But
    now
Why art thou Terrible? and yet I love thee in thy terror
    till
I am almost Extinct & soon shall be a shadow in Obliv-
    ion,
Unless some way can be found that I may look upon
    thee & live.
Hide me some shadowy semblance, secret whisp'ring in
    my Ear,
In secret of soft wings, in mazes of delusive beauty.
I have look'd into the secret soul of him I lov'd,
And in the Dark recesses found Sin & cannot return."

Trembling & pale sat Tharmas, weeping in his clouds.

"Why wilt thou Examine every little fibre of my soul,
Spreading them out before the sun like stalks of flax to
    dry?
The infant joy is beautiful, but its anatomy
Horrible, Ghast & Deadly; nought shalt thou find in it
But Death, Despair & Everlasting brooding Melancholy.
Thou wilt go mad with horror if thou dost Examine thus
Every moment of my secret hours. Yea, I know
That I have sinn'd, & that my Emanations are become
    harlots.

I am already distracted at their deeds. & if I look
Upon them more, Despair will bring self-murder on my
    soul.
O Enion, thou art thyself a root growing in hell,
Tho' thus heavenly beautiful to draw me to destruction."

[THE SOLITARY WANDERER]

Enion brooded o'er the rocks; the rough rocks groaning
    vegetate.
Such power was given to the Solitary wanderer:
The barked Oak. the long limb'd Beech, the Chestnut
    tree, the Pine,
The Pear tree mild, the frowning Walnut, the sharp
    Crab, & Apple sweet,
The rough bark opens; twittering peep forth little beaks
    & wings,
The Nightingale, the Goldfinch, Robin, Lark, Linnet &
    Thrush.
The Goat leap'd from the craggy cliff, the Sheep awoke
    from the mould,
Upon its green stalk rose the Corn, waving innumerable,
Infolding the bright Infants from the desolating winds.

[URIZEN THE GOD]

Los answer'd furious: "Art thou one of those who when
    most complacent
Mean mischief most? If you are such, Lo! I am also such.
One must be master. Try thy Arts. I also will try mine,
For I percieve thou hast Abundance which I claim as
    mine."

Urizen startled stood, but not Long; Soon he cried:

"Obey my voice, young Demon; I am God from Eternity
to Eternity.

*Art thou a visionary of Jesus, the soft delusion of Eter-
nity?*

Lo I am God, the terrible destroyer, & not the Saviour.

Why should the Divine Vision compell the sons of Eden

*To forego each his own delight, to war against his spec-
tre?*

*The Spectre is the Man. The rest is only delusion &
fancy."*

Thus Urizen spoke, collected in himself in awful pride.

Ten thousand thousand were his hosts of spirits on the
wind,

Ten thousand thousand glittering Chariots shining in
the sky.

They pour upon the golden shore beside the silent
ocean,

Rejoicing in the Victory, & the heavens were fill'd with
blood.

The Earth spread forth her table wide; the Night, a
silver cup

Fill'd with the wine of anguish, waited at the golden
feast.

But the bright Sun was not as yet; he, filling all the ex-
panse,

Slept as a bird in the blue shell that soon shall burst
away.

[THE SONG SUNG AT THE FEAST OF LOS AND ENITHARMON]

And This is the Song sung at The Feast of Los & Enitharmon:

"*Ephraim* call'd out to *Zion:* 'Awake, O Brother Mountain!
Let us refuse the Plow & Spade, the heavy Roller & spiked
Harrow; burn all these Corn fields, throw down all these fences!
Fatten'd on Human blood & drunk with wine of life is better far
Than all these labours of the harvest & the vintage. See the river,
Red with the blood of Men, swells lustful round my rocky knees;
My clouds are not the clouds of verdant fields & groves of fruit,
But Clouds of Human Souls: my nostrils drink the lives of Men.'

"The Villages lament: they faint, outstretch'd upon the plain.
Wailing runs round the Valleys from the Mill & from the Barn.
But most the polish'd Palaces, dark, silent, bow with dread,
Hiding their books & pictures underneath the dens of Earth.

"The Cities send to one another saying: 'My sons are Mad

With wine of cruelty. Let us plat a scourge, O Sister
  City.
Children are nourish'd for the Slaughter; once the Child
  was fed
With Milk, but wherefore now are Children fed with
  blood?

"The Horse is of more value than the Man. The Tyger
  fierce
Laughs at the Human form; the Lion mocks & thirsts for
  blood.
They cry, 'O Spider, spread thy web! Enlarge thy bones
  &, fill'd
With marrow, sinews & flesh, Exalt thyself, attain a
  voice.

" 'Call to thy dark arm'd hosts; for all the sons of Men
  muster together
To desolate their cities! Man shall be no more! Awake,
  O Hosts!'
The bow string sang upon the hills, 'Luvah & Vala ride
Triumphant in the bloody sky, & the Human form is no
  more.'

"The list'ning Stars heard, & the first beam of the morn-
  ing started back:
He cried out to his Father 'depart! depart!' but sudden
  Siez'd,
And clad in steel, & his Horse proudly neigh'd; he smelt
  the battle
Afar off. Rushing back, redd'ning with rage, the Mighty
  Father
Siez'd his bright sheephook studded with gems & gold;
  he swung it round

His head, shrill sounding in the sky; down rush'd the
    Sun with noise
Of war; the Mountains fled away; they sought a place
    beneath."

[THE MUNDANE SHELL]

Urizen rose from the bright Feast like a star thro' the
    evening sky,
Exulting at the voice that call'd him from the Feast of
    envy.
First he beheld the body of Man, pale, cold; the horrors
    of death
Beneath his feet shot thro' him as he stood in the Human
    Brain,
And all its golden porches grew pale with his sickening
    light,
No more exulting, for he saw Eternal Death beneath.
Pale, he beheld futurity: pale, he beheld the Abyss
Where Enion, blind & age bent, wept in direful hunger
    craving,
All rav'ning like the hungry worm & like the silent grave.
Mighty was the draught of Voidness to draw Existence
    in.

Terrific Urizen strode above in fear & pale dismay.
He saw the indefinite space beneath & his soul shrunk
    with horror,
His feet upon the verge of Non Existence; his voice went
    forth:

Luvah & Vala trembling & shrinking beheld the great
    Work master

And heard his Word: "Divide, ye bands, influence by
influence.
Build we a Bower for heaven's darling in the grizly
deep:
*Build we the Mundane Shell around the Rock of Al-
bion."*

The Bands of Heaven flew thro' the air singing & shout-
ing to Urizen.
Some fix'd the anvil, some the loom erected, some the
plow
And harrow form'd & fram'd the harness of silver &
ivory,
The golden compasses, the quadrant, & the rule & bal-
ance.
They erected the furnaces, they form'd the anvils of
gold beaten in mills
Where winter beats incessant, fixing them firm on their
base.
The bellows began to blow, & the Lions of Urizen stood
round the anvil
And the leopards cover'd with skins of beasts tended
the roaring fires,
*Sublime, distinct, their lineaments divine of human
beauty.*
The tygers of wrath called the horses of instruction from
their mangers,
They unloos'd them & put on the harness of gold & silver
& ivory,
In human forms distinct they stood round Urizen, prince
of Light,
Petrifying all the Human Imagination into rock & sand.
Groans ran along Tyburn's brook and along the River of
Oxford

Among the Druid Temples. Albion groan'd on Tyburn's
    brook:
Albion gave his loud death groan. The Atlantic Moun-
    tains trembled.
Aloft the Moon fled with a cry: the Sun with streams of
    blood.
From Albion's Loins fled all Peoples and Nations of the
    Earth,
Fled with the noise of Slaughter, & the stars of heaven
    fled.
Jerusalem came down in a dire ruin over all the Earth,
She fell cold from Lambeth's Vales in groans & dewy
    death—
The dew of anxious souls, the death-sweat of the dy-
    ing—
In every pillar'd hall & arched roof of Albion's skies.
The brother & the brother bathe in blood upon the
    Severn,
The Maiden weeping by. The father & the mother with
The Maiden's father & her mother fainting over the
    body,
And the Young Man, the Murderer, fleeing over the
    mountains.

[URIZEN'S WORK]

With trembling horror pale, aghast the Children of Man
Stood on the infinite Earth & saw these visions in the air,
In waters & in earth beneath; they cried to one another,
"What! are we terrors to one another? Come, O brethren,
    wherefore
Was this wide Earth spread all abroad? not. for wild
    beasts to roam."

But many stood silent, & busied in their families.

And many said, "We see no Visions in the darksom air.

Measure the course of that sulphur orb that lights the
darksom day;

Set stations on this breeding Earth & let us buy & sell."

Others arose & schools erected, forming Instruments

To measure out the course of heaven. Stern Urizen be-
held

In woe his brethren & his sons, in dark'ning woe lament-
ing

Upon the winds in clouds involv'd, Uttering his voice
in thunders,

Commanding all the work with care & power & severity.

Then seiz'd the Lions of Urizen their work, & heated in
the forge

Roar the bright masses; thund'ring beat the hammers,
many a pyramid

Is form'd & thrown down thund'ring into the deeps of
Non Entity.

Heated red hot they, hizzing, rend their way down
many a league

Till resting, each his basement finds; suspended there
they stand

Casting their sparkles dire abroad into the dismal deep.

For, measur'd out in order'd spaces, the Sons of Urizen

With compasses divide the deep; they the strong scales
erect

That Luvah rent from the faint Heart of the Fallen Man,

And weigh the massy Cubes, then fix them in their aw-
ful stations.

And all the time, in Caverns shut, the golden Looms
erected

First spun, then wove the Atmospheres; there the Spider
    & Worm
Plied the wing'd shuttle, piping shrill thro' all the list'n-
    ing threads;
Beneath the Caverns roll the weights of lead & spindles
    of iron,
The enormous warp & woof rage direful in the affrighted
    deep.

While far into the vast unknown the strong wing'd
    Eagles bend
Their venturous flight in Human forms distinct; thro'
    darkness deep
They bear the woven draperies; on golden hooks they
    hang abroad
The universal curtains & spread out from Sun to Sun
The vehicles of light; they separate the furious particles
Into mild currents as the water mingles with the wine.

While thus the Spirits of strongest wing enlighten the
    dark deep,
The threads are spun & the cords twisted & drawn out;
    then the weak
Begin their work, & many a net is netted, many a net
Spread, & many a Spirit caught: innumerable the nets,
Innumerable the gins & traps, & many a soothing flute
Is form'd, & many a corded lyre outspread over the im-
    mense.
In cruel delight they trap the listeners, & in cruel delight
Bind them, condensing the strong energies into little
    compass.
Some became seed of every plant that shall be planted;
    some
The bulbous roots, thrown up together into barns &
    garners.

Then rose the Builders. First the Architect divine his
plan

Unfolds. The wondrous scaffold rear'd all round the in-
finite,

Quadrangular the building rose, the heavens squared by
a line,

Trigons & cubes divide the elements in finite bonds.

Multitudes without number work incessant: the hewn
stone

Is plac'd in beds of mortar mingled with the ashes of
Vala.

Severe the labour; female slaves the mortar trod op-
pressed.

Twelve halls after the names of his twelve sons com-
pos'd

The wondrous building, & three Central Domes after
the Names

Of his three daughters were encompass'd by the twelve
bright halls.

Every hall surrounded by bright Paradises of Delight

In which were towns & Cities, Nations, Seas, Mountains
& Rivers.

Each Dome open'd toward four halls, & the Three
Domes Encompass'd

The Golden Hall of Urizen, whose western side glow'd
bright

With ever streaming fires beaming from his awful limbs.

His Shadowy Feminine Semblance here repos'd on a
White Couch,

Or hover'd over his starry head; & when he smil'd she
brighten'd

Like a bright Cloud in harvest; but when Urizen frown'd
she wept

In mists over his carved throne; & when he turned his
back
Upon his Golden hall & sought the Labyrinthine porches
Of his wide heaven, Trembling, cold, in jealous fears
she sat
A shadow of Despair; therefore toward the West, Uri-
zen form'd
A recess in the wall for fires to glow upon the pale
Female's limbs in his absence, & her Daughters oft upon
A Golden Altar burnt perfumes: with Art Celestial
form'd
Foursquare, sculptur'd & sweetly Engrav'd to please
their shadowy mother.
Ascending into her misty garments the blue smoke roll'd
to revive
Her cold limbs in the absence of her Lord. Also her sons,
With lives of Victims sacrificed upon an altar of brass
On the East side, Reviv'd her soul with lives of beasts &
birds
Slain on the Altar, up ascending into her cloudy bosom.
Of terrible workmanship the Altar, labour of ten thou-
sand Slaves,
One thousand Men of wondrous power spent their lives
in its formation.
It stood on twelve steps nam'd after the names of her
twelve sons,
And was erected at the chief entrance of Urizen's hall.
But infinitely beautiful the wondrous work arose·
In sorrow and care, a Golden World whose porches
round the heavens
And pillar'd halls & rooms reciev'd the eternal wander-
ing stars.
A wondrous golden Building, many a window, many a
door

And many a division let in & out the vast unknown.

Circled in infinite orb immoveable, within its walls & cielings

The heavens were clos'd, and spirits mourn'd their bondage night & day,

And the Divine Vision appear'd in Luvah's robes of blood.

Thus was the Mundane shell builded by Urizen's strong Power.

[THE SONG OF ENITHARMON OVER LOS]

"I sieze the sphery harp. I strike the strings.

"At the first sound the Golden sun arises from the deep
And shakes his awful hair,
The Eccho wakes the moon to unbind her silver locks,
The golden sun bears on my song
And nine bright spheres of harmony rise round the fiery king.

"The joy of woman is the death of her most best beloved
Who dies for Love of her
In torments of fierce jealousy & pangs of adoration.
The Lovers' night bears on my song
And the nine spheres rejoice beneath my powerful controll.

"They sing unceasing to the notes of my immortal hand.
The solemn, silent moon
Reverberates the living harmony upon my limbs,

The birds & beasts rejoice & play,
And every one seeks for his mate to prove his inmost joy.

"Furious & terrible they sport & red the nether deep;
The deep lifts up his rugged head,
And lost in infinite humming wings vanishes with a cry.
The fading cry is ever dying,
The living voice is ever living in its inmost joy.

"Arise, you little glancing wings & sing your infant joy!
Arise & drink your bliss!
For every thing that lives is holy; for the source of life
Descends to be a weeping babe;
For the Earthworm renews the moisture of the sandy
    plain.

"Now my left hand I stretch to earth beneath,
And strike the terrible string.
I wake sweet joy in dens of sorrow & I plant a smile
In forests of affliction,
And wake the bubbling springs of life in regions of dark
    death.

"O, I am weary! lay thine hand upon me or I faint,
I faint beneath these beams of thine,
For thou hast touch'd my five senses & they answer'd
    thee.
Now I am nothing, & I sink
And on the bed of silence sleep till thou awakest me."

Thus sang the Lovely one in Rapturous delusive trance.
Los heard, reviving; he siez'd her in his arms; delusive
    hopes
Kindling, she led him into shadows & thence fled out-
    stretch'd

Upon the immense like a bright rainbow, weeping &
  smiling & fading.

[ENION'S COMPLAINT]

"I am made to sow the thistle for wheat, the nettle for a
  nourishing dainty.
I have planted a false oath in the earth; it has brought
  forth a poison tree.
I have chosen the serpent for a councellor, & the dog
For a schoolmaster to my children.
I have blotted out from light & living the dove & night-
  ingale,
And I have caused the earth worm to beg from door to
  door.

"I have taught the thief a secret path into the house of
  the just.
I have taught pale artifice to spread his nets upon the
  morning.
My heavens are brass, my earth is iron, my moon a clod
  of clay,
My sun a pestilence burning at noon & a vapour of death
  in night.

"What is the price of Experience? do men buy it for a
  song?
Or wisdom for a dance in the street? No, it is bought
  with the price
Of all that a man hath, his house, his wife, his children.
Wisdom is sold in the desolate market where none come
  to buy,
And in the wither'd field where the farmer plows for
  bread in vain.

"It is an easy thing to triumph in the summer's sun
And in the vintage & to sing on the waggon loaded with
    corn.
It is an easy thing to talk of patience to the afflicted,
To speak the laws of prudence to the houseless wan-
    derer,
To listen to the hungry raven's cry in wintry season
When the red blood is fill'd with wine & with the mar-
    row of lambs.

"It is an easy thing to laugh at wrathful elements,
To hear the dog howl at the wintry door, the ox in the
    slaughter house moan;
To see a god on every wind & a blessing on every blast;
To hear sounds of love in the thunder storm that de-
    stroys our enemies' house;
To rejoice in the blight that covers his field, & the sick-
    ness that cuts off his children,
While our olive & vine sing & laugh round our door, &
    our children bring fruits & flowers.

"Then the groan & the dolor are quite forgotten, & the
    slave grinding at the mill,
And the captive in chains, & the poor in the prison, &
    the soldier in the field
When the shatter'd bone hath laid him groaning among
    the happier dead.

"It is an easy thing to rejoice in the tents of prosperity:
Thus could I sing & thus rejoice: but it is not so with
    me."

[THE SORROWS OF THARMAS]

And he said: "Wherefore do I feel such love & pity?
Ah, Enion! Ah, Enion! Ah, lovely, lovely Enion!
How is this? All my hope is gone! for ever fled!
Like a famish'd Eagle, Eyeless, raging in the vast expanse,
Incessant tears are now my food, incessant rage & tears.
Deathless for ever now I wander seeking oblivion
In torrents of despair: in vain; for if I plunge beneath,
Stifling I live: If dash'd in pieces from a rocky height,
I reunite in endless torment; would I had never risen
From death's cold sleep beneath the bottom of the raging Ocean.
And cannot those who once have lov'd ever forget their Love?
Are love & rage the same passion? they are the same in me.
Are those who love like those who died, risen again from death,
Immortal in immortal torment, never to be deliver'd?
Is it not possible that one risen again from death
Can die? When dark despair comes over, can I not
Flow down into the sea & slumber in oblivion? Ah Enion,
Deform'd I see these lineaments of ungratified desire.
The all powerful curse of an honest man be upon Urizen & Luvah.
But thou, My Son, Glorious in Brightness, comforter of Tharmas,
Go forth, Rebuild this Universe beneath my indignant power,
A Universe of Death & Decay. Let Enitharmon's hands

Weave soft delusive forms of Man above my wat'ry
    world;
Renew these ruin'd souls of Men thro' Earth, Sea, Air &
    Fire,
To waste in endless corruption, renew those I will de-
    stroy.
Perhaps Enion may resume some little semblance
To ease my pangs of heart & to restore some peace to
    Tharmas."

[THE BINDING OF URIZEN]

And thus began the binding of Urizen; day & night in
    fear
Circling round the dark Demon, with howlings, dismay
    & sharp blightings,
The Prophet of Eternity beat on his iron links & links
    of brass;
And as he beat round the hurtling Demon, terrified at
    the Shapes
Enslav'd humanity put on, he became what he beheld.
Raging against Tharmas his God, & uttering
Ambiguous words, blasphemous, fill'd with envy, firm
    resolv'd
On hate Eternal, in his vast disdain he labour'd beating
The Links of fate, link after link, an endless chain of
    sorrows.

[SUCH IS THE DEMON]

His limbs bound down mock at his chains, for over them
    a flame

Of circling fire unceasing plays; to feed them with life
    & bring
The virtues of the Eternal worlds, ten thousand thou-
    sand spirits
Of life lament around the Demon, going forth & return-
    ing.
At his enormous call they flee into the heavens of heav-
    ens
And back return with wine & food, or dive into the
    deeps
To bring the thrilling joys of sense to quell his ceaseless
    rage.
His eyes, the lights of his large soul, contract or else ex-
    pand:
Contracted they behold the secrets of the infinite moun-
    tains,
The veins of gold & silver & the hidden things of Vala,
Whatever grows from its pure bud or breathes a fra-
    grant soul:
Expanded they behold the terrors of the Sun & Moon,
The Elemental Planets & the orbs of eccentric fire.
His nostrils breathe a fiery flame, his locks are like the
    forests
Of wild beasts; there the lion glares, the tyger & wolf
    howl there,
And there the Eagle hides her young in cliffs & preci-
    pices.
His bosom is like starry heaven expanded; all the stars
Sing round; there waves the harvest & the vintage re-
    joices; the springs
Flow into rivers of delight; there the spontaneous flow-
    ers
Drink, laugh & sing, the grasshopper, the Emmet and
    the Fly;

The golden Moth builds there a house & spreads her
 silken bed.
His loins inwove with silken fires are like a furnace
 fierce:
As the strong Bull in summer time when bees sing round
 the heath
Where the herds low after the shadow & after the water
 spring,
The num'rous flocks cover the mountains & shine along
 the valley.
His knees are rocks of adament & rubie & emerald:
Spirits of strength in Palaces rejoice in golden armour
Armed with spear & shield they drink & rejoice over the
 slain.
Such is the Demon, such his terror on the nether deep.

[THE WOES OF URIZEN]

The Woes of Urizen shut up in the deep dens of Ur-
 thona:

"Ah! how shall Urizen the King submit to this dark man-
 sion?
Ah! how is this? Once on the heights I stretch'd my
 throne sublime;
The mountains of Urizen, once of silver, where the sons
 of wisdom dwelt,
And on whose tops the Virgins sang, are rocks of desola-
 tion.

"My fountains, once the haunt of swans, now breed the
 scaly tortoise,
The houses of my harpers are become a haunt of crows,

The gardens of wisdom are become a field of horrid
    graves,
And on the bones I drop my tears & water them in vain.

"Once how I walked from my palace in gardens of de-
    light,
The sons of wisdom stood around, the harpers follow'd
    with harps,
Nine virgins cloth'd in light compos'd the song to their
    immortal voices,
And at my banquets of new wine my head was crown'd
    with joy.

"Then in my ivory pavilions I slumber'd in the noon
And walked in the silent night among sweet smelling
    flowers,
Till on my silver bed I slept & sweet dreams round me
    hover'd,
But now my land is darken'd & my wise men are de-
    parted.

"My songs are turned into cries of Lamentation
Heard on my Mountains, & deep sighs under my palace
    roofs,
Because the Steeds of Urizen, once swifter than the
    light,
Were kept back from my Lord & from his chariot of
    mercies.

"O did I keep the horses of the day in silver pastures!
O I refus'd the lord of day the horses of his prince!
O did I close my treasuries with roofs of solid stone
And darken all my Palace walls with envyings & hate!

"O Fool! to think that I could hide from his all piercing
    eyes
The gold & silver & costly stone, his holy workmanship!
O Fool! could I forget the light that filled my bright
    spheres
Was a reflection of his face who call'd me from the deep!

"I well remember, for I heard the mild & holy voice
Saying, 'O light, spring up & shine,' & I sprang up from
    the deep.
He gave me a silver scepter, & crown'd me with a golden
    crown,
& said, 'Go forth & guide my Son who wanders on the
    ocean.'

"I went not forth: I hid myself in black clouds of my
    wrath;
I call'd the stars around my feet in the night of councils
    dark;
The stars threw down their spears & fled naked away.
We fell. I siez'd thee, dark Urthona. In my left hand
    falling

"I siez'd thee, beauteous Luvah; thou art faded like a
    flower
And like a lilly is thy wife Vala wither'd by winds.
When thou didst bear the golden cup at the immortal
    tables
Thy children smote their fiery wings, crown'd with the
    gold of heaven.

"Thy pure feet step'd on the steps divine, too pure for
    other feet,
And thy fair locks shadow'd thine eyes from the divine
    effulgence,

Then thou didst keep with Strong Urthona the living
    gates of heaven,
But now thou art bow'd down with him, even to the
    gates of hell.

"Because thou gavest Urizen the wine of the Almighty
For Steeds of Light, that they might run in thy golden
    chariot of pride,
I gave to thee the Steeds, I pour'd the stolen wine
And drunken with the immortal draught fell from my
    throne sublime.

"I will arise, Explore these dens, & find that deep pulsa-
    tion
That shakes my cavern with strong shudders; perhaps
    this is the night
Of Prophecy, & Luvah hath burst his way from Enithar-
    mon.
When Thought is clos'd in Caves Then love shall shew
    its root in deepest Hell."

[URIZEN'S BOOK OF BRASS]

And Urizen Read in his book of brass in sounding tones:
"Listen, O Daughters, to my voice. Listen to the Words
    of Wisdom,
So shall [you] govern over all; let Moral Duty tune your
    tongue,
But be your hearts harder than the nether millstone.
To bring the Shadow of Enitharmon beneath our won-
    drous tree,
That Los may Evaporate like smoke & be no more,
Draw down Enitharmon to the spectre of Urthona,
And let him have dominion over Los, the terrible shade.

Compell the poor to live upon a Crust of bread, by soft
    mild arts.
Smile when they frown, frown when they smile; & when
    a man looks pale
With labour & abstinence, say he looks healthy & happy;
And when his children sicken, let them die; there are
    enough
Born, even too many, & our Earth will be overrun
Without these arts. If you would make the poor live
    with temper[ance],
With pomp give every crust of bread you give; with
    gracious cunning
Magnify small gifts; reduce the man to want a gift, &
    then give with pomp.
Say he smiles if you hear him sigh. If pale, say he is
    ruddy.
Preach temperance: say he is overgorg'd & drowns his
    wit
In strong drink, tho' you know that bread & water are all
He can afford. Flatter his wife, pity his children, till we
    can
Reduce all to our will, as spaniels are taught with art."

[THE SONS OF URIZEN]

Then left the sons of Urizen the plow & harrow, the
    loom,
The hammer & the chisel & the rule & compasses.
They forg'd the sword, the chariot of war, the battle ax,
The trumpet fitted to the battle & the flute of summer,
And all the arts of life they chang'd into the arts of
    death.
The hour glass contemn'd because its simple workman-
    ship

Was as the workmanship of the plowman, & the water
   wheel
That raises water into Cisterns, broken & burn'd in fire
Because its workmanship was like the workmanship of
   the shepherd,
And in their stead intricate wheels invented, Wheel
   without wheel,
To perplex youth in their outgoings & to bind to labours
Of day & night the myriads of Eternity, that they might
   file
And polish brass & iron hour after hour, laborious work-
   manship,
Kept ignorant of the use that they might spend the days
   of wisdom
In sorrowful drudgery to obtain a scanty pittance of
   bread,
In ignorance to view a small portion & think that All,
And call it demonstration, blind to all the simple rules of
   life.

[URIZEN: KING OF PRIDE]

Darkness & sorrow cover'd all flesh. Eternity was dark-
   en'd.

Urizen sitting in his web of deceitful religion
Felt the female death, a dull & numming stupor, such as
   ne'er
Before assaulted the bright human form; he felt his
   pores
Drink in the deadly dull delusion; horrors of Eternal
   Death
Shot thro' him. Urizen sat stonied upon his rock.
Forgetful of his own Laws, pitying he began to embrace

The shadowy Female; since life cannot be quench'd,
    Life exuded;
His eyes shot outwards, then his breathing nostrils
    drawn forth,
Scales cover'd over a cold forehead & a neck outstretch'd
Into the deep to sieze the shadow; scales his neck &
    bosom
Cover'd & scales his hands & feet; upon his belly falling
Outstretch'd thro' the immense, his mouth wide opening,
    tongueless,
His teeth a triple row, he strove to sieze the shadow in
    vain,
And his immense tail lash'd the Abyss; his human form a
    Stone,
A form of Senseless Stone remain'd in terrors on the
    rock,
Abominable to the eyes of mortals who explore his
    books.
His wisdom still remain'd, & all his memory stor'd with
    woe.

And still his stony form remain'd in the Abyss immense,
Like the pale visage in its sheet of lead that cannot fol-
    low—
Incessant stern disdain his scaly form gnaws inwardly,
With deep repentance for the loss of that fair form of
    Man.
With Envy he saw Los, with Envy Tharmas & the
    Spectre,
With Envy & in vain he swam around his stony form.

No longer now Erect, the King of Light outstretch'd in
    fury
Lashes his tail in the wild deep: his eyelids, like the Sun
Arising in his pride, enlighten all the Grizly deeps,

His scales transparent give forth light like windows of
 the morning,
His neck flames with wrath & majesty, he lashes the
 Abyss,
Beating the desarts & the rocks; the desarts feel his
 power,
They shake their slumbers off, they wave in awful fear
Calling the Lion & the Tyger, the horse & the wild stag,
The Elephant, the wolf, the Bear, the Larma, the Satyr.
His Eyelids give their light around; his folding tail as-
 pires
Among the stars; the Earth & all the Abysses feel his
 fury
When as the snow covers the mountains, oft petrific
 hardness
Covers the deeps, at his vast fury moaning in his rock,
Hardens the Lion & the Bear; trembling in the solid
 mountain
They view the light & wonder; crying out in terrible ex-
 istence,
Up bound the wild stag & the horse: behold the King of
 Pride!

[THE GATES ARE BURST]

Trembling & strucken by the Universal stroke, the trees
 unroot,
The rocks groan horrible & run about; the mountains &
Their rivers cry with a dismal cry; the cattle gather to-
 gether,
Lowing they kneel before the heavens; the wild beasts
 of the forests
Tremble; the Lion shuddering asks the Leopard: "Feel-
 est thou

The dread I feel, unknown before? My voice refuses to
   roar,
And in weak moans I speak to thee. This night,
Before the morning's dawn, the Eagle call'd the Vulture,
The Raven call'd the hawk, I heard them from my for-
   ests black,
Saying: 'Let us go up far, for soon, I smell upon the
   wind,
A terror coming from the south.' The Eagle & Hawk fled
   away
At dawn, & e'er the sun arose, the raven & Vulture fol-
   low'd.
Let us flee also to the north." They fled. The Sons of
   Men
Saw them depart in dismal droves. The trumpet sounded
   loud
And all the Sons of Eternity Descended into Beulah.

In the fierce flames the limbs of Mystery lay consuming
   with howling
And deep despair. Rattling go up the flames around the
   Synagogue
Of Satan. Loud the Serpent Orc rag'd thro' his twenty
   seven
Folds. The tree of Mystery went up in folding flames.
Blood issu'd out in rushing volumes, pouring in whirl
   pools fierce
From out the flood gates of the Sky. The Gates are
   burst; down pour
The torrents black upon the Earth; the blood pours
   down incessant.
Kings in their palaces lie drown'd. Shepherds, their
   flocks, their tents,
Roll down the mountains in black torrents. Cities, Vil-
   lages,

High spires & Castles drown'd in the black deluge; shoal!
    on shoal
Float the dead carcases of Men & Beasts, driven to & fro
    on waves
Of foaming blood beneath the black incessant sky, till
    all
Mystery's tyrants are cut off & not one left on Earth.

And when all Tyranny was cut off from the face of the
    Earth,
Around the dragon form of Urizen, & round his strong
    form,
The flames rolling intense thro' the wide Universe
Began to enter the Holy City. Ent'ring, the dismal
    clouds
In furrow'd lightnings break their way, the wild flames
    licking up
The Bloody Deluge: living flames winged with intellect
And Reason, round the Earth they march in order, flame
    by flame.
From the clotted gore & from the hollow den
Start forth the trembling millions into flames of mental
    fire,
Bathing their limbs in the bright visions of Eternity.

Beyond this Universal Confusion, beyond the remotest
    Pole
Where their vortexes began to operate, there stands
A Horrible rock far in the South; it was forsaken when
Urizen gave the horses of Light into the hands of Luvah.
On this rock lay the faded head of the Eternal Man
Enwrapped round with weeds of death, pale cold in sor-
    row & woe.
He lifts the blue lamps of his Eyes & cries with heavenly
    voice:

Bowing his head over the consuming Universe, he cried:
"O weakness & O weariness! O war within my members!
My sons, exiled from my breast, pass to & fro before me.
My birds are silent on my hills, flocks die beneath my
    branches.
My tents are fallen, my trumpets & the sweet sound of
    my harp
Is silent on my clouded hills that belch forth storms &
    fire.
My milk of cows & honey of bees & fruit of golden har-
    vest
Are gather'd in the scorching heat & in the driving rain.
My robe is turned to confusion, & my bright gold to
    stone.
Where once I sat, I weary walk in misery & pain,
For from within my wither'd breast grown narrow with
    my woes
The Corn is turned to thistles & the apples into poison,
The birds of song to murderous crows, My joys to bitter
    groans,
The voices of children in my tents to cries of helpless
    infants,
And all exiled from the face of light & shine of morning
In this dark world, a narrow house, I wander up &
    down.
I hear Mystery howling in these flames of Consumma-
    tion.
When shall the Man of future times become as in days
    of old?
O weary life! why sit I here & give up all my powers
To indolence, to the night of death, when indolence &
    mourning
Sit hovering over my dark threshold? tho' I arise, look
    out

And scorn the war within my members, yet my heart is
     weak
And my head faint. Yet will I look again into the morn-
     ing.
Whence is this sound of rage of Men drinking each
     other's blood,
Drunk with the smoking gore, & red, but not with nour-
     ishing wine?"

The Eternal Man sat on the Rocks & cried with awful
     voice:
"O Prince of Light, where art thou? I behold thee not
     as once
In those Eternal fields, in clouds of morning stepping
     forth
With harps & songs when bright Ahania sang before thy
     face
And all thy sons & daughters gather'd round my ample
     table.
See you not all this wracking furious confusion?
Come forth from slumbers of thy cold abstraction! Come
     forth,
Arise to Eternal births! Shake off thy cold repose,
Schoolmaster of souls, great opposer of change, arise!
That the Eternal worlds may see thy face in peace &
     joy,
That thou, dread form of Certainty, maist sit in town
     & village
While little children play around thy feet in gentle awe,
Fearing thy frown, loving thy smile, O Urizen, Prince
     of Light."

He call'd; the deep buried his voice & answer none re-
     turn'd.

Then wrath burst round; the Eternal Man was wrath;
    again he cried:
"Arise, O stony form of death! O dragon of the Deeps!
Lie down before my feet, O Dragon! let Urizen arise.
O how couldst thou deform those beautiful proportions
Of life & person; for as the Person, so is his life propor-
    tion'd.
Let Luvah rage in the dark deep, even to Consumma-
    tion,
For if thou feedest not his rage, it will subside in peace.
But if thou darest obstinate refuse my stern behest,
Thy crown & scepter I will sieze, & regulate all my mem-
    bers
In stern severity, & cast thee out into the indefinite
Where nothing lives, there to wander; & if thou return-
    est weary,
Weeping at the threshold of Existence, I will steel my
    heart
Against thee to Eternity, & never recieve thee more.
Thy self-destroying, beast form'd Science shall be thy
    eternal lot.
My anger against thee is greater than against this Luvah,
For war is energy Enslav'd, but thy religion,
The first author of this war & the distracting of honest
    minds
Into confused perturbation & strife & horrour & pride,
Is a deciet so detestable that I will cast thee out
If thou repentest not, & leave thee as a rotten branch to
    be burn'd
With Mystery the Harlot & with Satan for Ever & Ever.
Error can never be redeemed in all Eternity,
But Sin, Even Rahab, is redeem'd in blood & fury &
    jealousy—
That line of blood that stretch'd across the windows of
    the morning—

Redeem'd from Error's power. Wake, thou dragon of
  the deeps!"

And the Eternal Man said: "Hear my words, O Prince of
  Light.
Behold Jerusalem in whose bosom the Lamb of God
Is seen; tho' slain before her Gates, he self-renew'd re-
  mains
Eternal, & I thro' him awake from death's dark vale.
The times revolve; the time is coming when all these de-
  lights
Shall be renew'd, & all these Elements that now con-
  sume
Shall reflourish. Then bright Ahania shall awake from
  death,
A glorious Vision to thine Eyes, a Self-renewing Vision:
The spring, the summer, to be thine; then sleep the win-
  try days
In silken garments spun by her own hands against her
  funeral.
The winter thou shalt plow & lay thy stores into thy
  barns
Expecting to recieve Ahania in the spring with joy.
Immortal thou, Regenerate She, & all the lovely Sex
From her shall learn obedience & prepare for a wintry
  grave,
That spring may see them rise in tenfold joy & sweet de-
  light
Thus shall the male & female live the life of Eternity,
Because the Lamb of God Creates himself a bride &
  wife
That we his Children evermore may live in Jerusalem
Which now descendeth out of heaven, a City, yet a
  Woman,

Mother of myriads redeem'd & born in her spiritual palaces,
By a New Spiritual birth Regenerated from Death."

[THE BURSTING UNIVERSE]

Urizen said: "I have Erred, & my Error remains with me.
What Chain encompasses? in what Lock is the river of light confin'd
That issues forth in the morning by measure & in the evening by carefulness?
Where shall we take our stand to view the infinite & unbounded?
Or where are human feet? for Lo, our eyes are in the heavens."

He ceas'd, for riv'n link from link, the bursting Universe explodes.
All things revers'd flew from their centers: rattling bones
To bones Join: shaking convuls'd, the shivering clay breathes:
Each speck of dust to the Earth's center nestles round & round
In pangs of an Eternal Birth: in torment & awe & fear,
All spirits deceas'd, let loose from reptile prisons, come in shoals:
Wild furies from the tyger's brain & from the lion's eyes,
And from the ox & ass come moping terrors, from the eagle
And raven: numerous as the leaves of autumn, every species
Flock to the trumpet, mutt'ring over the sides of the grave & crying

In the fierce wind round heaving rocks & mountains fill'd
with groans.

On rifted rocks, suspended in the air by inward fires,

Many a woful company & many on clouds & waters,

Fathers & friends, Mothers & Infants, Kings & Warriors,

Priests & chain'd Captives, met together in a horrible
fear;

And every one of the dead appears as he had liv'd be-
fore,

And all the marks remain of the slave's scourge & ty-
rant's Crown,

And of the Priest's o'ergorged Abdomen, & of the mer-
chant's thin

Sinewy deception, & of the warrior's outbraving &
thoughtlessness

In lineaments too extended & in bones too strait & long.

They shew their wounds: they accuse: they sieze the
opressor; howlings began

On the golden palace, songs & joy on the desart; the
Cold babe

Stands in the furious air; he cries: "The children of six
thousand years

Who died in infancy rage furious: a mighty multitude
rage furious,

Naked & pale standing in the expecting air, to be de-
liver'd.

Rend limb from limb the warrior & the tyrant, reuniting
in pain."

The furious wind still rends around; they flee in sluggish
effort;

They beg, they intreat in vain now; they listened not to
intreaty;

They view the flames red rolling on thro' the wide uni-
verse

From the dark jaws of death beneath & desolate shores
remote,

These covering vaults of heaven & these trembling
globes of earth.

One Planet calls to another & one star enquires of an-
other:

"What flames are these, coming from the South? what
noise, what dreadful rout

As of a battle in the heavens? hark! heard you not the
trumpet

As of fierce battle?" While they spoke, the flames come
on intense roaring.

They see him whom they have pierc'd, they wail be-
cause of him,

They magnify themselves no more against Jerusalem,
Nor

Against her little ones; the innocent, accused before the
Judges,

Shines with immortal glory; trembling, the judge springs
from his throne

Hiding his face in the dust beneath the prisoner's feet &
saying:

"Brother of Jesus, what have I done? intreat thy lord for
me:

Perhaps I may be forgiven." While he speaks the flames
roll on,

And after the flames appears the Cloud of the Son of
Man

Descending from Jerusalem with power and great
Glory.

All nations look up to the Cloud & behold him who was
crucified.

[MYSTERY IS NO MORE]

The morning dawn'd. Urizen rose, & in his hand the Flail
Sounds on the Floor, heard terrible by all beneath the
heavens.
Dismal loud redounding, the nether floor shakes with
the sound,
And all Nations were threshed out, & the stars thresh'd
from their husks.

Then Tharmas took the Winnowing fan; the winnowing
wind furious
Above, veer'd round by violent whirlwind, driven west
& south,
Tossed the Nations like chaff into the seas of Tharmas.

"O Mystery," Fieree Tharmas cries, "Behold thy end is
come!
Art thou she that made the nations drunk with the cup
of Religion?
Go down, ye Kings & Councellors & Giant Warriors,
Go down into the depths, go down & hide yourselves be-
neath,
Go down with horse & Chariots & Trumpets of hoarse
war.

"Lo, how the Pomp of Mystery goes down into the
Caves!
Her great men howl & throw the dust, & rend their hoary
hair.
Her delicate women & children shriek upon the bitter
wind,

Spoil'd of their beauty, their hair rent & their skin shriv-
el'd up.

"Lo, darkness covers the long pomp of banners on the
wind,
And black horses & armed men & miserable bound cap-
tives.
Where shall the graves recieve them all, & where shall
be their place?
And who shall mourn for Mystery who never loos'd her
Captives?

"Let the slave, grinding at the mill, run out into the
field;
Let him look up into the heavens & laugh in the bright
air.
Let the inchained soul, shut up in darkness & in sighing,
Whose face has never seen a smile in thirty weary years,
Rise & look out: his chains are loose, his dungeon doors
are open;
And let his wife & children return from the opressor's
scourge.

"They look behind at every step & believe it is a dream.
Are these the slaves that groan'd along the streets of
Mystery?
Where are your bonds & task masters? are these the
prisoners?
Where are your chains? where are your tears? why do
you look around?
If you are thirsty, there is the river: go, bathe your
parched limbs,
The good of all the Land is before you, for Mystery is
no more."

[THE SUN HAS LEFT HIS BLACKNESS]

The Sun has left his blackness & has found a fresher
    morning,
And the mild moon rejoices in the clear & cloudless
    night,
And Man walks forth from midst of the fires: the evil
    is all consum'd.
His eyes behold the Angelic spheres arising night & day;
The stars consum'd like a lamp blown out, & in their
    stead, behold
The Expanding Eyes of Man behold the depths of won-
    drous worlds!
One Earth, one sea beneath; nor Erring Globes wander,
    but Stars
Of fire rise up nightly from the Ocean; & one Sun
Each morning, like a New born Man, issues with songs
    & joy
Calling the Plowman to his Labour & the Shepherd to
    his rest.
He walks upon the Eternal Mountains, raising his heav-
    enly voice,
Conversing with the Animal forms of wisdom night &
    day,
That, risen from the Sea of fire, renew'd walk o'er the
    Earth;
For Tharmas brought his flocks upon the hills, & in the
    Vales
Around the Eternal Man's bright tent, the little Children
    play
Among the wooly flocks. The hammer of Urthona
    sounds

In the deep caves beneath; his limbs renew'd, his Lions
    roar
Around the Furnaces & in Evening sport upon the plains.
They raise their faces from the Earth, conversing with
    the Man:

"How is it we have walk'd thro' fires & yet are not con-
    sum'd?
How is it that all things are chang'd, even as in ancient
    times?"

The Sun arises from his dewy bed, & the fresh airs
Play in his smiling beams giving the seeds of life to
    grow,
And the fresh Earth beams forth ten thousand thousand
    springs of life.
Urthona is arisen in his strength, no longer now
Divided from Enitharmon, no longer the Spectre Los.
Where is the Spectre of Prophecy? where is the delusive
    Phantom?
Departed: & Urthona rises from the ruinous Walls
In all his ancient strength to form the golden armour of
    science
For intellectual War. The war of swords departed now,
The dark Religions are departed & sweet Science reigns.

[NOTES WRITTEN ON THE PAGES
OF THE FOUR ZOAS]

*Christ's Crucifix shall be made an excuse for Execut-
ing Criminals.*

*Till thou dost injure the distrest
Thou shalt never have peace within thy breast.*

The Christian Religion teaches that No Man is Indifferent to you, but that every one is Either your friend or your enemy; he must necessarily be either the one or the other, And that he will be equally profitable both ways if you treat him as he deserves.

Unorganiz'd Innocence: An Impossibility.
Innocence dwells with Wisdom, but never with Ignorance.

From MILTON

(1804–1808)

A POEM IN 2 BOOKS

To Justify the Ways of God to Men

PREFACE

The Stolen and Perverted Writings of Homer & Ovid,
of Plato & Cicero, which all men ought to contemn, are
set up by artifice against the Sublime of the Bible; but
when the New Age is at leisure to Pronounce, all will
be set right, & those Grand Works of the more ancient &
consciously & professedly Inspired Men will hold their
proper rank, & the Daughters of Memory shall become
the Daughters of Inspiration. Shakspeare & Milton were
both curb'd by the general malady & infection from the
silly Greek & Latin slaves of the Sword.

Rouze up, O Young Men of the New Age! set your
foreheads against the ignorant Hirelings! For we have
Hirelings in the Camp, the Court & the University, who
would, if they could, for ever depress Mental & prolong
Corporeal War. Painters! on you I call. Sculptors! Archi-
tects! Suffer not the fashonable Fools to depress your
powers by the prices they pretend to give for contempt-
ible works, or the expensive advertizing boasts that they
make of such works; believe Christ & his Apostles that
there is a Class of Men whose whole delight is in De-
stroying. We do not want either Greek or Roman Models

411

if we are but just & true to our own Imaginations, those
Worlds of Eternity in which we shall live for ever in
JESUS OUR LORD.

And did those feet in ancient time
Walk upon England's mountains green?
And was the holy Lamb of God
On England's pleasant pastures seen?

And did the Countenance Divine
Shine forth upon our clouded hills?
And was Jerusalem builded here
Among these dark Satanic Mills?

Bring me my Bow of burning gold:
Bring me my Arrows of desire:
Bring me my Spear: O clouds unfold!
Bring me my Chariot of fire.

I will not cease from Mental Fight,
Nor shall my Sword sleep in my hand
Till we have built Jerusalem
In England's green & pleasant Land.

"Would to God that all the Lord's people were Proph-
ets."

Numbers, xi. ch., 29 v.

[THE INVOCATION]

Daughters of Beulah! Muses who inspire the Poet's Song,
Record the journey of immortal Milton thro' your Realms
Of terror & mild moony lustre in soft sexual delusions

Of varied beauty, to delight the wanderer and repose

His burning thirst & freezing hunger! Come into my
    hand,

By your mild power descending down the Nerves of my
    right arm

From out the portals of my Brain, where by your minis-
    try

The Eternal Great Humanity Divine planted his Para-
    dise

And in it caus'd the Spectres of the Dead to take sweet
    forms

In likeness of himself. Tell also of the False Tongue!
    vegetated

Beneath your land of shadows, of its sacrifices and

Its offerings: even till Jesus, the image of the Invisible
    God,

Became its prey, a curse, an offering and an atonement

For Death Eternal in the heavens of Albion & before the
    Gates

Of Jerusalem his Emanation, in the heavens beneath
    Beulah.

Say first! what mov'd Milton, who walk'd about in Eter-
    nity

One hundred years, pond'ring the intricate mazes of
    Providence,

Unhappy tho' in heav'n—he obey'd, he murmur'd not,
    he was silent

Viewing his Sixfold Emanation scatter'd thro' the deep

In torment—To go into the deep her to redeem & him-
    self perish?

[WISDOM AND SILENCE]

"If you account it Wisdom when you are angry to be si-
    lent and
Not to shew it, I do not account that Wisdom, but Folly.
Every Man's Wisdom is peculiar to his own Individ-
    uality."

[THE HAMMER OF LOS]

Loud sounds the Hammer of Los & loud his Bellows is
    heard
Before London to Hampstead's breadths & Highgate's
    heights, To
Stratford & old Bow & across to the Gardens of Kensing-
    ton
On Tyburn's Brook: loud groans Thames beneath the
    iron Forge
Of Rintrah & Palamabron, of Theotorm & Bromion, to
    forge the instruments
Of Harvest, the Plow & Harrow to pass over the Nations.

The Surrey hills glow like the clinkers of the furnace;
    Lambeth's Vale
Where Jerusalem's foundations began, where they were
    laid in ruins,
Where they were laid in ruins from every Nation, & Oak
    Groves rooted,
Dark gleams before the Furnace-mouth a heap of burn-
    ing ashes.
When shall Jerusalem return & overspread all the Na-
    tions?

Return, return to Lambeth's Vale, O building of human
    souls!
Thence stony Druid Temples overspread the Island
    white,
And thence from Jerusalem's ruins, from her walls of
    salvation
And praise, thro' the whole Earth were rear'd from Ire-
    land
To Mexico & Peru west, & east to China & Japan, till
    Babel
The Spectre of Albion frown'd over the Nations in glory
    & war.
All things begin & end in Albion's ancient Druid rocky
    shore:
But now the Starry Heavens are fled from the mighty
    limbs of Albion.

Loud sounds the Hammer of Los, loud turn the Wheels
    of Enitharmon:
Her Looms vibrate with soft affections, weaving the
    Web of Life,
Out from the ashes of the Dead; Los lifts his iron Ladles
With molten ore: he heaves the iron cliffs in his rattling
    chains
From Hyde Park to the Alms-houses of Mile-end & old
    Bow.
Here the Three Classes of Mortal Men take their fix'd
    destinations,
And hence they overspread the Nations of the whole
    Earth, & hence
The Web of Life is woven & the tender sinews of life
    created . . .

[LOS IN HIS WRATH]

Los in his wrath curs'd heaven & earth; he rent up
    Nations,
Standing on Albion's rocks among high-rear'd Druid
    temples
Which reach the stars of heaven & stretch from pole to
    pole.
He displac'd continents, the oceans fled before his face:
He alter'd the poles of the world, east, west & north &
    south,
But he clos'd up Enitharmon from the sight of all these
    things.

[MILTON ROSE UP]

Then Milton rose up from the heavens of Albion ardor-
    ous.
The whole Assembly wept prophetic, seeing in Milton's
    face
And in his lineaments divine the shades of Death &
    Ulro:
He took off the robe of the promise & ungirded himself
    from the oath of God.

And Milton said: "I go to Eternal Death! The Nations
    still
Follow after the detestable Gods of Priam, in pomp
Of warlike selfhood contradicting and blaspheming.
When will the Resurrection come to deliver the sleeping
    body

From corruptibility? O when, Lord Jesus, wilt thou
    come?

Tarry no longer, for my soul lies at the gates of death.

I will arise and look forth for the morning of the grave:

I will go down to the sepulcher to see if morning
    breaks:

I will go down to self annihilation and eternal death,

Lest the Last Judgment come & find me unannihilate

And I be siez'd & giv'n into the hands of my own Self-
    hood.

The Lamb of God is seen thro' mists & shadows,
    hov'ring

Over the sepulchers in clouds of Jehovah & winds of
    Elohim,

A disk of blood distant, & heav'ns & earths roll dark
    between.

What do I here before the Judgment? without my
    Emanation?

With the daughters of memory & not with the daughters
    of inspiration?

I in my Selfhood am that Satan: I am that Evil One!

He is my Spectre! in my obedience to loose him from
    my Hells,

To claim the Hells, my Furnaces, I go to Eternal
    Death."

And Milton said: "I go to Eternal Death!" Eternity
    shudder'd,

For he took the outside course among the graves of the
    dead,

A mournful shade. Eternity shudder'd at the image of
    eternal death.

[THE NATURE OF INFINITY]

The nature of infinity is this: That every thing has its
Own Vortex, and when once a traveller thro' Eternity
Has pass'd that Vortex, he percieves it roll backward
behind
His path, into a globe itself infolding like a sun,
Or like a moon, or like a universe of starry majesty,
While he keeps onwards in his wondrous journey on the
earth,
Or like a human form, a friend with whom he liv'd
benevolent.
As the eye of man views both the east & west encom-
passing
Its vortex, and the north & south with all their starry
host,
Also the rising sun & setting moon he views surrounding
His corn-fields and his valleys of five hundred acres
square,
Thus is the earth one infinite plane, and not as apparent
To the weak traveller confin'd beneath the moony
shade.
Thus is the heaven a vortex pass'd already, and the
earth
A vortex not yet pass'd by the traveller thro' Eternity.

First Milton saw Albion upon the Rock of Ages,
Deadly pale outstretch'd and snowy cold, storm
cover'd,
A Giant form of perfect beauty outstretch'd on the rock
In solemn death: the Sea of Time & Space thunder'd
aloud

Against the rock, which was inwrapped with the weeds
    of death.
Hovering over the cold bosom in its vortex Milton bent
    down
To the bosom of death: what was underneath soon
    seem'd above:
A cloudy heaven mingled with stormy seas in loudest
    ruin;
But as a wintry globe descends precipitant thro' Beulah
    bursting
With thunders loud and terrible, so Milton's shadow fell
Precipitant, loud thund'ring into the Sea of Time &
    Space.

[THE MUNDANE SHELL]

The Mundane Shell is a vast Concave Earth, an im-
    mense
Harden'd shadow of all things upon our Vegetated
    Earth,
Enlarg'd into dimension & deform'd into indefinite
    space,
In Twenty-seven Heavens and all their Hells, with
    Chaos
And Ancient Night & Purgatory. It is a cavernous Earth
Of labyrinthine intricacy, twenty-seven-folds of opake-
    ness,
And finishes where the lark mounts.

[OPEN YOUR HUMAN GATES]

Now Albion's sleeping Humanity began to turn upon his
    Couch,

Feeling the electric flame of Milton's awful precipitate
  descent.
Seest thou the little winged fly, smaller than a grain of
  sand?
It has a heart like thee, a brain open to heaven & hell,
Withinside wondrous & expansive: its gates are not
  clos'd:
I hope thine are not: hence it clothes itself in rich array:
Hence thou art cloth'd with human beauty, O thou
  mortal man.
Seek not thy heavenly father then beyond the skies,
There Chaos dwells & ancient Night & Og & Anak old.
For every human heart has gates of brass & bars of
  adamant
Which few dare unbar, because dread Og & Anak guard
  the gates
Terrific: and each mortal brain is wall'd and moated
  round
Within, and Og & Anak watch here: here is the Seat
Of Satan in its Webs: for in brain and heart and loins
Gates open behind Satan's Seat to the City of Gol-
  gonooza,
Which is the spiritual fourfold London in the loins of
  Albion.

[BLAKE AND MILTON]

. . . Milton entering my Foot, I saw in the nether
Regions of the Imagination—also all men on Earth
And all in Heaven saw in the nether regions of the
  Imagination
In Ulro beneath Beulah—the vast breach of Milton's
  descent.

But I knew not that it was Milton, for man cannot
     know
What passes in his members till periods of Space & Time
Reveal the secrets of Eternity: for more extensive
Than any other earthly things are Man's earthly linea-
     ments.
And all this Vegetable World appear'd on my left Foot
As a bright sandal form'd immortal of precious stones &
     gold.
I stooped down & bound it on to walk forward thro'
     Eternity.

[THE PROPHET]

"I am that Shadowy Prophet who Six Thousand Years
     ago
Fell from my station in the Eternal bosom. Six Thousand
     Years
Are finish'd. I return! both Time & Space obey my will.
I in Six Thousand Years walk up and down; for not one
     Moment
Of Time is lost, nor one Event of Space unpermanent,
But all remain: every fabric of Six Thousand Years
Remains permanent, tho' on the Earth where Satan
Fell and was cut off, all things vanish & are seen no
     more,
They vanish not from me & mine, we guard them first &
     last.
The generations of men run on in the tide of Time,
But leave their destin'd lineaments permanent for ever
     & ever."

[AWAKE, ALBION, AWAKE!]

"Milton's Religion is the cause: there is no end to destruction.

Seeing the Churches at their Period in terror & despair,

Rahab created Voltaire, Tirzah created Rousseau,

Asserting the Self-righteousness against the Universal Saviour,

Mocking the Confessors & Martyrs, claiming Self-righteousness,

With cruel Virtue making War upon the Lamb's Redeemed

To perpetuate War & Glory, to perpetuate the Laws of Sin.

They perverted Swedenborg's Visions in Beulah & in Ulro

To destroy Jerusalem as a Harlot & her Sons as Reprobates,

To raise up Mystery the Virgin Harlot, Mother of War,

Babylon the Great, the Abomination of Desolation.

O Swedenborg! strongest of men, the Samson shorn by the Churches,

Shewing the Transgressors in Hell, the proud Warriors in Heaven,

Heaven as a Punisher, & Hell as One under Punishment,

With Laws from Plato & his Greeks to renew the Trojan Gods

In Albion, & to deny the value of the Saviour's blood.

But then I rais'd up Whitefield, Palamabron rais'd up Westley,

And these are the cries of the Churches before the two Witnesses.

Faith in God the dear Saviour who took on the likeness
    of men,
Becoming obedient to death, even the death of the
    Cross.
The Witnesses lie dead in the Street of the Great City:
No Faith is in all the Earth: the Book of God is trodden
    under Foot.
He sent his two Servants, Whitefield & Westley: were
    they Prophets,
Or were they Idiots or Madmen? shew us Miracles!

"Can you have greater Miracles than these? Men who
    devote
Their life's whole comfort to intire scorn & injury &
    death?
Awake, thou sleeper on the Rock of Eternity! Albion
    awake!
The trumpet of Judgment hath twice sounded: all
    Nations are awake,
But thou art still heavy and dull. Awake, Albion awake!"

[O GO NOT FORTH IN MARTYRDOMS & WARS!]

. . . Los thus spoke: "O noble Sons, be patient yet a
    little!
I have embrac'd the falling Death, he is become One
    with me:
O Sons, we live not by wrath, by mercy alone we live!
I recollect an old Prophecy in Eden recorded in gold
    and oft
Sung to the harp, That Milton of the land of Albion
Should up ascend forward from Felpham's Vale & break
    the Chain

Of Jealousy from all its roots; be patient therefore, O
    my Sons!
These lovely Females form sweet night and silence and
    secret
Obscurities to hide from Satan's Watch-Fiends Human
    loves
And graces, lest they write them in their Books & in the
    Scroll
Of mortal life to condemn the accused, who at Satan's
    Bar
Tremble in Spectrous Bodies continually day and night,
While on the Earth they live in sorrowful Vegetations.
O when shall we tread our Wine-presses in heaven and
    Reap
Our wheat with shoutings of joy, and leave the Earth in
    peace?
Remember how Calvin and Luther in fury premature
Sow'd War and stern division between Papists &
    Protestants.
Let it not be so now! O go not forth in Martyrdoms &
    Wars!
We were plac'd here by the Universal Brotherhood &
    Mercy
With powers fitted to circumscribe this dark Satanic
    death,
And that the Seven Eyes of God may have space for
    Redemption.
But how this is as yet we know not, and we cannot know
Till Albion is arisen; then patient wait a little while.
Six Thousand years are pass'd away, the end approaches
    fast:
This mighty one is come from Eden, he is of the Elect
Who died from Earth & he is return'd before the Judg-
    ment. This thing

Was never known, that one of the holy dead should will-
ing return.
Then patient wait a little while till the Last Vintage is
over. . . ."

[THE SPIRIT OF PROPHECY]

Los is by mortals nam'd Time, Enitharmon is nam'd
Space:
But they depict him bald & aged who is in eternal youth
All powerful and his locks flourish like the brows of
morning:
He is the Spirit of Prophecy, the ever apparent Elias.
Time is the mercy of Eternity; without Time's swiftness,
Which is the swiftest of all things, all were eternal tor-
ment.
All the Gods of the Kingdoms of Earth labour in Los's
Halls:
Every one is a fallen Son of the Spirit of Prophecy.

[THE GREAT VINTAGE AND HARVEST].

And Los stood & cried to the Labourers of the Vintage in
voice of awe:

"Fellow Labourers! The Great Vintage & Harvest is now
upon Earth.
The whole extent of the Globe is explored. Every
scatter'd Atom
Of Human Intellect now is flocking to the sound of the
Trumpet.
All the Wisdom which was hidden in caves & dens from
ancient

Time is now sought out from Animal & Vegetable &
    Mineral.
The Awakener is come outstretch'd over Europe: the
    Vision of God is fulfilled:
The Ancient Man upon the Rock of Albion Awakes,
He listens to the sounds of War astonish'd & ashamed,
He sees his Children mock at Faith and deny Provi-
    dence.
Therefore you must bind the Sheaves not by Nations or
    Families,
You shall bind them in Three Classes, according to their
    Classes
So shall you bind them, Separating What has been
    Mixed
Since Men began to be Wove into Nations by Rahab
    & Tirzah,
Since Albion's Death & Satan's Cutting off from our aw-
    ful Fields,
When under pretence to benevolence the Elect Subdu'd
    All
From the Foundation of the World. The Elect is one
    Class: You
Shall bind them separate: they cannot Believe in Eternal
    Life
Except by Miracle & a New Birth. The other two
    Classes,
The Reprobate who never cease to Believe, and the
    Redeem'd
Who live in doubts & fears perpetually tormented by
    the Elect,
These you shall bind in a twin-bundle for the Consum-
    mation:
But the Elect must be saved from fires of Eternal Death,
To be formed into the Churches of Beulah that they
    destroy not the Earth.

For in every Nation & every Family the Three Classes
    are born,
And in every Species of Earth, Metal, Tree, Fish, Bird &
    Beast.
We form the Mundane Egg, that Spectres coming by
    fury or amity,
All is the same, & every one remains in his own energy.
Go forth Reapers with rejoicing; you sowed in tears,
But the time of your refreshing cometh: only a little
    moment
Still abstain from pleasure & rest in the labours of
    eternity,
And you shall Reap the whole Earth from Pole to Pole,
    from Sea to Sea,
Beginning at Jerusalem's Inner Court, Lambeth . . ."

[THE VISIONS OF ETERNITY]

These are the Sons of Los, & these the Labourers of
    the Vintage.
Thou seest the gorgeous clothed Flies that dance &
    sport in summer
Upon the sunny brooks & meadows: every one the dance
Knows in its intricate mazes of delight artful to weave:
Each one to sound his instruments of music in the
    dance,
To touch each other & recede, to cross & change & re-
    turn:
These are the Children of Los; thou seest the Trees on
    mountains,
The wind blows heavy, loud they thunder thro' the
    darksom sky,
Uttering prophecies & speaking instructive words to the
    sons

Of men: These are the Sons of Los: These the Visions
    of Eternity,
But we see only as it were the hem of their garments
When with our vegetable eyes we view these wondrous
    Visions.

[THE WINE-PRESS OF LIFE]

. . . The Wine-press of Los is eastward of Golgonooza
    before the Seat
Of Satan: Luvah laid the foundation & Urizen finish'd it
    in howling woe.
How red the sons & daughters of Luvah! here they tread
    the grapes:
Laughing & shouting, drunk with odours many fall
    o'erwearied,
Drown'd in the wine is many a youth & maiden: those
    around
Lay them on skins of Tygers & of the spotted Leopard &
    the Wild Ass
Till they revive, or bury them in cool grots, making
    lamentation.

This Wine-press is call'd War on Earth: it is the
    Printing-Press
Of Los, and here he lays his words in order above the
    mortal brain,
As cogs are form'd in a wheel to turn the cogs of the
    adverse wheel.

Timbrels & violins sport round the Wine-presses; the
    little Seed,
The sportive Root, the Earth-worm, the gold Beetle, the
    wise Emmet

Dance round the Wine-presses of Luvah: the Centipede
is there,

The ground Spider with many eyes, the Mole clothed in
velvet,

The ambitious Spider in his sullen web, the lucky
golden Spinner,

The Earwig arm'd, the tender Maggot, emblem of im-
mortality,

The Flea, Louse, Bug, the Tape-Worm, all the Armies
of Disease,

Visible or invisible to the slothful vegetating Man.

The slow Slug, the Grasshopper that sings & laughs &
drinks:

Winter comes, he folds his slender bones without a mur-
mur.

The cruel Scorpion is there, the Gnat, Wasp, Hornet &
the Honey Bee,

The Toad & venomous Newt, the Serpent cloth'd in
gems & gold.

They throw off their gorgeous raiment: they rejoice with
loud jubilee

Around the Wine-presses of Luvah, naked & drunk with
wine.

There is the Nettle that stings with soft down, and
there

The indignant Thistle whose bitterness is bred in his
milk,

Who feeds on contempt of his neighbour: there all the
idle Weeds

That creep around the obscure places shew their various
limbs

Naked in all their beauty dancing round the Wine-
presses.

But in the Wine-presses the Human grapes sing not nor
    dance:
They howl & writhe in shoals of torment, in fierce flames
    consuming,
In chains of iron & in dungeons circled with ceaseless
    fires,
In pits & dens & shades of death, in shapes of torment &
    woe:
The plates & screws & wracks & saws & cords & fires &
    cisterns,
The cruel joys of Luvah's Daughters, lacerating with
    knives
And whips their Victims, & the deadly sport of Luvah's
    Sons.

They dance around the dying & they drink the howl &
    groan,
They catch the shrieks in cups of gold, they hand them
    to one another:
These are the sports of love, & these the sweet delights
    of amorous play,
Tears of the grape, the death sweat of the cluster, the
    last sigh
Of the mild youth who listens to the lureing songs of
    Luvah.

[THE FOUR FACES OF MAN]

These are the starry voids of night & the depths &
    caverns of earth.
These Mills are oceans, clouds & waters ungovernable
    in their fury:
Here are the stars created & the seeds of all things
    planted,

And here the Sun & Moon recieve their fixed destina-
   tions.

But in Eternity the Four Arts, Poetry, Painting, Music
And Architecture, which is Science, are the Four Faces
   of Man.
Not so in Time & Space: there Three are shut out, and
   only
Science remains thro' Mercy, & by means of Science the
   Three
Become apparent in Time & Space in the Three Profes-
   sions,
That Man may live upon Earth till the time of his
   awaking.

[THE BUILDING OF TIME]

The Sons of Ozoth within the Optic Nerve stand fiery
   glowing,
And the number of his Sons is eight millions & eight.
They give delights to the man unknown; artificial riches
They give to scorn, & their possessors to trouble & sor-
   row & care,
Shutting the sun & moon & stars & trees & clouds &
   waters
And hills out from the Optic Nerve, & hardening it into
   a bone
Opake and like the black pebble on the enraged beach,
While the poor indigent is like the diamond which, tho'
   cloth'd
In rugged covering in the mine, is open all within
And in his hallow'd center holds the heavens of bright
   eternity.
Ozoth here builds walls of rocks against the surging sea,

And timbers crampt with iron cramps bar in the joys of
life

From fell destruction in the Spectrous cunning or rage.
He Creates

The speckled Newt, the Spider & Beetle, the Rat &
Mouse.

The Badger & Fox: they worship before his feet in
trembling fear.

But others of the Sons of Los build Moments & Minutes
& Hours

And Days & Months & Years & Ages & Periods, won-
drous buildings;

And every Moment has a Couch of gold for soft repose,

(A Moment equals a pulsation of the artery),

And between every two Moments stands a Daughter of
Beulah

To feed the Sleepers on their Couches with maternal
care.

And every Minute has an azure Tent with silken Veils:

And every Hour has a bright golden Gate carved with
skill:

And every Day & Night has Walls of brass & Gates of
adamant,

Shining like precious Stones & ornamented with ap-
propriate signs:

And every Month a silver paved Terrace builded high:

And every Year invulnerable Barriers with high Towers:

And every Age is Moated deep with Bridges of silver &
gold:

And every Seven Ages is Incircled with a Flaming Fire.

Now Seven Ages is amounting to Two Hundred Years.

Each has its Guard, each Moment, Minute, Hour, Day,
Month & Year.

All are the work of Fairy hands of the Four Elements:

The Guard are Angels of Providence on duty evermore.
Every Time less than a pulsation of the artery
Is equal in its period & value to Six Thousand Years,

For in this Period the Poet's Work is Done, and all the
    Great
Events of Time start forth & are conciev'd in such a
    Period,
Within a Moment, a Pulsation of the Artery.

The Sky is an immortal Tent built by the Sons of Los:
And every Space that a Man views around his dwelling-
    place
Standing on his own roof or in his garden on a mount
Of twenty-five cubits in height, such space is his Uni-
    verse:
And on its verge the Sun rises & sets, the Clouds bow
To meet the flat Earth & the Sea in such an order'd
    Space:
The Starry heavens reach no further, but here bend and
    set
On all sides, & the two Poles turn on their valves of gold;
And if he move his dwelling-place, his heavens also
    move
Where'er he goes, & all his neighbourhood bewail his
    loss.
Such are the Spaces called Earth & such its dimension.
As to that false appearance which appears to the
    reasoner
As of a Globe rolling thro' Voidness, it is a delusion of
    Ulro.
The Microscope knows not of this nor the Telescope:
    they alter
The ratio of the Spectator's Organs, but leave Objects
    untouch'd.

For every Space larger than a red Globule of Man's
    blood
Is visionary, and is created by the Hammer of Los:
And every Space smaller than a Globule of Man's blood
    opens
Into Eternity of which this vegetable Earth is but a
    shadow.
The red Globule is the unwearied Sun by Los created
To measure Time and Space to mortal Men every morn-
    ing.

[THE ETERNAL GREAT HUMANITY]

And it is thus Created. Lo, the Eternal Great Humanity,
To whom be Glory & Dominion Evermore, Amen,
Walks among all his awful Family seen in every face:
As the breath of the Almighty such are the words of
    man to man
In the great Wars of Eternity, in fury of Poetic Inspira-
    tion,
To build the Universe stupendous, Mental forms Creat-
    ing.

[THE WEEPING OF THE NATIONS]

And all Nations wept in affliction, Family by Family:
Germany wept towards France & Italy, England wept
    & trembled
Towards America, India rose up from his golden bed
As one awaken'd in the night; they saw the Lord coming
In the Clouds of Ololon with Power & Great Glory.

[THE CHOIR OF DAY]

Thou hearest the Nightingale begin the Song of Spring.
The Lark sitting upon his earthy bed, just as the morn
Appears, listens silent; then springing from the waving
    Cornfield, loud
He leads the Choir of Day: trill, trill, trill, trill,
Mounting upon the wings of light into the Great Ex-
    panse,
Reecchoing against the lovely blue & shining heavenly
    Shell,
His little throat labours with inspiration; every feather
On throat & breast & wings vibrates with the effluence
    Divine.
All Nature listens silent to him, & the awful Sun
Stands still upon the Mountain looking on this little Bird
With eyes of soft humility & wonder, love & awe,
Then loud from their green covert all the Birds begin
    their Song:
The Thrush, the Linnet & the Goldfinch, Robin & the
    Wren
Awake the Sun from his sweet reverie upon the Moun-
    tain.
The Nightingale again assays his song, & thro the day
And thro' the night warbles luxuriant, every Bird of
    Song
Attending his loud harmony with admiration & love.
This is a Vision of the lamentation of Beulah over
    Ololon.

Thou percievest the Flowers put forth their precious
    Odours,

And none can tell how from so small a center comes
    such sweets,
Forgetting that within that Center Eternity expands
Its ever during doors that Og & Anak fiercely guard.
First, e'er the morning breaks, joy opens in the flowery
    bosoms,
Joy even to tears, which the Sun rising dries; first the
    Wild Thyme
And Meadow-sweet, downy & soft waving among the
    reeds,
Light springing on the air, lead the sweet Dance: they
    wake
The Honeysuckle sleeping on the Oak; the flaunting
    beauty
Revels along upon the wind; the White-thorn, lovely
    May,
Opens her many lovely eyes listening; the Rose still
    sleeps,
None dare to wake her; soon she bursts her crimson cur-
    tain'd bed
And comes forth in the majesty of beauty; every Flower,
The Pink, the Jessamine, the Wall-flower, the Carnation,
The Jonquil, the mild Lilly, opes her heavens; every
    Tree
And Flower & Herb soon fill the air with an innumerable
    Dance,
Yet all in order sweet & lovely. Men are sick with Love,
Such is a Vision of the lamentation of Beulah over
    Ololon.

[JUDGE THEN, OF THY OWN SELF]

"We are not Individuals but States, Combinations of
    Individuals.

We were Angels of the Divine Presence, & were Druids
in Annandale,

Compell'd to combine into Form by Satan, the Spectre
of Albion,

Who made himself a God & destroyed the Human Form
Divine.

But the Divine Humanity & Mercy gave us a Human
Form

Because we were combin'd in Freedom & holy Brother-
hood,

While those combin'd by Satan's Tyranny, first in the
blood of War

And Sacrifice & next in Chains of imprisonment, are
Shapeless Rocks

Retaining only Satan's Mathematic Holiness, Length,
Bredth & Highth,

Calling the Human Imagination, which is the Divine
Vision & Fruition

In which Man liveth eternally, madness & blasphemy
against

Its own Qualities, which are Servants of Humanity, not
Gods or Lords.

Distinguish therefore States from Individuals in those
States.

States Change, but Individual Identities never change
nor cease.

You cannot go to Eternal Death in that which can never
Die.

Satan & Adam are States Created into Twenty-seven
Churches,

And thou, O Milton, art a State about to be Created,

Called Eternal Annihilation, that none but the Living
shall

Dare to enter, & they shall enter triumphant over Death

And Hell & the Grave: States that are not, but ah! Seem
    to be.

Judge then of thy Own Self: thy Eternal Lineaments
    explore,
What is Eternal & what Changeable, & what Annihilable.
The Imagination is not a State: it is the Human Exist-
    ence itself.
Affection or Love becomes a State when divided from
    ·Imagination.
The Memory is a State always, & the Reason is a State
Created to be Annihilated & a new Ratio Created.
Whatever can be Created can be Annihilated: Forms
    cannot:
The Oak is cut down by the Ax, the Lamb falls by the
    Knife,
But their Forms Eternal Exist For-ever. Amen. Hal-
    lelujah!"

Thus they converse with the Dead, watching round the
    Couch of Death;
For God himself enters Death's Door always with those
    that enter
And lays down in the Grave with them, in Visions of
    Eternity,
Till they awake & see Jesus & the Linen Clothes lying
That the Females had Woven for them, & the Gates of
    their Father's House.

[THE LOOM OF DEATH]

. . . "How are the Wars of man, which in Great
    Eternity

Appear around in the External Spheres of Visionary
    Life,
Here render'd Deadly within the Life & Interior Vision?
How are the Beasts & Birds & Fishes & Plants & Minerals
Here fix'd into a frozen bulk subject to decay & death?
Those Visions of Human Life & Shadows of Wisdom &
    Knowledge
Are here frozen to unexpansive deadly destroying
    terrors,
And War & Hunting, the Two Fountains of the River
    of Life,
Are become Fountains of bitter Death & of corroding
    Hell,
Till Brotherhood is chang'd into a Curse & a Flattery
By Differences between Ideas, that Ideas themselves
    (which are
The Divine Members) may be slain in offerings for sin.
O dreadful Loom of Death! O piteous Female forms
    compell'd
To weave the Woof of Death! . . ."

[JERUSALEM BOUND]

I also stood in Satan's bosom & beheld its desolations:
A ruin'd Man, a ruin'd building of God, not made with
    hands:
Its plains of burning sand, its mountains of marble ter-
    rible:
Its pits & declivities flowing with molten ore & fountains
Of pitch & nitre: its ruin'd palaces & cities & mighty
    works:
Its furnaces of affliction, in which his Angels & Emana-
    tions

Labour with blacken'd visages among its stupendous
        ruins,
Arches & pyramids & porches, colonades & domes,
In which dwells Mystery, Babylon; here is her secret
        place,
From hence she comes forth on the Churches in delight;
Here is her Cup fill'd with its poisons in these horrid
        vales,
And here her scarlet Veil woven in pestilence & war;
Here is Jerusalem bound in chains in the Dens of Baby-
        lon.

In the Eastern porch of Satan's Universe Milton stood &
        said:

"Satan! my Spectre! I know my power thee to annihilate
And be a greater in thy place & be thy Tabernacle,
A covering for thee to do thy will, till one greater comes
And smites me as I smote thee & becomes my covering.
Such are the Laws of thy false Heav'ns; but Laws of
        Eternity
Are not such; know thou, I come to Self Annihilation.
Such are the Laws of Eternity, that each shall mutually
Annihilate himself for others' good, as I for thee.
Thy purpose & the purpose of thy Priests & of thy
        Churches
Is to impress on men the fear of death, to teach
Trembling & fear, terror, constriction, abject selfishness.
Mine is to teach Men to despise death & to go on
In fearless majesty annihilating Self, laughing to scorn
Thy Laws & terrors, shaking down thy Synagogues as
        webs.
I come to discover before Heav'n & Hell the Self
        righteousness

In all its Hypocritic turpitude, opening to every eye
These wonders of Satan's holiness, shewing to the Earth
The Idol Virtues of the Natural Heart, & Satan's Seat
Explore in all its Selfish Natural Virtue, & put off
In Self annihilation all that is not of God alone,
To put off Self & all I have, ever & ever. Amen."

Satan heard, Coming in a cloud, with trumpets & flam-
    ing fire,
Saying: "I am God the judge of all, the living & the
    dead.
Fall therefore down & worship me, submit thy supreme
Dictate to my eternal Will, & to my dictate bow.
I hold the Balances of Right & Just & mine the Sword.
Seven Angels bear my Name & in those Seven I appear,
But I alone am God & I alone in Heav'n & Earth
Of all that live dare utter this, others tremble & bow,
Till All Things become One Great Satan, in Holiness
Oppos'd to Mercy, and the Divine Delusion, Jesus, be
    no more."

[BATHE IN THE WATERS OF LIFE]

But turning toward Ololon in terrible majesty Milton
Replied: "Obey thou the Words of the Inspired Man.
All that can be annihilated must be annihilated
That the Children of Jerusalem may be saved from
    slavery.
There is a Negation, & there is a Contrary:
The Negation must be destroy'd to redeem the Con-
    traries.
The Negation is the Spectre, the Reasoning Power in
    Man:

This is a false Body, in Incrustation over my Immortal
Spirit, a Selfhood which must be put off & annihilated
  alway.
To cleanse the Face of my Spirit by Self-examination,
To bathe in the Waters of Life, to wash off the Not
  Human,
I come in Self-annihilation & the grandeur of Inspira-
  tion,
To cast off Rational Demonstration by Faith in the
  Saviour,
To cast off the rotten rags of Memory by Inspiration,
To cast off Bacon, Locke & Newton from Albion's cover-
  ing,
To take off his filthy garments & clothe him with
  Imagination,
To cast aside from Poetry all that is not Inspiration,
That it no longer shall dare to mock with the aspersion
  of Madness
Cast on the Inspired by the tame high finisher of paltry
  Blots
Indefinite, or paltry Rhymes, or paltry Harmonies,
Who creeps into State Government like a catterpiller to
  destroy;
To cast off the idiot Questioner who is always question-
  ing
But never capable of answering, who sits with a sly
  grin
Silent plotting when to question, like a thief in a cave,
Who publishes doubt & calls it knowledge, whose
  Science is Despair,
Whose pretence to knowledge is Envy, whose whole
  Science is
To destroy the wisdom of ages to gratify ravenous Envy
That rages round him like a Wolf day & night without
  rest:

He smiles with condescension, he talks of Benevolence
    & Virtue,
And those who act with Benevolence & Virtue they mur-
    der time on time.
These are the destroyers of Jerusalem, these are the
    murderers
Of Jesus, who deny the Faith & mock at Eternal Life,
Who pretend to Poetry that they may destroy Imagina-
    tion
By imitation of Nature's Images drawn from Remem-
    brance.
These are the Sexual Garments, the Abomination of
    Desolation,
Hiding the Human Lineaments as with an Ark & Cur-
    tains
Which Jesus rent & now shall wholly purge away with
    Fire
Till Generation is swallow'd up in Regeneration."

[THE LAST VISION]

And I beheld the Twenty-four Cities of Albion
Arise upon their Thrones to Judge the Nations of the
    Earth;
And the Immortal Four in whom the Twenty-four ap-
    pear Fourfold
Arose around Albion's body. Jesus wept & walked forth
From Felpham's Vale clothed in Clouds of blood, to
    enter into
Albion's Bosom, the bosom of death, & the Four sur-
    rounded him
In the Column of Fire in Felpham's Vale; then to their
    mouths the Four

Applied their Four Trumpets & them sounded to the
    Four winds.

Terror struck in the Vale I stood at that immortal sound.
My bones trembled, I fell outstretch'd upon the path
A moment, & my Soul return'd into its mortal state
To Resurrection & Judgment in the Vegetable Body,
And my sweet Shadow of Delight stood trembling by
    my side.

Immediately the Lark mounted with a loud trill from
    Felpham's Vale,
And the Wild Thyme from Wimbleton's green & im-
    purpled Hills,
And Los & Enitharmon rose over the Hills of Surrey:
Their clouds roll over London with a south wind; soft
    Oothoon
Pants in the Vales of Lambeth, weeping o'er her Human
    Harvest.
Los listens to the Cry of the Poor Man, his Cloud
Over London in volume terrific low bended in anger.

Rintrah & Palamabron view the Human Harvest be-
    neath.
Their Wine-presses & Barns stand open, the Ovens are
    prepar'd,
The Waggons ready; terrific Lions & Tygers sport &
    play.
All Animals upon the Earth are prepar'd in all their
    strength
To go forth to the Great Harvest & Vintage of the
    Nations

From JERUSALEM

(1804–1820)

THE EMANATION OF THE GIANT ALBION

SHEEP   TO THE PUBLIC   GOATS

After my three years slumber on the banks of the Ocean, I again display my Giant forms to the Public. My former Giants & Fairies having reciev'd the highest reward possible, the love and friendship of those with whom to be connected is to be blessed. I cannot doubt that this more consolidated & extended work will be as kindly recieved. . . . I also hope the Reader will be with me, wholly One in Jesus our Lord, who is the God of Fire and Lord of Love to whom the Ancients look'd and saw his day afar off, with trembling & amazement.

The Spirit of Jesus is continual forgiveness of Sin: he who waits to be righteous before he enters into the Saviour's kingdom, the Divine Body, will never enter there. I am perhaps the most sinful of men. I pretend not to holiness: yet I pretend to love, to see, to converse with daily as man with man, & the more to have an interest in the Friend of Sinners. Therefore, dear Reader, forgive what you do not approve, & love me for this energetic exertion of my talent.

Reader! lover of books! lover of heaven,
And of that God from whom all things are given,
Who in mysterious Sinai's awful cave

To Man the wondrous art of writing gave:
Again he speaks in thunder and in fire!
Thunder of Thought, & flames of fierce desire:
Even from the depths of Hell his voice I hear
Within the unfathom'd caverns of my Ear.
Therefore I print; nor vain my types shall be:
Heaven, Earth & Hell henceforth shall live in harmony.

Of the Measure in which
the following Poem is written.

We who dwell on Earth can do nothing of ourselves;
every thing is conducted by Spirits, no less than Diges-
tion or Sleep. . . . When this Verse was first dictated
to me, I consider'd a Monotonous Cadence, like that
used by Milton & Shakespeare & all writers of English
Blank Verse, derived from the modern bondage of
Rhyming, to be a necessary and indispensible part of
Verse. But I soon found that in the mouth of a true
Orator such monotony was not only awkward, but as
much a bondage as rhyme itself. I therefore have pro-
duced a variety in every line, both of cadences & num-
ber of syllables. Every word and every letter is studied
and put into its fit place; the terrific numbers are
reserved for the terrific parts, the mild & gentle for the
mild & gentle parts, and the prosaic for inferior parts;
all are necessary to each other. Poetry Fetter'd Fetters
the Human Race. Nations are Destroy'd or Flourish in
proportion as Their Poetry, Painting and Music are
Destroy'd or Flourish! The Primeval State of Man was
Wisdom, Art and Science.

TO THE JEWS

Jerusalem the Emanation of the Giant Albion! Can it be? Is it a Truth that the Learned have explored? Was Britain the Primitive Seat of the Patriarchal Religion? If it is true, my title-page is also True, that Jerusalem was & is the Emanation of the Giant Albion. It is True and cannot be controverted. Ye are united, O ye Inhabitants of Earth, in One Religion, The Religion of Jesus, the most Ancient, the Eternal & the Everlasting Gospel. The Wicked will turn it to Wickedness, the Righteous to Righteousness. Amen! Huzza! Selah!
"All things Begin & End in Albion's Ancient Druid
    Rocky Shore."

Your Ancestors derived their origin from Abraham, Heber, Shem and Noah, who were Druids, as the Druid Temples (which are the Patriarchal Pillars & Oak Groves) over the whole Earth witness to this day.

You have a tradition, that Man anciently contain'd in his mighty limbs all things in Heaven & Earth: this you recieved from the Druids.
"But now the Starry Heavens are fled from the mighty
    limbs of Albion."

Albion was the Parent of the Druids, & in his Chaotic State of Sleep, Satan & Adam & the whole World was Created by the Elohim.

The fields from Islington to Marybone,
To Primrose Hill and Saint John's Wood,
    Were builded over with pillars of gold,
And there Jerusalem's pillars stood.

Her Little-ones ran on the fields,
The Lamb of God among them seen,
    And fair Jerusalem his Bride,
Among the little meadows green.

Pancrass & Kentish-town repose
Among her golden pillars high,
    Among her golden arches which
Shine upon the starry sky.

The Jew's-harp-house & the Green Man,
The Ponds where Boys to bathe delight,
    The fields of Cows by Willan's farm.
Shine in Jerusalem's pleasant sight.

She walks upon our meadows green,
The Lamb of God walks by her side,
    And every English Child is seen
Children of Jesus & his Bride.

Forgiving trespasses and sins
Lest Babylon with cruel Og
    With Moral & Self-righteous Law
Should Crucify in Satan's Synagogue!

What are those golden Builders doing
Near mournful ever-weeping Paddington,
    Standing above that mighty Ruin
Where Satan the first victory won,

Where Albion slept beneath the Fatal Tree,
And the Druids' golden Knife
    Rioted in human gore,
In Offerings of Human Life?

They groan'd aloud on London Stone,
They groan'd aloud on Tyburn's Brook,
 Albion gave his deadly groan,
And all the Atlantic Mountains shook.

 Albion's Spectre from his Loins
Tore forth in all the pomp of War:
 Satan his name: in flames of fire
He stretch'd his Druid Pillars far.

 Jerusalem fell from Lambeth's Vale
Down thro' Poplar & Old Bow,
 Thro' Malden & across the Sea,
In War & howling, death & woe.

 The Rhine was red with human blood,
The Danube roll'd a purple tide,
 On the Euphrates Satan stood,
And over Asia stretch'd his pride.

 He wither'd up sweet Zion's Hill
From every Nation of the Earth;
 He wither'd up Jerusalem's Gates,
And in a dark Land gave her birth.

 He wither'd up the Human Form
By laws of sacrifice for sin,
 Till it became a Mortal Worm,
But O! translucent all within.

 The Divine Vision still was seen,
Still was the Human Form Divine,
 Weeping in weak & mortal clay,
O Jesus, still the Form was thine.

And thine the Human Face, & thine
The Human Hands & Feet & Breath,
    Entering thro' the Gates of Birth
And passing thro' the Gates of Death.

And O thou Lamb of God, whom I
Slew in my dark self-righteous pride,
    Art thou return'd to Albion's Land?
And is Jerusalem thy Bride?

Come to my arms & never more
Depart, but dwell for ever here:
    Create my Spirit to thy Love:
Subdue my Spectre to thy Fear.

Spectre of Albion! warlike Fiend!
In clouds of blood & ruin roll'd,
    I here reclaim thee as my own,
My Selfhood! Satan! arm'd in gold

Is this thy soft Family-Love,
Thy cruel Patriarchal pride,
    Planting thy Family alone,
Destroying all the World beside?

A man's worst enemies are those
Of his own house & family;
    And he who makes his law a curse,
By his own law shall surely die.

In my Exchanges every Land
Shall walk, & mine in every Land,
    Mutual shall build Jerusalem,
Both heart in heart & hand in hand.

If Humility is Christianity, you, O Jews, are the true Christians. If your tradition that Man contained in his Limbs all Animals is True, & they were separated from him by cruel Sacrifices, and when compulsory cruel Sacrifices had brought Humanity into a Feminine Tabernacle in the loins of Abraham & David, the Lamb of God, the Saviour became apparent on Earth as the Prophets had foretold, The Return of Israel is a Return to Mental Sacrifice & War. Take up the Cross, O Israel, & follow Jesus.

Rahab is an Eternal State. } **TO THE DEISTS** { The Spiritual States of the Soul are all Eternal. Distinguish between the Man & his present State.

He never can be a Friend to the Human Race who is the Preacher of Natural Morality or Natural Religion; he is a flatterer who means to betray, to perpetuate Tyrant Pride & the Laws of that Babylon which he foresees shall shortly be destroyed, with the Spiritual and not the Natural Sword. He is in the State named Rahab, which State must be put off before he can be the Friend of Man.

You, O Deists, profess yourselves the Enemies of Christianity, and you are so: you are also the Enemies of the Human Race & of Universal Nature. Man is born a Spectre or Satan & is altogether an Evil, & requires a New Selfhood continually, & must continually be changed into his direct Contrary. But your Greek Philosophy (which is a remnant of Druidism) teaches that Man is Righteous in his Vegetated Spectre: an Opinion of fatal & accursed consequence to Man, as the Ancients saw plainly by Revelation, to the intire abrogation of Experimental Theory; and many believed what they saw and Prophecied of Jesus.

Man must & will have Some Religion: if he has not the Religion of Jesus, he will have the Religion of Satan & will erect the Synagogue of Satan, calling the Prince of this World, God, and destroying all who do not worship Satan under the Name of God. Will any one say, "Where are those who worship Satan under the Name of God?" Where are they? Listen! Every Religion that Preaches Vengeance for Sin is the Religion of the Enemy & Avenger and not of the Forgiver of Sin, and their God is Satan, Named by the Divine Name. Your Religion, O Deists! Deism, is the Worship of the God of this World by the means of what you call Natural Religion and Natural Philosophy, and of Natural Morality or Self-Righteousness, the Selfish Virtues of the Natural Heart. This was the Religion of the Pharisees who murder'd Jesus. Deism is the same & ends in the same.

Voltaire, Rousseau, Gibbon, Hume, charge the Spiritually Religious with Hypocrisy; but how a Monk, or a Methodist either, can be a Hypocrite, I cannot concieve. We are Men of like passions with others & pretend not to be holier than others; therefore, when a Religious Man falls into Sin, he ought not to be call'd a Hypocrite; this title is more properly to be given to a Player who falls into Sin, whose profession is Virtue & Morality & the making Men Self-Righteous. Foote in calling Whitefield, Hypocrite, was himself one; for Whitefield pretended not to be holier than others, but confessed his Sins before all the World. Voltaire! Rousseau! You cannot escape my charge that you are Pharisees & Hypocrites, for you are constantly talking of the Virtues of the Human Heart and particularly of your own, that you may accuse others, & especially the Religious, whose errors you, by this display of pretended Virtue, chiefly design to expose. Rousseau thought Men Good by Nature: he found them Evil & found no friend. Friendship cannot exist without Forgiveness of Sins continually. The Book written by Rousseau call'd his Confessions, is an apology & cloke for his sin & not a confession.

But you also charge the poor Monks & Religious with being the causes of War, while you acquit & flatter the Alexanders & Caesars, the Lewis's & Fredericks, who alone are its causes & its actors. But the Religion of Jesus, Forgiveness of Sin, can never be the cause of a War nor of a single Martyrdom.

Those who Martyr others or who cause War are Deists, but never can be Forgivers of Sin. The Glory of Christianity is To Conquer by Forgiveness. All the Destruction, therefore, in Christian Europe has arisen from Deism, which is Natural Religion.

> I saw a Monk of Charlemaine
> Arise before my sight:
> I talk'd with the Grey Monk as we stood
> In beams of infernal light.
>
> Gibbon arose with a lash of steel,
> And Voltaire with a wracking wheel:
> The Schools, in clouds of learning roll'd,
> Arose with War in iron & gold.
>
> "Thou lazy Monk," they sound afar,
> "In vain condemning glorious War;

"And in your Cell you shall ever dwell:
"Rise, War, & bind him in his Cell!"

The blood red ran from the Grey Monk's side,
His hands & feet were wounded wide,
  His body bent, his arms & knees
Like to the roots of ancient trees.

When Satan first the black bow bent
And the Moral Law from the Gospel rent,
  He forg'd the Law into a Sword
And spill'd the blood of mercy's Lord.

Titus! Constantine! Charlemaine!
O Voltaire! Rousseau! Gibbon! Vain
  Your Grecian Mocks & Roman Sword
Against this image of his Lord!

For a Tear is an Intellectual thing,
And a Sigh is the Sword of an Angel King,
  And the bitter groan of a Martyr's woe
Is an Arrow from the Almightie's Bow.

TO THE CHRISTIANS

Devils are
False Religions.
    "Saul, Saul,
"Why persecutest thou me?"

I give you the end of a
  golden string,
Only wind it into a ball,
It will lead you in at Heaven's gate
Built in Jerusalem's wall.

We are told to abstain from fleshly desires that we
may lose no time from the Work of the Lord: Every mo-
ment lost is a moment that cannot be redeemed; every

pleasure that intermingles with the duty of our station
is a folly unredeemable, & is planted like the seed of a
wild flower among our wheat: All the tortures of re-
pentance are tortures of self-reproach on account of our
leaving the Divine Harvest to the Enemy, the struggles
of intanglement with incoherent roots. I know of no
other Christianity and of no other Gospel than the lib-
erty both of body & mind to exercise the Divine Arts of
Imagination, Imagination, the real & eternal World of
which this Vegetable Universe is but a faint shadow, &
in which we shall live in our Eternal or Imaginative
Bodies when these Vegetable Mortal Bodies are no more.
The Apostles knew of no other Gospel. What were all
their spiritual gifts? What is the Divine Spirit? is the
Holy Ghost any other than an Intellectual Fountain?
What is the Harvest of the Gospel & its Labours? What
is that Talent which it is a curse to hide? What are the
Treasures of Heaven which we are to lay up for our-
selves, are they any other than Mental Studies & Per-
formances? What are all the Gifts of the Gospel, are
they not all Mental Gifts? Is God a Spirit who must be
worshipped in Spirit & in Truth, and are not the Gifts of
the Spirit Every-thing to Man? O ye Religious, discoun-
tenance every one among you who shall pretend to de-
spise Art & Science! I call upon you in the Name of
Jesus! What is the Life of Man but Art & Science? is it
Meat & Drink? is not the Body more than Raiment?
What is Mortality but the things relating to the Body
which Dies? What is Immortality but the things relating
to the Spirit which Lives Eternally? What is the Joy of
Heaven but Improvement in the things of the Spirit?
What are the Pains of Hell but Ignorance, Bodily Lust,
Idleness & devastation of the things of the Spirit? An-
swer this to yourselves, & expel from among you those
who pretend to despise the labours of Art & Science,

which alone are the labours of the Gospel. Is not this plain & manifest to the thought? Can you think at all & not pronounce heartily That to Labour in Knowledge is to Build up Jerusalem, and to Despise Knowledge is to Despise Jerusalem & her Builders. And remember: He who despises & mocks a Mental Gift in another, calling it pride & selfishness & sin, mocks Jesus the giver of every Mental Gift, which always appear to the ignorance-loving Hypocrite as Sins; but that which is a Sin in the sight of cruel Man is not so in the sight of our kind God. Let every Christian, as much as in him lies, engage himself openly & publicly before all the World in some Mental pursuit for the Building up of Jerusalem.

I stood among my valleys of the south
And saw a flame of fire, even as a Wheel
Of fire surrounding all the heavens: it went
From west to east, against the current of
Creation, and devour'd all things in its loud
Fury & thundering course round heaven & earth.
By it the Sun was roll'd into an orb,
By it the Moon faded into a globe
Travelling thro' the night; for, from its dire
And restless fury, Man himself shrunk up
Into a little root a fathom long.
And I asked a Watcher & a Holy-One
Its Name; he answered: "It is the Wheel of Religion."
I wept & said: "Is this the law of Jesus,
This terrible devouring sword turning every way?"
He answer'd: "Jesus died because he strove
Against the current of this Wheel; its Name
Is Caiaphas, the dark preacher of Death,
Of sin, of sorrow & of punishment:
Opposing Nature! It is Natural Religion;
But Jesus is the bright Preacher of Life

Creating Nature from this fiery Law
By self-denial & forgiveness of Sin.
Go therefore, cast out devils in Christ's name,
Heal thou the sick of spiritual disease,
Pity the evil, for thou art not sent
To smite with terror & with punishments
Those that are sick, like to the Pharisees
Crucifying & encompassing sea & land
For proselytes to tyranny & wrath;
But to the Publicans & Harlots go,
Teach them True Happiness, but let no curse
Go forth out of thy mouth to blight their peace;
For Hell is open'd to Heaven: thine eyes beheld
The dungeons burst & the Prisoners set free."

    England! awake! awake! awake!
      Jerusalem thy Sister calls!
    Why wilt thou sleep the sleep of death
      And close her from thy ancient walls?

    Thy hills & valleys felt her feet
      Gently upon their bosoms move:
    Thy gates beheld sweet Zion's ways:
      Then was a time of joy and love.

    And now the time returns again:
      Our souls exult, & London's towers
    Recieve the Lamb of God to dwell
      In England's green & pleasant bowers.

[INTRODUCTION]

Of the Sleep of Ulro! and of the passage through
Eternal Death! and of the awaking to Eternal Life.

This theme calls me in sleep night after night, & ev'ry
    morn
Awakes me at sun-rise; then I see the Saviour over me
Spreading his beams of love & dictating the words of
    this mild song.

"Awake! awake O sleeper of the land of shadows, wake!
    expand!
I am in you and you in me, mutual in love divine:
Fibres of love from man to man thro' Albion's pleasant
    land.
In all the dark Atlantic vale down from the hills of Sur-
    rey
A black water accumulates; return Albion! return!
Thy brethren call thee, and thy fathers and thy sons,
Thy nurses and thy mothers, thy sisters and thy daugh-
    ters
Weep at thy soul's disease, and the Divine Vision is
    darken'd,
Thy Emanation that was wont to play before thy face,
Beaming forth with her daughters into the Divine
    bosom:

"Where hast thou hidden thy Emanation, lovely Jeru-
    salem,
From the vision and fruition of the Holy-one?
I am not a God afar off, I am a brother and friend:
Within your bosoms I reside, and you reside in me:
Lo! we are One, forgiving all Evil, Not seeking recom-
    pense.
Ye are my members, O ye sleepers of Beulah, land of
    shades!"

[BLAKE'S TASK]

Trembling I sit day and night, my friends are astonish'd
at me,
Yet they forgive my wanderings. I rest not from my
great task!
To open the Eternal Worlds, to open the immortal Eyes
Of Man inwards into the Worlds of Thought, into Eter-
nity
Ever expanding in the Bosom of God, the Human Imag-
ination.
O Saviour pour upon me thy Spirit of meekness & love!
Annihilate the Selfhood in me: be thou all my life!
Guide thou my hand, which trembles exceedingly upon
the rock of ages,
While I write. . . .

[THE FURNACE AND THE LOOM]

The Male is a Furnace of beryll; the Female is a golden
Loom.
I behold them, and their rushing fires overwhelm my
Soul
In London's darkness, and my tears fall day and night
Upon the Emanations of Albion's Sons, the Daughters
of Albion,
Names anciently remember'd, but now contemn'd as
fictions
Although in every bosom they controll our Vegetative
powers.

[THE CONTRARIES]

And this is the manner of the Sons of Albion in their
    strength:
They take the Two Contraries which are call'd Qualities,
    with which
Every Substance is clothed: they name them Good &
    Evil
From them they make an Abstract, which is a Negation
Not only of the Substance from which it is derived,
A murderer of its own Body, but also a murderer
Of every Divine Member: it is the Reasoning Power,
An Abstract objecting power that Negatives everything.
This is the Spectre of Man, the Holy Reasoning Power,
And in its Holiness is closed the Abomination of Desola-
    tion.

[BLAKE'S MOTTO]

"I must Create a System or be enslav'd by another
    Man's.
I will not Reason & Compare: my business is to Create."

[THE EARTH]

The Vegetative Universe opens like a flower from the
    Earth's center
In which is Eternity. It expands in Stars to the Mundane
    Shell
And there it meets Eternity again, both within and with-
    out,

And the abstract Voids between the Stars are the Satanic
  Wheels.

There is the Cave, the Rock, the Tree, the Lake of
  Udan Adan,
The Forest and the Marsh and the Pits of bitumen
  deadly,
The Rocks of solid fire, the Ice valleys, the Plains
Of burning sand, the rivers, cataract & Lakes of Fire,
The Islands of the fiery Lakes, the Trees of Malice, Re-
  venge
And black Anxiety, and the Cities of the Salamandrine
  men,
(But whatever is visible to the Generated Man
Is a Creation of mercy & love from the Satanic Void).
The land of darkness flamed, but no light & no repose:
The land of snows of trembling & of iron hail incessant:
The land of earthquakes, and the land of woven laby-
  rinths:
The land of snares & traps & wheels & pit-falls & dire
  mills:
The Voids, the Solids, & the land of clouds & regions of
  waters
With their inhabitants, in the Twenty-seven Heavens
  beneath Beulah:
Self-righteousness conglomerating against the Divine
  Vision:
A Concave Earth wondrous, Chasmal, Abyssal, Incoher-
  ent,
Forming the Mundane Shell: above, beneath, on all
  sides surrounding
Golgonooza. Los walks round the walls night and day.

[THE TWO GATES]

And Los beheld his Sons and he beheld his Daughters,
Every one a translucent Wonder, a Universe within,
Increasing inwards into length and breadth and heighth,
Starry & glorious; and they every one in their bright loins
Have a beautiful golden gate, which opens into the veg-
  etative world;
And every one a gate of rubies & all sorts of precious
  stones
In their translucent hearts, which opens into the vegeta-
  tive world;
And every one a gate of iron dreadful and wonderful
In their translucent heads, which opens into the vegeta-
  tive world;
And every one has the three regions, Childhood, Man-
  hood & Age;
But the gate of the tongue, the western gate, in them is
  clos'd,
Having a wall builded against it, and thereby the gates
Eastward & Southward & Northward are incircled with
  flaming fires.
And the North is Breadth, the South is Heighth &
  Depth,
The East is Inwards, & the West is Outwards every way.

[A VISION OF ALBION]

In every Nation of the Earth, till the Twelve Sons of
  Albion
Enrooted into every nation, a mighty Polypus growing

From Albion over the whole Earth: such is my awful
    Vision.

I see the Four-fold Man, The Humanity in deadly sleep
And its fallen Emanation, The Spectre & its cruel
    Shadow.
I see the Past, Present & Future existing all at once
Before me. O Divine Spirit, sustain me on thy wings,
That I may awake Albion from his long & cold repose;
For Bacon & Newton, sheath'd in dismal steel, their ter-
    rors hang
Like iron scourges over Albion: Reasonings like vast
    Serpents
Infold around my limbs, bruising my minute articula-
    tions.

I turn my eyes to the Schools & Universities of Europe
And there behold the Loom of Locke, whose Woof rages
    dire,
Wash'd by the Water-wheels of Newton: black the cloth
In heavy wreathes folds over every Nation: cruel Works
Of many Wheels I view, wheel without wheel, with cogs
    tyrannic
Moving by compulsion each other, not as those in Eden,
    which,
Wheel within Wheel, in freedom revolve in harmony &
    peace.

[THE GROANING CREATION]

Scotland pours out his Sons to labour at the Furnaces;
Wales gives his Daughters to the Looms; England, nurs-
    ing Mothers

Gives to the Children of Albion & to the Children of
Jerusalem.
From the blue Mundane Shell even to the Earth of Veg-
etation,
Throughout the whole Creation, which groans to be de-
liver'd,
Albion groans in the deep slumbers of Death upon his
Rock.

[MAN'S PILGRIMAGE]

All things acted on Earth are seen in the bright Sculp-
tures of
Los's Halls, & every Age renews its powers from these
Works
With every pathetic story possible to happen from Hate
or
Wayward Love; & every sorrow & distress is carved here,
Every Affinity of Parents, Marriages & Friendships are
here
In all their various combinations wrought with won-
drous Art,
All that can happen to Man is his pilgrimage of seventy
years.

[NEGATIONS ARE NOT CONTRARIES]

"They know not why they love nor wherefore they
sicken & die,
Calling that Holy Love which is Envy, Revenge & Cru-
elty,
Which separated the stars from the mountains, the
mountains from Man

And left Man, a little grovelling Root outside of Himself.
Negations are not Contraries: Contraries mutually Exist;
But Negations Exist Not. Exceptions & Objections & Un-
    beliefs
Exist not, nor shall they ever be Organized for ever &
    ever.
If thou separate from me, thou art a Negation, a meer
Reasoning & Derogation from me, an Objecting & Cruel
    Spite
And Malice & Envy; but my Emanation, Alas! will be-
    come
My Contrary. O thou Negation, I will continually com-
    pell
Thee to be invisible to any but whom I please, & when
And where & how I please, and never! never! shalt thou
    be Organized
But as a distorted & reversed Reflexion in the Darkness
And in the Non Entity: nor shall that which is above
Ever descend into thee, but thou shalt be a Non Entity
    for ever;
And if any enter into thee, thou shalt be an Unquench-
    able Fire,
And he shall be a never dying Worm, mutually tor-
    mented by
Those that thou tormentest: a Hell & Despair for ever
    & ever."

[THE OUTLINE OF IDENTITY]

From every-one of the Four Regions of Human Majesty
There is an Outside spread Without & an Outside spread
    Within,
Beyond the Outline of Identity both ways, which meet
    in One,

An orbed Void of doubt, despair, hunger & thirst & sorrow.

[THE SORROWS OF ALBION]

Hoarse turn'd the Starry Wheels rending a way in Albion's Loins:
Beyond the Night of Beulah, In a dark & unknown Night:
Outstretch'd his Giant beauty on the ground in pain & tears:
His Children exil'd from his breast pass to and fro before him,
His birds are silent on his hills, flocks die beneath his branches,
His tents are fall'n, his trumpets and the sweet sound of his harp
Are silent on his clouded hills that belch forth storms & fire.
His milk of Cows & honey of Bees & fruit of golden harvest
Is gather'd in the scorching heat & in the driving rain.
Where once he sat, he weary walks in misery and pain,
His Giant beauty and perfection fallen into dust,
Till, from within his wither'd breast, grown narrow with his woes,
The corn is turn'd to thistles & the apples into poison,
The birds of song to murderous crows, his joys to bitter groans,
The voices of children in his tents to cries of helpless infants,
And self-exiled from the face of light & shine of morning,

In the dark world, a narrow house! he wanders up and
    down
Seeking for rest and finding none! and hidden far within,
His Eon weeping in the cold and desolated Earth.

[BABYLON AND JERUSALEM]

O what is Life & what is Man? O what is Death?
    Wherefore
Are you, my Children, natives in the Grave to where I
    go?
Or are you born to feed the hungry ravenings of Destruc-
    tion,
To be the sport of Accident, to waste in Wrath & Love a
    weary
Life, in brooding cares & anxious labours that prove but
    chaff?
O Jerusalem, Jerusalem, I have forsaken thy Courts,
Thy Pillars of ivory & gold, thy Curtains of silk & fine
Linen, thy Pavements of precious stones, thy Walls of
    pearl
And gold, thy Gates of Thanksgiving, thy Windows of
    Praise,
Thy Clouds of Blessing, thy Cherubims of Tender-mercy
Stretching their Wings sublime over the Little-ones of
    Albion!
O Human Imagination, O Divine Body I have Crucified,
I have turned my back upon thee into the Wastes of
    Moral Law.
There Babylon is builded in the Waste, founded in Hu-
    man desolation.
O Babylon, thy Watchman stands over thee in the night,
Thy severe Judge all the day long proves thee, O Baby-
    lon,

With provings of destruction, with giving thee thy
    heart's desire;
But Albion is cast forth to the Potter, his Children to
    the Builders
To build Babylon because they have forsaken Jerusalem.
The Walls of Babylon are Souls of Men, her Gates the
    Groans
Of Nations, her Towers are the Miseries of once happy
    Families,
Her Streets are paved with Destruction, her Houses
    built with Death,
Her Palaces with Hell & the Grave, her Synagogues with
    Torments
Of ever-hardening Despair, squar'd & polish'd with
    cruel skill.
Yet thou wast lovely as the summer cloud upon my hills
When Jerusalem was thy heart's desire, in times of youth
    & love.
Thy Sons came to Jerusalem with gifts; she sent them
    away
With blessings on their hands & on their feet, blessings
    of gold
And pearl & diamond: thy Daughters sang in her Courts.
They came up to Jerusalem: they walked before Albion:
In the Exchanges of London every Nation walk'd,
And London walk'd in every Nation, mutual in love &
    harmony.
Albion cover'd the whole Earth, England encompass'd
    the Nations,
Mutual each within other's bosom in Visions of Regen-
    eration.
Jerusalem cover'd the Atlantic Mountains & the Ery-
    threan
From bright Japan & China to Hesperia, France & Eng-
    land.

Mount Zion lifted his head in every Nation under
  heaven,
And the Mount of Olives was beheld over the whole
  Earth.
The footsteps of the Lamb of God were there; but now
  no more,
No more shall I behold him. . . .

[THE PRAYER OF LOS]

And Los prayed and said, "O Divine Saviour, arise
Upon the Mountains of Albion as in ancient time! Be-
  hold!
The Cities of Albion seek thy face: London groans in
  pain
From Hill to Hill, & the Thames laments along the Val-
  leys:
The little Villages of Middlesex & Surrey hunger &
  thirst:
The Twenty-eight Cities of Albion stretch their hands to
  thee
Because of the Opressors of Albion in every City & Vil-
  lage.
They mock at the Labourer's limbs: they mock at his
  starv'd Children:
They buy his Daughters that they may have power to
  sell his Sons:
They compell the Poor to live upon a crust of bread by
  soft mild arts:
They reduce the Man to want, then give with pomp &
  ceremony:
The praise of Jehovah is chaunted from lips of hunger
  & thirst. . . ."

[THE MOCKERY OF MAN]

"I am your Rational Power, O Albion, & that Human
    Form
You call Divine is but a Wôrm seventy inches long
That creeps forth in a night & is dried in the morning
    sun,
In fortuitous concourse of memorys accumulated & lost.
It plows the Earth in its own conceit, it overwhelms the
    Hills
Beneath its winding labyrinths, till a stone of the brook
Stops it in midst of its pride among its hills & rivers.

[WOMAN AND MAN]

"I hear the screech of Childbirth loud pealing, & the
    groans
Of Death in Albion's clouds dreadful utter'd over all
    the Earth.
What may Man be? who can tell! but what may Woman
    be
To have power over Man from Cradle to corruptible
    Grave?
There is a Throne in every Man, it is the Throne of God;
This, Woman has claim'd as her own, & Man is no more!
Albion is the Tabernacle of Vala & her Temple,
And not the Tabernacle & Temple of the Most High.
O Albion, why wilt thou Create a Female Will?
To hide the most evident God in a hidden covert, even
In the shadows of a Woman & a secluded Holy Place,
That we may pry after him as after a stolen treasure,

Hidden among the Dead & mured up from the paths of
    life. . . ."

[THE PERCEPTIVE PATTERN]

If Perceptive Organs vary, Objects of Perception seem
    to vary:
If the Perceptive Organs close, their Objects seem to
    close also.

[THE WARS OF LIFE]

". . . Our wars are wars of life, & wounds of love
With intellectual spears, & long winged arrows of
    thought.
Mutual in one another's love and wrath all renewing
We live as One Man; for contracting our infinite senses
We behold multitude, or expanding, we behold as one,
As One Man all the Universal Family, and that One
    Man
We call Jesus the Christ; and he in us, and we in him
Live in perfect harmony in Eden, the land of life,
Giving, recieving, and forgiving each other's trespasses.
He is the Good shepherd, he is the Lord and master,
He is the Shepherd of Albion, he is all in all,
In Eden, in the garden of God, and in heavenly Jeru-
    salem.
If we have offended, forgive us; take not vengeance
    against us."

O! how the torments of Eternal Death waited on Man,
And the loud-rending bars of the Creation ready to
    burst,

That the wide world might fly from its hinges & the im-
mortal mansion
Of Man for ever be possess'd by monsters of the deeps,
And Man himself become a Fiend, wrap'd in an endless
curse,
Consuming and consum'd for-ever in flames of Moral
Justice.

[THE ENGLISH NAMES]

I call them by their English names: English, the rough
basement.
Los built the stubborn structure of the Language, acting
against
Albion's melancholy, who must else have been a Dumb
despair.

[MAN'S SPECTRE]

Each Man is in his Spectre's power
Until the arrival of that hour,
When his Humanity awake,
And cast his Spectre into the Lake.

[LOS'S FURY]

. . . Los grew furious, raging: "Why stand we here
trembling around
Calling on God for help, and not ourselves, in whom
God dwells,
Stretching a hand to save the falling Man? are we not
Four

Beholding Albion upon the Precipice ready to fall into
    Non-Entity?

Seeing these Heavens & Hells conglobing in the Void,
    Heavens over Hells

Brooding in holy hypocritic lust, drinking the cries of
    pain

From howling victims of Law, building Heavens
    Twenty-seven-fold,

Swell'd & bloated General Forms repugnant to the Di-
    vine-

Humanity who is the Only General and Universal Form,

To which all Lineaments tend & seek with love & sym-
    pathy.

All broad & general principles belong to benevolence

Who protects minute particulars every one in their own
    identity;

But here the affectionate touch of the tongue is clos'd in
    by deadly teeth,

And the soft smile of friendship & the open dawn of
    benevolence

Become a net & a trap, & every energy render'd cruel,

Till the existence of friendship & benevolence is denied:

The wine of the Spirit & the vineyards of the Holy-One

Here turn into poisonous stupor & deadly intoxication.

That they may be condemn'd by Law & the Lamb of
    God be slain;

And the two Sources of Life in Eternity, Hunting and
    War,

Are become the Sources of dark & bitter Death & of cor-
    roding Hell.

The open heart is shut up in integuments of frozen si-
    lence

That the spear that lights it forth may shatter the ribs &
    bosom.

A pretence of Art to destroy Art; a pretence of Liberty

To destroy Liberty; a pretence of Religion to destroy
   Religion. . . ."

[A MAN'S WORST ENEMIES]

Alas!—The time will come when a man's worst enemies
Shall be those of his own house and family, in a Religion
Of Generation to destroy, by Sin and Atonement, happy
   Jerusalem,
The Bride and Wife of the Lamb. O God, thou art Not
   an Avenger!

[JERUSALEM! JERUSALEM!]

"Jerusalem! Jerusalem! why wilt thou turn away?
. . . "The Gigantic roots & twigs of the vegetating Sons
   of Albion,
Fill'd with the little-ones, are consumed in the Fires of
   their Altars.
The vegetating Cities are burned & consumed from the
   Earth,
And the Bodies in which all Animals & Vegetations, the
   Earth & Heaven
Were contain'd in the All Glorious Imagination, are
   wither'd & darken'd.
The golden Gate of Havilah and all the Garden of God
Was caught up with the Sun in one day of fury and war.
The Lungs, the Heart, the Liver, shrunk away far dis-
   stant from Man
And left a little slimy substance floating upon the tides.
In one night the Atlantic Continent was caught up with
   the Moon

And became an Opake Globe far distant, clad with
   moony beams.
The Visions of Eternity, by reason of narrowed percep-
   tions,
Are become weak Visions of Time & Space, fix'd into
   furrows of death,
Till deep dissimulation is the only defence an honest
   man has left. . . ."

[THE SHUT FORM]

"Ah! weak & wide astray! Ah! shut in narrow doleful
   form!
Creeping in reptile flesh upon the bosom of the ground!
The Eye of Man, a little narrow orb, clos'd up & dark,
Scarcely beholding the Great Light, conversing with the
   ground:
The Ear, a little shell, in small volutions shutting out
True Harmonies & comprehending great as very small:
The Nostrils, bent down to the earth & clos'd with sense-
   less flesh
That odours cannot them expand, nor joy on them exult:
The Tongue, a little moisture fills, a little food it cloys,
A little sound it utters, & its cries are faintly heard. . . ."

[A MURDEROUS PROVIDENCE]

"A murderous Providence! A Creation that groans, liv-
   ing on Death,
Where Fish & Bird & Beast & Man & Tree & Metal &
   Stone
Live by Devouring, going into Eternal Death contin-
   ually!"

[COME, O LAMB OF GOD!]

"Come, O thou Lamb of God, and take away the re-
        membrance of Sin.
To Sin & to hide the Sin in sweet deceit is lovely!
To Sin in the open face of day is cruel & pitiless! But
To record the Sin for a reproach, to let the Sun go down
In a remembrance of the Sin, is a Woe & a Horror,
A brooder of an Evil Day and a Sun rising in blood!
Come then, O Lamb of God, and take away the remem-
        brance of Sin."

[ALBION'S SPECTRE]

. . . The Spectre, like a hoar frost & a Mildew, rose
        over Albion,
Saying, "I am God, O Sons of Men! I am your Rational
        Power!
Am I not Bacon & Newton & Locke who teach Humility
        to Man,
Who teach Doubt & Experiment? & my two Wings, Vol-
        taire, Rousseau?
Where is that Friend of Sinners? that Rebel against my
        Laws
Who teaches Belief to the Nations & an unknown Eter-
        nal Life?
Come hither into the Desart & turn these stones to
        bread.
Vain foolish Man! wilt thou believe without Experiment
And build a World of Phantasy upon my Great Abyss,
A World of Shapes in craving lust & devouring appe-
        tite?"

[IT IS BETTER TO PREVENT MISERY]

Silence remain'd & every one resum'd his Human Majesty.
And many conversed on these things as they labour'd at the furrow,
Saying: "It is better to prevent misery than to release from misery:
It is better to prevent error than to forgive the criminal.
Lábour well the Minute Particulars, attend to the Little-ones,
And those who are in misery cannot remain so long
If we do but our duty: labour well the teeming Earth."

They Plow'd in tears, the trumpets sounded before the golden Plow,
And the voices of the Living Creatures were heard in the clouds of heaven,
Crying: "Compell the Reasoner to Demonstrate with unhewn Demonstrations.
Let the Indefinite be explored, and let every Man be Judged
By his own Works. Let all Indefinites be thrown into Demonstrations,
To be pounded to dust & melted in the Furnaces of Affliction.
He who would do good to another must do it in Minute Particulars:
General Good is the plea of the scoundrel, hypocrite & flatterer,
For Art & Science cannot exist but in minutely organized Particulars

And not in generalizing Demonstrations of the Rational
    Power.
The Infinite alone resides in Definite & Determinate
    Identity;
Establishment of Truth depends on destruction of Fals-
    hood continually,
On Circumcision, not on Virginity, O Reasoners of Al-
    bion!"

[THE DIVINE VISION]

"What is a Wife & what is a Harlot? What is a Church
    & What
Is a Theatre? are they Two & not One? can they Exist
    Separate?
Are not Religion & Politics the Same Thing? Brother-
    hood is Religion,
O Demonstrations of Reason Dividing Families in Cru-
    elty & Pride!"

[THE DAUGHTERS OF LOS]

And in the North Gate, in the West of the North, to-
    ward Beulah,
Cathedron's Looms are builded, and Los's Furnaces in
    the South.
A wondrous golden Building immense with ornaments
    sublime
Is bright Cathedron's golden Hall, its Courts, Towers &
    Pinnacles.

And one Daughter of Los sat at the fiery Reel, & an-
    other

Sat at the shining Loom with her Sisters attending
    round,
Terrible their distress, & their sorrow cannot be utter'd;
And another Daughter of Los sat at the Spinning Wheel,
Endless their labour, with bitter food, void of sleep;
Tho' hungry, they labour: they rouze themselves anxious
Hour after hour labouring at the whirling Wheel,
Many Wheels & as many lovely Daughters sit weeping.

Yet the intoxicating delight that they take in their work
Obliterates every other evil; none pities their tears,
Yet they regard not pity & they expect no one to pity,
For they labour for life & love regardless of any one
But the poor Spectres that they work for always, inces-
    santly.

They are mock'd by every one that passes by; they re-
    gard not,
They labour, & when their Wheels are broken by scorn
    & malice
They mend them sorrowing with many tears & afflic-
    tions.

Other Daughters Weave on the Cushion & Pillow Net-
    work fine
That Rahab & Tirzah may exist & live & breathe & love.
Ah, that it could be as the Daughters of Beulah wish!

Other Daughters of Los, labouring at Looms less fine,
Create the Silk-worm & the Spider & the Catterpiller
To assist in their most grievous work of pity & compas-
    sion;
And others Create the wooly Lamb & the downy Fowl
To assist in the work; the Lamb bleats, the Sea-fowl
    cries:

Men understand not the distress & the labour & sorrow
That in the Interior Worlds is carried on in fear & trem-
bling,
Weaving the shudd'ring fears & loves of Albion's Fam-
ilies.
Thunderous rage the Spindles of iron, & the iron Distaff
Maddens in the fury of their hands, weaving in bitter
tears
The Veil of Goats-hair & Purple & Scarlet & fine twined
Linen.

[A VISION OF MARY AND JOSEPH]

". . . Behold, in the Visions of Elohim Jehovah, behold
Joseph & Mary
And be comforted, O Jerusalem, in the Visions of Je-
hovah Elohim."

She looked & saw Joseph the Carpenter in Nazareth &
Mary
His espoused Wife. And Mary said, "If thou put me
away from thee
Dost thou not murder me?" Joseph spoke in anger &
fury, "Should I
Marry a Harlot & an Adulteress?" Mary answer'd, "Art
thou more pure
Than thy Maker who forgiveth Sins & calls again Her
that is Lost?
Tho' She hates, he calls her again in love. I love my dear
Joseph,
But he driveth me away from his presence; yet I hear
the voice of God
In the voice of my Husband: tho' he is angry for a mo-
ment, he will not

Utterly cast me away; if I were pure, never could I
taste the sweets

Of the Forgiveness of Sins; if I were holy, I never could
behold the tears

Of love of him who loves me in the midst of his anger in
furnace of fire."

"Ah my Mary!" said Joseph, weeping over & embracing
her closely in

His arms: "Doth he forgive Jerusalem. & not exact Purity
from her who is

Polluted? I heard his voice in my sleep & his Angel in
my dream,

Saying, 'Doth Jehovah Forgive a Debt only on condi-
tion that it shall

Be Payed? Doth he Forgive Pollution only on conditions
of Purity?

That Debt is not Forgiven! That Pollution is not For-
given!

Such is the Forgiveness of the Gods, the Moral Virtues
of the

Heathen whose tender Mercies are Cruelty. But Jeho-
vah's Salvation

Is without Money & without Price, in the Continual For-
giveness of Sins,

In the Perpetual Mutual Sacrifice in Great Eternity; for
behold,

There is none that liveth & Sinneth not! And this is the
Covenant

Of Jehovah: If you Forgive one-another, so shall Jeho-
vah Forgive You,

That He Himself may Dwell among You. Fear not then
to take

To thee Mary thy Wife, for she is with Child by the
Holy Ghost.'"

Then Mary burst forth into a Song: she flowed like a
River of

Many Streams in the arms of Joseph & gave forth her
tears of joy

Like many waters, and Emanating into gardens & pal-
aces upon

Euphrates, & to forests & floods & animals wild & tame
from

Gihon to Hiddekel, & to corn fields & villages & inhabit-
ants

Upon Pison & Arnon & Jordan. And I heard the voice
among

The Reapers, Saying, "Am I Jerusalem the lost Adulter-
ess? or am I

Babylon come up to Jerusalem?" And another voice an-
swer'd, Saying,

"Does the voice of my Lord call me again? am I pure
thro' his Mercy

And Pity? Am I become lovely as a Virgin in his sight,
who am

Indeed a Harlot drunken with the Sacrifice of Idols?
does he

Call her pure as he did in the days of her Infancy when
She

Was cast out to the loathing of her person? The Chal-
dean took

Me from my Cradle. The Amalekite stole me away upon
his Camels

Before I had ever beheld with love the Face of Jehovah,
or known

That there was a God of Mercy. O Mercy, O Divine
Humanity!

O Forgiveness & Pity & Compassion! If I were Pure I
should never

Have known Thee: If I were Unpolluted I should never have
Glorified thy Holiness or rejoiced in thy great Salvation."

Mary leaned her side against Jerusalem: Jerusalem recieved
The Infant into her hands in the Visions of Jehovah. Times passed on.
Jerusalem fainted over the Cross & Sepulcher. She heard the voice:
"Wilt thou make Rome thy Patriarch Druid & the Kings of Europe his
Horsemen? Man in the Resurrection changes his Sexual Garments at Will.
Every Harlot was once a Virgin: every Criminal an Infant Love. . . .

[THE DESOLATE WORLD]

The inhabitants are sick to death: they labour to divide into Days
And Nights the uncertain Periods, and into Weeks & Months. In vain
They send the Dove & Raven & in vain the Serpent over the mountains
And in vain the Eagle & Lion over the four-fold wilderness:
They return not, but generate in rocky places desolate:
They return not, but build a habitation separate from Man.
The Sun forgets his course like a drunken man; he hesitates

Upon the Cheselden hills, thinking to sleep on the Sev-
ern.

In vain: he is hurried afar into an unknown Night:

He bleeds in torrents of blood as he rolls thro' heaven
above.

He chokes up the paths of the sky; the Moon is leprous
as snow,

Trembling & descending down, seeking to rest on high
Mona,

Scattering her leprous snows in flakes of disease over
Albion.

The Stars flee remote; the heaven is iron, the earth is
sulphur,

And all the mountains & hills shrink up like a withering
gourd

As the Senses of Men shrink together under the Knife of
flint

In the hands of Albion's Daughters among the Druid
Temples, . . .

And the Twelve Daughters of Albion united in Rahab
& Tirzah,

A Double Female; and they drew out from the Rocky
Stones

Fibres of Life to Weave, for every Female is a Golden
Loom,

The Rocks are opake hardnesses covering all Vegetated
things;

And as they Wove & Cut from the Looms, in various
divisions

Stretching over Europe & Asia from Ireland to Japan,

They divided into many lovely Daughters, to be counter-
parts

To those they Wove; for when they Wove a Male, they
divided

Into a Female to the Woven Male: in opake hardness

They cut the Fibres from the Rocks: groaning in pain
    they Weave,
Calling the Rocks Atomic Origins of Existence, denying
    Eternity
By the Atheistical Epicurean Philosophy of Albion's
    Tree.
Such are the Feminine & Masculine when separated
    from Man.
They call the Rocks Parents of Men, & adore the frown-
    ing Chaos,
Dancing around in howling pain, clothed in the bloody
    Veil,
Hiding Albion's Sons within the Veil, closing Jerusalem's
Sons without, to feed with their Souls the Spectres of
    Albion,
Ashamed to give Love openly to the piteous & merciful
    Man,
Counting him an imbecile mockery, but the Warrior
They adore & his revenge cherish with the blood of the
    Innocent.

[THE SPECTRE'S THREATS]

"O thou poor Human Form!" said she. "O thou poor
    child of woe!
Why wilt thou wander away from Tirzah? why me com-
    pel to bind thee?
If thou dost go away from me I shall consume upon
    these Rocks.
These fibres of thine eyes that used to beam in distant
    heavens
Away from me, I have bound down with a hot iron.
These nostrils that expanded with delight in morning
    skies

I have bent downward with lead melted in my roaring
    furnaces
Of affliction, of love, of sweet despair, of torment unen-
    durable.
My soul is seven furnaces; incessant roars the bellows
Upon my terribly flaming heart, the molten metal runs
In channels thro' my fiery limbs. O love, O pity, O fear,
O pain! O the pangs, the bitter pangs of love forsaken!"

[THE WARRIOR'S LAMENT]

". . . . Once Man was occupied in intellectual pleas-
    ures & energies,
But now my Soul is harrow'd with grief & fear & love &
    desire,
And now I hate & now I love, & Intellect is no more.
There is no time for any thing but the torments of love
    & desire. . . ."

[ALL ARE MEN IN ETERNITY]

For all are Men in Eternity, Rivers, Mountains, Cities,
    Villages,
All are Human, & when you enter into their Bosoms you
    walk
In Heavens & Earths, as in your own Bosom you bear
    your Heaven
And Earth & all you behold; tho' it appears Without,
    it is Within,
In your Imagination, of which this World of Mortality is
    but a Shadow.

[MEN AND STATES]

As the Pilgrim passes while the Country permanent re-
    mains,
So Men pass on, but States remain permanent for ever.

[SPECTRE AND IMAGINATION]

The Spectre is the Reasoning Power in Man, & when
    separated
From Imagination and closing itself as in steel in a Ratio
Of the Things of Memory, It thence frames Laws & Mo-
    ralities
To destroy Imagination, the Divine Body, by Martyr-
    doms & Wars.

Teach me, O Holy Spirit, the Testimony of Jesus! let me
Comprehend wonderous things out of the Divine Law!
I behold Babylon in the opening Streets of London. I
    behold
Jerusalem in ruins wandering about from house to house.
This I behold: the shudderings of death attend my steps.
I walk up and down in Six Thousand Years: their Events
    are present before me
To tell how Los in grief & anger, whirling round his
    Hammer on high,
Drave the Sons & Daughters of Albion from their an-
    cient mountains.

[LOS'S HAMMER]

The blow of his Hammer is Justice, the swing of his
    Hammer Mercy,
The force of Los's Hammer is eternal Forgiveness. . . .

[THE ETERNAL CIRCLE]

And where Luther ends Adam begins the Eternal Circle
To awake Prisoners of Death, to bring Albion again
With Luvah into light eternal in his eternal day.

But now the Starry Heavens are fled from the mighty
    limbs of Albion.

[WHAT GOD IS]

". . . . It is easier to forgive an Enemy than to forgive a
    Friend.
The man who permits you to injure him deserves your
    vengeance:
He also will recieve it; go Spectre! obey my most secret
    desire
Which thou knowest without my speaking. Go to these
    Fiends of Righteousness,
Tell them to obey their Humanities & not pretend Holi-
    ness
When they are murderers as far as my Hammer & Anvil
    permit.
Go, tell them that the Worship of God is honouring his
    gifts

In other men & loving the greatest men best, each according

To his Genius which is the Holy Ghost in Man; there is no other

God than that God who is the intellectual fountain of Humanity.

He who envies or calumniates, which is murder & cruelty,

Murders the Holy-one. Go, tell them this, & overthrow their cup,

Their bread, their altar-table, their incense & their oath,

Their marriage & their baptism, their burial & consecration.

I have tried to make friends by corporeal gifts but have only

Made enemies. I never made friends but by spiritual gifts,

By severe contentions of friendship & the burning fire of thought.

He who would see the Divinity must see him in his Children,

One first, in friendship & love, then a Divine Family, & in the midst

Jesus will appear; so he who wishes to see a Vision, a perfect Whole,

Must see it in its Minute Particulars, Organized, & not as thou,

O Fiend of Righteousness, pretendest; thine is a Disorganized

And snowy cloud, brooder of tempests & destructive War.

You smile with pomp & rigor, you talk of benevolence & virtue;

I act with benevolence & Virtue & get murder'd time after time.

You accumulate Particulars & murder by analyzing, that
you

May take the aggregate, & you call the aggregate Moral
Law,

And you call that swell'd & bloated Form a Minute
Particular;

But General Forms have their vitality in Particulars, &
every

Particular is a Man, a Divine Member of the Divine
Jesus. . . .

"I care not whether a Man is Good or Evil; all that I
care

Is whether he is a Wise Man or a Fool. Go, put off
Holiness

And put on Intellect, or my thund'rous Hammer shall
drive thee

To wrath which thou condemnest, till thou obey my
voice."

[THE BREATH DIVINE]

The Breath Divine went forth upon the morning hills.
Albion mov'd

Upon the Rock, he open'd his eyelids in pain, in pain he
mov'd

His stony members, he saw England. Ah! shall the Dead
live again?

The Breath Divine went forth over the morning hills.
Albion rose

In anger, the wrath of God breaking, bright flaming on
all sides around

His awful limbs; into the Heavens he walked, clothed in
flames,

Loud thund'ring, with broad flashes of flaming lightning
    & pillars

Of fire, speaking the Words of Eternity in Human
    Forms, in direful

Revolutions of Action & Passion, thro' the Four Ele-
    ments on all sides

Surrounding his awful Members. Thou seest the Sun in
    heavy clouds

Struggling to rise above the Mountains; in his burning
    hand

He takes his Bow, then chooses out his arrows of flaming
    gold;

Murmuring the Bowstring breathes with ardor! clouds
    roll round the

Horns of the wide Bow, loud sounding winds sport on
    the mountain brows,

Compelling Urizen to his Furrow & Tharmas to his
    Sheepfold

And Luvah to his Loom. Urthona he beheld, mighty
    labouring at

His Anvil, in the Great Spectre Los unwearied labour-
    ing & weeping:

Therefore the Sons of Eden praise Urthona's Spectre in
    songs,

Because he kept the Divine Vision in time of trouble.

[JESUS AND ALBION]

Then Jesus appeared standing by Albion as the Good
    Shepherd

By the lost Sheep that he hath found, & Albion knew
    that it

Was the Lord, the Universal Humanity; & Albion saw
    his Form

A Man, & they conversed as Man with Man in Ages of
    Eternity.
And the Divine Appearance was the likeness & simili-
    tude of Los.

Albion said: "O Lord, what can I do? my Selfhood cruel
Marches against thee, deceitful, from Sinai & from
    Edom
In to the Wilderness of Judah, to meet thee in his pride.
I behold the Visions of my deadly Sleep of Six Thousand
    Years
Dazling around thy skirts like a Serpent of precious
    stones & gold.
I know it is my Self, O my Divine Creator & Redeemer."

Jesus replied: "Fear not Albion: unless I die thou canst
    not live;
But if I die I shall arise again & thou with me.
This is Friendship & Brotherhood: without it Man Is
    Not."

So Jesus spoke: the Covering Cherub coming on in
    darkness
Overshadow'd them, & Jesus said: "Thus do Men in
    Eternity
One for another to put off, by forgiveness, every sin."

Albion reply'd: "Cannot Man exist without Mysterious
Offering of Self for Another? is this Friendship &
    Brotherhood?
I see thee in the likeness & similitude of Los my Friend."

Jesus said: "Wouldest thou love one who never died
For thee, or ever die for one who had not died for thee?
And if God dieth not for Man & giveth not himself

Eternally for Man, Man could not exist; for Man is Love
As God is Love: every kindness to another is a little
  Death
In the Divine Image, nor can Man exist but by Brother-
  hood."

So saying the Cloud overshadowing divided them
  asunder.
Albion stood in terror, not for himself but for his Friend
Divine; & Self was lost in the contemplation of faith
And wonder at the Divine Mercy & at Los's sublime
  honour.

"Do I sleep amidst danger to Friends? O my Cities &
  Counties,
Do you sleep? rouze up, rouze up! Eternal Death is
  abroad!"

So Albion spoke & threw himself into the Furnaces of
  affliction.
All was a Vision, all a Dream: the Furnaces became
Fountains of Living Waters flowing from the Humanity
  Divine.
And all the Cities of Albion rose from their Slumbers,
  and All
The Sons·& Daughters of Albion on soft clouds, waking
  from Sleep.
Soon all around remote the Heavens burnt with flaming
  fires,
And Urizen & Luvah & Tharmas & Urthona arose into
Albion's Bosom. Then Albion stood before Jesus in the
  Clouds
Of Heaven, Fourfold among the Visions of God in
  Eternity.

VII.

ON ART,
MONEY,
AND THE AGE

From THE LAOCOÖN GROUP

(1820)

If Morality was Christianity, Socrates was the Saviour.

Art Degraded, Imagination Denied, War Governed the Nations.

Spiritual War: Israel deliver'd from Egypt, is Art deliver'd from Nature & Imitation.

A Poet, a Painter, a Musician, an Architect: the Man
Or Woman who is not one of these is not a Christian.
You must leave Fathers & Mothers & Houses & Lands if they stand in the way of Art.
Prayer is the Study of Art.
Praise is the Practise of Art.
Fasting &c., all relate to Art.
The outward Ceremony is Antichrist.
The Eternal Body of Man is The Imagination, that is, God himself
The Divine Body } Jesus: we are his Members.
It manifests itself in his Works of Art (In Eternity All is Vision).
The True Christian Charity not dependent on Money (the life's blood of Poor Families), that is, on Caesar or Empire or Natural Religion: Money, which is The Great

Satan or Reason, the Root of Good & Evil In The Accusation of Sin.

Good & Evil are Riches & Poverty, a Tree of Misery, propagating Generation & Death.

Where any view of Money exists, Art cannot be carried on, but War only (Read Matthew, c. x: 9 & 10 v.) by pretences to the Two Impossibilities, Chastity & Abstinence, Gods of the Heathen.

He repented that he had made Adam (of the Female, the Adamah) & it grieved him at his heart.
What can be Created Can be Destroyed.
Adam is only The Natural Man & not the Soul or Imagination.

Hebrew Art is called Sin by the Deist Science.

All that we See is Vision, from Generated Organs gone as soon as come, Permanent in The Imagination, Consider'd as Nothing by the Natural Man.

Art can never exist without Naked Beauty displayed.

The Gods of Greece & Egypt were Mathematical Diagrams—See Plato's Works.

Divine Union Deriding, And Denying Immediate Communion with God, The Spoilers say, "Where are his Works That he did in the Wilderness? Lo, what are these? Whence came they?" These are not the Works Of Egypt nor Babylon, Whose Gods are the Powers Of this World, Goddess Nature, Who first spoil & then destroy Imaginative Art; for their Glory is War and Dominion.

Empire against Art—
Satan's Wife, The Goddess Nature, is War & Misery,
& Heroism a Miser.
For every Pleasure Money Is Useless.

There are States in which all Visionary Men are accounted Mad Men; such are Greece & Rome: Such is Empire or Tax—See Luke, Ch. 2, v. 1.

Without Unceasing Practise nothing can be done. Practise is Art. If you leave off you are Lost.

Jesus & his Apostles & Disciples were all Artists. Their Works were destroy'd by the Seven Angels of the Seven Churches in Asia, Antichrist Science.

The Old & New Testaments are the Great Code of Art.

Art is the Tree of Life. God is Jesus.

Science is the Tree of Death.

The Whole Business of Man Is The Arts, & All Things Common. No Secresy in Art.

The unproductive Man is not a Christian, much less the Destroyer.

Christianity is Art & not Money. Money is its Curse.

What we call Antique Gems are the Gems of Aaron's Breast Plate.

Is not every Vice possible to Man described in the
Bible openly?

All is not Sin that Satan calls so: all the Loves &
Graces of Eternity.

From A DESCRIPTIVE CATALOGUE

OF PICTURES, POETICAL AND HISTORI-
CAL INVENTIONS, PAINTED BY WILLIAM
BLAKE IN WATER COLOURS, BEING THE
ANCIENT METHOD OF FRESCO PAINTING
RESTORED: AND DRAWINGS, FOR PUBLIC
INSPECTION, AND FOR SALE BY PRIVATE
CONTRACT

(1809)

CONDITIONS OF SALE

I. *One third of the price to be paid at the time of Pur-
chase, and the remainder on Delivery.*
II. *The Pictures and Drawings to remain in the Exhibi-
tion till its close, which will be on the 29th of
September 1809; and the Picture of the Canterbury
Pilgrims, which is to be engraved, will be Sold only
on condition of its remaining in the Artist's hands
twelve months, when it will be delivered to the
Buyer.*

PREFACE

The eye that can prefer the Colouring of Titian and
Rubens to that of Michael Angelo and Rafael, ought to
be modest and to doubt its own powers. Connoisseurs
talk as if Rafael and Michael Angelo had never seen
the colouring of Titian or Correggio: They ought to
know that Correggio was born two years before Michael
Angelo, and Titian but four years after. Both Rafael and

Michael Angelo knew the Venetian, and contemned and rejected all he did with the utmost disdain, as that which is fabricated for the purpose to destroy art.

Mr. B. appeals to the Public, from the judgment of those narrow blinking eyes, that have too long governed art in a dark corner. The eyes of stupid cunning never will be pleased with the work any more than with the look of self-devoting genius. The quarrel of the Florentine with the Venetian is not because he does not understand Drawing, but because he does not understand Colouring. How should he, he who does not know how to draw a hand or a foot, know how to colour it?

Colouring does not depend on where the Colours are put, but on where the lights and darks are put, and all depends on Form or Outline, on where that is put; where that is wrong, the Colouring never can be right; and it is always wrong in Titian and Correggio, Rubens and Rembrandt. Till we get rid of Titian and Correggio, Rubens and Rembrandt, We never shall equal Rafael and Albert Durer, Michael Angelo, and Julio Romano.

*   *   *   *

NUMBER III.

Sir Jeffery Chaucer and the nine and twenty Pilgrims on their journey to Canterbury.

The time chosen is early morning, before sunrise, when the jolly company are just quitting the Tabarde Inn. The Knight and Squire with the Squire's Yeoman lead the Procession; next follow the youthful Abbess, her nun and three priests; her greyhounds attend her—

> Of small hounds had she, that she fed
> With roast flesh, milk and wastel bread.

Next follow the Friar and Monk; then the Tapiser, the Pardoner, and the Somner and Manciple. After these "Our Host," who occupies the center of the cavalcade, directs them to the Knight as the person who would be likely to commence their task of each telling a tale in their order. After the Host follows the Shipman, the Haberdasher, the Dyer, the Franklin, the Physician, the Plowman, the Lawyer, the poor Parson, the Merchant, the Wife of Bath, the Miller, the Cook, the Oxford Scholar, Chaucer himself, and the Reeve comes as Chaucer has described:

And ever he rode hinderest of the rout.

These last are issuing from the gateway of the Inn; the Cook and the Wife of Bath are both taking their morning's draft of comfort. Spectators stand at the gateway of the Inn, and are composed of an old Man, a Woman, and Children.

The Landscape is an eastward view of the country, from the Tabarde Inn, in Southwark, as it may be supposed to have appeared in Chaucer's time, interspersed with cottages and villages; the first beams of the Sun are seen above the horizon; some buildings and spires indicate the situation of the great City; the Inn is a gothic building, which Thynne in his Glossary says was the lodging of the Abbot of Hyde, by Winchester. On the Inn is inscribed its title, and a proper advantage is taken of this circumstance to describe the subject of the Picture. The words written over the gateway of the Inn are as follow: "The Tabarde Inn, by Henry Baillie, the lodgynge-house for Pilgrims, who journey to Saint Thomas's Shrine at Canterbury."

The characters of Chaucer's Pilgrims are the characters which compose all ages and nations: as one age falls, another rises, different to mortal sight, but to immortals only the same; for we see the same characters repeated again and again, in animals, vegetables, minerals, and in men; nothing new occurs in identical existence; Accident ever varies, Substance can never suffer change nor decay.

Of Chaucer's characters, as described in his Canterbury Tales, some of the names or titles are altered by time, but the characters themselves for ever remain unaltered, and consequently they are the physiognomies or lineaments of universal human life, beyond which Nature never steps. Names alter, things never alter. I have known multitudes of those who would have been monks in the age of monkery, who in this deistical age are deists. As Newton numbered the stars, and as Linneus numbered the plants, so Chaucer numbered the classes of men.

The Painter has consequently varied the heads and forms of his personages into all Nature's varieties; the Horses he has also varied to accord to their Riders; the costume is correct according to authentic monuments.

The Knight and Squire with the Squire's Yeoman lead the procession, as Chaucer has also placed them first in his prologue. The Knight is a true Hero, a good, great, and wise man; his whole length portrait on horseback, as written by Chaucer, cannot be surpassed. He has spent his life in the field; has ever been a conqueror, and is that species of character which in every age stands as the guardian of man against the oppressor. His son is like him with the germ of perhaps greater perfection still, as he blends literature and the arts with his warlike studies. Their dress and their horses are of the first rate, without ostentation, and with all the true grandeur that unaffected simplicity when in high rank always displays.

The Squire's Yeoman is also a great character, a man perfectly knowing in his profession:

And in his hand he bare a mighty bow.

Chaucer describes here a mighty man; one who in war is the worthy attendant on noble heroes.

The Prioress follows these with her female chaplain:

Another Nonne also with her had she,
That was her Chaplaine, and Priests three.

This Lady is described also as of the first rank, rich and honoured. She has certain peculiarities and little delicate affectations, not unbecoming in her, being accompanied with what is truly grand and really polite; her person and face Chaucer has described with minuteness; it is very elegant, and was the beauty of our ancestors, till after Elizabeth's time, when voluptuousness and folly began to be accounted beautiful.

Her companion and her three priests were no doubt all perfectly delineated in those parts of Chaucer's work which are now lost; we ought to suppose them suitable attendants on rank and fashion.

The Monk follows these with the Friar. The Painter has also grouped with these the Pardoner and the Sompnour and the Manciple, and has here also introduced one of the rich citizens of London: Characters likely to ride in company, all being above the common rank in life or attendants on those who were so.

For the Monk is described by Chaucer as a man of the first rank in society, noble, rich, and expensively attended; he is a leader of the age, with certain humorous accompaniments in his character, that do not degrade, but render him an object of dignified mirth, but also with other accompaniments not so respectable.

The Friar is a character also of a mixed kind:

> A friar there was, a wanton and a merry.

but in his office he is said to be a "full solemn man": eloquent, amorous, witty, and satyrical; young, handsome, and rich; he is a complete rogue, with constitutional gaiety enough to make him a master of all the pleasures of the world.

> His neck was white as the flour de lis,
> Thereto strong he was as a champioun.

It is necessary here to speak of Chaucer's own character, that I may set certain mistaken critics right in their conception of the humour and fun that occurs on the journey. Chaucer is himself the great poetical observer of men, who in every age is born to record and eternize its acts. This he does as a master, as a father, and superior, who looks down on their little follies from the Emperor to the Miller; sometimes with severity, oftener with joke and sport.

Accordingly Chaucer has made his Monk a great tragedian, one who studied poetical art. So much so, that the generous Knight is, in the compassionate dictates of his soul, compelled to cry out:

> Ho, quoth the Knyght,—good Sir, no more of this;
> That ye have said is right ynough I wis;
> And mokell more, for little heaviness
> Is right enough for much folk, as I guesse.
> I say, for me, it is a great disease,
> Whereas men have been in wealth and ease,
> To heare of their sudden fall, alas,
> And the contrary is joy and solas.

The Monk's definition of tragedy in the proem to his tale
is worth repeating:

> Tragedie is to tell a certain story,
> As old books us maken memory,
> Of hem that stood in great prosperity,
> And be fallen out of high degree,
> Into miserie, and ended wretchedly.

Though a man of luxury, pride and pleasure, he is a
master of art and learning, though affecting to despise it.
Those who can think that the proud Huntsman and
Noble Housekeeper, Chaucer's Monk, is intended for a
buffoon or a burlesque character, know little of Chaucer.

For the Host who follows this group, and holds the
center of the cavalcade, is a first rate character, and his
jokes are no trifles; they are always, though uttered with
audacity, and equally free with the Lord and the
Peasant, they are always substantially and weightily ex-
pressive of knowledge and experience; Henry Baillie,
the keeper of the greatest Inn of the greatest City, for
such was the Tabarde Inn in Southwark, near London:
our Host was also a leader of the age.

By way of illustration, I instance Shakspeare's
Witches in Macbeth. Those who dress them for the
stage, consider them as wretched old women, and not as
Shakspeare intended, the Goddesses of Destiny; this
shews how Chaucer has been misunderstood in his sub-
lime work. Shakspeare's Fairies also are the rulers of
the vegetable world, and so are Chaucer's; let them be
so considered, and then the poet will be understood,
and not else.

But I have omitted to speak of a very prominent char-
acter, the Pardoner, the Age's Knave, who always com-
mands and domineers over the high and low vulgar.
This man is sent in every age for a rod and scourge, and

for a blight, for a trial of men, to divide the classes of men; he is in the most holy sanctuary, and he is suffered by Providence for wise ends, and has also his great use, and his grand leading destiny.

His companion, the Sompnour, is also a Devil of the first magnitude, grand, terrific, rich and honoured in the rank of which he holds the destiny. The uses to Society are perhaps equal of the Devil and of the Angel, their sublimity, who can dispute.

> In daunger had he at his own gise,
> The young girls of his diocese,
> And he knew well their counsel, &c.

The principal figure in the next groupe is the Good Parson; an Apostle, a real Messenger of Heaven, sent in every age for its light and its warmth. This man is beloved and venerated by all, and neglected by all; He serves all, and is served by none; he is, according to Christ's definition, the greatest of his age. Yet he is a Poor Parson of a town. Read Chaucer's description of the Good Parson, and bow the head and the knee to him, who, in every age, sends us such a burning and a shining light. Search, O ye rich and powerful, for these men and obey their counsel, then shall the golden age return: But alas! you will not easily distinguish him from the Friar or the Pardoner; they, also, are "full solemn men", and their counsel you will continue to follow.

I have placed by his side the Sergeant at Lawe, who appears delighted to ride in his company, and between him and his brother, the Plowman; as I wish men of Law would always ride with them, and take their counsel, especially in all difficult points. Chaucer's Lawyer is a character of great venerableness, a Judge, and a real master of the jurisprudence of his age.

The Doctor of Physic is in this groupe, and the Franklin, the voluptuous country gentleman, contrasted with the Physician, and on his other hand, with two Citizens of London. Chaucer's characters live age after age. Every age is a Canterbury Pilgrimage; we all pass on, each sustaining one or other of these characters; nor can a child be born, who is not one of these characters of Chaucer. The Doctor of Physic is described as the first of his profession; perfect, learned, completely Master and Doctor in his art. Thus the reader will observe, that Chaucer makes every one of his characters perfect in his kind; every one is an Antique Statue; the image of a class, and not of an imperfect individual.

This groupe also would furnish substantial matter, on which volumes might be written. The Franklin is one who keeps open table, who is the genius of eating and drinking, the Bacchus; as the Doctor of Physic is the Esculapius, the Host is the Silenus, the Squire is the Apollo, the Miller is the Hercules, &c. Chaucer's characters are a description of the eternal Principles that exist in all ages. The Franklin is voluptuousness itself, most nobly pourtrayed:

It snewed in his house of meat and drink.

The Plowman is simplicity itself, with wisdom and strength for its stamina. Chaucer has divided the ancient character of Hercules between his Miller and his Plowman. Benevolence is the plowman's great characteristic; he is thin with excessive labour, and not with old age, as some have supposed:

He would thresh, and thereto dike and delve
For Christe's sake, for every poore wight,
Withouten hire, if it lay in his might.

Visions of these eternal principles or characters of human life appear to poets, in all ages; the Grecian gods were the ancient Cherubim of Phoenicia; but the Greeks, and since them the Moderns, have neglected to subdue the gods of Priam. These gods are visions of the eternal attributes, or divine names, which, when erected into gods, become destructive to humanity. They ought to be the servants, and not the masters of man, or of society. They ought to be made to sacrifice to Man, and not man compelled to sacrifice to them; for when separated from man or humanity, who is Jesus the Saviour, the vine of eternity, they are thieves and rebels, they are destroyers.

The Plowman of Chaucer is Hercules in his supreme eternal state, divested of his spectrous shadow; which is the Miller, a terrible fellow, such as exists in all times and places for the trial of men, to astonish every neighbourhood with brutal strength and courage, to get rich and powerful to curb the pride of Man.

The Reeve and the Manciple are two characters of the most consummate worldly wisdom. The Shipman, or Sailor, is a similar genius of Ulyssean art; but with the highest courage superadded.

The Citizens and their Cook are each leaders of a class. Chaucer has been somehow made to number four citizens, which would make his whole company, himself included, thirty-one. But he says there was but nine and twenty in his company:

Full nine and twenty in a company.

The Webbe, or Weaver, and the Tapiser, or Tapestry Weaver, appear to me to be the same person; but this is only an opinion, for full nine and twenty may signify one more or less. But I dare say that Chaucer wrote "A Webbe Dyer", that is, a Cloth Dyer:

A Webbe Dyer, and a Tapiser.

The Merchant cannot be one of the Three Citizens, as his dress is different, and his character is more marked, whereas Chaucer says of his rich citizens:

All were yclothed in o liverie.

The characters of Women Chaucer has divided into two classes, the Lady Prioress and the Wife of Bath. Are not these leaders of the ages of men? The lady prioress, in some ages, predominates; and in some the wife of Bath, in whose character Chaucer has been equally minute and exact, because she is also a scourge and a blight. I shall say no more of her, nor expose what Chaucer has left hidden; let the young reader study what he has said of her: it is useful as a scare-crow. There are of such characters born too many for the peace of the world.

I come at length to the Clerk of Oxenford. This character varies from that of Chaucer, as the contemplative philosopher varies from the poetical genius. There are always these two classes of learned sages, the poetical and the philosophical. The painter has put them side by side, as if the youthful clerk had put himself under the tuition of the mature poet. Let the Philosopher always be the servant and scholar of inspiration and all will be happy.

Such are the characters that compose this Picture, which was painted in self-defence against the insolent and envious imputation of unfitness for finished and scientific art; and this imputation, most artfully and industriously endeavoured to be propagated among the public by ignorant hirelings. The painter courts comparison with his competitors, who, having received fourteen hundred guineas and more, from the profits of his designs in that well-known work, Designs for Blair's Grave, have left him to shift for himself, while others, more obedient to an employer's opinions and directions, are employed, at a great expence, to produce works, in succession to his, by which they acquired public patronage. This has hitherto been his lot—to get patronage for others and then to be left and neglected, and his work, which gained that patronage, cried down as eccentricity and madness; as unfinished and neglected by the artist's violent temper; he is sure the works now exhibited will give the lie to such aspersions.

Those who say that men are led by interest are knaves. A knavish character will often say, "of what interest is it to me to do so and so?" I answer, "of none at all, but the contrary, as you well know. It is of malice and envy that you have done this; hence I am aware of you, because I know that you act, not from interest, but from malice, even to your own destruction." It is therefore become a duty which Mr. B. owes to the Public, who have always recognized him, and patronized him, however hidden by artifices, that he should not suffer such things to be done, or be hindered from the public Exhibition of his finished productions by any calumnies in future.

The character and expression in this picture could never have been produced with Rubens's light and shadow, or with Rembrandt's, or anything Venetian or Flemish. The Venetian and Flemish practice is broken lines, broken masses, and broken colours. Mr. B.'s practice is unbroken lines, unbroken masses, and unbroken colours. Their art is to lose form; his art is to find form, and to keep it. His arts are opposite to theirs in all things.

As there is a class of men whose whole delight is the destruction of men, so there is a class of artist, whose whole art and science is fabricated for the purpose of destroying art. Who these are is soon known: "by their works ye shall know them." All who endeavour to raise up a style against Rafael, Mich. Angelo, and the Antique; those who separate Painting from Drawing; who look if a picture is well Drawn, and, if it is, immediately cry out that it cannot be well Coloured,—those are the men.

But to shew the stupidity of this class of men nothing need be done but to examine my rival's prospectus.

The two first characters in Chaucer, the Knight and the Squire, he has put among his rabble; and indeed his prospectus calls the Squire the fop of Chaucer's age. Now hear Chaucer:

> Of his Stature, he was of even length,
> And wonderly deliver, and of great strength;
> And he had be sometime in Chivauchy,
> In Flanders, in Artois, and in Picardy,
> And borne him well, as of so litele space.

Was this a fop?

> Well could he sit a horse, and faire ride,
> He could songs make, and eke well indite
> Just, and eke dance, pourtray, and well write.

Was this a fop?

> Curteis he was, and meek, and serviceable;
> And kerft before his fader at the table.

Was this a fop?

It is the same with all his characters; he has done all by chance, or perhaps his fortune,—money, money. According to his prospectus he has Three Monks; these he cannot find in Chaucer, who has only One Monk, and that no vulgar character, as he has endeavoured to make him. When men cannot read they should not pretend to paint. To be sure Chaucer is a little difficult to him who has only blundered over novels, and catchpenny trifles of booksellers. Yet a little pains ought to be taken even by the ignorant and weak. He has put The Reeve, a vulgar fellow, between his Knight and Squire, as if he was resolved to go contrary in every thing to Chaucer, who says of the Reeve:

> And ever he rode hinderest of the rout.

In this manner he has jumbled his dumb dollies together and is praised by his equals for it; for both himself and his friend are equally masters of Chaucer's language. They both think that the Wife of Bath is a young, beautiful, blooming damsel, and H—— says, that she is the Fair Wife of Bath, and that the Spring appears in her Cheeks. Now hear what Chaucer has made her say of herself, who is no modest one:

> But Lord when it remembereth me
> Upon my youth and on my jollity
> It tickleth me about the heart root,
> Unto this day it doth my heart boot,
> That I have had my world as in my time;
> But age, alas, that all will envenime
> Hath me bireft my beauty and my pith
> Let go; farewell: the Devil go therewith,
> The flower is gone; there is no more to tell.
> The bran, as best I can, I now mote sell;
> And yet to be right merry will I fond,—
> Now forth to tell of my fourth husband.

She has had four husbands, a fit subject for this painter; yet the painter ought to be very much offended with his friend H——, who has called his "a common scene", and "very ordinary forms", which is the truest part of all, for it is so, and very wretchedly so indeed. What merit can there be in a picture of which such words are spoken with truth?

But the prospectus says that the Painter has represented Chaucer himself as a knave, who thrusts himself among honest people, to make game of and laugh at them; though I must do justice to the painter, and say that he has made him look more like a fool than a knave. But it appears in all the writings of Chaucer, and particularly in his Canterbury Tales, that he was very devout, and paid respect to true enthusiastic superstition. He has laughed at his knaves and fools, as I do now. But he has respected his True Pilgrims, who are a majority of his company, and are not thrown together in the random manner that Mr. S—— has done. Chaucer has no where called the Plowman old, worn out with age and labour, as the prospectus has represented him, and says that the picture has done so too. He is worn down with labour, but not with age. How spots of brown and yellow, smeared about at random, can be either young or old, I cannot see. It may be an old man; it may be a young one; it may be any thing that a prospectus pleases. But I know that where there are no lineaments there can be no character. And what connoisseurs call touch, I know by experience, must be the destruction of all character and expression, as it is of every lineament.

The scene of Mr. S——'s Picture is by Dulwich Hills, which was not the way to Canterbury; but perhaps the painter thought he would give them a ride round about, because they were a burlesque set of scare-crows, not worth any man's respect or care.

But the painter's thoughts being always upon gold, he has introduced a character that Chaucer has not; namely, a Goldsmith; for so the prospectus tells us. Why he introduced a Goldsmith, and what is the wit of it, the prospectus does not explain. But it takes care to mention the reserve and modesty of the Painter; this makes a good epigram enough:

> The fox, the owl, the spider, and the mole,
> By sweet reserve and modesty get fat.

But the prospectus tells us, that the painter has introduced a Sea Captain; Chaucer has a Ship-man, a Sailor, a Trading Master of a Vessel, called by courtesy Captain, as every master of a boat is; but this does not make him a sea Captain. Chaucer has purposely omitted such a personage, as it only exists in certain periods: it is the soldier by sea. He who would be a Soldier in inland nations is a sea captain in commercial nations.

All is misconceived, and its mis-execution is equal to its mis-conception. I have no objection to Rubens and Rembrandt being employed, or even to their living in a palace; but it shall not be at the expence of Rafael and Michael Angelo living in a cottage, and in contempt and derision. I have been scorned long enough by these fellows, who owe me all that they have; it shall be so no longer.

> I found them blind, I taught them how to see;
> And, now, they know me not, nor yet themselves.

NUMBER IV.

The Bard, from Gray.

On a rock, whose haughty brow
Frown'd o'er old Conway's foaming flood,
Robed in the sable garb of woe,
With haggard eyes the Poet stood;
Loose his beard, and hoary hair
Stream'd like a meteor to the troubled air.

Weave the warp, and weave the woof,
The winding sheet of Edward's race.

Weaving the winding sheet of Edward's race by means of sounds of spiritual music and its accompanying expressions of articulate speech is a bold, and daring, and most masterly conception, that the public have embraced and approved with avidity. Poetry consists in these conceptions; and shall Painting be confined to the sordid drudgery of fac-simile representations of merely mortal and perishing substances, and not be as poetry and music are, elevated into its own proper sphere of invention and visionary conception? No, it shall not be so! Painting, as well as poetry and music, exists and exults in immortal thoughts. If Mr. B.'s Canterbury Pilgrims had been done by any other power than that of the poetic visionary, it would have been just as dull as his adversary's.

The Spirits of the murdered bards assist in weaving the deadly woof:

With me in dreadful harmony they join
And weave, with bloody hands, the tissue of thy line.

The connoisseurs and artists who have made objections to Mr. B.'s mode of representing spirits with real bodies, would do well to consider that the Venus, the Minerva, the Jupiter, the Apollo, which they admire in Greek statues are all of them representations of spiritual existences, of Gods immortal, to the mortal perishing organ of sight; and yet they are embodied and organized in solid marble. Mr. B. requires the same latitude, and all is well. The Prophets describe what they saw in Vision as real and existing men, whom they saw with their imaginative and immortal organs; the Apostles the same; the clearer the organ the more distinct the object. A Spirit and a Vision are not, as the modern philosophy supposes, a cloudy vapour, or a nothing: they are organized and minutely articulated beyond all that the mortal and perishing nature can produce. He who does not imagine in stronger and better lineaments, and in stronger and better light than his perishing and mortal eye can see, does not imagine at all. The painter of this work asserts that all his imaginations appear to him infinitely more perfect and more minutely organized than any thing seen by his mortal eye. Spirits are organized men. Moderns wish to draw figures without lines, and with great and heavy shadows; are not shadows more unmeaning than lines, and more heavy? O who can doubt this!

NUMBER V.

The Ancient Britons

In the last Battle of King Arthur, only Three Britons escaped; these were the Strongest Man, the Beautifullest Man, and the Ugliest Man; these three

*marched through the field unsubdued, as Gods, and
the Sun of Britain set, but shall arise again with ten-
fold splendor when Arthur shall awake from sleep,
and resume his dominion over earth and ocean.*

The three general classes of men who are represented
by the most Beautiful, the most Strong, and the most
Ugly, could not be represented by any historical facts
but those of our own country, the Ancient Britons, with-
out violating costume. The Britons (say historians) were
naked civilized men, learned, studious, abstruse in
thought and contemplation; naked, simple, plain in their
acts and manners; wiser than after-ages. They were
overwhelmed by brutal arms, all but a small remnant;
Strength, Beauty, and Ugliness escaped the wreck, and
remain for ever unsubdued, age after age.

The British Antiquities are now in the Artist's hands;
all his visionary contemplations, relating to his own
country and its ancient glory, when it was, as it again
shall be, the source of learning and inspiration. Arthur
was a name for the constellation Arcturus or Boötes, the
keeper of the North Pole. And all the fables of Arthur
and his round table; of the warlike naked Britons; of
Merlin; of Arthur's conquest of the whole world; of his
death, or sleep, and promise to return again; of the
Druid monuments or temples; of the pavement of
Watling-street; of London stone; of the caverns in Corn-
wall, Wales, Derbyshire, and Scotland; of the Giants of
Ireland and Britain; of the elemental beings called by
us by the general name of Fairies; and of these three
who escaped, namely Beauty, Strength, and Ugliness.
Mr. B. has in his hands poems of the highest antiquity.
Adam was a Druid, and Noah; also Abraham was called
to succeed the Druidical age, which began to turn al-
legoric and mental signification into corporeal command,

whereby human sacrifice would have depopulated the earth. All these things are written in Eden. The artist is an inhabitant of that happy country; and if every thing goes on as it has begun, the world of vegetation and generation may expect to be opened again to Heaven, through Eden, as it was in the beginning.

The Strong Man represents the human sublime. The Beautiful Man represents the human pathetic, which was in the wars of Eden divided into male and female. The Ugly Man represents the human reason. They were originally one man, who was fourfold; he was self-divided, and his real humanity slain on the stems of generation, and the form of the fourth was like the Son of God. How he became divided is a subject of great sublimity and pathos. The Artist has written it under inspiration, and will, if God please, publish it; it is voluminous, and contains the ancient history of Britain, and the world of Satan and of Adam.

In the mean time he has painted this Picture, which supposes that in the reign of that British Prince, who lived in the fifth century, there were remains of those naked Heroes in the Welch Mountains; they are there now, Gray saw them in the person of his bard on Snowdon; there they dwell in naked simplicity; happy is he who can see and converse with them above the shadows of generation and death. The giant Albion, was Patriarch of the Atlantic; he is the Atlas of the Greeks, one of those the Greeks called Titans. The stories of Arthur are the acts of Albion, applied to a Prince of the fifth century, who conquered Europe, and held the Empire of the world in the dark age, which the Romans never again received. In this Picture, believing with Milton the ancient British History, Mr. B. has done as all the ancients did, and as all the moderns who are worthy of fame, given the historical fact in its poetical vigour so as it always happens, and not in that dull way that some Historians pretend, who, being weakly organized themselves, cannot see either miracle or prodigy; all is to them a dull round of probabilities and possibilities; but the history of all times and places is nothing else but improbabilities and impossibilities; what we should say was impossible if we did not see it always before our eyes.

The antiquities of every Nation under Heaven, is no less sacred than that of the Jews. They are the same thing, as Jacob Bryant and all antiquaries have proved. How other antiquities came to be neglected and disbelieved, while those of the Jews are collected and arranged, is an enquiry worthy both of the Antiquarian and the Divine. All had originally one language, and one religion: this was the religion of Jesus, the Everlasting Gospel. Antiquity preaches the Gospel of Jesus. The reasoning historian, turner and twister of causes and consequences, such as Hume, Gibbon, and Voltaire, cannot with all their artifice turn or twist one fact or disarrange self evident action and reality. Reasons and opinions concerning acts are not history. Acts themselves alone are history, and these are neither the exclusive property of Hume, Gibbon, nor Voltaire, Echard, Rapin, Plutarch, nor Herodotus. Tell me the Acts, O historian, and leave me to reason upon them as I please; away with your reasoning and your rubbish! All that is not action is not worth reading. Tell me the What; I do not want you to tell me the Why, and the How; I can find that out myself, as well as you can, and I will not be fooled by you into opinions, that you please to impose, to disbelieve what you think improbable or impossible. His opinions, who does not see spiritual agency, is not worth any man's reading; he who rejects a fact because it is improbable, must reject all History and retain doubts only.

It has been said to the Artist, "take the Apollo for the model of your beautiful Man, and the Hercules for your strong Man, and the Dancing Fawn for your Ugly Man." Now he comes to his trial. He knows that what he does is not inferior to the grandest Antiques. Superior they cannot be, for human power cannot go beyond either what he does, or what they have done; it is the gift of God, it is inspiration and vision. He had resolved to emulate those precious remains of antiquity; he has done so and the result you behold; his ideas of strength and beauty have not been greatly different. Poetry as it exists now on earth, in the various remains of ancient authors, Music as it exists in old tunes or melodies, Painting and Sculpture as it exists in the remains of Antiquity and in the works of more modern genius, is Inspiration, and cannot be surpassed; it is perfect and eternal. Milton, Shakspeare, Michael Angelo, Rafael, the finest specimens of Ancient Sculpture and Painting and Architecture, Gothic, Grecian, Hindoo and Egyptian, are the extent of the human mind. The human mind cannot go beyond the gift of God, the Holy Ghost. To suppose that Art can go beyond the finest specimens of Art that are now in the world, is not knowing what Art is; it is being blind to the gifts of the spirit.

It will be necessary for the Painter to say something concerning his ideas of Beauty, Strength and Ugliness.

The Beauty that is annexed and appended to folly, is a lamentable accident and error of the mortal and perishing life; it does but seldom happen; but with this unnatural mixture the sublime Artist can have nothing to do; it is fit for the burlesque. The Beauty proper for sublime art is lineaments, or forms and features that are capable of being the receptacles of intellect; accordingly the Painter has given in his Beautiful Man, his own idea of intellectual Beauty. The face and limbs that deviates or alters least, from infancy to old age, is the face and limbs of greatest Beauty and perfection.

The Ugly, likewise, when accompanied and annexed to imbecility and disease, is a subject for burlesque and not for historical grandeur; the Artist has imagined his Ugly Man, one approaching to the beast in features and form, his forehead small, without frontals; his jaws large; his nose high on the ridge, and narrow; his chest, and the stamina of his make, comparatively little, and his joints and his extremities large; his eyes, with scarce any whites, narrow and cunning, and every thing tending toward what is truly Ugly, the incapability of intellect.

The Artist has considered his strong Man as a receptacle of Wisdom, a sublime energizer; his features and limbs do not spindle out into length without strength, nor are they too large and unwieldly for his brain and bosom. Strength consists in accumulation of power to the principal seat, and from thence a regular gradation and subordination; strength is compactness, not extent nor bulk.

The strong Man acts from conscious superiority, and marches on in fearless dependence on the divine decrees, raging with the inspirations of a prophetic mind. The Beautiful Man acts from duty and anxious solicitude for the fates of those for whom he combats. The Ugly Man acts from love of carnage, and delight in the savage barbarities of war, rushing with sportive precipitation into the very jaws of the affrighted enemy.

The Roman Soldiers rolled together in a heap before

them: "Like the rolling thing before the whirlwind"; each shew a different character, and a different expression of fear, or revenge, or envy, or blank horror, or amazement, or devout wonder and unresisting awe.

The dead and the dying, Britons naked, mingled with armed Romans, strew the field beneath. Among these the last of the Bards who were capable of attending warlike deeds, is seen falling, outstretched among the dead and the dying, singing to his harp in the pains of death.

Distant among the mountains are Druid Temples, similar to Stone Henge. The Sun sets behind the mountains, bloody with the day of battle.

The flush of health in flesh exposed to the open air, nourished by the spirits of forests and floods in that ancient happy period, which history has recorded, cannot be like the sickly daubs of Titian or Rubens. Where will the copier of nature as it now is, find a civilized man, who is accustomed to go naked? Imagination only can furnish us with colouring appropriate, such as is found in the Frescos of Rafael and Michael Angelo: the disposition of forms always directs colouring in works of true art. As to a modern Man, stripped from his load of cloathing he is like a dead corpse. Hence Reubens, Titian, Correggio and all of that class, are like leather and chalk; their men are like leather, and their women like chalk, for the disposition of their forms will not admit of grand colouring; in Mr. B.'s Britons the blood is seen to circulate in their limbs; he defies competition in colouring.

NUMBER VI.

"A Spirit vaulting from a cloud to turn and wind a fiery Pegasus."—Shakspeare. The Horse of Intellect is leaping from the cliffs of Memory and Reasoning; it is

*a barren Rock: it is also called the Barren Waste of
Locke and Newton.*

This Picture was done many years ago, and was one
of the first Mr. B. ever did in Fresco; fortunately, or
rather, providentially, he left it unblotted and un-
blurred, although molested continually by blotting and
blurring demons; but he was also compelled to leave it
unfinished, for reasons that will be shewn in the follow-
ing.

NUMBER VIII.

The spiritual Preceptor, an experiment Picture.

The subject is taken from the Visions of Emanuel
Swedenborg, Universal Theology, No. 623. The
Learned, who strive to ascend into Heaven by means of
learning, appear to Children like dead horses, when
repelled by the celestial spheres. The works of this
visionary are well worthy the attention of Painters and
Poets; they are foundations for grand things; the reason
they have not been more attended to is because cor-
poreal demons have gained a predominance; who the
leaders of these are, will be shewn below. Unworthy
Men who gain fame among Men, continue to govern
mankind after death, and in their spiritual bodies op-
pose the spirits of those who worthily are famous; and,
as Swedenborg observes, by entering into disease and
excrement, drunkenness and concupiscence, they pos-
sess themselves of the bodies of mortal men, and shut
the doors of mind and of thought by placing Learning
above Inspiration. O Artist! you may disbelieve all this,
but it shall be at your own peril.

*Satan calling up his Legions, from Milton's Paradise
Lost; a composition for a more perfect Picture after-
ward executed for a Lady of high rank. An experi-
ment Picture.*

This Picture was likewise painted at intervals, for
experiment on colours without any oily vehicle; it may
be worthy of attention, not only on account of its com-
position, but of the great labour which has been be-
stowed on it, that is, three or four times as much as
would have finished a more perfect Picture; the labour
has destroyed the lineaments; it was with difficulty
brought back again to a certain effect, which it had at
first, when all the lineaments were perfect.

These Pictures, among numerous others painted for
experiment, were the result of temptations and pertur-
bations, labouring to destroy Imaginative power, by
means of that infernal machine called Chiaro Oscuro, in
the hands of Venetian and Flemish Demons, whose
enmity to the Painter himself, and to all Artists who
study in the Florentine and Roman Schools, may be re-
moved by an exhibition and exposure of their vile tricks.
They cause that every thing in art shall become a Ma-
chine. They cause that the execution shall be all blocked
up with brown shadows. They put the original Artist in
fear and doubt of his own original conception. The spirit
of Titian was particularly active in raising doubts con-
cerning the possibility of executing without a model,
and when once he had raised the doubt, it became easy
for him to snatch away the vision time after time, for,
when the Artist took his pencil to execute his ideas, his

power of imagination weakened so much and darkened, that memory of nature, and of Pictures of the various schools possessed his mind, instead of appropriate execution resulting from the inventions; like walking in another man's style, or speaking, or looking in another man's style and manner, unappropriate and repugnant to your own individual character; tormenting the true Artist, till he leaves the Florentine, and adopts the Venetian practice, or does as Mr. B. has done, has the courage to suffer poverty and disgrace, till he ultimately conquers.

Rubens is a most outrageous demon, and by infusing the remembrances of his Pictures and style of execution, hinders all power of individual thought: so that the man who is possessed by this demon loses all admiration of any other Artist but Rubens and those who were his imitators and journeymen; he causes to the Florentine and Roman Artist fear to execute; and though the original conception was all fire and animation, he loads it with hellish brownness, and blocks up all its gates of light except one, and that one he closes with iron bars, till the victim is obliged to give up the Florentine and Roman practice and adopt the Venetian and Flemish.

Correggio is a soft and effeminate, and consequently a most cruel demon, whose whole delight is to cause endless labour to whoever suffers him to enter his mind. The story that is told in all Lives of the Painters about Correggio being poor and but badly paid for his Pictures is altogether false; he was a petty Prince in Italy, and employed numerous Journeymen in manufacturing (as Rubens and Titian did) the Pictures that go under his name. The manual labour in these Pictures of Correggio is immense, and was paid for originally at the immense prices that those who keep manufactories of art always charge to their employers, while they themselves pay their journeymen little enough. But though Correggio was not poor, he will make any true artist so who permits him to enter his mind, and take possession of his affections; he infuses a love of soft and even tints without boundaries, and of endless reflected lights that confuse one another, and hinder all correct drawing from appearing to be correct; for if one of Rafael or Michael Angelo's figures was to be traced, and Correggio's reflections and refractions to be added to it, there would soon be an end of proportion and strength, and it would be weak, and pappy, and lumbering, and thick headed, like his own works; but then it would have softness and evenness by a twelvemonth's labour, where a month would with judgment have finished it better and higher; and the poor wretch who executed it, would be the Correggio that the life writers have written of: a drudge and a miserable man, compelled to softness by poverty. I say again, O Artist, you may disbelieve all this, but it shall be at your own peril.

Note. These experiment Pictures have been bruized and knocked about without mercy, to try all experiments.

NUMBER XIV.

The Angels hovering over the Body of Jesus in the Sepulchre.—A Drawing.

The above four drawings the Artist wishes were in Fresco on an enlarged scale to ornament the altars of churches, and to make England, like Italy, respected by respectable men of other countries on account of Art. It is not the want of Genius that can hereafter be laid to our charge; the Artist who has done these Pictures and Drawings will take care of that; let those who govern the Nation take care of the other. The times require that every one should speak out boldly; England expects that every man should do his duty, in Arts, as well as in Arms or in the Senate.

NUMBER XV.

Ruth.—A Drawing.

This Design is taken from that most pathetic passage in the Book of Ruth where Naomi, having taken leave of her daughters in law with intent to return to her own country, Ruth cannot leave her, but says, "Whither thou goest I will go; and where thou lodgest I will lodge; thy people shall be my people, and thy God my God; where thou diest I will die, and there will I be buried; God do so to me and more also, if ought but death part thee and me."

The distinction that is made in modern times between a Painting and a Drawing proceeds from ignorance of art. The merit of a Picture is the same as the merit of a Drawing. The dawber dawbs his Drawings; he who draws his Drawings draws his Pictures. There is no difference between Rafael's Cartoons and his Frescos, or Pictures, except that the Frescos, or Pictures, are more finished. When Mr. B. formerly painted in oil colours his Pictures were shewn to certain painters and connoisseurs, who said that they were very admirable Drawings on canvass, but not Pictures; but they said the same of Rafael's Pictures. Mr. B. thought this the greatest of compliments, though it was meant otherwise. If losing and obliterating the outline constitutes a Picture, Mr. B. will never be so foolish as to do one. Such art of losing the outlines is the art of Venice and Flanders; it loses all character, and leaves what some people call expression; but this is a false notion of expression; expression cannot exist without character as its stamina; and neither character nor expression can exist without firm and determinate outline. Fresco Painting is susceptible of higher finishing than Drawing on Paper, or than any other method of Painting. But he must have a strange organization of sight who does not prefer a Drawing on Paper to a Dawbing in Oil by the same master, supposing both to be done with equal care.

The great and golden rule of art, as well as of life, is this: That the more distinct, sharp, and wirey the bounding line, the more perfect the work of art, and the less keen and sharp, the greater is the evidence of weak imitation, plagiarism, and bungling. Great inventors, in all ages, knew this: Protogenes and Apelles knew each other by this line. Rafael and Michael Angelo and Albert Dürer are known by this and this alone. The want of this determinate and bounding form evidences the want of idea in the artist's mind, and the pretence of the plagiary in all its branches. How do we distinguish the oak from the beech, the horse from the ox, but by the bounding outline? How do we distinguish one face or countenance from another, but by the bounding line and its infinite inflexions and movements? What is it that builds a house and plants a garden, but the definite and determinate? What is it that distinguishes honesty from knavery, but the hard and wiry line of rectitude and certainty in the actions and intentions? Leave out this line, and you leave out life itself; all is chaos again, and the line of the almighty must be drawn out upon it before man or beast can exist. Talk no more then of Correggio, or Rembrandt, or any other of those plagiaries of Venice or Flanders. They were but the lame imitators of lines drawn by their predecessors, and their works prove themselves contemptible, disarranged imitations, and blundering, misapplied copies.

NUMBER XVI.

The Penance of Jane Shore in St. Paul's Church.—A Drawing.

This Drawing was done above Thirty Years ago, and proves to the Author, and he thinks will prove to any discerning eye, that the productions of our youth and of our maturer age are equal in all essential points. If a man is master of his profession, he cannot be ignorant that he is so; and if he is not employed by those who pretend to encourage art, he will employ himself, and laugh in secret at the pretences of the ignorant, while he has every night dropped into his shoe, as soon as he puts it off, and puts out the candle, and gets into bed, a reward for the labours of the day, such as the world cannot give, and patience and time await to give him all that the world can give.

FINIS

From PUBLIC ADDRESS

[*From the Rossetti MS.*]

(1810)

P. 1.

If Men of weak capacities have alone the Power of Execution in Art, Mr. B. has now put to the test. If to Invent & to draw well hinders the Executive Power in Art, & his strokes are still to be Condemn'd because they are unlike those of Artists who are Unacquainted with Drawing, is now to be Decided by The Public. Mr. B.'s Inventive Powers & his Scientific Knowledge of Drawing is on all hands acknowledg'd; it only remains to be Certified whether Physiognomic Strength & Power is to give Place to Imbecillity, and whether an unabated study & Practise of forty Years (for I devoted myself to engraving in my Earliest Youth) are sufficient to elevate me above the Mediocrity to which I have hitherto been the victim. In a work of Art it is not Fine Tints that are required, but Fine Forms; fine Tints without, are nothing. Fine Tints without Fine Forms are always the Subterfuge of the Blockhead.

I account it a Public Duty respectfully to address myself to The Chalcographic Society & to Express to them my opinion (the result of the constant Practise & Experience of Many Years) That Engraving as an art is Lost in England owing to an artfully propagated opinion that Drawing spoils an Engraver, which opinion has been held out to me by such men as Flaxman, Romney, Stothard. I request the Society to inspect my Print, of

which drawing is the Foundation & indeed the Super-
structure: it is drawing on copper, as Painting ought to
be drawing on canvas or any other surface, & nothing
Else. I request likewise that the Society will compare
the Prints of Bartolozzi, Woolett, Strange &c. with the
old English Portraits, that is, compare the Modern Art
with the Art as it existed Previous to the Enterance of
Vandyke and Rubens into this Country, since which
English Engraving is Lost, & I am sure the Result of the
comparison will be that the Society must be of my Opin-
ion that engraving, by Losing drawing, has Lost all the
character & all Expression, without which The Art is
Lost.

Pp. 51-57.

In this Plate Mr. B. has resumed the style with which
he set out in life, of which Heath & Stothard were the
awkward imitators at that time; it is the style of Alb.
Durer's Histories & the old Engravers, which cannot be
imitated by any one who does not understand drawing,
& which, according to Heath & Stothard, Flaxman, &
even Romney, spoils an Engraver; for Each of these
Men have repeatedly asserted this Absurdity to me in
Condemnation of my Work & approbation of Heath's
lame imitation, Stothard being such a fool as to suppose
that his blundering blurs can be made out & delineated
by any Engraver who knows how to cut dots & lozenges
equally well with those little prints which I engraved
after him five & twenty years ago by & which he got his
reputation as a draughtsman.

The manner in which my Character has been blasted
these thirty years, both as an artist & a Man, may be seen
particularly in a Sunday Paper cal'd the Examiner, Pub-
lish'd in Beaufort Buildings (We all know that Editors
of Newspapers trouble their heads very little about art

& science, & that they are always paid for what they put
in upon these ungracious Subjects), & the manner in
which I have routed out the nest of villains will be seen
in a Poem concerning my Three years' Herculean La-
bours at Felpham, which I will soon Publish. Secret
Calumny & open Professions of Friendship are common
enough all the world over, but have never been so good
an occasion of Poetic Imagery. When a Base Man means
to be your Enemy he always begins with being your
Friend. Flaxman cannot deny that one of the very first
Monuments he did, I gratuitously design'd for him; at
the same time he was blasting my character as an
Artist to Macklin, my Employer, as Macklin told me at
the time; how much of his Homer & Dante he will allow
to be mine I do not know, as he went far enough off to
Publish them, even to Italy, but the Public will know &
Posterity will know.

Many People are so foolish [as] to think that they can
wound Mr. Fuseli over my Shoulder; they will find
themselves mistaken; they could not wound even Mr.
Barry so.

A certain Portrait Painter said To me in a boasting
way, "Since I have Practised Painting I have lost all
idea of drawing." Such a Man must know that I look'd
upon him with contempt; he did not care for this any
more than West did, who hesitated & equivocated with
me upon the same subject, at which time he asserted
that Woolett's Prints were superior to Basire's because
they had more Labour & Care; now this is contrary to
the truth. Woolett did not know how to put so much
labour into a head or a foot as Basire did; he did not
know how to draw the Leaf of a tree; all his study was
clean strokes & mossy tints—how then should he be able
to make use of either Labour or Care, unless the Labour
& Care of Imbecillity? The Life's Labour of Mental

Weakness scarcely Equals one Hour of the Labour of Ordinary Capacity, like the full Gallop of the Gouty Man to the ordinary walk of youth & health. I allow that there is such a thing as high finish'd Ignorance, as there may be a fool or a knave in an Embroider'd Coat; but I say that the Embroidery of the Ignorant finisher is not like a Coat made by another, but is an Emanation from Ignorance itself, & its finishing is like its master—The Life's Labour of Five Hundred Idiots, for he never does the Work Himself.

What is Call'd the English Style of Engraving, such as proceeded from the Toilettes of Woolett & Strange (for theirs were Fribble's Toilettes) can never produce Character & Expression. I knew the Men intimately, from their Intimacy with Basire, my Master, & knew them both to be heavy lumps of Cunning & Ignorance, as their works shew to all the Continent, who laugh at the Contemptible Pretences of Englishmen to Improve Art before they even know the first Beginnings of Art. I hope this Print will redeem my Country from this Coxcomb situation & shew that it is only some Englishmen, and not All, who are thus ridiculous in their Pretences. Advertisements in Newspapers are no proof of Popular approbation, but often the Contrary. A Man who Pretends to Improve Fine Art does not know what Fine Art is. Ye English Engravers must come down from your high flights; ye must condescend to study Marc Antonio & Albert Durer. Ye must begin before you attempt to finish or improve, & when you have begun you will know better than to think of improving what cannot be improv'd. It is very true, what you have said for these thirty two Years. I am Mad or Else you are so; both of us cannot be in our right senses. Posterity will judge by our Works. Woolett's & Strange's works are like those of Titian & Correggio: the Life's Labour of Ignorant Journeymen, Suited to the Purposes of Commerce no doubt, for Commerce Cannot endure Individual Merit; its insatiable Maw must be fed by What all can do Equally well; at least it is so in England, as I have found to my Cost these Forty Years.

Commerce is so far from being beneficial to Arts, or to Empires, that it is destructive of both, as all their History shews, for the above Reason of Individual Merit being its Great hatred. Empires flourish till they become Commercial, & then they are scatter'd abroad to the four winds.

Woolett's best works were Etch'd by Jack Brown. Woolett Etch'd very bad himself. Strange's Prints were, when I knew him, all done by Aliamet & his french journeymen whose names I forget.

"The Cottagers", & "Jocund Peasants", the "Views in Kew Gardens", "Foots Cray", & "Diana", & "Acteon", & in short all that are Call'd Woolett's were Etch'd by Jack Browne, & in Woolett's works the Etching is All, tho' even in these, a single leaf of a tree is never correct.

Such Prints as Woolett & Strange produc'd will do for those who choose to purchase the Life's labour of Ignorance & Imbecillity, in Preference to the Inspired Moments of Genius & Animation.

P. 60.

I also knew something of Tom Cooke who Engraved after Hogarth. Cooke wished to Give to Hogarth what he could take from Rafael, that is Outline & Mass & Colour, but he could not.

P. 57.

I do not pretend to Paint better than Rafael or Mich. Angelo or Julio Romane or Alb. Durer, but I do Pretend to Paint finer than Rubens or Rembt. or Correggio or

Titian. I do not Pretend to Engrave finer than Alb.
Durer, Goltzius, Sadelar or Edelinck, but I do pretend to
Engrave finer than Strange, Woolett, Hall or Bartolozzi,
& all because I understand drawing which They under-
stood not.

P. 58.

In this manner the English Public have been imposed
upon for many Years under the impression that Engrav-
ing & Painting are somewhat Else besides drawing.
Painting is drawing on Canvas, & Engraving is drawing
on Copper, & Nothing Else; & he who pretends to be
either Painter or Engraver without being a Master of
drawing is an Imposter. We may be Clever as Pugilists,
but as Artists we are & have long been the Contempt of
the Continent. Gravelot once said to My Master, Basire,
"de English may be very clever in deir own opinions,
but dey do not draw de draw."

Resentment for Personal Injuries has had some share
in this Public Address, But Love to My Art & Zeal for
my Country a much Greater.

P. 59.

Men think they can Copy Nature as Correctly as I
copy Imagination; this they will find Impossible, & all
the Copies or Pretended Copiers of Nature, from Rem-
brandt to Reynolds, Prove that Nature becomes to its
Victim nothing but Blots & Blurs. Why are Copiers of
Nature Incorrect, while Copiers of Imagination are Cor-
rect? this is manifest to all.

Pp. 60-62.

The Originality of this Production makes it necessary
to say a few words.

While the Works of Pope & Dryden are look'd upon as

the same Art with those of Milton & Shakespeare, while
the works of Strange & Woollett are look'd upon as the
same Art with those of Rafael & Albert Durer, there can
be no Art in a Nation but such as is Subservient to the
interest of the Monopolizing Trader who Manufactures
Art by the Hands of Ignorant Journeymen till at length
Christian Charity is held out as a Motive to encourage a
Blockhead, & he is Counted the Greatest Genius who
can sell a Good-for-Nothing Commodity for a Great
Price. Obedience to the Will of the Monopolist is call'd
Virtue, and the really Industrious, Virtuous & Independ-
ent Barry is driven out to make room for a pack of Idle
Sycophants with whitlows on their fingers. Englishmen,
rouze yourselves from the fatal Slumber into which
Booksellers & Trading Dealers have thrown you, Under
the artfully propagated pretence that a Translation or a
Copy of any kind can be as honourable to a Nation as an
Original, Be-lying the English Character in that well
known Saying, "Englishmen Improve what others In-
vent." This Even Hogarth's Works Prove a detestable
Falshood. No Man Can Improve An Original Invention.
Since Hogarth's time we have had very few Efforts of
Originality. Nor can an Original Invention Exist without
Execution, Organized & minutely delineated & Articu-
lated, Either by God or Man. I do not mean smooth'd
up & Niggled & Poco-Pen'd, and all the beauties picked
out & blurr'd & blotted, but Drawn with a firm & de-
cided hand at once with all its Spots & Blemishes which
are beauties & not faults, like Fuseli & Michael Angelo,
Shakespeare & Milton.

Dryden in Rhyme cries, "Milton only Planned."
Every Fool shook his bells throughout the Land.
Tom Cooke cut Hogarth down with his clean Graving.
How many thousand Connoisseurs with joy ran raving!

Some blush at what others can see no crime in,
But Nobody at all sees harm in Rhyming.
Thus Hayley on his toilette seeing the sope
Says, "Homer is very much improv'd by Pope."
While I looking up to my Umbrella,
Resolv'd to be a very Contrary Fellow,
Cry, "Tom Cooke proves, from Circumference to Center,
No one can finish so high as the original inventor."

I have heard many People say, "Give me the Ideas. It
is no matter what Words you put them into," & others
say, "Give me the Design, it is no matter for the Ex-
ecution." These People know Enough of Artifice, but
Nothing Of Art. Ideas cannot be Given but in their min-
utely Appropriate Words, nor Can a Design be made
without its minutely Appropriate Execution. The un-
organized Blots & Blurs of Rubens & Titian are not Art,
nor can their Method ever express Ideas or Imaginations
any more than Pope's Metaphysical Jargon of Rhyming.
Unappropriate Execution is the Most nauseous of all
affectation & foppery. He who copies does not Execute;
he only Imitates what is already Executed. Execution is
only the result of Invention.

P. 63.
Whoever looks at any of the Great & Expensive Works
of Engraving that have been Publish'd by English Trad-
ers must feel a Loathing & disgust, & accordingly most
Englishmen have a Contempt for Art, which is the
Greatest Curse that can fall upon a Nation.

He who could represent Christ uniformly like a Dray-
man must have Queer Conceptions; consequently his
Execution must have been as Queer, & those must be
Queer fellows who give great sums for such nonsense &
think it fine Art.

The Modern Chalcographic Connoisseurs & Amateurs admire only the work of the journeyman, Picking out of whites & blacks in what is call'd Tints; they despise drawing, which despises them in return. They see only whether every thing is toned down but one spot of light.

Mr. B. submits to a more severe tribunal; he invites the admirers of old English Portraits to look at his Print.

P. 64.

I do not know whether Homer is a Liar & that there is no such thing as Generous Contention: I know that all those with whom I have Contended in Art have strove not to Excell, but to Starve me out by Calumny & the Arts of Trading Combination.

P. 66.

It is Nonsense for Noblemen & Gentlemen to offer Premiums for the Encouragement of Art when such Pictures as these can be done without Premiums; let them Encourage what Exists Already, & not endeavour to counteract by tricks; let it no more be said that Empires Encourage Arts, for it is Arts that Encourage Empires. Arts & Artists are Spiritual & laugh at Mortal Contingencies. It is in their Power to hinder Instruction but not to Instruct, just as it is in their Power to Murder a Man but not to make a Man.

Let us teach Buonaparte, & whomsoever else it may concern, That it is not Arts that follow & attend upon Empire, but Empire that attends upon & follows The Arts.

P. 67.

No Man of Sense can think that an Imitation of the Objects of Nature is The Art of Painting, or that such Imitation, which any one may easily perform, is worthy of Notice, much less that such an Art should be the Glory & Pride of a Nation. The Italians laugh at English Connoisseurs, who are most of them such silly Fellows as to believe this.

A Man sets himself down with Colours & with all the Articles of Painting; he puts a Model before him & he copies that so neat as to make it a deception: now let any Man of Sense ask himself one Question: Is this Art? can it be worthy of admiration to any body of Understanding? Who could not do this? what man who has eyes and an ordinary share of patience cannot do this neatly? Is this Art? Or is it glorious to a Nation to produce such contemptible Copies? Countrymen, Countrymen, do not suffer yourselves to be disgraced!

P. 66.

The English Artist may be assured that he is doing an injury & injustice to his Country while he studies & imitates the Effects of Nature. England will never rival Italy while we servilely copy what the Wise Italians, Rafael & Michael Angelo, scorned, nay abhorred, as Vasari tells us.

> Call that the Public Voice which is their Error,
> Like as a Monkey peeping in a Mirror
> Admires all his colours brown & warm
> And never once percieves his ugly form.

What kind of Intellects must he have who sees only the Colours of things & not the Forms of Things.

P. 71.

A Jockey that is anything of a Jockey will never buy a Horse by the Colour, & a Man who has got any brains will never buy a Picture by the Colour.

When I tell any Truth it is not for the sake of Convincing those who do not know it, but for the sake of defending those who do.

P. 76.

No Man of Sense ever supposes that copying from Nature is the Art of Painting; if Art is no more than this, it is no better than any other Manual Labour; anybody may do it & the fool often will do it best as it is a work of no Mind.

P. 78.

The Greatest part of what are call'd in England Old Pictures are Oil Colour Copies from Fresco originals; the Comparison is Easily made & the copy detected. Note, I mean Fresco, Easel, or Cabinet Pictures on Canvas & Wood & Copper &c.

P. 86.

The Painter hopes that his Friends Anytus, Melitus & Lycon will perceive that they are not now in Ancient Greece, & tho' they can use the Poison of Calumny, the English Public will be convinc'd that such a Picture as this Could never be Painted by a Madman or by one in a State of Outrageous manners, as these Bad Men both Print and Publish by all the means in their Power; the Painter begs Public Protection & all will be well.

P. 17.

I wonder who can say, Speak no Ill of the dead when it is asserted in the Bible that the name of the Wicked shall Rot. It is Deistical Virtue, I suppose, but as I have none of this I will pour Aqua fortis on the Name of the Wicked & turn it into an Ornament & an Example to be Avoided by Some & Imitated by Others if they Please.

Columbus discover'd America, but American Vesputius finish'd & smooth'd it over like an English Engraver or Corregio & Titian.

Pp. 18-19.

What Man of Sense will lay out his Money upon the Life's Labours of Imbecility & Imbecility's Journeyman, or think to Educate a Fool how to build a Universe with Farthing Balls? The Contemptible Idiots who have been call'd Great Men of late Years ought to rouze the Public Indignation of Men of Sense in all Professions.

There is not, because there cannot be, any difference of Effect in the Pictures of Rubens & Rembrandt: when you have seen one of their Pictures you have seen all. It is not so with Rafael, Julio Roman[o], Alb. d[ürer]. Mich. Ang. Every Picture of theirs has a different & appropriate Effect.

Yet I do not shrink from the comparison, in Either Relief or Strength of Colour, with either Rembrandt or Rubens; on the contrary I court the Comparison & fear not the Result, but not in a dark corner. Their Effects are in Every Picture the same. Mine are in every Picture different.

I hope my Countrymen will Excuse me if I tell them a Wholesome truth. Most Englishmen, when they look at a Picture, immediately set about searching for Points of Light & clap the Picture into a dark corner. This, when done by Grand Works, is like looking for Epigrams in Homer. A point of light is a Witticism; many are destructive of all Art. One is an Epigram only & no Grand Work can have them. They produce Dryness[?] & Monotony.

Rafael, Mich. Ag., Alb. d., & Jul. Rom. are accounted ignorant of that Epigrammatic Wit in Art because they avoid it as a destructive Machine, as it is.

That Vulgar Epigram in Art, Rembrandt's "Hundred Guelders", has entirely put an End to all Genuine & Appropriate Effect; all, both Morning & Night, is now a dark cavern. It is the Fashion. When you view a Collection of Pictures painted since Venetian Art was the Fashion, or Go into a Modern Exhibition, with a very few Exceptions, Every Picture has the same Effect, a Piece of Machinery of Points of Light to be put into a dark hole.

Mr. B. repeats that there is not one Character or Expression in this Print which could be Produced with the Execution of Titian, Rubens, Correggio, Rembrandt, or any of that Class. Character & Expression can only be Expressed by those who Feel Them. Even Hogarth's Execution cannot be Copied or Improved. Gentlemen of Fortune who give Great Prices for Pictures should consider the following. Rubens's Luxembourg Gallery is Confessed on all hands to be the work of a Blockhead: it bears this Evidence in its face. How can its Execution be any other than the Work of a Blockhead? Bloated Gods, Mercury, Juno, Venus, & the rattle traps of Mythology & the lumber of an awkward French Palace are thrown together around Clumsy & Ricketty Princes & Princesses higgledy piggledy. On the Contrary, Julio Rom[ano's] Palace of T at Mantua, is allow'd on all hands to be the Product of a Man of the Most Profound sense & Genius, & yet his Execution is pronounc'd by English Connoisseurs & Reynolds, their doll, to be unfit for the Study of the Painter. Can I speak with too great Contempt of such Contemptible fellows? If all the Princes in Europe, like Louis XIV & Charles the first, were to Patronize such Blockheads, I, William Blake, a Mental Prince, should decollate & Hang their Souls as Guilty of Mental High Treason.

Who that has Eyes cannot see that Rubens & Correg-

gio must have been very weak & Vulgar fellows? & we
are to imitate their Execution. This is like what Sr Fran-
cis Bacon says, that a healthy Child should be taught &
compell'd to walk like a Cripple, while the Cripple must
be taught to walk like healthy people. O rare wisdom!

I am really sorry to see my Countrymen trouble them-
selves about Politics. If Men were Wise, the Most arbi-
trary Princes could not hurt them. If they are not wise,
the Freest Government is compell'd to be a Tyranny.
Princes appear to me to be Fools. Houses of Commons &
Houses of Lords appear to me to be fools; they seem to
me to be something Else besides Human Life.

Pp. 20-21.
The wretched State of the Arts in this Country & in
Europe, originating in the wretched State of Political
Science, which is the Science of Sciences, Demands a
firm & determinate conduct on the part of Artists to Re-
sist the Contemptible Counter Arts Establish'd by such
contemptible Politicians as Louis XIV & originally set
on foot by Venetian Picture traders, Music traders, &
Rhime traders, to the destruction of all true art as it is
this Day. To recover Art has been the business of my
life to the Florentine Original & if possible to go beyond
that Original; this I thought the only pursuit worthy of
a Man. To Imitate I abhor. I obstinately adhere to the
true Style of Art such as Michael Angelo, Rafael, Jul.
Rom., Alb. Durer left it, the Art of Invention, not of
Imitation. Imagination is My World; this world of Dross
is beneath my Notice & beneath the Notice of the Pub-
lic. I demand therefore of the Amateurs of art the En-
couragement which is my due; if they continue to refuse,
theirs is the loss, not mine, & theirs is the Contempt of
Posterity. I have Enough in the Approbation of fellow

labourers; this is my glory & exceeding great reward. I
go on & nothing can hinder my course:

> and in Melodious Accents I
> Will sit me down & Cry I, I.

P. 20 (*sideways*).

An Example of these Contrary Arts is given us in the
Characters of Milton & Dryden as they are written in a
Poem signed with the name of Nat Lee, which perhaps
he never wrote & perhaps he wrote in a paroxysm of in-
sanity, In which it is said that Milton's Poem is a rough
Unfinish'd Piece & Dryden has finish'd it. Now let Dry-
den's Fall & Milton's Paradise be read, & I will assert
that every Body of Understanding must cry out Shame
on such Niggling & Poco-Pen as Dryden has degraded
Milton with. But at the same time I will allow that Stu-
pidity will Prefer Dryden, because it is in Rhyme &
Monotonous Sing Song, Sing Song from beginning to
end. Such are Bartolozzi, Woolett & Strange.

P. 23.

The Painters of England are unemploy'd in Public
Works, while the Sculptors have continual & superabun-
dant employment. Our Churches & Abbeys are treasures
of their producing for ages back, While Painting is ex-
cluded. Painting, the Principal Art, has no place among
our almost only public works. Yet it is more adapted to
solemn ornament than Marble can be, as it is capable
of beng Placed on any heighth & indeed would make a
Noble finish Placed above the Great Public Monuments
in Westminster, St. Pauls & other Cathedrals. To the
Society for Encouragement of Arts I address myself with
Respectful duty, requesting their Consideration of my

Plan as a Great Public means of advancing Fine Art in Protestant Communities. Monuments to the dead, Painted by Historical & Poetical Artists, like Barry & Mortimer (I forbear to name living Artists tho' equally worthy), I say, Monuments so Painted must make England What Italy is, an Envied Storehouse of Intellectual Riches.

Pp. 24-25.

It has been said of late years The English Public have no Taste for Painting. This is a Falsehood. The English are as Good Judges of Painting as of Poetry, & they prove it in their Contempt for Great Collections of all the Rubbish of the Continent brought here by Ignorant Picture dealers. An Englishman may well say, "I am no Judge of Painting," when he is sold these Smears & Dawbs at an immense price & told that such is the Art of Painting. I say the English Public are true Encouragers of real Art, while they discourage and look with Contempt on False Art.

In a Commercial Nation Impostors are abroad in all Professions; these are the greatest Enemies of Genius. In the Art of Painting these Impostors sedulously propagate an Opinion that Great Inventors Cannot Execute. This Opinion is as destructive of the true Artist as it is false by all Experience. Even Hogarth cannot be either Copied or Improved. Can Anglus never Discern Perfection but in the Journeyman's Labour?

Pp. 24-25 (*sideways*).

I know my Execution is not like Any Body Else. I do not intend it should be so; none but Blockheads Copy one another. My Conception & Invention are on all hands allow'd to be Superior. My Execution will be

found so too. To what is it that Gentlemen of the first
Rank both in Genius & Fortune have subscribed their
Names? To My Inventions: the Executive part they
never disputed; the Lavish praise I have recieved from
all Quarters for Invention & drawing has Generally been
accompanied by this: "he can concieve but he cannot
Execute"; this Absurd assertion has done me, & may still
do me, the greatest mischief. I call for Public protection
against these Villains. I am, like others, Just Equal in
Invention & in Execution as my works shew. I, in my
own defence, Challenge a Competition with the finest
Engravings & defy the most critical judge to make the
Comparison Honestly, asserting in my own Defence
that This Print is the Finest that has been done or is
likely to be done in England, where drawing, its foun-
dation, is Condemn'd, and absurd Nonsense about dots
& Lozenges & Clean Strokes made to occupy the atten-
tion to the Neglect of all real Art. I defy any Man to Cut
Cleaner Strokes than I do, or rougher where I please, &
assert that he who thinks he can Engrave, or Paint
either, without being a Master of drawing, is a Fool.
Painting is drawing on Canvas, & Engraving is drawing
on Copper, & nothing Else. Drawing is Execution, &
nothing Else, & he who draws best must be the best
Artist; to this I subscribe my name as a Public Duty.

—WILLIAM BLAKE

P.S.—I do not believe that this Absurd opinion ever was
set on foot till in my Outset into life it was artfully pub-
lish'd, both in whispers & in print, by Certain persons
whose robberies from me made it necessary to them that
I should be hid in a corner; it never was supposed that
a Copy could be better than an original, or near so Good,
till a few Years ago it became the interest of certain
envious Knaves.

ADDITIONAL PASSAGES

P. 38.

There is just the same Science in Lebrun or Rubens, or even Vanloo, that there is in Rafael or Mich. Angelo, but not the same Genius. Science is soon got; the other never can be acquired, but must be Born.

P. 39.

I do not condemn Rubens, Rembrandt or Titian because they did not understand drawing, but because they did not Understand Colouring; how long shall I be forced to beat this into Men's Ears? I do not condemn Strange or Woolett because they did not understand drawing, but because they did not understand Graving. I do not condemn Pope or Dryden because they did not understand Imagination, but because they did not understand Verse. Their Colouring, Graving & Verse can never be applied to Art—That is not either Colouring, Graving or Verse which is Unappropriate to the Subject. He who makes a design must know the Effect & Colouring Proper to be put to that design & will never take that of Rubens, Rembrandt or Titian to turn that which is Soul & Life into a Mill or Machine.

P. 44.

Let a Man who has made a drawing go on & on & he will produce a Picture or Painting, but if he chooses to leave it before he has spoil'd it, he will do a Better Thing.

Pp. 46-47.

They say there is no Strait Line in Nature; this Is a

Lie, like all that they say. For there is Every Line in Nature. But I will tell them what is Not in Nature. An Even Tint is not in Nature; it produces Heaviness. Nature's Shadows are Ever varying, & a Ruled Sky that is quite Even never can Produce a Natural Sky; the same with every Object in a Picture, its Spots are its beauties. Now, Gentlemen Critics, how do you like this? You may rage, but what I say, I will prove by Such Practise & have already done, so that you will rage to your own destruction. Woolett I knew very intimately by his intimacy with Basire, & I knew him to be one of the most ignorant fellows that I ever knew. A Machine is not a Man nor a Work of Art; it is destructive of Humanity & of Art; the word Machination. Woolett I know did not know how to Grind his Graver. I know this; he has often proved his Ignorance before me at Basire's by laughing at Basire's knife tools & ridiculing the Forms of Basire's other Gravers till Basire was quite dash'd & out of Conceit with what he himself knew, but his Impudence had a Contrary Effect on me. Englishmen have been so used to Journeymen's undecided bungling that they cannot bear the firmness of a Master's Touch.

Every Line is the Line of Beauty; it is only fumble & Bungle which cannot draw a Line; this only is Ugliness. That is not a Line which doubts & Hesitates in the Midst of its Course.

ON HOMER'S POETRY &
ON VIRGIL

(1820)

ON HOMER'S POETRY

Every Poem must necessarily be a perfect Unity, but why Homer's is peculiarly so, I cannot tell; he has told the story of Bellerophon & omitted the Judgment of Paris, which is not only a part, but a principal part, of Homer's subject.

But when a Work has Unity, it is as much in a Part as in the Whole: the Torso is as much a Unity as the Laocoon.

As Unity is the cloke of folly, so Goodness is the cloke of knavery. Those who will have Unity exclusively in Homer come out with a Moral like a sting in the tail. Aristotle says Characters are either Good or Bad; now Goodness or Badness has nothing to do with Character: an Apple tree, a Pear tree, a Horse, a Lion are Characters, but a Good Apple tree or a Bad is an Apple tree still; a Horse is not more a Lion for being a Bad Horse: that is its Character: its Goodness or Badness is another consideration.

It is the same with the Moral of a whole Poem as with the Moral Goodness of its parts. Unity & Morality are secondary considerations, & belong to Philosophy & not to Poetry, to Exception & not to Rule, to Accident & not to Substance; the Ancients call'd it eating of the tree of good & evil.

The Classics! it is the Classics, & not Goths nor Monks, that Desolate Europe with Wars.

ON VIRGIL

Sacred Truth has pronounced that Greece & Rome, as Babylon & Egypt, so far from being parents of Arts & Sciences as they pretend, were destroyers of all Art. Homer, Virgil & Ovid confirm this opinion & make us reverence The Word of God, the only light of antiquity that remains unperverted by War. Virgil in the Eneid, Book vi, line 848, says "Let others study Art: Rome has somewhat better to do, namely War & Dominion."

Rome & Greece swept Art into their maw & destroy'd it; a Warlike State never can produce Art. It will Rob & Plunder & accumulate into one place, & Translate & Copy & Buy & Sell & Criticise, but not Make. Grecian is Mathematic Form: Gothic is Living Form. Mathematic Form is Eternal in the Reasoning Memory: Living Form is Eternal Existence.

MARGINALIA, I

(1788)

From ANNOTATIONS TO
LAVATER'S "APHORISMS ON MAN"
LONDON 1788

Who begins with severity, in judging of another, ends
commonly with falsehood.

False! Severity of judgment is a great virtue.

Who, without pressing temptation, tells a lie, will, without
pressing temptation, act ignobly and meanly.

Uneasy.

False! A man may lie for his own pleasure, but if any
one is hurt by his lying, will confess his lie.

Frequent laughing has been long called a sign of a little
mind—whilst the scarcer smile of harmless quiet has been
complimented as the mark of a noble heart—But to abstain
from laughing, and exciting laughter, merely not to offend,
or to risk giving offence, or not to debase the inward dignity
of character—is a power unknown to many a vigorous mind.

I hate scarce smiles: I love laughing.

None can see the man in the enemy; if he is igno-
rantly so, he is not truly an enemy; if maliciously, not a

553

man. I cannot love my enemy, for my enemy is not man, but beast or devil, if I have any. I can love him as a beast & wish to beat him.

Mark that I do not believe there is such a thing litterally, but hell is the being shut up in the possession of corporeal desires which shortly weary the man, *for* ALL LIFE IS HOLY.

Lie is the contrary to Passion

Take here the grand secret—if not of pleasing all, yet of displeasing none—court mediocrity, avoid originality, and sacrifice to fashion.

& go to hell.

I hope no one will call what I have written cavilling because he may think my remarks of small consequence. For I write from the warmth of my heart, & cannot resist the impulse I feel to rectify what I think false in a book I love so much & approve so generally.

Man is bad or good as he unites himself with bad or good spirits: tell me with whom you go & I'll tell you what you do.

As we cannot experience pleasure but by means of others, who experience either pleasure or pain thro' us, And as all of us on earth are united in thought, for it is impossible to think without images of somewhat on earth—So it is impossible to know God or heavenly things without conjunction with those who know God & heavenly things; therefore all who converse in the spirit, converse with spirits.

For these reasons I say that this Book is written by consultation with Good Spirits, because it is Good, & that the name Lavater is the amulet of those who purify the heart of man.

There is a strong objection to Lavater's principles (as I understand them) & that is He makes every thing originate in its accident; he makes the vicious propensity not only a leading feature of the man, but the stamina on which all his virtues grow. But as I understand Vice it is a Negative. It does not signify what the laws of Kings & Priests have call'd Vice; we who are philosophers ought not to call the Staminal Virtues of Humanity by the same name that we call the omissions of intellect springing from poverty.

Every man's leading propensity ought to be call'd his leading Virtue & his good Angel. But the Philosophy of Causes & Consequences misled Lavater as it has all his Cotemporaries. Each thing is its own cause & its own effect. Accident is the omission of act in self & the hindering of act in another; This is Vice, but all Act is Virtue. To hinder another is not an act; it is the contrary; it is a restraint on action both in ourselves & in the person hinder'd, for he who hinders another omits his own duty at the same time.

Murder is Hindering Another.

Theft is Hindering Another.

Backbiting, Undermining, Circumventing, & whatever is Negative is Vice. But the origin of this mistake in Lavater & his cotemporaries is, They suppose that Woman's Love is Sin; in consequence all the Loves & Graces with them are Sins.

From ANNOTATIONS TO SWEDENBORG'S
"WISDOM OF ANGELS CONCERNING
DIVINE LOVE AND DIVINE WISDOM"
LONDON 1788

(1788)

Man can have no idea of any thing greater than Man,
as a cup cannot contain more than its capaciousness. But
God is a man, not because he is so perceiv'd by man, but
because he is the creator of man.

Think of a white cloud as being holy, you cannot love
it; but think of a holy man within the cloud, love springs
up in your thoughts, for to think of holiness distinct from
man is impossible to the affections. Thought alone can
make monsters, but the affections cannot.

Page 33.
Appearances are the first Things from which the human
Mind forms its Understanding, and it cannot shake them
off but by an Investigation of the Cause, and if the Cause is
very deep, it cannot investigate it, *without keeping the
Understanding some Time in spiritual Light*. . . .

This Man can do while in the body.

Pages 195-6.
These three Degrees of Altitude are named Natural,
Spiritual and Celestial. . . . Man, at his Birth, first comes
into the natural Degree, and this increases in him by Con-
tinuity according to the Sciences, and according to the Un-
derstanding acquired by them, to the Summit of Under-
standing which is called Rational.

Study Sciences till you are blind, Study intellectuals till you are cold, Yet science cannot teach intellect. Much less can intellect teach Affection. How foolish then is it to assert that Man is born in only one degree, when that one degree is reception of the 3 degrees, two of which he must destroy or close up or they will descend; if he closes up the two superior, then he is not truly in the 3d, but descends out of it into meer Nature or Hell. . . . Is it not also evident that one degree will not open the other, & that science will not open intellect, but that they are discrete & not continuous so as to explain each other except by correspondence, which has nothing to do with demónstration; for you cannot demonstrate one degree by the other; for how can science be brought to demonstrate intellect without making them continuous & not discrete?

Page 220.
But still Man, in whom the spiritual Degree is open, comes into that Wisdom when he dies, and may also come into it by laying asleep the Sensations of the Body, and by Influx from above at the Same time into the Spirituals of his Mind.

This is while in the Body.
This is to be understood as unusual in our time, but common in ancient.

Page 233.
. . . for the natural Man can elevate his Understanding to superior Light as far as he desires it, but he who is principled in Evils and thence in Things false, does not elevate it higher than to the superior Region of his natural Mind; . . .

Who shall dare to say after this that all elevation is of self & is Enthusiasm & Madness, & is it not plain that self-derived intelligence is worldly demonstration?

Heaven & Hell are born together.

From ANNOTATIONS TO
"AN APOLOGY FOR THE BIBLE
IN A SERIES OF LETTERS ADDRESSED
TO THOMAS PAINE
BY R. WATSON, D.D., F.R.S."
LONDON 1797

(1798)

Notes on the Bishop of Leicester's Apology for the Bible
by William Blake

To defend the Bible in this year 1798 would cost a man his life.

The Beast & the Whore rule without control.

It is an easy matter for a Bishop to triumph over Paine's attack, but it is not so easy for one who loves the Bible.

The Perversions of Christ's words & acts, are attack'd by Paine & also the perversions of the Bible; Who dare defend either the Acts of Christ or the Bible Unperverted?

But to him who sees this mortal pilgrimage in the light that I see it, Duty to his country is the first consideration & safety the last.

Read patiently: take not up this Book in an idle hour: the consideration of these things is the whole duty of man & the affairs of life & death trifles, sports of time.

But these considerations [are the] business of Eternity.

I have been commanded from Hell not to print this, as it is what our Enemies wish. . . .

If this first Letter is written without Railing & Illiberality I have never read one that is. To me it is all Daggers & Poison; the sting of the serpent is in every Sentence as well as the glittering Dissimulation. Achilles' wrath is blunt abuse: Thersites' sly insinuation; such is the Bishop's. If such is the Characteristic of a modern polite gentleman we may hope to see Christ's discourses Expung'd. I have not the Charity for the Bishop that he pretends to have for Paine. I believe him to be a State trickster. Dishonest Misrepresentation. Priestly Impudence. Contemptible Falsehood & Detraction. Presumptuous Murderer. Dost thou, O Priest, wish thy brother's death when God has preserved him? Mr. Paine has not extinguish'd, & cannot Extinguish, Moral rectitude; he has Extinguish'd Superstition, which took the Place of Moral Rectitude. What has Moral Rectitude to do with Opinions concerning historical fact?

To what does the Bishop attribute the English Crusade against France? Is it not to State Religion? Blush for shame. Folly & Impudence. Does the thorough belief of Popery hinder crimes, or can the man who writes the latter sentiment be in the good humour the bishop Pretends to be? If we are to expect crimes from Paine & his followers, are we to believe that Bishops do not Rail? I should Expect that the man who wrote this sneaking sentence *would be as good an inquisitor as any other Priest*. Conscience in those that have it is unequivocal. It is the voice of God. Our judgment of right & wrong is Reason. I believe that the Bishop laught at the Bible in his slieve & so did Locke. Virtue is not Opinion.

Virtue & honesty, or the dictates of Conscience, are of
no doubtful Signification to anyone. Opinion is one
Thing. Principle another. No Man can change his Prin-
ciples. Every Man changes his opinions. He who
supposes that his Principles are to be changed is a Dis-
sembler, who Disguises his Principles & calls that
change. Paine is either a Devil or an Inspired man. Men
who give themselves to their Energetic Genius in the
manner that Paine does are no Examiners. If they are
not determinately wrong they must be Right or the
Bible is false; as to Examiners in these points they will
be spewed out. The Man who pretends to be a modest
enquirer into the truth of a self evident thing is a Knave.
The truth & certainty of Virtue & Honesty, *i.e.* Inspira-
tion, needs no one to prove it; it is Evident as the Sun &
Moon. He who stands doubting of what he intends,
whether it is Virtuous or Vicious, knows not what Virtue
means. No man can do a Vicious action & think it to be
Virtuous. No man can take darkness for light. He may
pretend to do so & may pretend to be a modest En-
quirer, but he is a Knave.

The Bible says that God formed Nature perfect, but
that Man perverted the order of Nature, since which
time the Elements are fill'd with the Prince of Evil, who
has the power of the air. Natural Religion is the voice
of God & not the result of reasoning on the Powers of
Satan. Horrible! The Bishop is an Inquisitor. God never
makes one man murder another, nor one nation. There
is a vast difference between an accident brought on by
a man's own carelessness & a destruction from the
designs of another. The Earthquakes at Lisbon etc. were
the Natural result of Sin, but the distruction of the
Canaanites by Joshua was the Unnatural design of

wicked men. To Extirpate a nation by means of another is as wicked as to destroy an individual by means of another individual, which God considers (in the Bible) as Murder & commands that it shall not be done. Therefore the Bishop has not answer'd Paine. . . .

That the Jews assumed a right Exclusively to the benefits of God will be a lasting witness against them & the same will it be against Christians. . . .

Jesus could not do miracles where unbelief hindered, hence we must conclude that the man who holds miracles to be ceased puts it out of his own power to ever witness one. The manner of a miracle being performed is in modern times considered as an arbitrary command of the agent upon the patient, but this is an impossibility, not a miracle, neither did Jesus ever do such a miracle. Is it a greater miracle to feed five thousand men with five loaves than to overthrow all the armies of Europe with a small pamphlet? Look over the events of your own life & if you do not find that you have both done such miracles & lived by such you do not see as I do. True, I cannot do a miracle thro' experiment & to domineer over & prove to others my superior power, as neither could Christ. But I can & do work such as both astonish & comfort me & mine. How can Paine, the worker of miracles, ever doubt Christ's in the above sense of the word miracle? But how can Watson ever believe the above sense of a miracle, who considers it as an arbitrary act of the agent upon an unbelieving patient, whereas the Gospel says that Christ could not do a miracle because of Unbelief?

If Christ could not do miracles because of Unbelief, the reason alledged by Priests for miracles is false; for those who believe want not to be confounded by miracles. Christ & his Prophets & Apostles were not Ambitious miracle mongers. . . .

Prophets, in the modern sense of the word, have never existed. Jonah was no prophet in the modern sense, for his prophecy of Nineveh failed. Every honest man is a Prophet; he utters his opinion both of private & public matters. Thus: If you go on So, the result is So. He never says, such a thing shall happen let you do what you will. A Prophet is a Seer, not an Arbitrary Dictator. It is man's fault if God is not able to do him good, for he gives to the just & to the unjust, but the unjust reject his gift. . . .

Nothing can be more contemptible than to suppose Public RECORDS to be True. Read, then, & Judge, if you are not a Fool.

Of what consequence is it whether Moses wrote the Pentateuch or no? If Paine trifles in some of his objections it is folly to confute him so seriously in them & leave his more material ones unanswered. Public Records! As if Public Records were True! Impossible; for the facts are such as none but the actor could tell. If it is True, Moses & none but he could write it, unless we allow it to be Poetry & that poetry inspired.

If historical facts can be written by inspiration, Milton's Paradise Lost is as true as Genesis or Exodus; but the Evidence is nothing, for how can he who writes what he has neither seen nor heard of be an Evidence of The Truth of his history. . . .

I cannot concieve the Divinity of the books in the Bible to consist either in who they were written by, or at what time, or in the historical evidence which may be all false in the eyes of one man & true in the eyes of another, but in the Sentiments & Examples, which, whether true or Parabolic, are Equally useful as Examples given to us of the perverseness of some & its consequent evil & the honesty of others & its consequent good. This sense of the Bible is equally true to all & equally plain to all. None can doubt the impression which he receives from a book of Examples. If he is good he will abhor wickedness in David or Abraham; if he is wicked he will make their wickedness an excuse for his & so he would do by any other book. . . .

. . . The importance of revelation is by nothing rendered more apparent, than by the discordant sentiments of learned and good men (for I speak not of the *ignorant and immoral*) on this point.

It appears to me Now that Tom Paine is a better Christian than the Bishop.

I have read this Book with attention & find that the Bishop has only hurt Paine's heel while Paine has broken his head. The Bishop has not answer'd one of Paine's grand objections.

(Written on the last page)

From ANNOTATIONS TO "BACON'S ESSAYS"
LONDON 1798

(1798)

Good advice for Satan's Kingdom [*on the title-page*].
Is it true or is it false that the wisdom of the world is
foolishness with God? This is certain: if what Bacon
says is true, what Christ says is false. If Caesar is right,
Christ is wrong, both in politics and religion, since they
will divide themselves in two.

Everybody knows that this is epicurism and libertin-
ism, and yet everybody says that it is Christian philoso-
phy. How is this possible? Everybody must be a liar and
deceiver? No! "Everybody" does not do this; but the
hirelings of Kings and Courts, who made themselves
"everybody", and knowingly propagate falsehood. It
was a common opinion in the Court of Queen Elizabeth
that knavery is wisdom. Cunning plotters were con-
sidered as wise Machiavels. . . .

Did not Jesus descend and become a servant? The
Prince of Darkness is a gentleman and not a man: he is
a Lord Chancellor.

What do these knaves mean by virtue? Do they mean
war and its horrors, and its heroic villains?

Thought is act. Christ's acts were nothing to Caesar's if this is not so.

The increase of a State, as of a man, is from internal improvement or intellectual acquirement. Man is not improved by the hurt of another. States are not improved at the expense of foreigners.

Bacon calls intellectual arts unmanly: and so they are for kings and wars, and shall in the end annihilate them.

What is fortune but an outward accident, for a few years, sixty at the most, and then gone?

King James was Bacon's primum mobile.

A tyrant is the worst disease, and the cause of all others.

Everybody hates a king! David was afraid to say that the envy was upon a king: but is this envy or indignation?

From ANNOTATIONS TO
SIR JOSHUA REYNOLDS'S DISCOURSES
LONDON 1798

(1808)

This Man was Hired to Depress Art.
This is the Opinion of Will Blake: my Proofs of this Opinion are given in the following Notes.

Advice of the Popes who succeeded the Age of Rafael

Degrade first the Arts if you'd Mankind Degrade.
Hire Idiots to Paint with cold light & hot shade:
Give high Price for the worst, leave the best in disgrace,
And with Labours of Ignorance fill every place.

Having spent the Vigour of my Youth & Genius under the Opression of Sr Joshua & his Gang of Cunning Hired Knaves Without Employment & as much as could possibly be Without Bread, The Reader must Expect to Read in all my Remarks on these Books Nothing but Indignation & Resentment. While Sr Joshua was rolling in Riches, Barry was Poor & Unemploy'd except by his own Energy; Mortimer was call'd a Madman, & only Portrait Painting applauded & rewarded by the Rich & Great. Reynolds & Gainsborough Blotted & Blurred one against the other & Divided all the English World between them. Fuseli, Indignant, almost hid himself. I am hid.

The Arts & Sciences are the Destruction of Tyrannies or Bad Governments. Why should A Good Government endeavour to Depress what is its Chief & only Support?

The Foundation of Empire is Art & Science. Remove them or Degrade them, & the Empire is No More. Empire follows Art & Not Vice Versa as Englishmen suppose.

Who will Dare to Say that Polite Art is Encouraged or Either Wished or Tolerated in a Nation where The Society for the Encouragement of Art Suffer'd Barry to Give them his Labour for Nothing, A Society Composed of the Flower of the English Nobility & Gentry?—

Suffering an Artist to Starve while he Supported Really what They, under Pretence of Encouraging, were Endeavouring to Depress.—Barry told me that while he Did that Work, he Lived on Bread & Apples.

O Society for Encouragement of Art! O King & Nobility of England! Where have you hid Fuseli's Milton? Is Satan troubled at his Exposure?

To learn the Language of Art, "Copy for Ever" is My Rule.

The Bible says That Cultivated Life Existed First. Uncultivated Life comes afterwards from Satan's Hirelings. Necessaries, Accomodations & Ornaments are the whole of Life. Satan took away Ornament First. Next he took away Accomodations, & Then he became Lord & Master of Necessaries.

Liberality! we want not Liberality. We want a Fair Price & Proportionate Value & a General Demand for Art.

Let not that Nation where Less than Nobility is the Reward, Pretend that Art is Encouraged by that Nation. Art is First in Intellectuals & Ought to be First in Nations.

Invention depends Altogether upon Execution or Organization; as that is right or wrong so is the Invention perfect or imperfect. Whoever is set to Undermine the Execution of Art is set to destroy Art. Michael Angelo's Art depends on Michael Angelo's Execution Altogether.

Men who have been Educated with Works of Venetian Artists under their Eyes cannot see Rafael unless they are born with Determinate Organs.

I am happy I cannot say that Rafael Ever was, from my Earliest Childhood, hidden from Me. I Saw & I Knew immediately the difference between Rafael & Rubens.

> Some look to see the sweet Outlines
> And beauteous Forms that Love does wear.
> Some look to find out Patches, Paint,
> Bracelets & Stays & Powder'd Hair.

A Lie! The Florid Style, such as the Venetian & the Flemish, Never Struck Me at Once nor At-All.

The Style that Strikes the Eye is the True Style, But A Fool's Eye is Not to be a Criterion.

If he means that Copying Correctly is a hindrance, he is a Liar, for that is the only School to the Language of Art.

The Contradictions in Reynolds's Discourses are Strong Presumptions that they are the Work of Several Hands, But this is no Proof that Reynolds did not Write them. The Man, Either Painter or Philosopher, who Learns or Acquires all he knows from Others, Must be full of Contradictions.

I was once looking over the Prints from Rafael & Michael Angelo in the Library of the Royal Academy. Moser came to me & said: "You should not Study these old Hard, Stiff & Dry, Unfinish'd Works of Art—Stay a little & I will shew you what you should Study." He then went & took down Le Brun's & Rubens's Galleries. How I did secretly Rage! I also spoke my Mind. . . .

I said to Moser, "These things that you call Finish'd are not Even Begun; how can they then be Finish'd?

The Man who does not know The Beginning never can
know the End of Art."

A Lie! Working up Effect is more an operation of
Indolence than the Making out of the Parts, as far as
Greatest is more than Least. I speak here of Rem-
brandt's & Rubens's & Reynolds's Effects. For Real
Effect is Making out the Parts, & it is Nothing Else but
That.

If Reynolds had Really admired Mich. Angelo, he
never would have follow'd Rubens.

Such Men as Goldsmith ought not to have been Ac-
quainted with such Men as Reynolds.

To Generalize is to be an Idiot. To Particularize is the
Alone Distinction of Merit. General Knowledges are
those Knowledges that Idiots possess.

The Man who does not Labour more than the Hire-
ling must be a poor Devil.

[To a footnote giving a quotation from Pope appropriate to "the
ferocious and enslaved Republick of France", ending with the lines:]

> They led their wild desires to woods and caves
> And thought that all but savages were slaves

When France got free, Europe, 'twixt Fool & Knaves,
Were Savage first to France, & after—Slaves.

This Whole Book was Written to Serve Political Pur-
poses.

When Sr Joshua Reynolds died
All Nature was degraded;
The King drop'd a tear into the Queen's Ear
And all his Pictures Faded.

I consider Reynolds's Discourses to the Royal Academy as the Simulations of the Hypocrite who smiles particularly where he means to Betray. His Praise of Rafael is like the Hysteric Smile of Revenge. His Softness & Candour, the hidden trap & the poisoned feast. He praises Michel Angelo for Qualities which Michel Angelo abhorr'd, & He blames Rafael for the only Qualities which Rafael Valued. Whether Reynolds knew what he was doing is nothing to me: the Mischief is just the same whether a Man does it Ignorantly or Knowingly. I always consider'd True Art & True Artists to be particularly Insulted & Degraded by the Reputation of these Discourses, As much as they were Degraded by the Reputation of Reynolds's Paintings, & that Such Artists as Reynolds are at all times Hired by the Satans for the Depression of Art—A Pretence of Art, To destroy Art.

The Neglect of Fuseli's Milton in a Country pretending to the Encouragement of Art is a Sufficient Apology for My Vigorous Indignation, if indeed the Neglect of My own Powers had not been. Ought not the Employers of Fools to be Execrated in future Ages? They Will and Shall! Foolish Men, your own real Greatness depends on your Encouragement of the Arts, & your Fall will depend on their Neglect & Depression. What you Fear is your true Interest. Leo X was advised not to Encourage the Arts; he was too Wise to take this Advice.

The Rich Men of England form themselves into a Society to Sell & Not to Buy Pictures. The Artist who does not throw his Contempt on such Trading Exhibitions, does not know either his own Interest or his Duty.

When Nations grow Old, The Arts grow Cold
And Commerce settles on every Tree,
And the Poor & the Old can live upon Gold,
For all are Born Poor, Aged Sixty three.

Reynolds's Opinion was that Genius May be Taught & that all Pretence to Inspiration is a Lie & a Deceit, to say the least of it. For if it is a Deceit, the whole Bible is Madness. This Opinion originates in the Greeks' calling the Muses Daughters of Memory.

The Enquiry in England is not whether a Man has Talents & Genius, But whether he is Passive & Polite & a Virtuous Ass & obedient to Noblemen's Opinions in Art & Science. If he is, he is a Good Man. If Not, he must be Starved.

Minute Discrimination is Not Accidental. All Sublimity is founded on Minute Discrimination.

I do not believe that Rafael taught Mich. Angelo, or that Mich. Angelo taught Rafael, any more than I believe that the Rose teaches the Lilly how to grow, or the Apple tree teaches the Pear tree how to bear Fruit. I do not believe the tales of Anecdote writers when they militate against Individual Character.

Imitation is Criticism.

Are we to understand him to mean that Facility in Composing is a Frivolous pursuit? A Facility in Composing is the Greatest Power of Art, & Belongs to None but the Greatest Artists, the Most Minutely Discriminating & Determinate.

Mechanical Excellence is the Only Vehicle of Genius.

Execution is the Chariot of Genius.

The Lives of Painters say that Rafael Died of Dissipation. Idleness is one Thing & Dissipation Another. He who has Nothing to Dissipate Cannot Dissipate; the Weak Man may be Virtuous Enough, but will Never be an Artist.
Painters are noted for being Dissipated & Wild.

The Labour'd Works of Journeymen employ'd by Correggio, Titian, Veronese & all the Venetians, ought not to be shewn to the Young Artist as the Works of original Conception any more than the Engravings of Strange, Bartolozzi, or Wollett. They are Works of Manual Labour.

After having been a Fool, a Student is to amass a Stock of Ideas, &, knowing himself to be a Fool, he is to assume the Right to put other Men's Ideas into his Foolery.

Instead of Following One Great Master he is to follow a Great Many Fools.

Contemptible Mocks!

Reynolds Depreciates the Efforts of Inventive Genius. Trifling Conceits are better than Colouring without any meaning at all.

No one can ever Design till he has learn'd the Language of Art by making many Finish'd Copies both of Nature & Art & of whatever comes in his way from Earliest Childhood. The difference between a bad Artist & a Good One Is: the Bad Artist Seems to copy a Great deal. The Good one Really does Copy a Great deal.

Nonsense! Every Eye sees differently. As the Eye, Such the Object.

General Principles Again! Unless you Consult Particulars you Cannot even Know or See Mich. Ango. or Rafael or any Thing Else.

But as mere enthusiasm will carry you but a little way . . .

Meer Enthusiasm is the All in All! Bacon's Philosophy has Ruin'd England. Bacon is only Epicurus over again.

The Man who asserts that there is no such Thing as Softness in Art, & that every thing in Art is Definite & Determinate, has not been told this by Practise, but by Inspiration & Vision, because Vision is Determinate & Perfect, & he Copies That without Fatigue, Every thing being Definite & determinate. Softness is Produced alone by Comparative Strength & Weakness in the Marking out of the Forms. I say These Principles could never be found out by the Study of Nature with Con—, or Innate, Science.

A work of Genius is a Work "Not to be obtain'd by the Invocation of Memory & her Syren Daughters, but by Devout prayer to that Eternal Spirit, who can enrich with all utterance & knowledge & sends out his Seraphim with the hallowed fire of his Altar to touch & purify the lips of whom he pleases." MILTON.

The following Discourse is particularly Interesting to Block heads, as it endeavours to prove That there is No such thing as Inspiration & that any Man of a plain Understanding may by Thieving from Others become a Mich. Angelo.

Without Minute Neatness of Execution The Sublime cannot Exist! Grandeur of Ideas is founded on Precision of Ideas.

Enthusiastic Admiration is the first Principle of Knowledge & its last. Now he begins to Degrade, to Deny & to Mock.

The Man who on Examining his own Mind finds nothing of Inspiration ought not to dare to be an Artist, & he is a Fool & a Cunning Knave suited to the Purposes of Evil Demons.

The Man who never in his Mind & Thoughts travel'd to Heaven Is No Artist.

Artists who are above a plain Understanding are Mock'd & Destroy'd by this President of Fools.

It is Evident that Reynolds Wish'd none but Fools to be in the Arts & in order to this, he calls all others Vague Enthusiasts or Madmen.

What has Reasoning to do with the Art of Painting?

Singular & Particular Detail is the Foundation of the Sublime.

Knowledge of Ideal Beauty is Not to be Acquired. It is Born with us. Innate Ideas are in Every Man, Born with him; they are truly Himself. The Man who says that we have No Innate Ideas must be a Fool & Knave, Having No Con-Science or Innate Science.

One Central Form composed of all other Forms being Granted, it does not therefore follow that all other Forms are Deformity.

All Forms are Perfect in the Poet's Mind, but these are not Abstracted nor compounded from Nature, but are from Imagination.

The Great Bacon—he is Call'd: I call him the Little Bacon—says that Every thing must be done by Experiment; his first principle is Unbelief, and yet here he says that Art must be produc'd Without such Method. He is Like Sr Joshua, full of Self-Contradiction & Knavery.

What is General Nature? is there Such a Thing? what is General Knowledge? is there such a Thing? Strictly Speaking All Knowledge is Particular.

The Symmetry of Deformity is a Pretty Foolery. Can any Man who Thinks Talk so? Leanness or Fatness is not Deformity, but Reynolds thought Character Itself Extravagance & Deformity. Age & Youth are not Classes, but Properties of Each Class; so are Leanness & Fatness.

Generalizing in Every thing, the Man would soon be a Fool, but a Cunning Fool.

What does this mean, *"Would have been"* one of the *first Painters of his Age?* Albert Durer *Is,* Not would have been. Besides, let them look at Gothic Figures &

Gothic Buildings & not talk of Dark Ages or of any Age. Ages are all Equal. But Genius is Always Above The Age.

He is for Determinate & yet for Indeterminate.

Distinct General Form Cannot Exist. Distinctness is Particular, Not General.

. . . Bacon's Philosophy makes both Statesmen & Artists Fools & Knaves.

The Two Following Discourses [IV & V] are Particularly Calculated for the Setting Ignorant & Vulgar Artists as Models of Execution in Art. Let him who will, follow such advice. I will not. I know that The Man's Execution is as his Conception & No better.

All but Names of Persons & Places is Invention both in Poetry & Painting.

Sacrifice the Parts, What becomes of the Whole?

To produce an Effect of True Light & Shadow is Necessary to the Ornamental Style, which altogether depends on Distinctness of Form. The Venetian ought not to be call'd the Ornamental Style.

The Language of Painters cannot be allow'd them if Reynolds says right at p. 97; he there says that the Venetian Will Not Correspond with the Great Style. The Greek Gems are in the Same Style as the Greek Statues.

Reynolds contradicts what he says continually. He makes little Concessions that he may take Great Advantages.

Venetian Attention is to a Contempt & Neglect of Form Itself & to the Destruction of all Form or Outline Purposely & Intentionally.

On the Venetian Painter

He makes the Lame to walk we all agree,
But then he strives to blind those who can see.

Mich. Ang. knew & despised all that Titian could do.

If the Venetian's Outline was Right, his Shadows would destroy it & deform its appearance.

A Pair of Stays to mend the Shape
Of crooked, Humpy Woman
Put on, O Venus! now thou art
Quite a Venetian Roman.

Titian, as well as the other Venetians, so far from Senatorial Dignity appears to me to give always the Characters of Vulgar Stupidity.

Why should Titian & The Venetians be Named in a discourse on Art? Such Idiots are not Artists.

Venetian, all thy Colouring is no more
Than Boulster'd Plasters on a Crooked Whore.

Broken Colours & Broken Lines & Broken Masses are Equally Subversive of the Sublime.

Well Said Enough!

How can that be call'd the Ornamental Style of which Gross Vulgarity forms the Principal Excellence?

A History Painter Paints The Hero, & not Man in General, but most minutely in Particular.

Of what consequence is it to the Arts what a Portrait Painter does?

There is No Such a Thing as A Composite Style.

Genius has no Error; it is Ignorance that is Error.

All Equivocation & Self-Contradiction!

Gainsborough told a Gentleman of Rank & Fortune that the Worst Painters always chose the Grandest Subjects. I desired the Gentleman to Set Gainsborough about one of Rafael's Grandest Subjects, Namely Christ delivering the Keys to St. Peter, & he would find that in Gainsborough's hands it would be a Vulgar Subject of Poor Fishermen & a Journeyman Carpenter.

The following Discourse is written with the same End in View that Gainsborough had in making the Above assertion, Namely To Represent Vulgar Artists as the Models of Executive Merit.

Passion & Expression is Beauty Itself. The Face that is Incapable of Passion & Expression is deformity Itself. Let it be Painted & Patch'd & Praised & Advertised for Ever, it will only be admired by Fools.

If Reynolds could not see variety of Character in Rafael, Others Can.

Reynolds cannot bear Expression.

Fresco Painting is the Most Minute. Fresco Painting is Like Miniature Painting; a Wall is a Large Ivory.

The Man who can say that Rafael knew not the smaller beauties of the Art ought to be contemn'd, & I accordingly hold Reynolds in Contempt . . .

Rafael did as he Pleased. He who does not admire Rafael's Execution does not Even see Rafael.

According to Reynolds Mich. Angelo was worse still & knew Nothing at all about Art as an object of Imitation. Can any Man be such a fool as to believe that Rafael & Michael Angelo were Incapable of the meer Language of Art & That Such Idiots as Rubens, Correggio & Titian knew how to Execute what they could not Think or Invent?

Damned Fool!

The Great Style is always Novel or New in all its Operations.

Original & Characteristical are the Two Grand Merits of the Great Style.

Salvator Rosa was precisely what he Pretended not to be. His Pictures are high Labour'd pretensions to Expeditious Workmanship. He was the Quack Doctor of Painting. His Roughnesses & Smoothnesses are the Production of Labour & Trick. As to Imagination, he was totally without Any.

Savages are Fops & Fribbles more than any other Men.

All Rubens's Pictures are Painted by Journeymen &, so far from being all of a Piece, are The most wretched Bungles.

To My Eye Rubens's Colouring is most Contemptible. His Shadows are of a Filthy Brown somewhat of the Colour of Excrement; these are fill'd with tints & messes of yellow & red. His lights are all the Colours of the Rainbow, laid on Indiscriminately & broken one into another. Altogether his Colouring is Contrary to The Colouring of Real Art & Science.

Opposed to Rubens's Colouring Sr Joshua has placed Poussin, but he ought to put All Men of Genius who ever Painted. Rubens & the Venetians are Opposite in every thing to True Art & they Meant to be so; they were hired for this Purpose.

Why then does he talk in other places of pleasing Every body?

When a Man talks of Acquiring Invention & of learning how to produce Original Conception, he must expect to be call'd a Fool by Men of Understanding; but such a Hired Knave cares not for the Few. His Eye is on the Many, or, rather, the Money.

Bacon's Philosophy has Destroy'd [*word cut away*] Art & Science. The Man who says that the Genius is not Born, but Taught—Is a Knave.

O Reader, behold the Philosopher's Grave!
He was born quite a Fool, but he died quite a Knave.

How ridiculous it would be to see the Sheep Endeavouring to walk like the Dog, or the Ox striving to trot like the Horse; just as Ridiculous it is to see One Man Striving to Imitate Another. Man varies from Man more than Animal from Animal of different Species.

If Art was Progressive We should have had Mich. Angelos & Rafaels to Succeed & to Improve upon each other. But it is not so. Genius dies with its Possessor & Comes not again till Another is Born with It.

Identities or Things are Neither Cause nor Effect. They are Eternal.

Reynolds Thinks that Man Learns all that he knows. I say on the Contrary that Man Brings All that he has or can have Into the World with him. Man is Born Like a Garden ready Planted & Sown. This World is too poor to produce one Seed.

Reynolds: The mind is but a barren soil; a soil which is soon exhausted, and will produce no crop, . . .

The mind that could have produced this Sentence must have been a Pitiful, a Pitiable Imbecillity. I always thought that the Human Mind was the most Prolific of All Things & Inexhaustible. I certainly do Thank God that I am not like Reynolds.

A Very Clever Sentence; who wrote it, God knows.

No Man who can see Michael Angelo can say that he wants either Colouring or Ornamental parts of Art in the highest degree, for he has Every Thing of Both.

He who Admires Rafael Must admire Rafael's Execution. He who does not admire Rafael's Execution Cannot Admire Rafael.

A Polish'd Villain who Robs & Murders!

He who can be bound down is No Genius. Genius cannot be Bound; it may be Render'd Indignant & Outrageous.

> "Opression makes the Wise Man Mad."
>
> SOLOMON.

The Purpose of the following discourse [VII] is to Prove That Taste & Genius are not of Heavenly Origin & that all who have supposed that they Are so, are to be Consider'd as Weak headed Fanatics.

The Obligations Reynolds has laid on Bad Artists of all Classes will at all times make them his Admirers, but most especially for this discourse, in which it is proved that the Stupid are born with Faculties Equal to other Men, Only they have not Cultivated them because they thought it not worth the trouble.

Obscurity is Neither the Source of the Sublime nor of any Thing Else.

The Ancients did not mean to Impose when they affirm'd their belief in Vision & Revelation. Plato was in Earnest: Milton was in Earnest. They believ'd that God did Visit Man Really & Truly & not as Reynolds pretends.

How very Anxious Reynolds is to Disprove & Contemn Spiritual Perception!

He states Absurdities in Company with Truths & calls both Absurd.

The Artifice of the Epicurean Philosophers is to Call all other Opinions Unsolid & Unsubstantial than those which are derived from Earth.

It is not in Terms that Reynolds & I disagree. Two Contrary Opinions can never by any Language be made alike. I say, Taste & Genius are Not Teachable or Acquirable, but are born with us. Reynolds says the Contrary.

Demonstration, Similitude & Harmony are Objects of Reasoning. Invention, Identity & Melody are Objects of Intuition.

God forbid that Truth should be Confined to Mathematical Demonstration!

He who does not Know Truth at Sight is unworthy of Her Notice.

Here is a great deal to do to Prove that All Truth is Prejudice, for All that is Valuable in Knowledge is Superior to Demonstrative Science, such as is Weighed or Measured.

He thinks he has proved that Genius & Inspiration are All a Hum.

He may as well say that if Man does not lay down settled Principles, The Sun will not rise in a Morning.

Here is a Plain Confession that he Thinks Mind & Imagination not to be above the Mortal & Perishing Nature. Such is the End of Epicurean or Newtonian Philosophy; it is Atheism.

Reynolds's Eye could not bear Characteristic Colouring or Light & Shade.

Reynolds: A picture should please at first sight, and appear to invite the spectator's attention; . . .

Please Whom? Some Men cannot see a Picture except in a Dark Corner.

Violent Passions Emit the Real, Good & Perfect Tones.

A Fool's Balance is no Criterion because, tho' it goes down on the heaviest side, we ought to look what he puts into it.

Reynolds: In the midst of the highest flights of fancy or imagination, reason ought to preside from first to last, . . .

If this is True, it is a devilish Foolish Thing to be an Artist.

Burke's Treatise on the Sublime & Beautiful is founded on the Opinions of Newton & Locke; on this Treatise Reynolds has grounded many of his assertions in all his Discourses. I read Burke's Treatise when very Young; at the same time I read Locke on Human Understanding & Bacon's Advancement of Learning; on Every one of these Books I wrote my Opinions, & on looking them over find that my Notes on Reynolds in this Book are exactly Similar. I felt the Same Contempt & Abhorrence then that I do now. They mock Inspiration & Vision. Inspiration & Vision was then, & now is, & I hope will always Remain, my Element, my Eternal Dwelling place; how can I then hear it Contemned without returning Scorn for Scorn?

Rembrandt was a Generalizer. Poussin was a Particularizer.

Poussin knew better than to make all his Pictures have the same light & shadows. Any fool may concentrate a light in the Middle.

If you Endeavour to Please the Worst, you will never Please the Best. To please All Is Impossible.

Bad Pictures are always Sr Joshua's Friends.

EPIGRAMS AND VERSES
CONCERNING
SIR JOSHUA REYNOLDS

(1808–1811)

Can there be any thing more mean,
More Malice in disguise,
Than Praise a Man for doing what
That Man does most despise?
Reynolds Lectures Exactly so
When he praises Michael Angelo.

Sir Joshua Praises Michael Angelo:
'Tis Christian Mildness when Knaves Praise a Foe;
But 'Twould be Madness all the World would say
Should Michael Angelo praise Sir Joshua—
Christ us'd the Pharisees in a rougher way.

FLORENTINE INGRATITUDE

Sir Joshua sent his own Portrait to
The birth Place of Michael Angelo,
And in the hand of the simpering fool
He put a dirty paper scroll,
And on the paper, to be polite,
Did "Sketches by Michael Angelo" write.
The Florentines said, " 'Tis a Dutch English bore,
Michael Angelo's Name writ on Rembrandt's door."

586

The Florentines call it an English Fetch,
For Michael Angelo did never sketch.
Every line of his has Meaning
And needs neither Suckling nor Weaning.
'Tis the trading English Venetian cant
To speak Michael Angelo & Act Rembrandt.
It will set his Dutch friends all in a roar
To write "Mich. Ang." on Rembrandt's Door.
But You must not bring in your hand a Lie
If you mean the Florentines should buy.

Ghiotto's Circle or Apelles' Line
Were not the Work of Sketchers drunk with Wine,
Nor of the City Clark's warm hearted Fashion,
Nor of Sir Isaac Newton's Calculation,
Nor of the City Clark's Idle Facilities
Which sprang from Sir Isaac Newton's great Abilities.

These Verses were written by a very Envious Man,
Who, whatever likeness he may have to Michael Angelo,
Never can have any to Sir Jehoshuan.

A PITIFUL CASE

The Villain at the Gallows tree
When he is doom'd to die,
To assuage his misery
In Virtue's praise does cry.

So Reynolds when he came to die,
To assuage his bitter woe
Thus aloud does howl & cry:
"Michael Angelo! Michael Angelo!"

The Cripple every Step Drudges & labours,
And says: "Come, learn to walk of me, Good Neigh-
    bours."
Sir Joshua in astonishment cries out:
"See, what Great Labour! Pain in Modest Doubt!"

Newton & Bacon cry, being badly Nurst:
"He is all Experiments from last to first.
He walks & stumbles as if he crep,
And how high labour'd is every step!"

TO VENETIAN ARTISTS

That God is Colouring Newton does shew,
And the devil is a Black outline, all of us know.
Perhaps this little Fable may make us merry:
A dog went over the water without a wherry:
A bone which he had stolen he had in his mouth;
He cared not whether the wind was north or south.
As he swam he saw the reflection of the bone.
"This is quite Perfection, one Generalizing Tone!
Outline! There's no outline! There's no such thing!
All is Chiaro Scuro, Poco Pen, it's all colouring."
Snap, Snap! he has lost shadow & substance too.
He had them both before: now how do ye do?
"A great deal better than I was before.
Those who taste colouring love it more & more."
"O dear Mother outline, of knowledge most sage,
What's the First Part of Painting?" she said: "Patron-
    age."
"And what is the second?" to please & Engage,
She frown'd like a Fury & said: "Patronage."
"And what is the Third?" she put off Old Age,
And smil'd like a Syren & said: "Patronage."

MARGINALIA, II

From NOTES ON
SPURZHEIM'S "OBSERVATIONS ON
THE DERANGED MANIFESTATIONS
OF THE MIND, OR INSANITY"
LONDON 1817

(1819)

Cowper came to me and said: "O that I were insane
always. I will never rest. Can you not make me truly
insane? I will never rest till I am so. O that in the bosom
of God I was hid. You retain health and yet are as mad
as any of us all—over us all—mad as a refuge from un-
belief—from Bacon, Newton and Locke."

From ANNOTATIONS TO
"POEMS" BY WILLIAM WORDSWORTH
VOL. I, LONDON 1815

(1826)

I see in Wordsworth the Natural Man rising up
against the Spiritual Man Continually, & then he is No
Poet but a Heathen Philosopher at Enmity against all
true Poetry or Inspiration.

There is no such Thing as Natural Piety Because The Natural Man is at Enmity with God.

I cannot think that Real Poets have any competition. None are greatest in the Kingdom of Heaven; it is so in Poetry.

Natural Objects always did & now do weaken, deaden & obliterate Imagination in Me. Wordsworth must know that what he Writes Valuable is Not to be found in Nature.

I Believe both Macpherson & Chatterton, that what they say is Ancient Is so.

I own myself an admirer of Ossian equally with any other Poet whatever, Rowley & Chatterton also.

Imagination has nothing to do with Memory.

From ANNOTATIONS TO DR. THORNTON'S "NEW TRANSLATION OF THE LORD'S PRAYER" LONDON 1827

(1827)

I look upon this as a Most Malignant & Artful attack upon the Kingdom of Jesus By the Classical Learned, thro' the Instrumentality of Dr. Thornton. The Greek & Roman Classics is the Anthichrist. I say Is & Not Are as most expressive & correct too. [*on the title-page*]

Christ & his Apostles were Illiterate Men; Caiaphas, Pilate & Herod were Learned.

If Morality was Christianity, Socrates was The Savior.

The Beauty of the Bible is that the most Ignorant & Simple Minds Understand it Best—Was Johnson hired to Pretend to Religious Terrors while he was an Infidel, or how was it?

The only thing for Newtonian & Baconian Philosophers to Consider is this: Whether Jesus did not suffer himself to be Mock'd by Caesar's Soldiers Willingly, & to Consider this to all Eternity will be Comment Enough.

It is the learned that Mouth, & not the Vulgar.

Lawful Bread, Bought with Lawful Money, & a Lawful Heaven, seen thro' a Lawful Telescope, by means of Lawful Window Light! The Holy Ghost, & whatever cannot be Taxed, is Unlawful & Witchcraft.

Spirits are Lawful, but not Ghosts; especially Royal Gin is Lawful Spirit. No Smuggling real British Spirit & Truth!

Give us the Bread that is our due & Right, by taking away Money, or a Price, or Tax upon what is Common to all in thy Kingdom.

Jesus, our Father, who art in thy heaven call'd by thy Name the Holy Ghost, Thy Kingdom on Earth is Not, nor thy Will done, but Satan's, who is God of this World, the Accuser. Let his Judgment be Forgiveness that he may be cursed on his own throne.

Give us This Eternal Day our own right Bread by taking away Money or debtor Tax & Value or Price, as [words illegible] have all the Common [several words *illegible*] among us. Every thing has as much right to Eternal Life as God, who is the Servant of Man. His Judgment shall be Forgiveness that he may be consum'd on his own Throne.

Leave us not in Parsimony, Satan's Kingdom; liberate us from the Natural Man & [*words illegible*] Kingdom.

For thine is the Kingdom & the Power & the Glory & not Ceasar's or Satan's. Amen.

Doctor Thornton's Tory Translation, Translated out of its disguise in the Classical & Scotch languages into the vulgar English.

Our Father Augustus Ceasar, who art in these thy Substantial Astronomical Telescopic Heavens, Holiness to thy Name or Title, & reverence to thy Shadow. Thy Kingship come upon Earth first & then in Heaven. Give us day by day our Real Taxed Substantial Money bought Bread; deliver from the Holy Ghost whatever cannot be Taxed; for all is debts & Taxes between Caesar & us & one another; lead us not to read the Bible, but let our Bible be Virgil & Shakespeare; & deliver us from Poverty in Jesus, that Evil One. For thine is the Kingship, [or] Allegoric Godship, & the Power, or War, & the Glory, or Law, Ages after Ages in thy descendants; for God is only an Allegory of Kings & nothing Else. AMEN.

MIRTH AND HER COMPANIONS

(1820)

[*Engraved beneath a print of the first subject illustrating Milton's L'Allegro.*]

Solomon says, "Vanity of Vanities, all is Vanity," & What can be Foolisher than this?

NOTE IN CENNINI'S
"TRATTATO DELLA PITTURA"
ROMA. MDCCCXXI

(1822)

The Pope supposes Nature & the Virgin Mary to be the same allegorical personages, but the Protestant considers Nature as incapable of bearing a Child.

NOTES ON THE ILLUSTRATIONS
TO DANTE

(1825-1827)

[On design no. 7, a map of the classical conception of the Universe, written in the circles surrounding the central figure of Homer.]

Every thing in Dante's Comedia shews That for Tyrannical Purposes he has made This World the Foundation of All, & the Goddess Nature Mistress; Nature is his Inspirer & not . . . the Holy Ghost. As Poor Shakspeare said: "Nature, thou art my "Goddess."

Round Purgatory is Paradise, & round Paradise is Vacuum or Limbo, so that Homer is the Center of All—I mean the Poetry of the Heathen, Stolen & Perverted from the Bible, not by Chance but by design, by the Kings of Persia & their Generals, The Greek Heroes & lastly by the Romans.

Swedenborg does the same in saying that in this World is the Ultimate of Heaven. This is the most damnable Falshood of Satan & his Antichrist.

On design no. 16, The Goddess Fortune.

The Goddess Fortune is the devil's servant, ready to Kiss any one's Arse.

On design no. 101, a diagram of the Circles of Hell.

It seems as if Dante's supreme Good was something Superior to the Father or Jesus; for if he gives his rain to the Evil & the Good, & his Sun to the Just & the Unjust, He could never have Built Dante's Hell, nor the Hell of the Bible neither, in the way our Parsons explain it—It must have been originally Formed by the devil Himself; & So I understand it to have been.

This [*the diagram*] is Upside Down When view'd from Hell's gate, which ought to be at top, But right When View'd from Purgatory after they have passed the Center.

In Equivocal Worlds Up & Down are Equivocal.

Whatever Book is for Vengeance for Sin & Whatever Book is Against the Forgiveness of Sins is not of the Father, but of Satan the Accuser & Father of Hell.

EPIGRAMS, VERSES, AND
FRAGMENTS

(1808–1811)

You don't believe—I won't attempt to make ye:
You are asleep—I won't attempt to wake ye.
Sleep on, Sleep on! while in your pleasant dreams
Of Reason you may drink of Life's clear streams.
Reason and Newton, they are quite two things;
For so the Swallow & the Sparrow sings.
Reason says "Miracle": Newton says "Doubt".
Aye! that's the way to make all Nature out.
"Doubt, Doubt, & don't believe without experiment":
That is the very thing that Jesus meant,
When he said, "Only Believe! Believe & try!
"Try, Try, and never mind the Reason why."

Anger & Wrath my bosom rends:
I thought them the Errors of friends.
But all my limbs with warmth glow:
I find them the Errors of the foe.

"Madman" I have been call'd: "Fool" they call thee
I wonder which they Envy, Thee or Me?

TO GOD

If you have form'd a Circle to go into,
Go into it yourself & see how you would do.

I am no Homer's Hero, you all know;
I profess not Generosity to a Foe.
My Generosity is to my Friends,
That for their Friendship I may make amends.
The Generous to Enemies promotes their Ends
And becomes the Enemy & Betrayer of his Friends.

TO F[LAXMAN]

I mock thee not, tho' I by thee am Mocked.
Thou call'st me Madman, but I call thee Blockhead.

Of H(ayley)'s birth this was the happy lot,
His Mother on his Father him begot.

He's a Blockhead who wants a proof of what he can't
Percieve,
And he's a Fool who tries to make such a Blockhead
believe.

C(romek) loves artists, as he loves his Meat.
He loves the Art, but 'tis the Art to Cheat.

A petty Sneaking Knave I knew—
O Mr. Cr(omek), how do ye do?

He has observ'd the Golden Rule
Till he's become the Golden Fool.

ON F[LAXMAN] & S[TOTHARD]

I found them blind: I taught them how to see;
And now they know neither themselves nor me.
'Tis Excellent to turn a thorn to a pin,
A Fool to a bolt, a Knave to a glass of gin.

P[hillips] loved me not as he lov'd his Friends,
For he lov'd them for gain to serve his Ends.
He loved me and for no Gain at all
But to rejoice & triumph in my fall.

Some Men, created for destruction, come
Into the World & make the World their home.
Be they as Vile & Base as E'er they can,
They'll still be called "The World's honest man".

ON S[TOTHARD]

You say reserve & modesty he has,
Whose heart is iron, his head wood, & his face brass.
The Fox, the Owl, the Beetle & the Bat
By sweet reserve & modesty get Fat.

TO H[AYLEY]

Thy Friendship oft has made my heart to ake:
Do be my Enemy for Friendship's sake.

Cosway, Frazer & Baldwin of Egypt's Lake
Fear to associate with Blake.
This Life is a Warfare against Evils;
They heal the sick; he casts out devils.
Hayley, Flaxman & Stothard are also in doubt
Lest their Virtue should be put to the rout.
One grins, t'other spits & in corners hides,
And all the Virtuous have shewn their backsides.

EPITAPH

I was buried near this Dike,
That my Friends may weep as much as they like.

ANOTHER

Here lies John Trot, the Friend of all mankind:
He has not left one Enemy behind.
Friends were quite hard to find, old authors say;
But now they stand in every bodies way.

My title as a Genius thus is prov'd:
Not Prais'd by Hayley nor by Flaxman lov'd.

I, Rubens, am a Statesman & a Saint.
Deceptions? And so I'll learn to Paint.

TO ENGLISH CONNOISSEURS

You must agree that Rubens was a Fool,
And yet you make him master of your School
And give more money for his slobberings
Than you will give for Rafael's finest Things.
I understood Christ was a Carpenter
And not a Brewer's Servant, my good Sir.

A PRETTY EPIGRAM FOR THE ENTERTAINMENT OF THOSE WHO HAVE PAID GREAT SUMS IN THE VENETIAN & FLEMISH OOZE

Nature & Art in this together Suit:
What is Most Grand is always most Minute.
Rubens thinks Tables, Chairs & Stools are Grand,
But Rafael thinks A Head, a foot, a hand.

These are the Idiot's chiefest arts,
To blend & not define the Parts.
The Swallow sings in Courts of Kings
That Fools have their high finishings,
And this the Princes' golden rule,
The Laborious stumble of a Fool.
To make out the parts is the wise man's aim,
But to lose them the Fool makes his foolish Game.

Rafael Sublime, Majestic, Graceful, Wise,
His Executive Power must I despise?
Rubens Low, Vulgar, Stupid, Ignorant,
His power of Execution I must grant?
Learn the Laborious stumble of a Fool,
And from an Idiot's Actions form my rule?
Go send your Children to the Slobbering School!

If I e'er Grow to Man's Estate,
O, Give to me a Woman's fate!
May I govern all, both great & small,
Have the last word & take the wall.

ON THE GREAT ENCOURAGEMENT GIVEN BY ENGLISH NOBILITY & GENTRY TO CORREGGIO, RUBENS, REMBRANDT, REYNOLDS, GAINS-BOROUGH, CATALANI, DU CROWE, & DILBURY DOODLE

As the Ignorant Savage will sell his own Wife
For a Sword or a Cutlass, a dagger or Knife,
So the Taught, Savage Englishman spends his whole
    Fortune
On a smear or a squall to destroy Picture or Tune,
And I call upon Colonel Wardle
To give these Rascals a dose of Cawdle.

Give pensions to the Learned Pig
Or the Hare playing on a Tabor;
Anglus can never see Perfection
But in the Journeyman's Labour.

All Pictures that's Painted with Sense & with Thought
Are Painted by Madmen as sure as a Groat;
For the Greater the Fool in the Pencil more blest,
And when they are drunk they always paint best.
They never can Rafael it, Fuseli it, nor Blake it;
If they can't see an outline, pray how can they make it?
When Men will draw outlines begin you to jaw them;
Madmen see outlines & therefore they draw them.

ON H[AYLEY] THE PICK THANK

I write the Rascal Thanks till he & I
With Thanks & Compliments are quite drawn dry.

CROMEK SPEAKS

I always take my judgment from a Fool
Because his judgment is so very Cool,
Not prejudic'd by feelings great or small.
Amiable state! he cannot feel at all.

ENGLISH ENCOURAGEMENT OF ART: CROMEK'S OPINIONS PUT INTO RHYME

If you mean to Please Every body you will
Set to work both Ignorance & skill;
For a great multitude are Ignorant,
And skill to them seems raving & rant;
Like putting oil & water into a lamp,
'Twill make a great splutter with smoke & damp;
For there is no use, as it seems to me,
Of Lighting a Lamp when you don't wish to see.

And, when it smells of the Lamp, we can
Say all was owing to the Skilful Man.
For the smell of water is but small,
So e'en let Ignorance do it all.

You say their Pictures well Painted be,
And yet they are Blockheads you all agree.
Thank God, I never was sent to school
To be Flog'd into following the Style of a Fool.

The Errors of a Wise Man make your Rule
Rather than the Perfections of a Fool.

THE WASHERWOMAN'S SONG

I wash'd them out & wash'd them in,
And they told me it was a great Sin.

When I see a Rubens, Rembrandt, Correggio,
I think of the Crippled Harry & Slobbering Joe;
And then I question thus: are artists' rules
To be drawn from the works of two manifest fools?
Then God defend us from the Arts I say!
Send Battle, Murder, Sudden death, O pray!
Rather than be such a blind Human Fool
I'd be an Ass, a Hog, a worm, a Chair, a Stool!

Great things are done when Men & Mountains meet;
This is not done by Jostling in the Street

If you play a Game of Chance, know, before you begin,
If you are benevolent you will never win.

WILLIAM COWPER, ESQRE

For this is being a Friend just in the nick,
Not when he's well, but waiting till he's sick.
He calls you to his help: be you not mov'd
Untill, by being Sick, his wants are prov'd.

You see him spend his Soul in Prophecy.
Do you believe it a confounded lie
Till some Bookseller & the Public Fame
Proves there is truth in his extravagant claim.

For 'tis atrocious in a Friend you love
To tell you any thing that he can't prove,
And 'tis most wicked in a Christian Nation
For any Man to pretend to Inspiration.

The only Man that e'er I knew
Who did not make me almost spew
Was Fuseli: he was both Turk & Jew—
And so, dear Christian Friends, how do you do?

BLAKE'S APOLOGY FOR HIS CATALOGUE

Having given great offence by writing in Prose,
I'll write in Verse as soft as Bartolloze.
Some blush at what others can see no crime in,

But nobody sees any harm in Rhyming.
Dryden in Rhyme cries, "Milton only plann'd!"
Every Fool shook his bells throughout the land.
Tom Cooke cut Hogarth down with his clean graving.
Thousands of Connoisseurs with joy ran raving.
Thus Hayley on his Toilette seeing the sope,
Cries, "Homer is very much improv'd by Pope."
Some say I've given great Provision to my foes,
And that now I lead my false friends by the nose.
Flaxman & Stothard smelling a sweet savour
Cry, "Blakified drawing spoils painter & Engraver,"
While I, looking up to my Umbrella,
Resolv'd to be a very contrary fellow,
Cry, looking quite from Skumference to Center,
"No one can finish so high as the original Inventor."
Thus Poor Schiavonetti died of the Cromek,
A thing that's tied around the Examiner's neck.
This is my sweet apology to my friends,
That I may put them in mind of their latter ends.

If Men will act like a maid smiling over a Churn,
They ought not, when it comes to another's turn,
To grow sower at what a friend may utter,
Knowing & feeling that we all have need of Butter.
False Friends! fie! fie! our Friendship you shan't sever,
In spite we will be greater friends than ever.

Some people admire the work of a Fool,
For it's sure to keep your judgment cool;
It does not reproach you with want of wit;
It is not like a lawyer serving a writ.

"Now Art has lost its mental Charms
France shall subdue the World in Arms."
So spoke an Angel at my birth,
Then said, "Descend thou upon Earth.
Renew the Arts on Britain's Shore,
And France shall fall down & adore.
With works of Art their Armies meet,
And War shall sink beneath thy feet.
But if thy Nation Arts refuse,
And if they scorn the immortal Muse,
France shall the arts of Peace restore,
And save thee from the Ungrateful shore."

Spirit, who lov'st Brittannia's Isle
Round which the Fiends of Commerce smile . . .

VIII.

THE OLD BLAKE

FRAGMENTS

INSCRIPTION IN THE AUTOGRAPH ALBUM OF WILLIAM UPCOTT

(January 16, 1826)

William Blake, one who is very much delighted with being in good Company.

Born 28 Novr 1757 in London & has died several times since.

23 May, 1810, found the Word Golden.

Jesus does not bear . . . he makes a Wide distinction between the Sheep & the Goats; consequently he is Not Charitable.

THE EVERLASTING GOSPEL

(1818)

There is not one Moral Virtue that Jesus Inculcated but Plato & Cicero did Inculcate before him; what then did Christ Inculcate? Forgiveness of Sins. This alone is the Gospel, & this is the Life & Immortality brought to light by Jesus, Even the Covenant of Jehovah, which is This: If you forgive one another your Trespasses, so shall Jehovah forgive you, That he himself may dwell among you; but if you Avenge, you Murder the Divine Image, & he cannot dwell among you; because you Murder him he arises again, & you deny that he is Arisen, & are blind to Spirit.

1

If Moral Virtue was Christianity,
Christ's Pretensions were all Vanity,
And Cai[a]phas & Pilate, Men
Praise Worthy, & the Lion's Den
And not the Sheepfold, Allegories
Of God & Heaven & their Glories.
The Moral Christian is the Cause
Of the Unbeliever & his Laws.
The Roman Virtues, Warlike Fame,
Take Jesus' & Jehovah's Name;
For what is Antichrist but those
Who against Sinners Heaven close

610

With Iron bars, in Virtuous State,
And Rhadamanthus at the Gate?

2

What can this Gospel of Jesus be?
What Life & Immortality,
What was it that he brought to Light
That Plato & Cicero did not write?
The Heathen Deities wrote them all,
These Moral Virtues, great & small.
What is the Accusation of Sin
But Moral Virtues' deadly Gin?
The Moral Virtues in their Pride
Did o'er the World triumphant ride
In Wars & Sacrifice for Sin,
And Souls to Hell ran trooping in.
The Accuser, Holy God of All
This Pharisaic Worldly Ball,
Amidst them in his Glory Beams
Upon the Rivers & the Streams.
Then Jesus rose & said to Me,
"Thy Sins are all forgiven thee."
Loud Pilate Howl'd, loud Caiphas yell'd,
When they the Gospel Light beheld.
It was when Jesus said to Me,
"Thy Sins are all forgiven thee."
The Christian trumpets loud proclaim
Thro' all the World in Jesus' name
Mutual forgiveness of each Vice,
And oped the Gates of Paradise.
The Moral Virtues in Great fear
Formed the Cross & Nails & Spear,
And the Accuser standing by
Cried out, "Crucify! Crucify!

Our Moral Virtues ne'er can be,
Nor Warlike pomp & Majesty;
For Moral Virtues all begin
In the Accusations of Sin,
And all the Heroic Virtues End
In destroying the Sinners' Friend.
Am I not Lucifer the Great,
And you my daughters in Great State,
The fruit of my Mysterious Tree
Of Good & Evil & Misery
And Death & Hell, which now begin
On everyone who Forgives Sin?"

a

The Vision of Christ that thou dost see
Is my Vision's Greatest Enemy:
Thine has a great hook nose like thine,
Mine has a snub nose like to mine:
Thine is the friend of All Mankind,
Mine speaks in parables to the Blind:
Thine loves the same world that mine hates,
Thy Heaven doors are my Hell Gates.
Socrates taught what Meletus
Loath'd as a Nation's bitterest Curse,
And Caiaphas was in his own Mind
A benefactor to Mankind:
Both read the Bible day & night,
But thou read'st black where I read white.

b

Was Jesus gentle, or did he
Give any marks of Gentility?
When twelve years old he ran away
And left his Parents in dismay.
When after three days' sorrow found,

Loud as Sinai's trumpet sound:
"No Earthly Parents I confess—
My Heavenly Father's business!
Ye understand not what I say,
And, angry, force me to obey."
Obedience is a duty then,
And favour gains with God & Men.
John from the Wilderness loud cried;
Satan gloried in his Pride.
"Come," said Satan, "come away,
I'll soon see if you'll obey!
John for disobedience bled,
But you can turn the stones to bread.
God's high king & God's high Priest
Shall Plant their Glories in your breast
If Caiaphas you will obey,
If Herod you with bloody Prey
Feed with the sacrifice, & be
Obedient, fall down, worship me."
Thunders & lightnings broke around,
And Jesus' voice in thunders' sound:
"Thus I seize the Spiritual Prey.
Ye smiters with disease, make way.
I come your King & God to sieze.
Is God a smiter with disease?"
The God of this World raged in vain:
He bound Old Satan in his Chain,
And bursting forth, his furious ire
Became a Chariot of fire.
Throughout the land he took his course,
And traced diseases to their source:
He curs'd the Scribe & Pharisee,
Trampling down Hipocrisy:
Where'er his Chariot took its way,
There Gates of death let in the day,

Broke down from every Chain & Bar;
And Satan in his Spiritual War
Drag'd at his Chariot wheels: loud howl'd
The God of this World: louder roll'd
The Chariot Wheels, & louder still
His voice was heard from Zion's hill,
And in his hand the Scourge shone bright;
He scourg'd the Merchant Canaanite
From out the Temple of his Mind,
And in his Body tight does bind
Satan & all his Hellish Crew;
And thus with wrath he did subdue
The Serpent Bulk of Nature's dross,
Till He had nail'd it to the Cross.
He took on Sin in the Virgin's Womb,
And put it off on the Cross & Tomb
To be Worship'd by the Church of Rome.

c

Was Jesus Humble? or did he
Give any proofs of Humility?
When but a Child he ran away
And left his Parents in dismay.
When they had wonder'd three days long
These were the words upon his Tongue:
"No Earthly Parents I confess:
I am doing my Father's business."
When the rich learned Pharisee
Came to consult him secretly,
Upon his heart with Iron pen
He wrote, "Ye must be born again."
He was too Proud to take a bribe;
He spoke with authority, not like a Scribe.
He says with most consummate Art,

"Follow me, I am meek & lowly of heart,"
As that is the only way to Escape
The Miser's net & the Glutton's trap.
He who loves his Enemies, hates his Friends;
This is surely not what Jesus intends;
He must mean the meer love of Civility,
And so he must mean concerning Humility;
But he acts with triumphant, honest pride,
And this is the Reason Jesus died.
If he had been Antichrist, Creeping Jesus,
He'd have done anything to please us:
Gone sneaking into the Synagogues
And not used the Elders & Priests like Dogs,
But humble as a Lamb or an Ass,
Obey himself to Caiaphas.
God wants not Man to humble himself:
This is the Trick of the Ancient Elf.
Humble toward God, Haughty toward Man,
This is the Race that Jesus ran,
And when he humbled himself to God,
Then descended the cruel rod.
"If thou humblest thyself, thou humblest me;
Thou also dwelst in Eternity.
Thou art a Man, God is no more,
Thine own Humanity learn to Adore
And thy Revenge Abroad display
In terrors at the Last Judgment day.
God's Mercy & Long Suffering
Are but the Sinner to Judgment to bring.
Thou on the Cross for them shalt pray
And take Revenge at the last Day.

"Do what you will, this Life's a Fiction
And is made up of Contradiction."

d

Was Jesus Humble? or did he
Give any Proofs of Humility?
Boast of high Things with Humble tone,
And give with Charity a Stone?
When but a Child he ran away
And left his Parents in dismay.
When they had wander'd three days long
These were the words upon his tongue:
"No Earthly Parents I confess:
"I am doing my Father's business."
When the rich learned Pharisee
Came to consult him secretly,
Upon his heart with Iron pen
He wrote, "Ye must be born again."
He was too proud to take a bribe;
He spoke with authority, not like a Scribe.
He says with most consummate Art,
"Follow me, I am meek & lowly of heart,"
As that is the only way to escape
The Miser's net & the Glutton's trap.
What can be done with such desperate Fools
Who follow after the Heathen Schools?
I was standing by when Jesus died;
What I call'd Humility, they call'd Pride.
He who loves his Enemies betrays his Friends;
This surely is not what Jesus intends,
But the sneaking Pride of Heroic Schools,
And the Scribes' & Pharisees' Virtuous Rules;
For he acts with honest, triumphant Pride,
And this is the cause that Jesus died.
He did not die with Christian Ease,
Asking pardon of his Enemies:
If he had, Caiaphas would forgive;

Sneaking submission can always live.
He had only to say that God was the devil,
And the devil was God, like a Christian Civil:
Mild Christian regrets to the devil confess
For affronting him thrice in the Wilderness;
He had soon been bloody Caesar's Elf,
And at last he would have been Caesar himself.
Like dr. Priestly & Bacon & Newton—
Poor Spiritual Knowledge is not worth a button!
For thus the Gospel Sir Isaac confutes:
"God can only be known by his Attributes;
And as for the Indwelling of the Holy Ghost
Or of Christ & his Father, it's all a boast
And Pride & Vanity of the imagination,
That disdains to follow this World's Fashion.'
To teach doubt & Experiment
Certainly was not what Christ meant.
What was he doing all that time,
From twelve years old to manly prime?
Was he then Idle, or the Less
About his Father's business?
Or was nis wisdom held in scorn
Before his wrath began to burn
In Miracles throughout the Land,
That quite unnerv'd Caiaphas' hand?
If he had been Antichrist, Creeping Jesus,
He'd have done any thing to please us—
Gone sneaking into Synagogues
And not us'd the Elders & Priests like dogs,
But Humble as a Lamb or Ass
Obey'd himself to Caiaphas.
God wants not Man to Humble himself:
This is the trick of the ancient Elf.
This is the Race that Jesus ran:
Humble to God, Haughty to Man,

Cursing the Rulers before the People
Even to the temple's highest Steeple;
And when he Humbled himself to God,
Then descended the Cruel Rod.
"If thou humblest thyself, thou humblest me;
Thou also dwell'st in Eternity.
Thou art a Man, God is no more,
Thy own humanity learn to adore,
For that is my Spirit of Life.
Awake, arise to Spiritual Strife
And thy Revenge abroad display
In terrors at the Last Judgment day
God's Mercy & Long Suffering
Is but the Sinner to Judgment to bring.
Thou on the Cross for them shalt pray
And take Revenge at the Last Day.
This Corporeal life's a fiction
And is made up of Contradiction."
Jesus replied & thunders hurl'd:
"I never will Pray for the World.
Once I did so when I pray'd in the Garden;
I wish'd to take with me a Bodily Pardon."
Can that which was of woman born
In the absence of the Morn,
When the Soul fell into Sleep
And Archangels round it weep,
Shooting out against the Light
Fibres of a deadly night,
Reasoning upon its own dark Fiction,
In doubt which is Self Contradiction?
Humility is only doubt,
And does the Sun & Moon blot out,
Rooting over with thorns & stems
The buried Soul & all its Gems.
This Life's dim Windows of the Soul

Distorts the Heavens from Pole to Pole
And leads you to Believe a Lie
When you see with, not thro', the Eye
That was born in a night to perish in a night,
When the Soul slept in the beams of Light.
Was Jesus Chaste? or did he, &c.

e

Was Jesus Chaste? or did he
Give any Lessons of Chastity?
The morning blush'd fiery red:
Mary was found in Adulterous bed;
Earth groan'd beneath, & Heaven above
Trembled at discovery of Love.
Jesus was sitting in Moses' Chair,
They brought the trembling Woman There.
Moses commands she be stoned to death,
What was the sound of Jesus' breath?
He laid His hand on Moses' Law:
The Ancient Heavens, in Silent Awe
Writ with Curses from Pole to Pole,
All away began to roll:
The Earth trembling & Naked lay
In secret bed of Mortal Clay,
On Sinai felt the hand divine
Putting back the bloody shrine,
And she heard the breath of God
As she heard by Eden's flood:
"Good & Evil are no more!
Sinai's trumpets, cease to roar!
Cease, finger of God, to write!
The Heavens are not clean in thy Sight.
Thou art Good, & thou Alone;
Nor may the sinner cast one stone.
To be Good only, is to be

A God or else a Pharisee.
Thou Angel of the Presence Divine
That didst create this Body of Mine,
Wherefore hast thou writ these Laws
And Created Hell's dark jaws?
My Presence I will take from thee:
A Cold Leper thou shalt be.
Tho' thou wast so pure & bright
That Heaven was Impure in thy Sight,
Tho' thy Oath turn'd Heaven Pale,
Tho' thy Covenant built Hell's Jail,
Tho' thou didst all to Chaos roll
With the Serpent for its soul,
Still the breath Divine does move
And the breath Divine is Love.
Mary, Fear Not! Let me see
The Seven Devils that torment thee:
Hide not from my Sight thy Sin,
That forgiveness thou maist win.
Has no Man Condemned thee?"
No Man, Lord:" "Then what is he
Who shall Accuse thee? Come Ye forth,
Fallen fiends of Heav'nly birth
That have forgot your Ancient love
And driven away my trembling Dove.
You shall bow before her feet;
You shall lick the dust for Meat;
And tho' you cannot Love, but Hate,
Shall be beggars at Love's Gate.
What was thy Love? Let me see it;
Was it love or dark deceit?"
Love too long from Me has fled;
'Twas dark deceit, to Earn my bread;
'Twas Covet, or 'twas Custom, or
Some trifle not worth caring for;

That they may call a shame & Sin
Love's temple that God dwelleth in,
And hide in secret hidden shrine
The Naked Human form divine,
And render that a Lawless thing
On which the Soul Expands its wing.
But this, O Lord, this was my Sin
When first I let these devils in
In dark pretence to Chastity:
Blaspheming Love, blaspheming thee.
Thence Rose Secret Adulteries,
And thence did Covet also rise.
My sin thou hast forgiven me,
Canst thou forgive my Blasphemy?
Canst thou return to this dark Hell,
And in my burning bosom dwell?
And canst thou die that I may live?
And canst thou Pity & forgive?"
Then Roll'd the shadowy Man away
From the Limbs of Jesus, to make them his prey,
An Ever devouring appetite
Glittering with festering venoms bright,
Crying, "Crucify this cause of distress,
Who don't keep the secrets of holiness!
All Mental Powers by Diseases we bind,
But he heals the deaf & the dumb & the Blind.
Whom God has afflicted for Secret Ends,
He Comforts & Heals & calls them Friends."
But, when Jesus was Crucified,
Then was perfected his glitt'ring pride:
In three Nights he devour'd his prey,
And still he devours the Body of Clay;
For dust & Clay is the Serpent's meat,
Which never was made for Man to Eat.

f

I am sure this Jesus will not do
Either for Englishman or Jew.

g

Seeing this False Christ, In fury & Passion
I made my Voice heard all over the Nation.
What are those, &c.

h

This was spoke by My Spectre to Voltaire, Bacon, &c.

Did Jesus teach doubt? or did he
Give any lessons of Philosophy,
Charge Visionaries with decieving,
Or call Men wise for not Believing?

i

Was Jesus Born of a Virgin Pure
With narrow Soul & looks demure?
If he intended to take on Sin
The Mother should an Harlot been,
Just such a one as Magdalen
With seven devils in her Pen;
Or were Jew Virgins still more Curst,
And more sucking devils nurst?
Or what was it which he took on
That he might bring Salvation?
A Body subject to be Tempted,
From neither pain nor grief Exempted?
Or such a body as might not feel
The passions that with Sinners deal?
Yes, but they say he never fell.
Ask Caiaphas; for he can tell.

"He mock'd the Sabbath, & he mock'd
The Sabbath's God, & he unlock'd
The Evil spirits from their Shrines,
And turn'd Fishermen to Divines;
O'erturn'd the Tent of Secret Sins,
& its Golden cords & Pins—
'Tis the Bloody Shrine of War
Pinn'd around from Star to Star,
Halls of justice, hating Vice,
Where the devil Combs his lice.
He turn'd the devils into Swine
That he might tempt the Jews to dine;
Since which, a Pig has got a look
That for a Jew may be mistook.
'Obey your parents.'—What says he?
'Woman, what have I to do with thee?
No Earthly Parents I confess:
I am doing my Father's Business.'
He scorn'd Earth's Parents, scorn'd Earth's God,
And mock'd the one & the other's Rod;
His Seventy Disciples sent
Against Religion & Government:
They by the Sword of Justice fell
And him their Cruel Murderer tell.
He left his Father's trade to roam
A wand'ring Vagrant without Home;
And thus he others' labour stole
That he might live above Controll.
The Publicans & Harlots he
Selected for his Company,
And from the Adulteress turn'd away
God's righteous Law, that lost its Prey."

A VISION OF
THE BOOK OF JOB

The following twenty-one plates are not "illustrations" to *The Book of Job*, but Blake's vision of its meaning to him. It is rival to the Bible lesson, though it occasionally seems to complement it. Were it not for the fact that Blake is so intent upon divulging its "real" theme, as he conceived it, his own work could be taken for a parody of the complacency with which the Bible story ends.

The Bible tells the story of a man "perfect and upright, and one that feared God and eschewed evil." His "substance" was very great, and his piety so preeminent among men that Satan was allowed to try it, to see whether his faith in God could withstand deprivation and bitter physical suffering. Job nearly reached the bottom of the pit of desolation; he lost everything. Indeed, he nearly failed the test. When his pious friends, shocked by his lamentations and reproaches against the Divine will, sought to convince him that his suffering was a punishment for sin, Job rebelled. Only when the voice of the Lord came to him out of the whirlwind and overwhelmed Job by His power and majesty, did he submit to God's mysterious permission of evil. Yet it is the human cries with which Job struggles to believe in so inscrutable a violation of human happiness and good faith that give the story in the Bible its eloquence and its poetry.

Blake's vision begins with an attack on Job himself for *his own love* of worldly goods and his consequent self-righteousness. The Bible portrays a man who was virtuous and who was made an example, despite his own goodness, of God's eternal dominion. Blake portrays a man who went wrong from the beginning, for he sought prosperity rather than vision. The drama takes place all within his own soul. In the Bible Satan is an agent of God, albeit a jealous agent; and as an agent, has liberty to try men for the edification of God. The Biblical Satan, in short, is really a court jester to Majesty. Blake's Satan is the God of this world, the God who tempts men to yield their real humanity by leading them after material goals. Satan is beaten only when Job recovers his spiritual sight, his true human understanding that his material "substance," which in the Bible is the reward for goodness and the mark of human success, is sterile and corrupting.

We owe the elucidation of Blake's symbolism in this work to the English scholar, Joseph Wicksteed. He discovered that the theme of Blake's designs—the struggle between the "natural" and the spiritual, or visionary man—is plotted on the difference between right and left. The right hand or foot stands for the visionary, unmaterial, prophetic character; the left hand or foot for the worldly, the conformist and the material. Where Job is shown with his right hand or foot ahead of his left, it means that the spiritual side of his human nature is in the ascendancy. This scheme is followed in every design, and by all the characters. It is a key to Blake's fundamental belief in the integral character of human nature, in which alone all of life's struggles are waged, that the right and left should be part of the same body.

In the Bible God, Satan and man are three different characters, on three different levels of power, knowledge and creativity. In Blake's vision, the only character is man himself, in whom the right, which is spiritual, and the left, which is materialist, conflict for ultimate domination.

In the first illustration all is seemingly calm and prosperous before the storm. But the sun is setting on the left, in the West—evidence that Job is living in a world of approaching night and darkness. The musical instruments that hang on the tree are the symbols of art, creativity and joy that have been put away. We see here a Job prosperous, pious but in danger of losing his inner gift, his soul. For while the musical instruments have been put away, he is reading evening prayers to his family "from the books," as Foster Damon said, "written by others."

In the last illustration, the twenty-first, Job and his human flock stand before the tree, this time playing upon their instruments. It is the sunrise; the real life of man's creative powers, of his joyous acceptance of his true nature, is just beginning. But between the first and twenty-first illustrations Job goes through hell, the hell that is in all men when they close their eyes to their own divinity. As Wicksteed pointed out, the Jehovah who appears at the crest of the second illustration, the "Poetic Genius" who is at the head of man, is the same image as Job himself. He is Job, when Job accepts his inner nature. In that light the true unity of the Creation appears everywhere in the picture, emphasized by the border designs. But with the third illustration Satan appears; and it is an introduction to the subtle inner drama that Blake introduces into every design to study the mocking contortions of the Demon's figure.

In the greatest of these designs, "When The Morning

Stars Sang Together," XIV, Blake created what must remain forever one of the great testaments to man's craving for spiritual fulfillment. Level upon level the whole creation rises out of the poetic genius of man, and the world sings in the joy of its beholding and in the wonder of man himself, who has so much greatness within him.

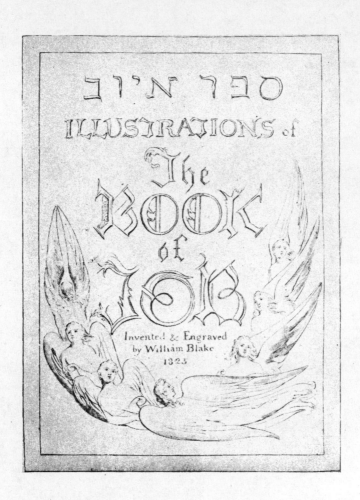

ספר איוב

ILLUSTRATIONS of

The BOOK of JOB

Invented & Engraved
by William Blake
1825

1.

The Letter Killeth
The Spirit giveth Life
It is Spiritually Discerned

2.

When the Almighty was yet with me. When my Children were about me

3.

The Fire of God is fallen from Heaven

4.

And I only am escaped alone to tell thee

5.

Then went Satan forth from the presence of the Lord

6.

And smote Job with sore Boils from the sole of his foot to the crown of his head

7.

*And when they lifted up their eyes afar off & knew
him not they lifted up their voice & wept*

8.

Let the Day perish wherein I was Born

9.

Then a Spirit passed before my face

10.

Have pity upon me! Have pity upon me! O ye my friends
for the hand of God hath touched me

11.

With Dreams upon my bed thou scarest me & affrightest me with Visions

12.

I am Young & ye are very Old wherefore I was afraid

13.

Then the Lord answered Job out of the Whirlwind

14.

*When the morning Stars sang together & all the Sons of
God shouted for joy*

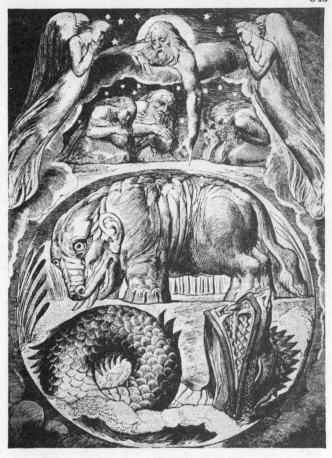

15.

Behold now Behemoth which I made with thee

16.

Hell is naked before him & Destruction has no covering

17.

I have heard thee with the hearing of the Ear but now my Eye seeth thee

18.

Also the Lord accepted Job

19.

Every one also gave him a piece of Money

20.

There were not found Women fair as the Daughters of Job

21.

*So the Lord blessed the latter end of Job more than the
beginning*

From A VISION OF THE LAST JUDGMENT

[From the Rossetti MS]

FOR THE YEAR 1810
ADDITIONS TO BLAKE'S CATALOGUE OF PICTURES & C

P. 70.

The Last Judgment [will be] when all those are Cast away who trouble Religion with Questions concerning Good & Evil or Eating of the Tree of those Knowledges or Reasonings which hinder the Vision of God, turning all into a Consuming Fire. When Imagination, Art & Science & all Intellectual Gifts, all the Gifts of the Holy Ghost, are look'd upon as of no use & only Contention remains to Man, then the Last Judgment begins, & its Vision is seen by the Imaginative Eye of Every one according to the situation he holds.

P. 68.

The Last Judgment is not Fable or Allegory, but Vision. Fable or Allegory are a totally distinct & inferior kind of Poetry. Vision or Imagination is a Representation of what Eternally Exists, Really & Unchangeably. Fable or Allegory is Form'd by the daughters of Memory. Imagination is surrounded by the daughters of Inspiration, who in the aggregate are call'd Jerusalem. Fable is allegory, but what Critics call The Fable, is Vision itself. The Hebrew Bible & the Gospel of Jesus are not Allegory, but Eternal Vision or Imagination of All that Exists. Note here that Fable or Allegory is seldom without some Vision. Pilgrim's Progress is full of it, the Greek Poets the same; but Allegory & Vision ought to be known as Two Distinct Things, & so call'd for the Sake of Eternal Life. Plato has made Socrates say that Poets & Prophets do not know or Understand what they write or Utter; this is a most Pernicious Falshood. If they do not, pray is an inferior kind to be call'd Knowing? Plato confutes himself.

Pp. 68-69.

The Last Judgment is one of these Stupendous Visions. I have represented it as I saw it; to different People it appears differently as every thing else does; for tho' on Earth things seem Permanent, they are less permanent than a Shadow, as we all know too well.

The Nature of Visionary Fancy, or Imagination, is very little known, & the Eternal nature & permanence of its ever Existent Images is consider'd as less permanent than the things of Vegetative & Generative Nature; yet the Oak dies as well as the Lettuce, but Its Eternal Image & Individuality never dies, but renews by its seed; just so the Imaginative Image returns by the seed of Contemplative Thought; the Writings of the Prophets illustrate these conceptions of the Visionary Fancy by their various sublime & Divine Images as seen in the Worlds of Vision.

Pp. 71-72.

The Learned m . . . or Heroes; this is an . . . & not Spiritual . . . while the Bible . . . of Virtue & Vice . . . as they are Ex . . . is the Real Di . . . Things. The . . . when they Assert that Jupiter usurped the Throne of his Father, Saturn, & brought on an Iron Age & Begat on Mnemosyne, or Memory, The Greek Muses, which are not Inspiration as the Bible is. Reality was Forgot, & the Vanities of Time & Space only Remember'd & call'd Reality. Such is the Mighty difference between Allegoric Fable & Spiritual Mystery. Let it here be Noted that the Greek Fables originated in Spiritual Mystery & Real Visions, which are lost & clouded in Fable & Allegory, while the Hebrew Bible & the Greek Gospel are Genuine, Preserv'd by the Saviour's Mercy. The Nature of my Work is Visionary or Imaginative; it is an Endeavour to Restore what the Ancients call'd the Golden Age.

Pp. 69-70.

This world of Imagination is the world of Eternity; it is the divine bosom into which we shall all go after the death of the Vegetated body. This World of Imagination is Infinite & Eternal, whereas the world of Generation, or Vegetation, is Finite & Temporal. There Exist in that Eternal World the Permanent Realities of Every Thing which we see reflected in this Vegetable Glass of Nature. All Things are comprehended in their Eternal Forms in the divine body of the Saviour, the True Vine of Eternity, The Human Imagination, who appear'd to Me as Coming to Judgment among his Saints & throwing off the Temporal that the Eternal might be Establish'd; around him were seen the Images of Existences according to a certain order Suited to my Imaginative Eye as follows.

P. 76.

Jesus seated between the Two Pillars, Jachin & Boaz, with the Word of divine Revelation on his knees, & on

each side the four & twenty Elders sitting in judgment;
the Heavens opening around him by unfolding the
clouds around his throne. The Old H[eave]n & O[ld]
Earth are passing away & the N[ew] H[eaven] & N[ew]
Earth descending. The Just arise on his right & the
wicked on his Left hand. A sea of fire issues from before
the throne. Adam & Eve appear first, before the Judg-
ment seat in humiliation. Abel surrounded by Innocents,
& Cain, with the flint in his hand with which he slew his
brother, falling with the head downward. From the
Cloud·on which Eve stands, Satan is seen falling head-
long wound round by the tail of the serpent whose bulk,
nail'd to the Cross round which he wreathes, is falling
into the Abyss. Sin is also represented as a female
bound in one of the Serpent's folds, surrounded by her
fiends. Death is Chain'd to the Cross, & Time falls to-
gether with death, dragged down by a demon crown'd
with Laurel; another demon with a Key has the charge
of Sin & is dragging her down by the hair; beside them
a figure is seen, scaled with iron scales from head to feet,
precipitating himself into the Abyss with the Sword &
Balances: he is Og, King of Bashan.

On the Right, Beneath the Cloud on which Abel
Kneels, is Abraham with Sarah & Isaac, also Hagar &
Ishmael. Abel kneels on a bloody Cloud &c. (*to come in
here as two leaves forward*).

P. 80.
Abel kneels on a bloody cloud descriptive of those
Churches before the flood, that they were fill'd with
blood & fire & vapour of smoke; even till Abraham's time
the vapor & heat was not extinguished; these States
Exist now. Man Passes on, but States remain for Ever;
he passes thro' them like a traveller who may as well
suppose that the places he has passed thro' exist no

more, as a Man may suppose that the States he has pass'd thro' Exist no more. Every thing is Eternal.

P. 79.

In Eternity one Thing never Changes into another Thing. Each Identity is Eternal: consequently Apuleius's Golden Ass & Ovid's Metamorphosis & others of the like kind are Fable; yet they contain Vision in a sublime degree, being derived from real Vision in More ancient Writings. Lot's Wife being Changed into [a] Pillar of Salt alludes to the Mortal Body being render'd a Permanent Statue, but not Changed or Transformed into Another Identity while it retains its own Individuality. A Man can never become Ass nor Horse; some are born with shapes of Men, who may be both, but Eternal Identity is one thing & Corporeal Vegetation is another thing. Changing Water into Wine by Jesus & into Blood by Moses relates to Vegetable Nature also.

Pp. 76-77.

Ishmael is Mahomed, & on the left, beneath the falling figure of Cain, is Moses casting his tables of stone into the deeps. It ought to be understood that the Persons, Moses & Abraham, are not here meant, but the States Signified by those Names, the Individuals being representatives or Visions of those States as they were reveal'd to Mortal Man in the Series of Divine Revelations as they are written in the Bible; these various States I have seen in my Imagination; when distant they appear as One Man, but as you approach they appear Multitudes of Nations. Abraham hovers above his posterity, which appear as Multitudes of Children ascending from the Earth, surrounded by Stars, as it was said: "As the Stars of Heaven for Multitude." Jacob & his Twelve Sons hover beneath the feet of Abraham & receive their children from the Earth. I have seen, when at a distance, Multitudes of Men in Harmony appear like a single Infant, sometimes in the Arms of a Female; this represented the Church.

But to proceed with the description of those on the Left hand—beneath the Cloud on which Moses kneels is two figures, a Male & Female, chain'd together by the feet; they represent those who perish'd by the flood; beneath them a multitude of their associates are seen falling headlong; by the side of them is a Mighty fiend with a Book in his hand, which is Shut; he represents the person nam'd in Isaiah, xxii c. & 20 v., Eliakim, the Son of Hilkiah: he drags Satan down headlong: he is crown'd with oak; by the side of the Scaled figure representing Og, King of Bashan, is a Figure with a Basket, emptying out the vanities of Riches & Worldly Honours: he is Araunah, the Jebusite, master of the threshing floor; above him are two figures, elevated on a Cloud, representing the Pharisees who plead their own Righteousness before the throne; they are weighed down by two fiends. Beneath the Man with the Basket are three fiery fiends with grey beards & scourges of fire: they represent Cruel Laws; they scourge a groupe of figures down into the deeps; beneath them are various figures in attitudes of contention representing various States of Misery, which, alas, every one on Earth is liable to enter into, & against which we should all watch. The Ladies will be pleas'd to see that I have represented the Furies by Three Men & not by three Women. It is not because I think the Ancients wrong, but they will be pleas'd to remember that mine is Vision & not Fable. The Spectator may suppose them Clergymen in the Pulpit, scourging Sin instead of Forgiving it.

The Earth beneath these falling Groupes of figures is

rocky & burning, and seems as if convuls'd by Earth-quakes; a Great City on fire is seen in the distance; the armies are fleeing upon the Mountains. On the fore-ground, hell is opened & many figures are descending into it down stone steps & beside a Gate beneath a rock where sin & death are to be closed Eternally by that Fiend who carries the key in one hand & drags them down with the other. On the rock & above the Gate a fiend with wings urges the wicked onwards with fiery darts; he is Hazael, the Syrian, who drives abroad all those who rebell against their Saviour; beneath the steps [is] Babylon, represented by a King crowned, Grasping his Sword and his Sceptre: he is just awaken'd out of his Grave; around him are other Kingdoms arising to Judg-ment, represented in this Picture as Single Personages according to the descriptions in the Prophets. The Figure dragging up a Woman by her hair represents the Inquisition, as do those contending on the sides of the Pit, & in Particular the Man strangling two women represents a Cruel Church.

P. 78.

Two persons, one in Purple, the other in Scarlet, are descending down the steps into the Pit; these are Caiaphas & Pilate—Two States where all those reside who Calumniate & Murder under Pretence of Holiness & Justice. Caiaphas has a Blue Flame like a Miter on his head. Pilate has bloody hands that never can be cleansed; the Females behind them represent the Females belonging to such States, who are under per-petual terrors & vain dreams, plots & secret deceit. Those figures that descend into the Flames before Caiaphas & Pilate are Judas & those of his Class. Achitophel is also here with the cord in his hand.

Pp. 80-81.

Between the Figures of Adam & Eve appears a fiery Gulph descending from the sea of fire before the throne; in this Cataract Four Angels descend headlong with four trumpets to awake the dead; beneath these is the Seat of the Harlot, nam'd Mystery in the Revelations. She is siezed by Two Beings each with three heads; they represent Vegetative Existence; as it is written in Revelations, they strip her naked & burn her with fire; it represents the Eternal Consummation of Vegetable Life & Death with its Lusts. The wreathed Torches in their hands represents Eternal Fire which is the fire of Generation or Vegetation; it is an Eternal Consummation. Those who are blessed with Imaginative Vision see This Eternal Female & tremble at what others fear not, while they despise & laugh at what others fear. Her Kings & Councellors & Warriors descend in Flames, Lamenting & looking upon her in astonishment & Terror, & Hell is open'd beneath her Seat on the Left hand. Beneath her feet is a flaming Cavern in which is seen the Great Red Dragon with seven heads & ten Horns; he has Satan's book of Accusations lying on the Rock open before him; he is bound in chains by Two strong demons; they are Gog & Magog, who have been compell'd to subdue their Master (Ezekiel, xxxviii c, 8 v.) with their Hammer & Tongs, about to new-Create the Seven-Headed Kingdoms. The Graves beneath are open'd, & the dead awake & obey the call of the Trumpet; those on the Right hand awake in joy, those on the Left in Horror; beneath the Dragon's Cavern a Skeleton begins to Animate, starting into life at the Trumpet's sound, while the Wicked contend with each other on the brink of perdition. On the Right a Youthful couple are awaked by their Children; an Aged patriarch is awaked by his aged wife—He is Albion, our Ancestor, patriarch of the Atlantic Continent, whose History Preceded that of the Hebrews & in whose Sleep, or Chaos, Creation began; at their head the Aged Woman is Brittannica, the Wife of Albion: Jerusalem is their daughter. Little Infants creep out of the flowery mould into the Green fields of the blessed who in various joyful companies embrace & ascend to meet Eternity.

The Persons who ascend to Meet the Lord, coming in the Clouds with power & great Glory, are representations of those States described in the Bible under the Names of the Fathers before & after the Flood. Noah is seen in the Midst of these, canopied by a Rainbow, on his right hand Shem & on his Left Japhet; these three Persons represent Poetry, Painting & Music, the three Powers in Man of conversing with Paradise, which the flood did not Sweep away. Above Noah is the Church Universal, represented by a Woman Surrounded by Infants. There is such a State in Eternity: it is composed of the Innocent civilized Heathen & the Uncivilized Savage, who, having not the Law, do by Nature the things contain'd in the Law. This State appears like a Female crown'd with stars, driven into the Wilderness; she has the Moon under her feet. The Aged Figure with Wings, having a writing tablet & taking account of the numbers who arise, is That Angel of the Divine Presence mention'd in Exodus, xiv c., 19 v. & in other Places; this Angel is frequently call'd by the Name of Jehovah Elohim, The "I am" of the Oaks of Albion.

Around Noah & beneath him are various figures Risen into the Air; among these are Three Females, representing those who are not of the dead but of those found alive at the Last Judgment; they appear to be innocently gay & thoughtless, not being among the condemn'd because ignorant of crime in the midst of a corrupted Age; the Virgin Mary was of this Class. A Mother Meets her

THE OLD BLAKE

numerous Family in the Arms of their Father; these are
representations of the Greek Learned & Wise, as also of
those of other Nations, such as Egypt & Babylon, in
which were multitudes who shall meet the Lord coming
in the Clouds.

The Children of Abraham, or Hebrew Church, are
represented as a Stream of Figures, on which are seen
Stars somewhat like the Milky way; they ascend from
the Earth where Figures kneel Embracing above the
Graves, & Represent Religion, or Civilized Life such
as it is in the Christian Church, who are the Offspring
of the Hebrew.

Pp. 82-84.

Just above the graves & above the spot where the
Infants creep out of the Ground stand two, a Man &
Woman; these are the Primitive Christians. The two
Figures in purifying flames by the side of the dragon's
cavern represents the Latter state of the Church when
on the verge of Perdition, yet protected by a Flaming
Sword. Multitudes are seen ascending from the Green
fields of the blessed in which a Gothic Church is repre-
sentative of true Art, Call'd Gothic in All Ages by those
who follow'd the Fashion, as that is call'd which is with-
out Shape or Fashion. On the right hand of Noah a
Woman with Children Represents the State Call'd
Laban the Syrian; it is the Remains of Civilization in
the State from whence Abraham was taken. Also on the
right hand of Noah A Female descends to meet her
Lover or Husband, representative of that Love, call'd
Friendship, which Looks for no other heaven than their
Beloved & in him sees all reflected as in a Glass of
Eternal Diamond.

On the right hand of these rise the diffident &
Humble, & on their left a solitary Woman with her

infant: these are caught up by three aged Men who appear as suddenly emerging from the blue sky for their help. These three Aged Men represent divine Providence as oppos'd to, & distinct from, divine vengeance, represented by three Aged men on the side of the Picture among the Wicked, with scourges of fire.

If the Spectator could enter into these Images in his Imagination, approaching them on the Fiery Chariot of his Contemplative Thought, if he could Enter into Noah's Rainbow or into his bosom, or could make a Friend & Companion of one of these Images of wonder, which always intreats him to leave mortal things (as he must know), then would he arise from his Grave, then would he meet the Lord in the Air & then he would be happy. General Knowledge is Remote Knowledge; it is in Particulars that Wisdom consists & Happiness too. Both in Art & in Life, General Masses are as Much Art as a Pasteboard Man is Human. Every Man has Eyes, Nose & Mouth; this Every Idiot knows, but he who enters into & discriminates most minutely the Manners & Intentions, the Characters in all their branches, is the alone Wise or Sensible Man, & on this discrimination All Art is founded. I intreat, then, that the Spectator will attend to the Hands & Feet, to the Lineaments of the Countenances; they are all descriptive of Character, & not a line is drawn without intention, & that most discriminate & particular. As Poetry admits not a Letter that is Insignificant, so Painting admits not a Grain of Sand or a Blade of Grass Insignificant—much less an Insignificant Blur or Mark.

*   *   *

A Last Judgment is Necessary because Fools flourish. Nations Flourish under Wise Rulers & are depress'd under foolish Rulers; it is the same with Individuals as

Nations; works of Art can only be produc'd in Perfection
where the Man is either in Affluence or is Above the
Care of it. Poverty is the Fool's Rod, which at last is
turn'd on his own back; this is A Last Judgment—when
Men of Real Art Govern & Pretenders Fall. Some People
& not a few Artists have asserted that the Painter of this
Picture would not have done so well if he had been
properly Encourag'd. Let those who think so, reflect on
the State of Nations under Poverty & their incapability
of Art; tho' Art is Above Either, the Argument is better
for Affluence than Poverty; & tho' he would not have
been a greater Artist, yet he would have produc'd
Greater works of Art in proportion to his means. A Last
Judgment is not for the purpose of making Bad Men
better, but for the Purpose of hindering them from
opressing the Good with Poverty & Pain by means of
Such Vile Arguments & Insinuations.

Around the Throne Heaven is open'd & the Nature of
Eternal Things Display'd, All Springing from the Divine
Humanity. All beams from him & as he himself has said,
All dwells in him. He is the Bread & the Wine; he is the
Water of Life; accordingly on Each Side of the opening
Heaven appears an Apostle; that on the Right Repre-
sents Baptism, that on the Left Represents the Lord's
Supper. All Life consists of these Two, Throwing off
Error & Knaves from our company continually & Reciev-
ing Truth or Wise Men into our Company continually.
He who is out of the Church & opposes it is no less an
Agent of Religion than he who is in it; to be an Error &
to be Cast out is a part of God's design. No man can
Embrace True Art till he has Explor'd & cast out False
Art (such is the Nature of Mortal Things), or he will be
himself Cast out by those who have Already Embraced
True Art. Thus My Picture is a History of Art & Science,
the Foundation of Society, Which is Humanity itself.

What are all the Gifts of the Spirit but Mental Gifts? Whenever any Individual Rejects Error & Embraces Truth, a Last Judgment passes upon that Individual.

*   *   *

Pp. 90-91.

Here they are no longer talking of what is Good & Evil, or of what is Right or Wrong, & puzzling themselves in Satan's Labyrinth, But are Conversing with Eternal Realities as they Exist in the Human Imagination. We are in a World of Generation & death, & this world we must cast off if we would be Painters such as Rafael, Mich. Angelo & the Ancient Sculptors; if we do not cast off this world we shall be only Venetian Painters, who will be cast off & Lost from Art.

P. 85.

Jesus is surrounded by Beams of Glory in which are seen all around him Infants emanating from him; these represent the Eternal Births of Intellect from the divine Humanity. A Rainbow surrounds the throne & the Glory, in which youthful Nuptials recieve the infants in their hands. In Eternity Woman is the Emanation of Man; she has No Will of her own. There is no such thing in Eternity as a Female Will, & Queens.

On the Side next Baptism are seen those call'd in the Bible Nursing Fathers & Nursing Mothers; they represent Education. On the Side next the Lord's Supper The Holy Family, consisting of Mary, Joseph, John the Baptist, Zacharias & Elizabeth, recieving the Bread & Wine, among other Spirits of the Just made perfect. Beneath these a Cloud of Women & Children are taken up, fleeing from the rolling Cloud which separates the Wicked from the Seats of Bliss. These represent those who, tho' willing, were too weak to Reject Error without the Assistance & Countenance of those Already in the Truth; for a Man Can only Reject Error by the Advice of a Friend or by the Immediate Inspiration of God; it is for this Reason among many others that I have put the Lord's Supper on the Left hand of the Throne, for it appears so at the Last Judgment, for a Protection.

Pp. 91-92.

Many suppose that before the Creation All was Solitude & Chaos. This is the most pernicious Idea that can enter the Mind, as it takes away all sublimity from the Bible & Limits All Existence to Creation & to Chaos, To the Time & Space fixed by the Corporeal Vegetative Eye, & leaves the Man who entertains such an Idea the habitation of Unbelieving demons. Eternity Exists, and All things in Eternity, Independent of Creation which was an act of Mercy. I have represented those who are in Eternity by some in a Cloud within the Rainbow that Surrounds the Throne; they merely appear as in a Cloud when any thing of Creation, Redemption or Judgment are the Subjects of Contemplation, tho' their Whole Contemplation is concerning these things; the Reason they so appear is The Humiliation of the Reason & doubting Self-hood, & the Giving all up to Inspiration. By this it will be seen that I do not consider either the Just or the Wicked to be in a Supreme State, but to be every one of them States of the Sleep which the Soul may fall into in its deadly dreams of Good and Evil when it leaves Paradise following the Serpent.

P. 91.

The Greeks represent Chronos or Time as a very Aged Man; this is Fable, but the Real Vision of Time is in Eternal Youth. I have, however, somewhat accomodated my Figure of Time to the common opinion, as I myself am also infected with it & my Visions also infected, & I see Time aged, alas, too much so.

Allegories are things that Relate to Moral Virtues. Moral Virtues do not Exist; they are Allegories & dissimulations. But Time & Space are Real Beings, a Male & a Female. Time is a Man, Space is a Woman, & her Masculine Portion is Death.

Pp. 86, 90.

The Combats of Good & Evil is Eating of the Tree of Knowledge. The Combats of Truth & Error is Eating of the Tree of Life; these are not only Universal, but Particular. Each are Personified. There is not an Error but it has a Man for its Agent, that is, it is a Man. There is not a Truth but it has also a Man. Good & Evil are Qualities in Every Man, whether a Good or Evil Man. These are Enemies & destroy one another by every Means in their power, both of deceit & of open Violence. The deist & the Christian are but the Results of these Opposing Natures. Many are deists who would in certain Circumstances have been Christians in outward appearance. Voltaire was one of this number; he was as intolerant as an Inquisitor. Manners make the Man, not Habits. It is the same in Art: by their Works ye shall know them; the Knave who is Converted to Deism & the Knave who is Converted to Christianity is still a Knave, but he himself will not know it, tho' Every body else does. Christ comes, as he came at first, to deliver those who were bound under the Knave, not to deliver the Knave. He Comes to deliver Man, the Accused, & not Satan, the Accuser. We do not find any where that Satan is Accused of Sin; he is only accused of Unbelief & thereby drawing Man into Sin that he may accuse him. Such is the Last Judgment—a deliverance from Satan's Accusation. Satan thinks that Sin is displeasing to God; he ought to know that Nothing is displeasing to God but Unbelief & Eating of the Tree of Knowledge of Good & Evil.

P. 87.

Men are admitted into Heaven not because they have curbed & govern'd their Passions or have No Passions, but because they have Cultivated their Understandings. The Treasures of Heaven are not Negations of Passion, but Realities of Intellect, from which all the Passions Emanate Uncurbed in their Eternal Glory. The Fool shall not enter into Heaven let him be ever so Holy. Holiness is not The Price of Enterance into Heaven. Those who are cast out are All Those who, having no Passions of their own because No Intellect, Have spent their lives in Curbing & Governing other People's by the Various arts of Poverty & Cruelty of all kinds. Wo, Wo, Wo to you Hypocrites. Even Murder, the Courts of Justice, more merciful than the Church, are compell'd to allow is not done in Passion, but in Cool Blooded design & Intention.

The Modern Church Crucifies Christ with the Head Downwards.

Pp. 92-95.

Many Persons, such as Paine & Voltaire, with some of the Ancient Greeks, say: "we will not converse concerning Good & Evil; we will live in Paradise & Liberty." You may do so in Spirit, but not in the Mortal Body as you pretend, till after the Last Judgment; for in Paradise they have no Corporeal & Mortal Body—that originated with the Fall & was call'd Death & cannot be removed but by a Last Judgment. While we are in the world of Mortality we Must Suffer. The Whole Creation Groans to be deliver'd; there will always be as many Hypocrites

born as Honest Men, & they will always have superior
Power in Mortal Things. You cannot have Liberty in this
World without what you call Moral Virtue, & you can-
not have Moral Virtue without the Slavery of that half
of the Human Race who hate what you call Moral
Virtue.

The Nature of Hatred & Envy & of All the Mischiefs
in the World are here depicted. No one Envies or Hates
one of his Own Party; even the devils love one another
in their Way; they torment one another for other
reasons than Hate or Envy; these are only employ'd
against the Just. Neither can Seth Envy Noah, or Elijah
Envy Abraham, but they may both of them Envy the
Success of Satan or of Og or Molech. The Horse never
Envies the Peacock, nor the Sheep the Goat, but they
Envy a Rival in Life & Existence whose ways & means
exceed their own, let him be of what Class of Animals
he will; a dog will envy a Cat who is pamper'd at the
expense of his comfort, as I have often seen. The Bible
never tells us that devils torment one another thro'
Envy; it is thro' this that they torment the Just—but
for what do they torment one another? I answer: For
the Coercive Laws of Hell, Moral Hypocrisy. They tor-
ment a Hypocrite when he is discover'd; they punish a
Failure in the tormentor who has suffer'd the Subject
of his torture to Escape. In Hell all is Self Righteous-
ness; there is no such thing there as Forgiveness of Sin;
he who does Forgive Sin is Crucified as an Abettor of
Criminals, & he who performs Works of Mercy in Any
shape whatever is punish'd &, if possible, destroy'd, not
thro' envy or Hatred or Malice, but thro' Self Righteous-
ness that thinks it does God service, which God is Satan.
They do not Envy one another: They contemn & despise
one another: Forgiveness of Sin is only at the Judgment
Seat of Jesus the Saviour, where the Accuser is cast out,

not because he Sins, but because he torments the Just & makes them do what he condemns as Sin & what he knows is opposite to their own Identity.

It is not because Angels are Holier than Men or Devils that makes them Angels, but because they do not Expect Holiness from one another, but from God only.

The Player is a liar when he says: "Angels are happier than Men because they are better." Angels are happier than Men & Devils because they are not always Prying after Good & Evil in one another & eating the Tree of Knowledge for Satan's Gratification.

Thinking as I do that the Creator of this World is a very Cruel Being, & being a Worshipper of Christ, I cannot help saying: "the Son, O how unlike the Father!" First God Almighty comes with a Thump on the Head. Then Jesus Christ comes with a balm to heal it.

The Last Judgment is an Overwhelming of Bad Art & Science. Mental Things are alone Real; what is call'd Corporeal, Nobody Knows of its Dwelling Place: it is in Fallacy, & its Existence an Imposture. Where is the Existence Out of Mind or Thought? Where is it but in the Mind of a Fool? Some People flatter themselves that there will be No Last Judgment & that Bad Art will be adopted & mixed with Good Art, That Error or Experiment will make a Part of Truth, & they Boast that it is its Foundation; these People flatter themselves: I will not Flatter them. Error is Created. Truth is Eternal. Error, or Creation, will be Burned up, & then, & not till Then, Truth or Eternity will appear. It is Burnt up the Moment Men cease to behold it. I assert for My Self that I do not behold the outward Creation & that to me it is hindrance & not Action; it is as the dirt upon my feet, No part of Me. "What," it will be Question'd, "When the Sun rises, do you not see a round disk of fire somewhat like a Guinea?" O no, no, I see an Innumerable company of the Heavenly host crying, "Holy, Holy, Holy is the Lord God Almighty." I question not my Corporeal or Vegetative Eye any more than I would Question a Window concerning a Sight. I look thro' it & not with it.

APPENDIX

From CRABB ROBINSON'S
REMINISCENCES, 1869

19/2/52.

WILLIAM BLAKE

It was at the latter end of the year 1825 that I put in writing my recollections of this most remarkable man. The larger portions are under the date of the 18th of December. He died in the year 1827. I have therefore now revised what I wrote on the 10th of December and afterwards, and without any attempt to reduce to order, or make consistent the wild and strange rhapsodies uttered by this insane man of genius, thinking it better to put down what I find as it occurs, though I am aware of the objection that may justly be made to the recording the ravings of insanity in which it may be said there can be found no principle, as there is no ascertainable law of mental association which is obeyed; and from which therefore nothing can be learned.

This would be perfectly true of *mere* madness—but does not apply to that form of insanity ordinarily called monomania, and may be disregarded in a case like the present in which the subject of the remark was unquestionably what a German would call a *Verunglückter Genie,* whose theosophic dreams bear a close resemblance to those of Swedenborg—whose genius as an artist was praised by no less men than Flaxman and Fuseli—and whose poems were thought worthy republication by the biographer of Swedenborg (Wilkinson),

and of which Wordsworth said after reading a number
—they were the "Songs of Innocence and Experience
showing the two opposite sides of the human soul"—
"There is no doubt this poor man was mad, but there is
something in the madness of this man which interests
me more than the sanity of Lord Byron and Walter
Scott!" The German painter Götzenberger (a man in-
deed who ought not to be named *after the others* as an
authority for my writing about Blake) said, on his re-
turning to Germany about the time at which I am now
arrived, "I saw in England many men of talents, but
only three men of genius, Coleridge, Flaxman, and
Blake, and of these Blake was the greatest." I do not
mean to intimate my assent to this opinion, nor to do
more than supply such materials as my intercourse with
him furnish to an uncritical narrative to which I shall
confine myself. I have written a few sentences in these
reminiscences already, those of the year 1810. I had not
then begun the regular journal which I afterwards kept.
I will therefore go over the ground again and introduce
these recollections of 1825 by a reference to the slight
knowledge I had of him before, and what occasioned my
taking an interest in him, not caring to repeat what
Cunningham has recorded of him in the volume of his
Lives of the British Painters, etc. etc. . . .

Dr. Malkin, our Bury Grammar School Headmaster,
published in the year 1806 a Memoir of a very pre-
cocious child who died . . . years old, and he prefixed
to the Memoir an account of Blake, and in the volume
he gave an account of Blake as a painter and poet, and
printed some specimens of his poems, viz. "The Tyger,"
and ballads and mystical lyrical poems, all of a wild
character, and M. gave an account of Visions which
Blake related to his acquaintance. I knew that Flaxman

thought highly of him, and though he did not venture to extol him as a genuine seer, yet he did not join in the ordinary derision of him as a madman. Without having seen him, yet I had already conceived a high opinion of him, and thought he would furnish matter for a paper interesting to Germans, and therefore when Fred. Perthes, the patriotic publisher at Hamburg, wrote to me in 1810 requesting me to give him an article for his *Patriotische Annalen,* I thought I could do no better than send him a paper on Blake, which was translated into German by Dr. Julius, filling, with a few small poems copied and translated, 24 pages. . . .

In order to enable me to write this paper, which, by the bye, has nothing in it of the least value, I went to see an exhibition of Blake's original paintings in Carnaby Market, at a hosier's, Blake's brother. These paintings filled several rooms of an ordinary dwelling-house, and for the sight a half-crown was demanded of the visitor, for which he had a catalogue. This catalogue I possess, and it is a very curious exposure of the state of the artist's mind. I wished to send it to Germany and to give a copy to Lamb and others, so I took four, and giving 10s., bargained that I should be at liberty to go again. "Free! as long as you live," said the brother, astonished at such a liberality, which he had never experienced before, nor I dare say did afterwards. Lamb was delighted with the catalogue, especially with the description of a painting afterwards engraved, and connected with which is an anecdote that, unexplained, would reflect discredit on a most amiable and excellent man, but which Flaxman considered to have been not the wilful act of Stodart. It was after the friends of Blake had circulated a subscription paper for an engraving of his "Canterbury Pilgrims," that Stodart was made a party to an engraving of a painting of the same subject by himself. Stodart's work is well known, Blake's is known by very few. Lamb preferred it greatly to Stodart's, and declared that Blake's description was the finest criticism he had ever read of Chaucer's poem.

In this catalogue Blake writes of himself in the most outrageous language—says, "This artist defies all competition in colouring"—that none can beat him, for none can beat the Holy Ghost—that he and Raphael and Michael Angelo were under divine influence—while Corregio and Titian worshipped a lascivious and therefore cruel deity—Reubens a proud devil, etc. etc. He declared, speaking of colour, Titian's men to be of leather and his women of chalk, and ascribed his own perfection in colouring to the advantage he enjoyed in seeing daily the primitive men walking in their native nakedness in the mountains of Wales. There were about thirty oil-paintings, the colouring excessively dark and high, the veins black, and the colour of the primitive men very like that of the Red Indians. In his estimation they would probably be the primitive men. Many of his designs were unconscious imitations. This appears also in his published works—the designs of "Blair's Grave," which Fuseli and Schiavonetti highly extolled—and in his designs to illustrate "Job," published after his death for the benefit of his widow.

23/2/52.

To this catalogue and in the printed poems, the small pamphlet which appeared in 1783, the edition put forth by Wilkinson of "The Songs of Innocence," and other works already mentioned, to which I have to add the first four books of Young's Night Thoughts, and Allan Cunningham's Life of him, I now refer, and will confine myself to the memorandums I took of his conversation. I had heard of him from Flaxman, and for the first time dined in his company at the Aders'. Linnell the painter also was there—an artist of considerable talent, and who professed to take a deep interest in Blake and his work, whether of a perfectly disinterested character may be doubtful, as will appear hereafter. This was on the 10th of December.

I was aware of his idiosyncracies and therefore to a great degree prepared for the sort of conversation which took place at and after dinner, an altogether unmethodical rhapsody on art, poetry, and religion—he saying the most strange things in the most unemphatic manner, speaking of his *Visions* as any man would of the most ordinary occurrence. He was then 68 years of age. He had a broad, pale face, a large full eye with a benignant expression—at the same time a look of languor, except when excited, and then he had an air of inspiration. But not such as without a previous acquaintance with him, or attending to *what* he said, would suggest the notion that he was insane. There was nothing *wild* about his look, and though very ready to be drawn out to the assertion of his favourite ideas, yet with no warmth as if he wanted to make proselytes. Indeed one of the peculiar features of his scheme, as far as it was consistent, was indifference and a very extraordinary degree of tolerance and satisfaction with what had taken place. A sort of pious and humble optimism, not the scornful optimism of Candide. But at the same time that he was very ready to praise he seemed incapable of envy, as he was of discontent. He warmly praised some composition of Mrs. Aders, and having brought for Aders an engraving of his "Canterbury Pilgrims," he remarked that one of the figures resembled a figure in one of the works then in Aders's room, so that he had been accused of having stolen from it. But he added that he had drawn the figure in question 20 years before he had seen the *original* picture. However, there is "no wonder in the resemblance, as in my youth I was always studying that class of painting." I have forgotten what it was, but his taste was in close conformity with the old German school.

This was somewhat at variance with what he said both this day and afterwards—implying that he copies his Visions. And it was on this first day that, in answer to a question from me, he said, *"The Spirits told me."* This lead me to say: Socrates used pretty much the same language. He spoke of his Genius. Now, what affinity or resemblance do you suppose was there between the *Genius* which inspired Socrates and your *Spirits?* He smiled, and for once it seemed to me as if he had a feeling of vanity gratified. "The same as in our countenances." He paused and said, "I was Socrates"—and then as if he had gone too far in that—"or a sort of brother. I must have had conversations with him. So I had with Jesus Christ. I have an obscure recollection of having been with both of them." As I had for many years been familiar with the idea that an eternity *a parte post* was inconceivable without an eternity *a parte ante,* I was naturally led to express that thought on this occasion. His eye brightened on my saying this. He eagerly assented: "To be sure. We are all coexistent with God; members of the Divine body, and partakers of the Divine nature." Blake's having adopted this Platonic idea led me on our *tête-à-tête* walk home at night to put the popular question to him, concerning the imputed Divinity of Jesus Christ. He answered: "He is the only God"—but then he added—"And so am I and so are you." He had before said—and that led me to put the question—that Christ ought not to have suffered himself to be crucified. "He should not have attacked the Government. He had no business with such matters." On my representing this to be inconsistent with the sanctity of divine qualities, he said Christ was not yet become the Father. It is hard on bringing together these fragmentary recollections to fix Blake's position in relation to Christianity, Platonism, and Spinozism.

It is one of the subtle remarks of Hume on the tendency of certain religious notions to reconcile us to whatever occurs, as God's will. And applying this to something Blake said, and drawing the inference that there is no use in education, he hastily rejoined: "There is no use in education. I hold it wrong. It is the great Sin. It is eating of the tree of knowledge of Good and Evil. That was the fault of Plato: he knew of nothing but the Virtues and Vices. There is nothing in all that. Everything is good in God's eyes." On my asking whether there is nothing absolutely evil in what man does, he answered: "I am no judge of that—perhaps not in God's eyes." Notwithstanding this, he, however, at the same time spoke of error as being in heaven; for on my asking whether Dante was pure in writing his *Vision*, "Pure," said Blake. "Is there any purity in God's eyes? No. 'He chargeth his angels with folly.'" He even extended this liability to error to the Supreme Being. "Did he not repent him that he had made Nineveh?" My journal here has the remark that it is easier to retail his personal remarks than to reconcile those which seemed to be in conformity with the most opposed abstract systems. He spoke with seeming complacency of his own life in connection with Art. In becoming an artist he "acted by command." The Spirits said to him, "Blake, be an artist." His eye glistened while he spoke of the joy of devoting himself to *divine art* alone. "Art is inspiration. When Mich. Angelo or Raphael, in their day, or Mr. Flaxman, does any of his fine things, he does them in the Spirit." Of fame he said: "I should be sorry if I had any earthly fame, for whatever natural glory a man has is so much detracted from his spiritual glory. I wish to do nothing for profit. I want nothing—I am quite happy." This was confirmed to me on my subsequent interviews with him. His distinction between the Natural and Spiritual worlds was very confused. Incidentally, Swedenborg was mentioned—he declared him to be a Divine Teacher. He had done, and would do, much good. Yet he did wrong in endeavouring to explain to the *reason* what it could not comprehend. He seemed to consider, but that was not clear, the visions of Swedenborg and Dante as of the same kind. Dante was the greater poet. He too was wrong in occupying his mind about political objects. Yet this did not appear to affect his estimation of Dante's genius, or his opinion of the truth of Dante's visions. Indeed, when he even declared Dante to be an Atheist, it was accompanied by expression of the highest admiration; though, said he, Dante saw Devils where I saw none.

I put down in my journal the following insulated remarks. Jacob Böhmen was placed among the divinely inspired men. He praised also the designs to Law's translation of Böhmen. Michael Angelo could not have surpassed them.

"Bacon, Locke, and Newton are the three great teachers of Atheism, or Satan's Doctrine," he asserted.

"Irving is a higly gifted man—he is a *sent* man; but they who are sent sometimes go further than they ought."

Calvin. I saw nothing but good in Calvin's house. In Luther's there were Harlots. He declared his opinion that the earth is flat, not round, and just as I had objected the circumnavigation dinner was announced. But objections were seldom of any use. The wildest of his assertions was made with the veriest indifference of

tone, as if altogether insignificant. It respected the nat-
ural and spiritual worlds. By way of example of the dif-
ference between them, he said, "*You* never saw the
spiritual Sun. I have. I saw him on Primrose Hill." He
said, "Do you take me for the Greek Apollo?" "No!" I
said. "*That* (pointing to the sky) that is the Greek
Apollo. He is Satan."

Not everything was thus absurd. There were glimpses
and flashes of truth and beauty: as when he compared
moral with physical evil. "Who shall say what God
thinks evil? That is a wise tale of the Mahometans—of
the Angel of the Lord who murdered the Infant."—The
Hermit of Parnell, I suppose.—"Is not every infant that
dies of a natural death in reality slain by an Angel?"

And when he joined to the assurance of his happiness,
that of his having suffered, and that it was necessary, he
added, "There is suffering in Heaven; for where there
is the capacity of enjoyment, there is the capacity of
pain."

I include among the glimpses of truth this assertion,
"I know what is true by internal conviction. A doctrine
is stated. My heart tells me It *must* be true." I remarked,
in confirmation of it, that, to an unlearned man, what
are called the *external* evidences of religion can carry
no conviction with them; and this he assented to.

After my first evening with him at Aders's, I made the
remark in my journal, that his observations, apart from
his Visions and references to the spiritual world, were
sensible and acute. In the sweetness of his countenance
and gentility of his manner he added an indescribable
grace to his conversation. I added my regret, which I
must now repeat, at my inability to give more than in-
coherent thoughts. Not altogether my fault perhaps.

On the 17th I called on him in his house in Fountain's Court in the Strand. The interview was a short one, and what I saw was more remarkable than what I heard. He was at work engraving in a small bedroom, light, and looking out on a mean yard. Everything in the room squalid and indicating poverty, except himself. And there was a natural gentility about him, and an insensibility to the seeming poverty, which quite removed the impression. Besides, his linen was clean, his hand white, and his air quite unembarrassed when he begged me to sit down as if he were in a palace. There was but one chair in the room besides that on which he sat. On my putting my hand to it, I found that it would have fallen to pieces if I had lifted it, so, as if I had been a Sybarite, I said with a smile, "Will you let me indulge myself?" and I sat on the bed, and near him, and during my short stay there was nothing in him that betrayed that he was aware of what to other persons might have been even offensive, not in his person, but in all about him.

His wife I saw at this time, and she seemed to be the very woman to make him happy. She had been formed by him. Indeed, otherwise, she could not have lived with him. Notwithstanding her dress, which was poor and dirty, she had a good expression in her countenance, and, with a dark eye, had remains of beauty in her youth. She had that virtue of virtues in a wife, an implicit reverence of her husband. It is quite certain that she believed in all his visions. And on one occasion, not this day, speaking of his Visions, she said, "You know, dear, the first time you saw God was when you were four years old, and he put his head to the window and set you a-screaming." In a word, she was formed on the Miltonic model, and like the first Wife Eve worshipped

God in her husband. He being to her what God was to him. Vide Milton's Paradise Lost—*passim.*

26/2/52.

He was making designs or engravings, I forget which. Carey's Dante was before [him]. He showed me some of his designs from Dante, of which I do not presume to speak. They were too much above me. But Götzenberger, whom I afterwards took to see them, expressed the highest admiration of them. They are in the hands of Linnell the painter, and, it has been suggested, are reserved by him for publication when Blake may have become an object of interest to a greater number than he could be at this age. Dante was again the subject of our conversation. And Blake declared him a mere politician and atheist, busied about this world's affairs; as Milton was till, in his (M.'s) old age, he returned back to the God he had abandoned in childhood. I in vain endeavoured to obtain from him a qualification of the term atheist, so as not to include him in the ordinary reproach. And yet he afterwards spoke of Dante's being *then* with God. I was more successful when he also called Locke an atheist, and imputed to him wilful deception, and seemed satisfied with my admission, that Locke's philosophy led to the Atheism of the French school. He reiterated his former strange notions on morals—would allow of no other education than what lies in the cultivation of the fine arts and the imagination. "What are called the Vices in the natural world, are the highest sublimities in the spiritual world." And when I supposed the case of his being the father of a vicious son and asked him how he would feel, he evaded the question by saying that in trying to think correctly he must not regard his own weaknesses any more than other people's.

And he was silent to the observation that his doctrine
denied evil. He seemed not unwilling to admit the Mani-
chæan doctrine of two principles, as far as it is found in
the idea of the Devil. And said expressly he did not
believe in the omnipotence of God. The language of the
Bible is only poetical or allegorical on the subject, yet he
at the same time denied the *reality* of the natural world.
Satan's empire is the empire of nothing.

As he spoke of frequently seeing Milton, I ventured
to ask, half ashamed at the time, which of the three or
four portraits in Hollis's Memoirs (vols. in 4to) is the
most like. He answered, "They are all like, at different
ages. I have seen him as a youth and as an old man with
a long flowing beard. He came lately as an old man—he
said he came to ask a favour of me. He said he had com-
mitted an error in his *Paradise Lost*, which he wanted
me to correct, in a poem or picture; but I declined. I
said I had my own duties to perform." It is a presump-
tuous question, I replied—might I venture to ask—
what that could be. "He wished me to expose the false-
hood of his doctrine, taught in the *Paradise Lost*, that
sexual intercourse arose out of the Fall. Now that can-
not be, for no good can spring out of evil." But, I replied,
if the consequence were evil, mixed with good, then the
good might be ascribed to the common cause. To this
he answered by a reference to the *androgynous* state, in
which I could not possibly follow him. At the time that
he asserted his own possession of this gift of Vision, he
did not boast of it as peculiar to himself; all men might
have it if they would.

27/2/52.

On the 24th I called a second time on him. And on
this occasion it was that I read to him Wordsworth's
Ode on the supposed pre-existent State, and the subject

of Wordsworth's religious character was discussed when we met on the 18th of Feb., and the 12th of May. I will here bring together Blake's declarations concerning Wordsworth, and set down his marginalia in the 8vo. edit. A.D. 1815, vol. i. I had been in the habit, when reading this marvellous Ode to friends, to omit one or two passages, especially that beginning:

But there's a Tree, of many one,

lest I should be rendered ridiculous, being unable to explain precisely *what* I admired. Not that I acknowledged this to be a fair test. But with Blake I could fear nothing of the kind. And it was this very stanza which threw him almost into a hysterical rapture. His delight in Wordsworth's poetry was intense. Nor did it seem less, notwithstanding the reproaches he continually cast on Wordsworth for his imputed worship of nature; which in the mind of Blake constituted Atheism.

28/2/52.

The combination of the warmest praise with imputations which from another would assume the most serious character, and the liberty he took to interpret as he pleased, rendered it as difficult to be offended as to reason with him. The eloquent descriptions of Nature in Wordsworth's poems were conclusive proofs of atheism, for whoever believes in Nature, said Blake, disbelieves in God. For Nature is the work of the Devil. On my obtaining from him the declaration that the Bible was the Word of God, I referred to the commencement of Genesis—In the beginning God created the Heavens and the Earth. But I gained nothing by this, for I was triumphantly told that this God was not Jehovah, but the

Elohim; and the doctrine of the Gnostics repeated with sufficient consistency to silence one so unlearned as myself.

The Preface to the Excursion, especially the verses quoted from book i. of the Recluse, so troubled him as to bring on a fit of illness. These lines he singled out:

> Jehovah with his thunder, and the Choir
> Of shouting Angels, and the Empyreal throne,
> I pass them unalarmed.

Does Mr. Wordsworth think he can surpass Jehovah? There was a copy of the whole passage in his own hand, in the volume of Wordsworth's poems sent to my chambers after his death. There was this note at the end: "Solomon, when he married Pharaoh's daughter, and became a convert to the Heathen Mythology, talked exactly in this way of Jehovah, as a very inferior object of Man's contemplations; he also passed him unalarmed, and was permitted. Jehovah dropped a tear and followed him by his Spirit into the abstract void. It is called the Divine Mercy. Sarah dwells in it, but Mercy does not dwell in Him."

Some of Wordsworth's poems he maintained were from the Holy Ghost, others from the Devil. I lent him the 8vo edition, two vols., of Wordsworth's poems, which he had in his possession at the time of his death. They were sent me then. I did not recognise the pencil notes he made in them to be his for some time, and was on the point of rubbing them out under that impression, when I made the discovery.

The following are found in the 3rd vol., in the fly-leaf under the words: Poems referring to the Period of Childhood.

29/2/52.

"I see in Wordsworth the Natural man rising up against the Spiritual man continually, and then he is no poet, but a Heathen Philosopher at Enmity against all true poetry or inspiration."

Under the first poem:

> And I could wish my days to be
> Bound each to each by natural piety,

he had written, "There is no such thing as natural piety, because the natural man is at enmity with God." P. 43, under the Verses "To H. C., six years old"—"This is all in the highest degree imaginative and equal to any poet, but not superior. I cannot think that real poets have any competition. None are greatest in the kingdom of heaven. It is so in poetry." P. 44, "On the Influence of Natural Objects," at the bottom of the page. "Natural objects always did and now do weaken, deaden, and obliterate imagination in me. Wordsworth must know that what he writes valuable is not to be found in Nature. Read Michael Angelo's sonnet, vol. iv. p. 179." That is, the one beginning

> No mortal object did these eyes behold
> When first they met the placid light of thine.

It is remarkable that Blake, whose judgements were on most points so very singular, on one subject closely connected with Wordsworth's poetical reputation should have taken a very commonplace view. Over the heading of the "Essay Supplementary to the Preface" at the end of the vol. he wrote, "I do not know who wrote these Prefaces; they are very mischievous, and direct contrary to Wordsworth's own practice" (p. 341). This is not the defence of his own style in opposition to what is called

Poetic Diction, but a sort of historic vindication of the
unpopular poets. On Macpherson, p. 364, Wordsworth
wrote with the severity with which all great writers have
written of him. Blake's comment below was, "I believe
both Macpherson and Chatterton, that what they say is
ancient is so." And in the following page, "I own myself
an admirer of Ossian equally with any other poet what-
ever. Rowley and Chatterton also." And at the end of
this Essay he wrote, "It appears to me as if the last para-
graph beginning 'Is it the spirit of the whole,' etc., was
written by another hand and mind from the rest of these
Prefaces; they are the opinions of [a] landscape-painter.
Imagination is the divine vision not of the world, nor of
man, nor from man as he is a natural man, but only as he
is a spiritual man. Imagination has nothing to do with
memory."

1826

1/3/52.

19th Feb. It was this day in connection with the as-
sertion that the Bible is the Word of God and all truth
is to be found in it, he using language concerning man's
reason being opposed to grace very like that used by the
Orthodox Christian, that he qualified, and as the same
Orthodox would say utterly nullified all he said by de-
claring that he understood the Bible in a Spiritual sense.
As to the natural sense, he said Voltaire was commis-
sioned by God to expose that. "I have had," he said,
"much intercourse with Voltaire, and he said to me, 'I
blasphemed the Son of Man, and it shall be forgiven me,
but they (the enemies of Voltaire) blasphemed the Holy
Ghost in me, and it shall not be forgiven to them.'" I
ask him in what language Voltaire spoke. His answer
was ingenious and gave no encouragement to cross-
questioning: "To my sensations it was English. It was
like the touch of a musical key; he touched it probably

French, but to my ear it became English." I also enquired as I had before about the form of the persons who appeared to him, and asked why he did not *draw* them. "It is not worth while," he said. "Besides there are so many that the labour would be too great. And there would be no use in it." In answer to an enquiry about Shakespeare, "he is exactly like the old engraving —which is said to be a bad one. I think it very good." I enquired about his own writings. "I have written," he answered, "more than Rousseau or Voltaire—six or seven Epic poems as long as Homer and 20 Tragedies as long as Macbeth." He shewed me his 'Version of Genesis,' for so it may be called, as understood by a Christian Visionary. He read a wild passage in a sort of Bible style. "I shall print no more," he said. "When I am commanded by the Spirits, then I write, and the moment I have written, I see the words fly about the room in all directions. It is then published. The Spirits can read, and my MS. is of no further use. I have been tempted to burn my MS., but my wife won't let me." She is right, I answered; you write not from yourself but from higher order. The MSS. are their property, not yours. You cannot tell what purpose they may answer. This was addressed *ad hominem*. And it indeed amounted only to a deduction from his own principles. He incidentally denied *causation*, every thing being the work of God or Devil. Every man has a Devil in himself, and the conflict between his *Self* and God is perpetually going on. I ordered of him to-day a copy of his songs for 5 guineas. My manner of receiving his mention of price pleased him. He spoke of his horror of money and of turning pale when it was offered him, and this was certainly unfeigned.

In the No. of the *Gents. Magazine* for last Jan. there is a letter by Cromek to Blake printed in order to convict Blake of selfishness. It cannot possibly be substantially true. I may elsewhere notice it.

13th June. I saw him again in June. He was as wild as ever, says my journal, but he was led to-day to make assertions more palpably mischievous, if capable of influencing other minds, and immoral, supposing them to express the will of a responsible agent, than anything he had said before. As, for instance, that he had learned from the Bible that Wives should be in common. And when I objected that marriage was a Divine institution, he referred to the Bible—"that from the beginning it was not so." He affirmed that he had committed many murders, and repeated his doctrine, that reason is the only sin, and that careless, gay people are better than those who think, etc. etc.

It was, I believe, on the 7th of December that I saw him last. I had just heard of the death of Flaxman, a man whom he professed to admire, and was curious to know how he would receive the intelligence. It was as I expected. He had been ill during the summer, and he said with a smile, "I thought I should have gone first." He then said, "I cannot think of death as more than the going out of one room into another." And Flaxman was no longer thought of. He relapsed into his ordinary train of thinking. Indeed I had by this time learned that there was nothing to be gained by frequent intercourse. And therefore it was that after this interview I was not anxious to be frequent in my visits. This day he said, "Men are born with an Angel and a Devil." This he himself interpreted as Soul and Body, and as I have long since said of the strange sayings of a man who enjoys a high reputation, "it is more in the language than the thought that this singularity is to be looked for." And this day he spoke of the Old Testament as if [it] were the evil element. Christ, he said, took much after his mother, and

in so far was one of the worst of men. On my asking him
for an instance, he referred to his turning the money-
changers out of the Temple—he had no right to do that.
He digressed into a condemnation of those who sit in
judgement on others. "I have never known a very bad
man who had not something very good about him."

Speaking of the Atonement in the ordinary Calvinistic
sense, he said, "It is a horrible doctrine; if another pay
your debt, I do not forgive it."

I have no account of any other call—but there is
probably an omission. I took Götzenberger to see him,
and he met the Masqueriers in my chambers. Masquerier
was not the man to meet him. He could not humour
Blake nor understand the peculiar sense in which he was
to be received.

1827

My journal of this year contains nothing about Blake.
But in January 1828 Barron Field and myself called on
Mrs. Blake. The poor old lady was more affected than I
expected she would be at the sight of me. She spoke of
her husband as dying like an angel. She informed me
that she was going to live with Linnell as his house-
keeper. And we understood that she would live with
him, and he, as it were, to farm her services and take
all she had. The engravings of Job were his already.
Chaucer's "Canterbury Pilgrims" were hers. I took two
copies—one I gave to C. Lamb. Barron Field took a
proof.

Mrs. Blake died within a few years, and since Blake's
death Linnell has not found the market I took for
granted he would seek for Blake's works. Wilkinson
printed a small edition of his poems, including the
"Songs of Innocence and Experience," a few years ago,
and Monkton Mylne talks of printing an edition. I have
a few coloured engravings—but Blake is still an object

of interest exclusively to men of imaginative taste and psychological curiosity. I doubt much whether these mems. will be of any use to this small class. I have been reading since the Life of Blake by Allan Cuningham, vol. ii. p. 143 of his Lives of the Painters. It recognises more perhaps of Blake's merit than might be expected of a *Scotch* realist.

BLAKE CHRONOLOGY

1757. November 28. William Blake born at 28 Broad Street, Golden Square, London, to James and Catherine Blake.

1765. First Visions.

1767. First lessons in drawing at Pars' Drawing School in the Strand.

1768. Earliest poems in *Poetical Sketches* written.

1771. Apprenticed to James Basire, engraver to the Society of Antiquaries.

1773. Begins training in Gothic. Employed in sketching monuments in Westminster Abbey.

1776 or –77 Latest of the *Poetical Sketches* written.

1778. Ends apprenticeship. Studies under George Moser in the Antique School of the Royal Academy.
Begins water-color painting. "Penance of Jane Shore."

1779. Employed as an engraver by Joseph Johnson, a radical bookseller, and by other booksellers in London.

1780. Meets Thomas Stothard, an illustrator, who introduces him to the Swiss-born painter, Henry Fuseli —"the only Man that e'er I knew Who did not make me almost spew." Fuseli, a neighbor in Broad Street, becomes one of Blake's closest friends.
Exhibits for the first time at the Royal Academy.

1781. Falls in love with "a lively little girl" named Polly Wood, who rejects him. Becomes ill and recuperates from his illness in the house of a market-gardener named Boucher. His daughter, Catherine, consoles him.

1782. August 18. Marries Catherine Sophia Boucher at

695

Battersea Church. They make their first home at 23 Green Street, Leicester Fields.

Is introduced by another painter friend, John Flaxman, to Mrs. Henry Mathew, the bluestocking wife of a minister, and begins to attend her salon.

1783. *Poetical Sketches* printed at the expense of John Flaxman and the Reverend Henry Mathew.

1784. Blake's father dies.

Opens a print-seller's shop at 27 Broad Street in partnership with James Parker, a former fellow-apprentice. His brother Robert, the only member of his family Blake ever felt close to, becomes a pupil of his.

1784. *An Island In The Moon,* a burlesque of London highbrows written at the expense of the *illuminati* at the salon of Mrs. Mathew. This work contains the earliest of *Songs of Innocence,* and mentions a scheme of "Illuminated Printing."

1787. Death of Robert Blake. Gives up print shop, dissolving partnership with James Parker, and moves to 28 Poland Street.

1788. First use of new process of relief-engraving used in "Illuminated Printing."

There Is No Natural Religion and *All Religions Are One,* "tractates" which first set forth Blake's mature philosophy, are engraved.

1788–89. Marginalia to the *Aphorisms* of John Casper Lavater. Marginalia to Swedenborg's *Wisdom of Angels.*

Writes *Tiriel.*

1789. *Songs of Innocence.*

Book of Thel.

1790. About this time begins to use a sketch book, later known as the "Rossetti Manuscript," for illustrations.

Marriage of Heaven and Hell.

1791. *The French Revolution,* Book I, set up in type by Joseph Johnson. The work was not published.

1792. Blake's mother dies.

Warns Thomas Paine, a member of the group of radical intellectuals around Joseph Johnson, that he is in danger of arrest. Paine escapes just in time to Dover, and gets to France.

A Song of Liberty probably written at this time.

1793. "The Rossetti Manuscript" notebook now used for poems.

Visions of the Daughters of Albion.

Moves to 13 Hercules Buildings, Lambeth.

Publishes the little book of engravings: *For Children: The Gates of Paradise.*

America: A Prophecy.

Prospectus, "To The Public," giving a list of "Works now published and on sale at Mr. Blake's."

Meets his future patron, Thomas Butts.

1794. *Songs of Experience.*

Europe: A Prophecy.

The First Book of Urizen.

1795. *The Song of Los.*

The Book of Los.

The Book of Ahania.

1796. Engaged on designs and engravings to Young's *Night Thoughts.*

1797–99. Lack of commissions. Begins to design in watercolor. Thomas Butts commissions some works from him.

1800. John Flaxman introduces Blake to William Hayley, a tedious squire and versifier, who invites him to settle at Felpham, in Sussex.

1800–03. Felpham period, the only time Blake lived out of London. Works at various commissions for Hayley.

1803. Quarrels with a dragoon who has entered his garden. The dragoon accuses Blake of insulting the king, and a warrant is issued for his arrest on the charge of sedition.

Returns to London in September.

1804. Tried at Chichester and is acquitted.

Begins engraving *Milton* and *Jerusalem.*

1804–05. Letters to Hayley.

1805. Designs to Blair's *The Grave,* purchased by an art-dealer and agent, R. H. Cromek, who cheats him.

1806. Cromek sees Blake's design of "The Canterbury Pilgrims," and commissions Stothard to do a picture on the same subject.

1807. Stothard's picture is exhibited. Blake attacks Cromek.

1807–08. Illustrations to *Paradise Lost*.

1807–10. Epigrams in the "Rossetti Manuscript."

1808. Completes water-color of "The Last Judgment." Publication of illustrations to *The Grave*. Marginalia to Reynolds's *Discourses*.

1808–09. Probably at this time wrote two works now lost: *Barry: A Poem* and *Book of Moonlight*. Completes engraving of *Milton*.

1809. Unsuccessful exhibition of his pictures at 28 Broad Street, May to September, under the grudging hospitality of his brother James. *A Descriptive Catalogue*.

1810. Writes in the "Rossetti Manuscript" "Advertisements to Blake's Canterbury Pilgrims From Chaucer Containing Anecdotes of Artists." Publication of his engraving of *The Canterbury Pilgrims*. "The Everlasting Gospel." Re-issues *Gates of Paradise: For The Sexes*, with Prologue, Epilogue, and Keys Of The Gates.

1811–17. Years of obscurity.

1817. Engraves *Laocoön, On Homer's Poetry, On Virgil*.

1818. Meets John Linnell, a young artist and admirer, who becomes a link with the young artists of the period.

1820. Begins his "fresco" of *The Last Judgment*.

1820. Designs and executes woodcuts to Thornton's *Pastorals of Virgil*. Completes engraving of *Jerusalem*.

1821. Moves to 3 Fountain Court, The Strand.

1821. Water-color designs to *The Book of Job* for Thomas Butts.

1822. Receives a donation of £25 from the Royal Academy. *The Ghost of Abel*.

1823. John Linnell commissions him to paint and engrave replicas of the designs to "Job."

1825. Completion of engravings for "Job," published March 1826.

First meeting with Crabb Robinson, December 10th.

1825–26. Executes designs in illustration of Dante for John Linnell.

1826. Illness, February and May.

1827. August 12. Dies.

1831. October 18. Death of Catherine Blake.

1863. Publication of Alexander Gilchrist's *Life of Blake*, a work completed after Gilchrist's death in 1861 by his widow, Anne Gilchrist, with the aid of Dante Gabriel Rossetti and William Michael Rossetti.

1905. *Blake's Poetical Works* edited John Sampson for the Clarendon Press, Oxford. The first accurate and completely trustworthy edition of Blake's poems, based upon his own writings.

1921. *A Bibliography of William Blake.* Prepared by the distinguished British surgeon and bibliophile, Geoffrey Keynes, and printed for the Grolier Club of New York.

1924. *Blake's Vision of the Book of Job.* By Joseph Wicksteed. Second Edition. Discovery of the plan on which Blake arranged his symbols in his Job. *William Blake: His Philosophy and Symbols.* By S. Foster Damon. One of the great landmarks in Blake scholarship.

1925. *The Writings of William Blake.* Edited by Geoffrey Keynes. First complete and authoritative edition of all Blake's writings, in poetry and prose.

1926. *The Prophetic Writings of William Blake.* Two volumes. Edited by D. J. Sloss and J. P. R. Wallis for the Clarendon Press, Oxford, to supplement John Sampson's edition of the shorter poems.

1927. *The Life of William Blake.* By Mona Wilson. The Nonesuch Press, London. First modern life of Blake to be based on a careful check of all the sources.

BIBLIOGRAPHY

The Complete Writings of William Blake, ed. Geoffrey Keynes. London and New York, 1957; rev. ed., 1966. The standard text, with variant readings.

The Poetry and Prose of William Blake, ed. David V. Erdman and Harold Bloom. New York, 1965. A scholarly text, with Blake's original punctuation, full textual notes, and critical commentary.

Blake Trust Facsimiles. London. *Jerusalem,* 1951 (black and white, 1952); *Songs of Innocence,* 1954; *Songs of Innocence and Experience,* 1955; *The Book of Urizen,* 1958; *Visions of the Daughters of Albion,* 1959; *The Marriage of Heaven and Hell,* 1960; *America,* 1963; *The Book of Thel,* 1965; *Milton,* 1967. Superb color reproductions, invaluable for study of the poems.

Bentley, G. E., Jr., and Martin K. Nurmi. *A Blake Bibliography.* Minneapolis, Minn., 1964; London, 1965.

Gilchrist, Alexander. *The Life of William Blake, Pictor Ignotus,* ed. Ruthven Todd. London and New York, 1945. Everyman's Library. The earliest (1863) and still the most important biography

Wilson, Mona. *The Life of William Blake.* London, 1927; rev. ed., 1948. The standard modern biography.

Binyon, Laurence. *The Drawings and Engravings of William Blake.* London, 1922.

Damon, S. Foster. *William Blake's Illustrations of the Book of Job.* Providence, R.I., 1966.

Figgis, Darrell. *The Paintings of William Blake* London, 1925.

Blunt, Anthony. *The Art of William Blake.* New York and London, 1959.

Digby, George Wingfield. *Symbol and Image in William Blake*. Oxford, 1957.

Hagstrum, Jean H. *William Blake, Poet and Painter: An Introduction to the Illuminated Verse*. Chicago and London, 1964.

Roe, Albert S. *Blake's Illustrations to the Divine Comedy*. Princeton, N.J., and London, 1953.

Wicksteed, Joseph H. *Blake's Vision of the Book of Job*. London, 1910; rev. ed., 1924.

Adams, Hazard. *William Blake: A Reading of the Shorter Poems*. Seattle, Wash., 1963.

Blackstone, Bernard. *English Blake*. Cambridge, 1949. A study of the eighteenth-century intellectual background.

Bloom, Harold. *Blake's Apocalypse*. New York and London, 1963. A close reading of the Prophetic Books.

Bronowski, Jacob. *William Blake and the Age of Revolution*. New York, 1965. Revision of *A Man Without a Mask*, 1943. Illuminating on the social and political background.

Damon, S. Foster. *William Blake: His Philosophy and Symbols*. Boston and London, 1924. A monumental work of explication.

———— *A Blake Dictionary*. Providence, R.I., 1965.

Davies, J. G. *The Theology of William Blake*. Oxford, 1948.

Erdman, David V. *Blake: Prophet Against Empire*. Princeton, N.J., and London, 1954. A detailed and illuminating study of the historical background.

Fisher, Peter F. *The Valley of Vision*. Toronto, 1961.

Frye, Northrop. *Fearful Symmetry*. Princeton, N.J., and London, 1947. A brilliant study of Blake's mythology and symbolism.

————, ed. *William Blake: Modern Essays in Criticism*. Englewood Cliffs, N.J., and London, 1966.

Gardner, Stanley. *Infinity on the Anvil: A Critical Study of Blake's Poetry*. Oxford, 1964.

Gleckner, Robert F. *The Piper and the Bard*. Detroit, 1959. A close reading of the earlier poems.

Grant, John E., ed. *Discussions of William Blake*. Boston, 1961.

Harper, George Mills. *The Neoplatonism of William Blake*. Chapel Hill, N.C., and London, 1961.

Hirsch, E. D., Jr. *Innocence and Experience: An Introduction to Blake.* New Haven, Conn., and London, 1964.

Hirst, Désirée. *Hidden Riches: Traditional Symbolism from the Renaissance to Blake.* London, 1964.

Lowery, Margaret Ruth. *Windows of the Morning.* New Haven, 1940. A study of the *Poetical Sketches.*

Margoliouth, H. M. *William Blake.* London, 1951. A good brief introduction.

Murry, John Middleton. *William Blake.* London, 1933.

Nurmi, Martin K. *Blake's "Marriage of Heaven and Hell."* Kent, Ohio, 1957.

Ostriker, Alicia. *Vision and Verse in William Blake.* Madison, Wisc., 1965; London, 1966.

Percival, Milton O. *William Blake's Circle of Destiny.* New York, 1938. A study of occult traditions in Blake.

Pinto, Vivian de Sola, ed. *The Divine Vision.* London, 1957. A collection of important critical essays.

Raine, Kathleen. "Blake's Debt to Antiquity," *Sewanee Review,* LXXI (1963), 352–450.

Saurat, Denis. *Blake and Modern Thought.* London, 1929.

Schorer, Mark. *William Blake: The Politics of Vision.* New York, 1946. A valuable study of Blake's radical background.

Swinburne, Algernon Charles. *William Blake.* London, 1868.

White, Helen C. *The Mysticism of William Blake.* Madison, Wisc., 1927.

Wicksteed, Joseph H. *Blake's Innocence and Experience.* London, 1928.

AILEEN WARD

INDEX

OF TITLES AND FIRST LINES OF POEMS

FOR THE BEST IN PAPERBACKS, LOOK FOR THE

In every corner of the world, on every subject under the sun, Penguin represents quality and variety—the very best in publishing today.

For complete information about books available from Penguin—including Penguin Classics, Penguin Compass, and Puffins—and how to order them, write to us at the appropriate address below. Please note that for copyright reasons the selection of books varies from country to country.

In the United States: Please write to *Penguin Group (USA), P.O. Box 12289 Dept. B, Newark, New Jersey 07101-5289* or call 1-800-788-6262.

In the United Kingdom: Please write to *Dept. EP, Penguin Books Ltd, Bath Road, Harmondsworth, West Drayton, Middlesex UB7 0DA.*

In Canada: Please write to *Penguin Books Canada Ltd, 10 Alcorn Avenue, Suite 300, Toronto, Ontario M4V 3B2.*

In Australia: Please write to *Penguin Books Australia Ltd, P.O. Box 257, Ringwood, Victoria 3134.*

In New Zealand: Please write to *Penguin Books (NZ) Ltd, Private Bag 102902, North Shore Mail Centre, Auckland 10.*

In India: Please write to *Penguin Books India Pvt Ltd, 11 Panchsheel Shopping Centre, Panchsheel Park, New Delhi 110 017.*

In the Netherlands: Please write to *Penguin Books Netherlands bv, Postbus 3507, NL-1001 AH Amsterdam.*

In Germany: Please write to *Penguin Books Deutschland GmbH, Metzlerstrasse 26, 60594 Frankfurt am Main.*

In Spain: Please write to *Penguin Books S. A., Bravo Murillo 19, 1° B, 28015 Madrid.*

In Italy: Please write to *Penguin Italia s.r.l., Via Benedetto Croce 2, 20094 Corsico, Milano.*

In France: Please write to *Penguin France, Le Carré Wilson, 62 rue Benjamin Baillaud, 31500 Toulouse.*

In Japan: Please write to *Penguin Books Japan Ltd, Kaneko Building, 2-3-25 Koraku, Bunkyo-Ku, Tokyo 112.*

In South Africa: Please write to *Penguin Books South Africa (Pty) Ltd, Private Bag X14, Parkview, 2122 Johannesburg.*